Pra

"A fast-paced [...]
right out of Ja[...] [...]nds."
—Andrew Gross, #1 *New York Times* bestselling author
of *Reckless* and *Don't Look Twice*

"*The Silence of the Lambs* meets *The Bourne Identity*."
—Brian S. Wheeler, author of *Mr. Hancock's Signature*

"An intense novel that will have you locking your
windows and doors, installing a safe room and taking
Ambien so you can sleep through the night after
finishing."
—Jeremy Robinson, author of *Pulse* and *Instinct*

"A superbly crafted thriller skillfully delving into the
twisted mind of a psychopath and the tormented soul
of the man destined to bring him down."
—D. B. Henson, bestselling author of *Deed to Death*

"A taut, violent and relentless nightmare."
—A. J. Hartley, bestselling author of
What Time Devours and *Act of Will*

"This powerful thriller keeps the pace at a rapid fire.
Once I started reading, it was difficult to put the book
down.... It is a must-have for the action and thriller
fan, and a great addition to any library. *The Shepherd*
is full of surprises to the very end—you won't be
disappointed and you won't see it coming."
—*Blogcritics*

ETHAN CROSS

When a fireman or a policeman would visit his school, most of his classmates' heads would swim with aspirations of growing up and catching bad guys or saving someone from a blazing inferno. When these moments came for Ethan Cross, however, his dreams weren't to someday be a cop or put out fires; he just wanted to write about it.

In addition to writing and working in the publishing industry, Ethan has also served as the chief technology officer for a national franchise, recorded albums and opened for national recording artists as lead singer and guitar player in a musical group, and been an active and highly involved member of the International Thriller Writers organization.

Ethan Cross is the pen name of an author who lives and writes in Illinois with his wife, three kids and two Shih Tzus.

THE
PROPHET

ETHAN
CROSS

W☉RLDWIDE®

TORONTO • NEW YORK • LONDON
AMSTERDAM • PARIS • SYDNEY • HAMBURG
STOCKHOLM • ATHENS • TOKYO • MILAN
MADRID • WARSAW • BUDAPEST • AUCKLAND

To my beautiful wife, Gina, for walking ten miles with me through a Chicago snowstorm…

Recycling programs
for this product may
not exist in your area.

ISBN-13: 978-0-373-18970-0

The Prophet

Copyright © 2012 by Aaron Brown

A Worldwide Library Suspense/April 2015

First published by The Story Plant

THE
PROPHET

Acknowledgments

First of all, I want to thank my wife, Gina, and my daughters, Madison and Calissa, for their love and support (especially Gina, who has to endure a lot of craziness in the name of the research and put up with me in general).

Next, I wish to thank my parents, Leroy and Emily, for taking me to countless movies as a child and instilling in me a deep love of stories. Also, thank you to my mother, Emily, for always being my first beta reader and my mother-in-law, Karen, for being my best saleswoman.

While conducting research for this novel, I trained and rode with several law enforcement personnel. Without their invaluable help, this book could not have been completed. They include the Montgomery County Sheriff's Department, Montgomery County Sheriff Jim Vazzi and Undersheriff Rick Robbins, the DuPage County Sheriff's Office and Deputy Andrew Barnish, the Matteson Police Department and Officer Aaron Dobrovits, and author and retired officer Michael A. Black.

Thank you so very much to John and Gayle Hanafin for their support at the Montgomery County Cancer Association benefit by placing the highest bid of the night on a character name in this book (the name of Eleanor Adare Schofield, honoring their mothers and grandchildren—Adam, Danielle, Ashleigh, Rebecca and Elizabeth).

Unfortunately, there is always a great deal of research that never makes it into the book for one reason or another. One of these cases in particular that still deserves my thanks is that of the Thornton Quarry and Dave Wenslauskis. I'm sure that the fascinating info I learned during my visit there will end up in another book down the road.

And, as always, none of this would be possible without the help of my mentor/publisher/friend, Lou Aronica, and my wonderful agents, Danny Baror and Heather Baror-Shapiro. Also, big thanks to my friend across the pond and UK editor, Tim Vanderpump, for all his hard work on this book (even amid the birth of his son, Oskar). In addition, I wouldn't be here without the guidance and friendship of all my fellow authors at the International Thriller Writers organization. To all of these and my extraordinary readers, thank you so much. I couldn't be living my dream without your support.

1

FRANCIS ACKERMAN JR. stared out the window of the dark copper and white bungalow on Macarthur Boulevard. Across the street, a green sign with yellow letters read *Mosswood Playground—Oakland Recreation Department.* Children laughed and played while mothers and fathers pushed swings and sat on benches reading paperback novels or fiddling with cell phones. He had never experienced such things as a child. The only games his father had ever played were the kind that scarred the body and soul. The young Ackerman had never been nurtured; he had never been loved. But he had come to accept that. He had found purpose and meaning born from the pain and chaos that had consumed his life.

He watched the sun reflect off all the smiling faces and imagined how different the scene would be if the sun suddenly burned out and fell from the heavens. The cleansing cold of an everlasting winter would sweep across the land, sterilizing it, purifying it. He pictured the faces forever etched in torment, their screams silent, and their eyes like crystal balls reflecting what lay beyond death.

He let out a long sigh. It would be beautiful. He wondered if normal people ever thought of such things. He wondered if they ever found beauty in death.

Ackerman turned back to the three people bound to chairs in the room behind him. The first two were men—plainclothes cops who had been watching the house. The older officer had a pencil-thin mustache and thinning brown hair while his younger counterpart's head was topped with a greasy mop of dark black. The younger man's bushy eyebrows matched his hair, and a hooked nose sat above thin pink lips and a recessed chin. The first man struck Ackerman to be like any other cop he had met, honest and hardworking. But there was something about the younger man that he didn't like, something in his eyes.

He suppressed the urge to smack the condescending little snarl from the younger cop's ferret-like face.

But, instead of hitting him, Ackerman just smiled at the cop. He needed a demonstration to get the information he wanted, and the ferret would be perfect. His eyes held the ferret's gaze a moment longer, and then he winked and turned to the last of his three captives.

Rosemary Phillips wore a faded Oakland Raiders sweatshirt. She had salt-and-pepper hair, and ancient pockmarks marred her smooth dark-chocolate complexion. Her eyes burned with a self-assurance and inner strength that Ackerman respected.

Unfortunately, he needed to find her grandson, and if necessary, he would kill all three of them to accomplish his goal.

He reached up to her mouth and pulled down the gag. She didn't scream. "Hello, Rosemary. I apologize that I didn't properly introduce myself earlier when I tied you up, but my name is Francis Ackerman Jr. Have you ever heard of me?"

Rosemary met his gaze. "I've seen you on television. You're the serial killer whose father experimented on him as a child, trying to prove that he could create a monster. I guess he succeeded. But I'm not afraid of you."

Ackerman smiled. "That's wonderful. It means that I can skip the introductions and get straight to the point. Do you know why I asked these two gentlemen to join us?"

Rosemary's head swiveled toward the two officers. Her gaze lingered on the ferret. Ackerman saw disgust in her eyes. Apparently she didn't like him either. That would make things even more interesting once he started to torture the young cop.

"I've seen these two around," she said. "I've already told

the cops that my grandson ain't no damn fool. He wouldn't just show up here, and I haven't heard from him since this mess started. But they wouldn't listen. Apparently they think it's a good idea to stake out an old lady's house instead of being out there on the streets doing what the people of this city pay them to do. Typical government at work."

Ackerman smiled. "I know exactly what you mean. I've never had much respect for authority. But, you see, I'm looking for your grandson as well. I, however, don't have the time or patience to sit around here on the off chance that he might show up. I prefer the direct approach, and so I'm going to ask you to level with me. Where can I find your grandson?"

"Like I told them, I have no idea."

He walked over to a tall mahogany hutch resting against the wall. It was old and well built. Family pictures lined its surface and shelves. He picked up a picture of a smiling young black man with his arm around Rosemary. A blue and gold birthday cake sat in front of them. "Rosemary, I've done my homework, and I've learned that your grandson thinks the world of you. You were his anchor in the storm. Maybe the one good thing in his life. The one person who loved him. You know where he's hiding, and you are going to share that information with me. One way or another."

"Why do you even care? What's he to you?"

"He's nothing to me. I could care less about your grandson. But someone that I do care about is looking for him, and I try to be useful where I can. And, like you said, sometimes bureaucracy and red tape are just too damn slow. We're going to speed along the process."

Rosemary shook her head and tugged on the ropes. "I don't know where he is, and if I did, I'd never tell a monster like you."

His father's words tumbled through his mind.

You're a monster... Kill her and the pain will stop... No one will ever love you...

"Oh, my dear, words hurt. But you're right. I am a monster." Ackerman grabbed a duffel bag from the floor and tossed it onto a small end table. As he unzipped the bag and rifled through the contents, he said, "Are you familiar with the Spanish Inquisition? I've been reading a lot about it lately. It's a fascinating period of history. The Inquisition was basically a tribunal established by the Catholic monarchs Ferdinand II of Aragon and Isabella I of Castile in order to maintain Catholic orthodoxy within their kingdoms, especially among the new converts from Judaism and Islam. But that's not what fascinates me. What fascinates me are the unspeakable acts of barbarism and torture that were carried out in the name of God upon those deemed to be heretics. We think that we live in a brutal age, but our memories are very short-sighted. Any true student of history can tell you that this is the age of enlightenment compared with other periods throughout time. The things the Inquisitors did to wrench confessions from their victims were nothing less than extraordinary. Those Inquisitors displayed fabulous imagination."

Ackerman brought a strange device up out of the duffel bag. "This is an antique. Its previous owner claimed that it's an exact replica of one used during the Inquisition. You've got to love eBay."

He held up the device—made from two large, spiked blocks of wood connected by two threaded metal rods an inch in diameter each— for their inspection. "This was referred to as the Knee Splitter. Although it was used on more than just knees. When the Inquisitor turned these screws, the two blocks would push closer together and the spikes would first pierce the flesh of the victim. Then the Inquisitor would continue to twist the screws tighter and tighter until they received the answers they wanted or until the affected appendage was rendered useless."

Rosemary spat at him. As she spoke, her words were strong and confident. He detected a slight hint of a Georgia accent and suspected that it was from her youth and only presented itself when she was especially flustered. "You're going to kill us anyway. No matter what I do. I can't save these men any more than I can save myself. The only thing that I can control is the way that I go out. And I won't grovel and beg to the likes of you. I won't give you the satisfaction."

Ackerman nodded. "I respect that. So many people blame the world or society or others for the way that they are. But we're all victims of circumstance to a certain extent. We like to think that we're in control of our own destinies, but the truth is that much of our lives is dictated by forces far beyond our control and comprehension. We all have our strings pulled by someone or something. It's unavoidable. The only place that we have any real control is right here." He tapped the tip of his fifteen-inch survival knife against his right temple. "Within our minds. Most people don't understand that, but you do. I didn't come here to kill you, Rosemary. It will give me no pleasure to remove you from the world. But my strings get pulled just like everyone else's. In this case, circumstances dictate that I hurt you and these men in order to achieve my goal. I'm good at what I do, my dear. I've been schooled in pain and suffering my entire life. Time will only allow me to share a small portion of my expertise with you, but I can tell you that it will be enough. You will tell me.

That's beyond your control. The only aspect of this situation that you can influence is the duration of the suffering you must endure. So I'll ask again: where is your grandson?"

Her lips trembled, but she didn't speak.

The smell of cinnamon permeated the air but was unable to mask a feral aroma of sweat and fear. Ackerman had missed that smell. He had missed the fear, the power. But he needed to keep his excitement contained. He couldn't lose control. This was about information, not about satisfying his own hunger.

"Time to begin. As they say, I'm going to put the screws

to this officer. Makes you wonder if this device is responsible for such a saying, doesn't it?"

AFTER SEVERAL MOMENTS of playing with his new toy, Ackerman looked at Rosemary, but she had diverted her gaze. He twisted the handles again, and the officer's thrashing increased.

"Okay, I'll tell you!" she said. "He's in Spokane, Washington. They're set up in an abandoned metal-working shop of some kind. Some crooked realtor set it up for them. I've tried to get him to turn himself in. I even considered calling the police myself, but I know that he and his friends won't allow themselves to be captured alive. He's the only family I have left." Tears ran down her cheeks.

Ackerman reached down to relieve the pressure on the officer's legs. The man's head fell back against the chair. "Thank you. I believe you, and I appreciate your situation. Your grandson has been a bad boy. But he's your flesh and blood, and you still love him."

He walked over to the table and pulled up another chair in front of Rosemary. As he sat, he pulled out a small notepad. It was spiral-bound from the top and had a bloodred cover. "Since you've been so forthcoming with me, and out of respect, I'll give you a genuine chance to save your lives." He flipped up the notepad's cover, retrieved a small pen from within the spiral, and started to write. As the pen traveled over the page, he said, "I'm going to let you pick the outcome of our little game. On this first sheet, I've written 'ferret' to represent our first officer." He tore off the page, wadded it up, and placed it between his legs. "On the second, we'll write 'Jackie Gleason' to represent the next officer. Then 'Rosemary'. Then 'all live'. And 'all die'." He mixed up the wadded pieces of paper and placed them on the floor in front of her. "I think the game is self-explanatory. But to make sure that there's no confusion, you pick the piece of paper, and I kill whoever's name is on it. But you do have a twenty percent chance that you all live. And just to be clear, if you refuse to pick or take too long, I'll be happy to kill all three of you. So please don't try to fight fate. The only thing you have control over here is which piece of paper you choose. Have no illusions that you have any other options. It will only serve to make the situation even less manageable for you. Pick one."

Rosemary's eyes were full of hate. They burrowed into him. Her gaze didn't waver. A doctor named Kendrick from the Cedar Mill Psychiatric Hospital had once told Ackerman that he had damage to a group of interconnected brain structures, known as the paralimbic system, that were involved in processing emotion, goal-seeking, motivation, and self-control. The doctor had studied his brain using functional magnetic resonance imaging technology and had also found damage to an area known as the amygdala that generated emotions such as fear. Monkeys in the wild with damage to the amygdala had been known to walk right up to people or even predators. The doctor had said this explained why Ackerman didn't feel fear in the way that other people did. He wondered if Rosemary had a similar impairment or if her strength originated from somewhere else entirely.

She looked down at the pieces of paper, then back into his eyes. "Third one. The one right in the center."

He reached down and uncrumpled the small piece of paper. He smiled. "It's your lucky day. You all get to live. I'm sorry that you had to endure this due to the actions of someone else. But, as I said, we're all victims of circumstance."

Then he stood, retrieved his things, and exited onto Macarthur Boulevard.

ACKERMAN TOSSED HIS duffel bag into the trunk of a light-blue Ford Focus. He wished he could travel in more style, but the ability to blend in outweighed his own sense of flare. He pulled open the driver's door, slipped inside, and dropped some jewelry and the wallets and purse of his former captives on the seat next to him. He hated to lower himself to common thievery, but everything cost money. And his skill set didn't exactly look good on a résumé. Besides, he didn't have time for such things.

He retrieved a disposable cell phone from the glove box and activated the device. As he dialed and pressed send, he looked down at the small slip of paper that Rosemary had chosen. The words *All Die* stared back at him.

After a few rings, the call connected, and the voice on the other end said, "What do you want?"

Ackerman smiled. "Hello, Marcus. Please forgive me, for I have sinned. But I do it all for you."

2

MARCUS WILLIAMS STARED down at the brutalized body of a dead woman and could tell by the bruising and ligature marks that she had been raped before being murdered. The small maintenance office connected to the back of the factory was in general disrepair. The plaster had crumbled from water damage, and the roof was bare in several spots, exposing a clear night sky. Snow had fallen through the gaps, and a light dusting of it covered everything. A large section of shelving attached to the back wall had broken free from its mounts. Its former contents littered the floor—rusted pipe fittings, bailing wire, half-dissolved cardboard boxes, old equipment manuals. The body had been discarded like just another piece of junk intended to be disposed of more thoroughly at a later time. Judging by the body's lividity and rigor, Marcus suspected that she'd been dead only a few hours and had been killed using some small, blunt object like a hammer. If only he had arrived just a little sooner…

He pushed the anger and guilt from his mind. It did him no good now. Stepping through the exterior entrance of the office, he pushed the door shut and wedged a rock against it to keep it from swinging back open. The door had been padlocked, and he had popped it using a Hallaghan Tool, a device similar to a crowbar used for breaching and entries. He didn't want the door to catch in the wind and slam against the frame. He wanted to maintain the element of surprise.

He crossed the parking lot, scaled a chain-link fence, and dropped onto the sidewalk. There were other, newer factories nearby, but this business had gone bankrupt and abandoned its facility. The Bank Crew had been paying the realtor under the table for access to the crumbling brick structure. It hadn't taken much convincing to obtain the information from the operator of the realty office. He had crumbled like a house of cards at the mention of lawyers and prison sentences for aiding and abetting.

Marcus had been tracking the Bank Crew for several weeks now, but they had gone underground after their last job. Then, two days ago, they had struck again, taking the wife and two daughters of a jewelry-store owner. The Bank Crew, as the press had come to call them, had worked out a violent money-making scheme whereby they kidnapped the family of someone with access to a great deal of cash or valuable assets. Then they would force the person to bring them the money by threatening to kill the family. It was a pretty straightforward extortion-and-ransom gambit, but the thing that set the Crew apart was their brutal nature. Their victims almost always complied, but they killed them anyway. First, they killed the father once they had the money. Then they had some fun with the female members of the family before ending their lives as well.

The police knew that the group had four members, but they had been pretty good so far at leaving behind little evidence. The only piece of useful information came from a fingerprint left at one of the scenes. The man's name popped up in the system, but no one had seen or heard from him since the Crew had started up. The cops in Oakland who had questioned his grandmother believed that she knew more than she was telling them, but they couldn't do anything more than stake out her place.

Marcus had planned to pay her a visit himself, but Ackerman had beaten him to it.

Jerking open the door to the black GMC Yukon, he dropped in behind the wheel, pressed the button to activate the heated seats, and blew into his hands. After a moment, the passenger-side door opened as well, and Andrew

Garrison pulled himself inside. Andrew ripped a stocking cap from his head, revealing short sandy-blond hair. Unlike Marcus, whose face was covered by three days of dark beard growth, Andrew had a clean-cut and well-kept appearance.

"Anything?" Marcus said.

"Yeah, I think I found the room where they're keeping the daughters and saw at least one of the Crew passed out on a futon in the main building. It looks like they've brought in a folding table and a couple pieces of furniture to make some kind of makeshift living area. They've covered up the windows of the front offices, and I was afraid I'd make too much noise breaking in there. How about you?"

"I found the mother."

Andrew seemed to be waiting for more of an explanation, but after a moment's silence, none was needed. Andrew looked through the front windshield and said, "Dammit. How do you want to play it?"

"We go in the back. Standard tether formation, me in the front and you in the rear. We work our way through the building." Marcus sighed. "I'm going to call it in."

He pulled a cell phone from his pocket and dialed. The Director of the Shepherd Organization answered with no preamble after the first ring. "Did you find them?"

"Yeah. The mother's dead. We're ready to breach."

"Okay, the council's convened and have granted you full authority to move forward with this operation. Be careful and Godspeed." The Director clicked off without another word.

Marcus laid down the phone and stared out at the snow. He had been a Shepherd for over a year now, and he still wasn't sure if he'd made the right decision. The Shepherd Organization operated out of the Department of Justice under the guise of a think-tank and consulting agency specializing in violent offenders, mostly serial killers. But their primary mandate separated them from other law-enforcement agencies like the FBI's Behavioral Analysis Unit. They weren't charged with simply capturing and convicting killers. Their goal was to get them off the streets in any way possible, and they usually bent or outright broke any law necessary to do so. They had been designed as a no-holds-barred task force that could bypass all the red tape and get the job done without worrying about evidence and due process. It wasn't all that different from operations that the CIA and military had been conducting for years, eliminating hostile targets overseas. The difference being that the Shepherd Organization carried out its activities on US soil and against US citizens.

The organization consisted of small cell groups, and Marcus had been recruited to head one of the teams due to certain talents he had displayed during his time as a homicide detective with the NYPD. While on the force, he had shown great promise and deductive aptitude, but he had also thrown away his future by choosing not to look the other way. A wealthy senator from a powerful family had a penchant for abusing and murdering young girls, and Marcus had refused to let him get away with it. Instead, he had put a bullet in the senator's brain and had only avoided prosecution so that the senator's dark deeds would not see the light of day.

Marcus had operational command of his unit but reported to a man he knew only as the Director and some council of faceless men or women whose existence he couldn't even verify.

"What's wrong?" Andrew said.

"Other than the current Attorney General and the Director, have you ever met anyone high up the chain of command? Any members of the council?"

"Why the sudden interest?"

"It's not a sudden interest. It's a nagging suspicion. Haven't you ever wondered about how we get away with the things we do? Or who's pulling the strings?"

Andrew shrugged. "Sure. But I believe in what we do. I think the world's a better place with us on the streets. So

I try to focus on that. Keep my mind on the things that I have control over."

"You really think what we do is right?"

"We save people's lives, protect the average Joe from monsters that he doesn't even want to know exist. What can be wrong about that?"

"Gandhi said, 'I object to violence because when it appears to do good, the good is only temporary; the evil it does is permanent.'" Andrew laughed. "How do you think Gandhi would feel if that was one of his loved ones lying dead in there? A lot of people in this world would say that we're every bit as bad as the men we hunt. They'd say that we violate these men's human rights. But those people have also never had to put their own kid in the ground after their baby girl's life was stolen by a man just like the ones in that building. They can't say how they'd feel then. Until you're in that position, you can never understand the depth of what we do. You think Gandhi ever met a man like Ackerman?"

Andrew looked away and leaned back against the seat.

Marcus reached up and rubbed his temples. The migraines had been getting steadily worse, and he barely slept fifteen hours in a good week. He couldn't go on like this, and the situation with Ackerman didn't help matters. The killer had been used in Marcus's recruitment to show him the true face of the type of men that the Shepherd Organization hunted. But the demonstration had backfired. The killer escaped and became convinced that his and Marcus's destinies were linked. Ackerman's fixation on him resulted in frequent calls and unwanted attempts at helping with active investigations. But the worst part was that Marcus and the other members of his team had no idea how Ackerman even knew what case they were investigating or how the killer had learned his number. All attempts at finding and tracking Ackerman had turned up nothing.

Andrew said, "Maybe we should thank Ackerman. He did

find the Bank Crew for us. He may end up saving the lives of those two girls." Marcus's arm shot out and he grabbed a fistful of Andrew's coat.

He jerked him up and off the seat, pulling him in close. "And he tortured two cops and an old woman in the process! It's only a matter of time before he starts killing again. If he isn't already. But I suppose that's okay as long as the ends justify the means, right?"

He shoved Andrew back against his seat and looked toward the abandoned factory. Silence stretched within the vehicle.

"We'll get him, Marcus."

"Whatever."

Andrew was silent for a moment more and then added, "If things go south in there and the cops show up, remember to let me do the talking."

Marcus cocked his head to the side and said, "What are you trying to say?"

"I'm just saying that, you know, you're not much of a people person."

"'A people person'? What is that supposed to mean?"

"Well, it's what's known as a euphemism or a nice way of saying that you're a bit of an asshole."

"Thanks. I'm so lucky to have you as my wingman."

Andrew raised his hands in surrender. "I just call it the way I see it."

Marcus ignored the comment and tried to prepare his mind for what they were about to do. Pole lights surrounded the structure, illuminating most of the exterior. The building was white block with a metal roof. It was in need of a coat of paint and a pole jutted up in front of the offices, but the sign on top had been removed. It looked like any other nondescript building within the industrial park, only it had been sitting empty for years.

"You wearing your vest?"

"Of course. I sleep with the damn thing," Andrew replied. Marcus took a deep breath, cocked his head to the side, cracked his neck, and then threw open his door. "We've got work to do."

MARCUS ENTERED FIRST, leading the way with a silenced 9 mm Sig Sauer P226 Tactical Operations pistol gripped in his hand. Andrew followed close behind with a Glock in his right hand and his left touching Marcus's back. They moved forward in tandem as if they were connected by a tether. It allowed them to cover all angles. In a space like this one, with big open rooms and several points of ingress, they needed to monitor their backs as much as their fronts. And the bottom line was that no matter how cautious or well trained they were, a man with a little luck and a handful of bullets could end their lives as easily as they could his.

The back of the warehouse opened into a pale green hallway with two wood-grain hollow-core doors on the right and one on the left. Then the corridor came to a door in front and an intersection that veered off to the right. They had acquired a floor plan from the realtor's office, and through a window, Andrew had glimpsed one of the girls being taken to the large office on their left-hand side.

The girls' names were Paula and Kristy, their ages sixteen and twelve.

Marcus nodded toward the right door. They took up positions along each side of the entryway with Andrew monitoring the rest of the corridor. Marcus twisted the knob and gave the door a gentle push. Using a law enforcement technique known as "pieing", he used the door frame as a pivot and kept himself positioned so that anyone in the room would only be able to see him as soon as he saw them.

The room was empty.

They repeated the same procedure at the next door. A bathroom. No one inside.

Marcus gestured with two fingers toward the door on the left. They took up their positions, and he twisted the knob.

It was locked. Nodding silently, Andrew prepared to kick in the door. Marcus hated to make the extra noise, but their first priority was getting the girls out safe. They had done this sort of thing enough times to know the procedure. Andrew's blow would clear the way, and Marcus would swing into the room.

A glance passed between them, and then Andrew kicked the door near the handle. The striker plate burst from the jamb, and the door swung inward. Marcus followed it through the opening.

He analyzed the scene within a millisecond. A bare mattress lay on the floor. It was yellowed and stained. The whole room stank of body odor and urine. The girl sat atop the filthy mattress, and duct tape bound her hands and feet and covered her mouth. Her blond hair was greasy with sweat, and her eyes were red from crying. A purple bruise covered her cheek. To her right, a dark-skinned man in a faded black Raiders sweatshirt sat in a dirty old recliner that looked like it had been left on the curb for the garbage man to retrieve. An Ithaca shotgun with a pistol grip rested across his lap.

The man's eyes went wide, and his hand flew toward the shotgun.

Marcus squeezed the trigger, the P226 bucked, and the man fell back into the chair. Marcus fired two more shots into the man's chest, just to be sure.

Andrew was already at the girl's side, cutting through her restraints. She pulled away from him like a wounded animal that didn't understand he was trying to help. The girl's head jerked around as if she was searching for a way to escape. Her once beautiful blue eyes had gone feral. It was the sixteen-year-old, Paula. Andrew reached for her, and some part of her finally realized what was happening. She started to sob.

"Get her out of here. I'll find the other girl and meet you back at the car."

"You can't go up against these guys on your own."

"Look at her, Andrew. We can't just leave her here. Besides, I know what I'm doing." Marcus pulled off his leather jacket and tossed it to Andrew, who wrapped it around the girl's trembling shoulders.

Without another word, Andrew lifted Paula from the mattress and headed toward the back door.

The sight of the girl and the thought of her sister in a similar condition somewhere in the building propelled Marcus forward. The rage was building in him now, but he tried to beat it down and stay calm. He needed to remain objective and focused, but the feral look in Paula's eyes kept filling his mind. Physically, she would be fine. But the events of the past two days would stay with her for the rest of her life. On the surface she might appear normal, but she would never again feel safe. Her body would heal, but a piece of her soul would never return. He knew from experience.

He entered the main part of the warehouse and could hear rap music thumping and crackling out of a set of small underpowered speakers. The ceiling of bare supports and metal loomed thirty feet above his head, and tall shelves containing bins for parts lined the space. The smell of old oil and rust hung in the air. Past the end of a row of shelving he could see dust-covered tables and machinery. Vise-grips, sanders, and various metalworking tools still covered the work benches. Apparently, they had been trying to sell the equipment along with the real estate. The hum of a portable space heater droned within the open area in between the shelving. He could see a heavyset man in a red puffy coat sitting at a beige card table playing solitaire next to the heater. His large legs jutted over the sides of the small chair. The man's dark brown hair stuck up at odd angles, and a skullcap rested on the table next to the rows of cards.

Marcus quietly worked his way behind the man and raised his gun. A scream cut through the air. High and shrill, the sound of a young girl crying out in pain or fear. Or both.

The man in the red coat chuckled at the sound of the girl's pain and played a ten of clubs on a jack of diamonds.

The anger in Marcus welled up again.

He placed the barrel two inches behind the man's skull—sighting in on the medulla oblongata, where the spinal cord broadens at the base of the brain—and squeezed the trigger. The sharp thump wasn't the little plink that was typically portrayed in the movies. It was difficult to truly silence anything more powerful than a .22 caliber pistol. But he refused to wield anything beneath a 9mm, and usually carried a .45 for stopping power. Opting for stealth on this operation, he had loaded the P226 with subsonic ammunition and an SWR Trident suppressor. It made little difference to the end result.

The fat man fell forward onto the card table, and its legs bent inward under his substantial bulk. The table shot out to the side as the man slammed to the concrete floor.

"Jeff? You okay over there?"

Marcus swore under his breath and ran forward into the rows of shelving on the opposite side of the open area. He knelt low so that no one walking down the adjoining rows would be able to see him through the shelving. Heavy footfalls slapped against the concrete, the sound moving in his direction. He aimed back toward the fat man, hoping that his accomplice would go to check on him.

But the man must have been smarter than that.

The muscles in Marcus's forearm started to burn as time stretched out. His prey knew he was there and was waiting for him to make a mistake.

He heard a grunt and the sound of metal clacking onto concrete. At first, the domesticated side of his brain didn't know what had just happened, but the animal part registered the danger.

The crashing noises cascaded toward him, and he rolled out into the open just as the row of shelving where he had been hiding collapsed over onto its neighbor.

His gaze darted around the room, and he glimpsed a black

man in jeans and a gray hooded sweatshirt at the far end of the rows of shelving. The man raised a Heckler and Koch MP5-K and, with the gun on full auto, unleashed a spray of 9 mm bullets in Marcus's direction.

He ran toward the opposite side of the shelving past the dead man in the red coat. The bullets sparked all around him, ricocheting off the concrete and striking the parts bins. He reached the door leading to the back offices and scrambled inside as bullets chewed into the frame. The hallway stretched ahead, and he instinctively ran toward the room where they'd found Paula. The sound of tennis shoes slamming down onto concrete chased him inside.

Once in the room, Marcus grabbed the Ithaca shotgun from the dead man's lap and pumped back the forestock to make sure that the weapon was loaded and ready. Then he grabbed hold of the filthy mattress, pulled it up onto its end, and shoved it toward the room's entrance. Before the mattress had even struck the door frame, he had slid to the floor to the left. He lay there flat against the concrete with the shotgun pointed at the doorway.

Bullets struck the door and mattress. He heard the sound of an empty MP5-K magazine striking the concrete and a new one being slammed home. More rounds ripped through the walls, blanketing the room with drywall dust, the tiny particles filling his eyes and nostrils.

He waited.

Time stretched out.

Then the man in the hoodie pushed the mattress away from the doorway and started to step over it. He hadn't made it a foot into the room when Marcus fired. The man's chest exploded into red, and he flew back against the door frame, landing in the hallway.

Marcus dropped the Ithaca and followed the man into the hall, with his Sig Sauer held out in front of him. The man's eyes stared into oblivion, and crimson stained the center of his gray sweatshirt. Marcus stepped over him and headed back to the main section of the warehouse to find Kristy.

He passed the dead heavyset man, the broken card table, the downed shelving, and the scattered and rusty parts. A set of stairs that led up to what he guessed was the factory manager's office sat next to another series of workstations. Windows were set all around the raised room so that the manager could look out over his workers and supervise their activities.

Marcus had no illusions that Ty Phillips wouldn't be ready for him. Rosemary's grandson was smart and bloodthirsty, so there was little doubt that he was the leader of the Bank Crew. Ty would be set up in the manager's office with his choice of the girls.

Marcus ascended the stairs and listened for any movement from above, but he could detect nothing beyond the hum of the space heater and the thump of rap music. A suspicion of what he would find within the office crept through his mind, and he thought about how he should handle the situation.

He stayed to the left on the stairs and kept his weapon at the ready. At the top, he pushed through a glass-fronted door into the manager's office. An empty desk sat along the back wall with several blank corkboards hanging above it. The room smelled musty, and the walls were a pale yellow.

Ty Phillips stood next to the desk with his left arm wrapped tight around Kristy's neck, a Glock 19 pressed against her right temple. Phillips stood two feet taller than the girl. He was shirtless, and Kristy was crying. Phillips was thin and prison tattoos snaked across his arms and chest. Kristy was still dressed, but her clothes were torn and her lip was bleeding.

Phillips smiled and tightened his grip around her. "Stupid cop. You should've known to bring the SWAT team if you were coming after me. Now drop the heat, or I'll splatter this girl and do the same to you."

Marcus's aim didn't waver. "I'm not a cop. I'm a Shepherd. I keep wolves like you from hurting good people like this girl."

Phillips laughed. "A Shepherd? That's the craziest sh—"

The Sig Sauer bucked in Marcus's hand. Phillips's head jerked back, and he dropped to the floor of the office. Kristy twitched at the sound but barely reacted beyond that. She just stood there, glassy-eyed, like a trembling statue.

Marcus approached and kicked Phillips's gun away. There was a nice neat hole above his left eye. A pool of blood was forming behind his head where Marcus imagined the medical examiner would find a large and ragged exit wound. The eyes were blank and lifeless.

Marcus put his arms around the girl. She tried to pull back, but he held firm. Eventually, she fell against him, gripping a handful of his shirt and burying her face in his chest. He placed a hand on the back of her head and said, "You're safe now. We're going to get you home."

Even as he spoke the words, he realized that she no longer had a home to return to. Her parents were gone. Her old life was gone. The person she was and would become had been forever changed.

His gaze drifted down to the body of Ty Phillips. Maybe these men deserved to die for what they'd done, but was it his place to carry out their punishment? He caught sight of his reflection in the office's many windows. He looked into the eyes of his doppelganger and wondered what he had become, what he was becoming. There was no one to blame for his choices other than himself. He was a killer. He was a monster.

Marcus wondered what separated him from men like the Bank Crew. Was he any better than them? Was he any better than Ackerman?

SANDRA LUTRELL FELT a pinch on her arm and awakened from a horrible dream. She felt strange and groggy. Her head ached. She tried to reach up to rub the sleep from her eyes, but she couldn't move her arms.

Her eyes fluttered as she tried to pull herself into full awareness. At first she didn't recognize her surroundings. The space around her was small with gray metal walls. There was a Coleman lamp on the floor that cast a sparse puddle of illumination onto the concrete. The room was longer than it was wide, and eventually she recognized it as the interior of a storage container like the one she had used to store some extra furniture when she had first moved to Chicago from Nebraska. The job had been an upgrade, but the apartment had been a downgrade. She hadn't been able to find a house she liked right off and had used a storage facility outside Jackson's Grove for six months until she found the perfect place. She had fallen asleep in that same house last night.

Sandra tried to move her head but discovered that it was restrained as well. She felt cold and glanced down to find that she was still in her pajamas. Her mouth opened to scream for help, but then she saw the man in the shadows at the opposite end of the container. The darkness obscured his face, but she could see that he was dressed all in black. A syringe dangled from his right hand.

She remained completely still, her eyes wide and her muscles frozen with fear.

His words cut through the cold, moist air and sent shivers through her body. His voice was soft and lacked confidence, as if he were vying for her approval. "I just injected you with a small dose of adrenaline to counteract the other drugs that I gave you and speed up your recovery."

Other drugs? Awareness of the implication of those words came slowly. Sandra's thoughts were still scattered and only semi-coherent. But when realization struck her, it hit with the force of a freight train. She had been kidnapped. A man had come into her home while she slept and had stolen her away. But what would happen now? What did he plan to do with her?

She opened her mouth to plead with him, but the words wouldn't come. Fear gripped her tongue.

He stepped forward into the light. A pair of oval wire-rimmed glasses rested on his nose, and his face was thin and pale. His brown hair was short and combed neatly to the side. All of which gave him a bookish appearance betrayed only by the above-average muscle tone showing beneath his tight black clothes. He had one of those ageless faces where he could have passed for early twenties or late thirties without anyone questioning him. He could even have passed for a teenager if it hadn't been for the thick shadow of stubble that covered his cheeks and chin. He didn't appear angry or insane in any way. In fact, if Sandra had passed him on a lonely street at night, she wouldn't have felt the least bit threatened by him.

His quiet appearance gave her a boost in confidence, and she said, "Please, just let me go, and we can forget that any of this ever happened. No harm, no foul. You don't want to go down a road that you can't come back from."

His gaze strayed away from hers, but then he said, "I'm sorry. I wish it didn't have to be this way."

He reached into a small leather bag sitting near the Coleman lamp and brought out two clamp-like devices that seemed vaguely familiar. He moved toward her.

"What are you doing? Please don't—"

Her words became a scream as his left hand grabbed her

face with surprising strength. Using his thumb and fore-finger, he held her eyelids open. She tried to blink and pull away, but the restraints held her in place. With his right hand, he inserted one device into her eye, and she remembered where she had seen such an instrument before. Her eye doctor had used something similar to hold her lids open during her last visit.

Sandra bucked and cried out for help, but she could do little to prevent him from repeating the procedure with her left eye. Tears rolled down both her cheeks and clouded her vision, but she was unable to blink them away.

The man reached back toward the leather bag, and she caught the glint of something shiny in his hand.

"Please don't do this. I'll do whatever you want."

"There's no point in screaming. No one can hear you. I realize you'll try anyway, but I would suggest that you use your last breaths for a more useful purpose."

His hand moved toward her leg, and Sandra saw the scalpel. Her screams reverberated off the metal walls. A terrible pain sliced through her inner thigh. Then he leaned in close, and his eyes burrowed deep into hers.

"I've just made a deep diagonal incision through your femoral artery. It's one of the primary paths of blood flow. You'll be dead within a moment unless I seal the wound."

Sobs racked her body. "Please, no. I—"

"I'll stop the bleeding and release you if you answer my questions honestly."

"Anything you want! Just let me go."

"Okay, Sandra. Why are you happy?"

"What? I don't understand."

"We don't have time, Sandra. You only have a moment before you die from blood loss. Tell me now. What is the key to your happiness?"

She was beginning to feel light-headed, her leg pulsing and gushing blood with each beat of her heart. The room spun, and a nauseous feeling snaked through her abdomen. Her mind fought for an answer.

"I don't know. I guess I just try to focus on the good things in life and see the best in people."

He smiled. "That's a good, simple answer. Thank you, Sandra. Maybe, after I take your soul, I'll be able to do the same."

"What? You said you'd let me go." Her leg throbbed and ached. "You need to stop the bleeding!"

"Again, I'm sorry, but I lied. Even if we were sitting in a hospital right now, there's little they could do for you at this point."

He reached back to the leather bag and retrieved a small cup. He filled it with some of the blood gushing from her leg. Sandra watched in horror as he raised the cup to his lips and dumped its contents down his throat.

A part of her couldn't believe this was actually happening. This was something that happened in the movies or in those true-crime documentaries. It wasn't something that she had ever even considered could actually happen to her. Was this really the end? There was so much that she still wanted to do. So much life left.

Her vision faded in and out, but she fought against the coming darkness.

He pulled up another chair across from her, and then she felt a cool liquid splashing over her bare skin. The strong smell touched her nostrils, but her mind couldn't identify it.

His stare drilled deep into her, and Sandra was unable to look away. For the first time, she noticed his beautiful green eyes. Those eyes were the last thing she saw before he sparked a match and flames engulfed her body.

AFTER THE GIRL was dead, Harrison Schofield recited the words and painted the symbols onto the walls of the storage container, always following the Prophet's exacting specifications. Then he left the storage yard. He passed a beige and white guardhouse, where he had killed the night watchman, and made his way down the street to his blue Toyota Camry. The neighborhood was quiet and mostly industrial—a lumberyard, a block building that housed some produce supplier. It was painted bright green and red like a watermelon. The only residences were a row of cheap town houses on the far side of the street. The storage yard had camera surveillance, but Schofield had disabled the unit. He was familiar with the model, an AVMS 2500. No remote backups, just a simple digital recording onto an onsite hard drive.

He walked past a row of cast-iron street lamps that looked down on him like angry sentinels, watching him, accusing him. He pulled open the car door and slid in behind the wheel. The Prophet was sitting in the passenger seat.

"How do you feel?" the Prophet said. His slow Southern drawl was deep and hypnotic. The words flowed from his mouth like warm honey.

Schofield knew what the Prophet wanted to hear, but it was also the truth. "I feel powerful. Stronger."

"That's good. Very good. Did you carry out the ritual exactly as I've taught you?"

In a more aggressive tone than he'd intended, Schofield snapped, "I know what I'm doing."

Before he could react, the Prophet's hand shot out and

struck him hard across the left cheek. "Remember your place, boy. Once you ascend, you'll sit at the right hand of the father and rule this world. But until then, I speak for the father. Don't ever forget that. You show me respect at all times."

Schofield felt like a little boy again. Visions of the Prophet striking him with a barbed whip flashed through his mind. He could almost feel the flesh tearing from his back. He hung his head low and mumbled a quiet apology.

The Prophet placed a hand on his shoulder. His tone softened. "It's only a matter of days before the *Darkest Night*. We need your spirit to be ready for the ascension. You're sure that you carried out the ritual properly?"

"I followed your instructions to the letter."

"Good. Have you chosen the sacrifice for tomorrow night?" Schofield nodded, and his pulse quickened with anticipation.

"Everything's in place."

A sound of deep elation reverberated in the Prophet's throat. The older man reached up and flicked on the Camry's radio. The Rolling Stones boomed out of the speakers with Mick Jagger's voice crooning *Sympathy for the Devil*.

Schofield put the vehicle in gear and pulled away from the curb. As they drove away, he wondered how he would feel in the morning when he looked into the eyes of his children.

LOCATED TWENTY MILES northwest of downtown Chicago, Elk Grove Village was known as one of the most business-friendly suburbs in the country and was home to one of the largest business parks in North America. The town's schools ranked among the top educational establishments in Illinois, and the local administration had worked hard to make the city look picturesque and serene.

FBI Special Agent Victoria Vasques reckoned that the peaceful suburb wasn't the sort of place a person would usually expect to find a human-trafficking ring, but looks were often deceiving. And in her experience, every community, just like every person, had many complex levels that often never saw the light of day. Her partner, Troy La-Paglia, punched a few keys on the keyboard and brought up the video feed for the Starbright Motel—a place that could unofficially be rented by the hour and had a mirror above every bed. She fidgeted in her chair, leaning back and trying to stretch out her legs as best she could. The surveillance van—marked on the outside with block letters cut from white vinyl that read MASCONI PLUMBING AND HEATING—didn't offer much space, and her legs were starting to fall asleep. The rock-hard little stools didn't help the situation. Next time, Vasques planned to buy one of those butt pads that old ladies brought to basketball games when they sat in the bleachers. The smell of stale coffee and greasy take-out food floated through the cramped space and was making her feel nauseous. She needed to get out, and she really needed a cigarette. But she had gone two weeks without a drag, and she wasn't about to let the urges get the better of her now. She popped in another piece of gum and worked it around her jaw.

LaPaglia must have read her mind. "Got a feeling that we won't be in this van much longer. They should be here any minute."

"They better be," she said. "I have to take a piss."

LaPaglia shook his head. "You're like a delicate flower, Vasques. So genteel and reserved."

"I was raised by a single dad who was also a homicide detective. Words like that aren't in my vocabulary."

LaPaglia leaned forward, and the light from the display monitor made his face glow bright white. Vasques had always found his surname somewhat comical since LaPaglia was as pasty white as they come, with short blond hair, nothing like his Italian surname would have suggested. She, on the other hand, had inherited bronze skin and dark hair from her Brazilian-American parents, and her Portuguese surname fitted her perfectly. She looked at another of the monitors and saw the pair of officers from the Cook County Sheriff's Vice Unit sitting in an unmarked beige sedan and waiting for the word to move in and assist with the arrest.

They had been staking out the motel for several days, but their work was about to come to fruition. They were awaiting the arrival of a driver named Oscar Wilhelm. His passenger would be a big Jamaican man who went simply by the name Mr. Chains. Vasques had often found that creeps like Chains had an odd flair for the dramatic. Chains was the operator of a human-trafficking and prostitution ring comprised of Guatemalan illegals ranging in ages from twelve to the mid-twenties. These girls and young women had been promised legitimate work in America when they'd been taken from their poor communities back in Guatemala, but instead they had found themselves sold as sex slaves and were being forced to entertain anywhere from five to twenty-five clients every day.

The driver, Wilhelm, had been hired to provide discreet transportation and security for Chains, but he hadn't signed on for the world he encountered. He had called in a tip to a group called CAST—Coalition to Abolish Slavery and Trafficking. CAST had immediately contacted the Chicago Area Task Force on Human Trafficking, a multi-jurisdictional team trying to stamp out the trade in their communities. And that was where Vasques and LaPaglia had come on board. They had convinced Wilhelm to wear a wire, the plan being to gather evidence against Chains and then liberate his harem.

"There they are," LaPaglia said.

Vasques watched as Wilhelm parked the car and opened the door for Chains. Then they ascended the stairs of the motel to the bank of rooms they rented out for entertaining clients and housing the girls. She wondered how much money it had taken to convince the motel owners to sell their souls and look the other way. In front of the rooms, a big guy with a shaved head stood watch over the area that, according to Wilhelm, Chains referred to as the holding pen. There were usually anywhere from five to ten girls held inside the single room.

The big guard's voice hissed out over the small speakers inside the van. His words were faint and somewhat muffled, coming as they did from the wire secured under Wilhelm's shirt. Vasques leaned in close to hear. "One of the girls tried to run this morning. She didn't make it twenty feet, but she made a real scene. Lucky nobody called it in and brought round the heat."

Chains issued a string of what must have been curses in some language that Vasques didn't understand. She looked back at the monitor as Chains threw open the door of the motel room and stormed inside. Wilhelm followed him in, and Chains's enraged voice crackled and reverberated around the van's interior. He screamed out more angry phrases in the strange dialect, and then in Spanish, he said,

"I'm not even going to ask which one of you it was. It doesn't matter. One of you betrays me, you all betray me. You all suffer. If I had other girls lined up to replace you, I'd kill every last one of you and dump your bodies into the land-fill with the rest of the garbage. Unfortunately, I don't have replacements, and I do have a business to run. But you need to see what happens when you betray our little family."

Vasques leaned forward to the edge of her stool, translat-ing the Spanish in her head as best she could. Then one of the girls issued a shrill scream, and, probably for their ben-efit, Wilhelm said, "Chains, you don't need to use a knife on her, do you?"

It was all that Vasques needed to hear. She lunged toward the back doors of the van. They flew open, and her .45 cali-ber Sig Sauer 1911 Stainless was in her hand before her feet touched the pavement. She stumbled forward and almost fell, her legs asleep from sitting for so long in the cramped space.

"Vasques! Wait!"

She ignored her partner and, regaining her balance, sprinted across the Starbright's parking lot. She hit the stairs and flew up them two at a time. She reached the top, and before the bald guard could register her presence or react, the side of her pistol slammed against his left temple and her knee found his groin. She shoved past the dazed man and heard her partner at her back telling the guard to kiss the ground.

She took up position next to the door of Chains's holding pen. Looking back, she saw LaPaglia slap the cuffs onto the bald guard and noticed the two Cook County deputies racing up the stairs. But she wouldn't allow herself to wait. Even a second's hesitation at this point could be the difference be-tween life and death for a young Guatemalan girl who only wanted a better life for herself and her family.

Vasques spun her body round, and her foot struck the door. It splintered inward. "FBI," she screamed into the room. She slipped inside and caught sight of Chains against the back wall. He held a tiny girl in front of his large Jamaican frame. His arms had snaked around her waist, and her feet dangled two feet above the floor. His right hand held a Glock 9 mm. The rest of the room was empty except for the girls, Wilhelm, and a few blankets. The usual bed, television, desk, and cheap photo prints typically found in a room such as this had been removed. The girls hadn't even been given mattresses to sleep on. An all-too-familiar stench of abuse and fear permeated the air.

"Come any closer, and she dies." Even as Chains spoke, he began to back toward the bathroom.

Vasques sighted down her weapon and wanted badly to squeeze the trigger, but she couldn't risk it. The big man held the girl in front of his head, and anything other than a head shot could get the hostage killed. Chains continued to back away into the open door of the bathroom. This had quickly become a hostage situation. The plan had been to apprehend him after he left the motel. This was the very situation they had hoped to avoid. Vasques's guts churned, and she knew that her rash actions might have done as much harm as good.

"Now get out, or I'll kill her. I'll only talk to someone who can meet my demands. You bring me someone in charge!" Chains said, and she watched helplessly as he slammed the door to the bathroom.

"Dammit!"

LaPaglia appeared at her side, and the Cook County deputies started to shuffle the other women and Wilhelm from the room. LaPaglia said, "That didn't go quite as planned."

Vasques shook her head in disgust and opened her mouth to comment. But then a thought struck her. She had been focused on Chains in the bathroom, but as the images replayed through her mind, she realized that she had seen a large window over his left shoulder. He hadn't backed himself into a corner with a hostage. He had been trying to buy enough time to slip out the back and escape.

She lunged toward the stairs. "He's going out the back,"

she screamed over her shoulder. At the bottom of the steps, she scanned the front of the motel. The doors were painted a faded red and the walls were a dingy cream. The row of rooms stretched out fifteen units from her position down to the office. She didn't have time to run completely around the building. Chains would be long gone. She wheeled around and saw a corridor slicing through the back section of rooms.

Vasques rounded the stairs and sprinted down the corridor. An ice machine from the 1950s, a vending machine stocked with candy bars and chips, and a Pepsi machine sat inside a niche on her left, but she could see daylight ahead. Her arms pumped, and her feet slapped hard against the cracked concrete walkway. The corridor spilled out into a courtyard containing an empty pool filled at one end with a small puddle of greenish water and withered brown leaves. Her stare darted upward and searched for the back of Chains's room.

Then she saw him. Chains had made his way out the window and was running across the crumbling reddish-brown rooftop heading toward the alley. He hadn't seen her.

She raced round the empty pool and hugged the wall, shadowing Chains's movements from the ground. They reached the end of the building, and she slipped around the corner just as he dropped from the roof onto a nearby dumpster. The large container was blue with white lettering on its side. The lid was made of a black plastic that bent under his substantial weight. He slid off the dumpster and stumbled to the pavement of the alley. His back was to her.

Vasques leveled her 1911 at his back and said, "That's far enough, Chains. It's over."

His large black frame turned slowly in her direction. He had an angry, almost animal look in his eyes. The Glock dangled from his right hand. His nostrils flared in and out like those of a bull about to charge.

"Put it down." She spoke slowly and emphasized each

word. He snorted a laugh, and his right arm started upward.
Vasques fired.

The .45 caliber bullet tore deeply into the meat of his
right shoulder, and he folded in on himself with a shout of
pain. Within a second, she was at his side, kicking his gun
away and covering him as he writhed on the alley's surface.
Speaking again in the strange language, the big Jamaican
clutched his shoulder and uttered what she guessed were
curses upon her and her family.

She heard LaPaglia's feet on the pavement behind her. She
looked down on the creep and felt a little twinge of regret for
not aiming at his head. "You're going to spend Christmas in
jail this year, Chains. And I'm personally going to spread the
word that you have a taste for young girls. So don't worry—
you'll still have a love life when you get on the inside."

VASQUES SLAMMED THE door of the ambulance carrying Chains off for treatment at Alexian Brothers Medical Center. She glanced around at the assortment of police cars and officers. They were taking statements, gathering evidence, and cordoning off the area. The INS counselors had also arrived to take the girls into custody. They had been waiting on standby. Vasques didn't know what the future held for the young women that Chains had forced into slavery, but she knew anything had to be better than the hell they had been enduring.

A familiar voice cut through the confusion. "Seems like trouble follows you wherever you go, Vicky."

Only a couple of people in the world ever called her "Vicky". She turned to find Detective Sergeant Trevor Belacourt leaning against the hood of a red metallic Chevy Impala. His arms were folded across his chest, and he wore a lopsided grin. Belacourt was a big, older man with a hairline somewhere between thinning and bald. A thick mustache hung under a long nose, and one of his front teeth bent outward. He wore khakis and a light brown cape-wool sports coat over a white button-down shirt. Belacourt had been her father's partner during the three years before his death and had since been promoted to head of the Jackson's Grove PD homicide division.

Seeing him here could mean only one thing, but Vasques thought it rude to raise the subject without any preamble. She walked over and gave him a quick hug. "How have you been, Trevor?"

His voice was deep but nasal. "Doing fine. I've been checking the mail every day for an invitation to your wedding."

"I'd have to find a guy first. What about you? You going to spend your golden years as a bachelor?"

He laughed. "Marriage would just cramp my style at the nursing home, little girl. Don't worry. I've got it planned out. I'll be beating the widows off with a stick."

She just nodded as she searched for something more to say.

"Go ahead and speak your mind, kid," Belacourt said. "You know why I'm here."

"The Anarchist is back. He's killing again."

"Found the first one last night. He killed the security guy at a storage yard, then set up his freak show in one of the empty containers. Same MO as before. I already spoke to your SAC and requested that he assign you to consult on the case. He took some convincing but, given your first-hand knowledge of how this guy works and your background in profiling, he finally gave me what I wanted."

Vasques's chest tightened, and memories of her father's death flooded back to her. The Anarchist case had been the last he had worked before his death. She had reviewed the files exhaustively. Somehow, finishing his last case had seemed like the best thing she could do to honor his memory. But she hadn't been able to make any headway. Then the killer had gone underground, and there had been no trace of him for nearly a year and a half.

Vasques nodded as a fierce wave of determination swept over her. She would catch this guy, whatever it took. "What are we waiting for? Let's go look at a crime scene."

IN ANOTHER LIFE, Emily Morgan had been a clinical psychologist helping police officers work through traumatic events. She had married a man named Jim, a trooper with the Colorado State Patrol. They'd had a little girl and a beautiful green and brown two-story colonial that nestled among the trees of Southeastern Colorado. Then, through pure random chance, Francis Ackerman had come into their lives and changed everything.

But through her battle with Ackerman, she'd met a man named Marcus Williams, who had introduced her to another man he referred to only as the Director. She had shown what they had called *great strength* during the confrontation with the killer, and the Director had offered her a position within the Shepherd Organization as a counselor to the field agents.

It had been a chance to start over, a chance to leave behind the memories of Jim and their old lives, and she had packed up her daughter and moved to a small town in northern Virginia.

That had been almost a year ago, and she still had made little progress with her main subject: Marcus Williams. Marcus had a good heart, but he also had a tendency to torture himself and let the weight of the world's problems fall squarely onto his shoulders. In the field, he was a man of action, but when it came to his personal issues, he was a ponderer. She worried about him, and so did the Director.

"Would you like to try another session of hypnosis? See if you can remember any more details from that night?"

"What's the point?" he said.

Marcus sat across from Emily on a tan leather sofa. She had tried to fill the office attached to the back of her home with soothing colors—neutrals and pastels—and peaceful images—babbling brooks, children laughing, forests, sunsets. She had studied the psychology of color and imagery in detail and was constantly experimenting with it, swapping out pictures, gauging the results. It wasn't an exact science, but she desperately wanted to create a bastion for these men and women where they could feel safe and protected. The others seemed calm and relaxed here. But not Marcus. She often wondered if he would feel more at home in her office if she painted the walls black and replaced the babbling brooks with photos of crime scenes. "I think we've made good progress. When we first started, you could barely remember anything except darkness and fear."

"And what do I remember now? A voice in the darkness that you say probably wasn't even there, and my parents screaming. We haven't accomplished anything. It's been a big waste of time. Mine and yours." Emily reached up and removed her glasses, laid them and her notebook on a nearby table. Then she leaned forward in her chair and braced her elbows against her knees. "I disagree completely, but you have never told me why you wanted to remember more about that night. Had you hoped to find their killer somehow? To remember some clue that would lead you to him?"

An unreadable emotion flashed through Marcus's eyes, and for the briefest of moments, she thought that he was actually going to open up. Then he pulled his phone from his pocket and showed her the time. "I think our session is over, Doc. I wouldn't want to have the taxpayers charged overtime."

She leaned back in her chair and sighed. "I've told you before. I'm here for you, day or night. Holding on to anger is like grasping a hot coal with the intent of throwing it at someone else. You are the one who gets burned."

Marcus cocked an eyebrow. "You read that on a fortune cookie?"

"My grandfather was Japanese and a Buddhist. He taught me that phrase. It was a teaching of Buddha. My grandmother was Irish Catholic. She taught me to love your enemies and pray for those who persecute you. That one's from Jesus."

He said nothing.

Emily considered another teaching of Buddha that her grandfather had taught her. *Better than a thousand hollow words is one word that brings peace.* Unfortunately, she had yet to find anything to bring peace to Marcus Williams.

"How long has it been since you've slept?"

"Why? You offering to tuck me in?"

She didn't respond. She had seen him like this before. Any attempt at real conversation would be answered by a smart-ass comment to deflect attention from the issues at hand. She simply stood and walked back to her desk. She pulled open a drawer, took out a bottle of pills, and tossed them in his direction.

He snatched them from the air and stared down at the bottle. "What the hell is this?"

Emily sat down at her desk and started to make some notes. "I picked you up something to help you sleep."

"Thanks, Doc. But no thanks. I need to be focused. I can't be taking crap like this." Marcus tossed the pill bottle in her direction. She caught it and immediately threw it back at him with as much force as she could muster. It bounced off his chest.

"Focused? How focused do you think you are, running on fumes? Exhaustion reduces your operational efficiency to zero. It's as bad as being drunk. You take those damn pills and get some sleep, or I'll pull your ass from active duty. Is that clear enough for you?"

He stared at her for a moment, but then he reached down and retrieved the bottle of pills. He headed toward the door.

She stared down at her notes for a second, but then said, "Marcus, be careful out there."

Without turning back, he said, "You know that Buddha also taught, 'The whole secret of existence is to have no fear. Never fear what will become of you, depend on no one. Only the moment you reject all help are you freed.'"

Emily opened her mouth to respond but couldn't find the words. She simply watched his back as he pulled open her door and slipped out into the night.

MARCUS WALKED INTO his office and threw his leather jacket over the back of one of the black visitor chairs in front of his desk. The whole room smelled of new leather and old vinyl. The leather scent originated from the new furniture he had purchased on the Shepherd Organization's tab. The old-vinyl smell came from his collection of records sitting in one corner. Movie posters lined the walls—Jack Nicholson films, the first *Predator*, the second *Aliens*, the first three Indiana Jones movies, *Die Hard*, and an assortment of his other favorites. All were signed by the cast and crew. A growing collection of screen-used film props rested in a display case in one corner. He had a lot of disposable income and spent what little downtime he had on eBay. The office contained no family photos.

He had sensed the man sitting on his couch as he entered, but he feigned ignorance until he sat down at his desk and started to open his mail. Without looking up from a package in a padded manila mailer, he let the other man know that he was aware of his presence. "You should be careful who you sneak up on. I typically shoot first and ask questions later."

"How do you know that I haven't already removed the firing pin from your Sig?"

Marcus looked up at the Director of the Shepherd Organization and almost reached to his shoulder holster to check. "That sounds like something you'd do."

"I've told you, kid. Most situations you face are far beyond your control. So you need to control the ones you can." The Director nudged a pillow and blanket resting against the arm of the couch. "I heard you got rid of the apartment we leased for you and moved into your office."

"The apartment was pointless. I'm on the road ninety percent of the time, and when I'm not I spend all my time here. Think of all the taxpayer dollars we're saving."

"It's hard to have a home life when you don't have a home, Marcus."

He spread his arms. "This is my home."

The Director looked around the office at the various collections, then his eyes settled on stacks of crime-scene photos resting on the desktop. "Are things any better between you and Maggie?"

Marcus said nothing. He stared expressionlessly at the Director for a moment and then pointed at a file folder tucked under the older man's arm. "We have a new case?"

"Old case, actually. New developments. But you didn't answer my question."

He didn't respond.

"She loves you. You know that, don't you?" the Director said.

Marcus stuck out his hand. "Are you going to give me the file? If it's anything like the other cases we work, there's no time to screw around."

The Director stood statue-still, the file pressed firmly under his left arm. "How have you been sleeping?"

Marcus blew out a frustrated breath and came around the desk. "You brought me in to do a job, and that's what I've been doing nonstop for the past year. I live and breathe it. I've brought down every bad guy you've put on my desk. Do you have any doubts that I can do the job you recruited me for?"

The Director's gaze didn't waver. "You know I don't."

"Then give me the damn file, and let me do my job. If you've got a problem with the way I'm handling things on a professional level, feel free to bust my ass for it. Anything beyond that, keep it to yourself."

The Director was quiet for a moment. Neither of them moved. Then the Director's right hand reached across his chest and took hold of the file. His arm straightened, and he stuck the file out between them. Marcus snatched it from the Director's grasp, leaned back on the corner of his desk, and opened it at the first page. "The Anarchist?"

"That's right. We don't actually know how many he's killed, but there's definitely some type of an occult connection. Details are in the file. He's been dormant for about a year and a half. Allen worked the case briefly before the killer went under and is planning on meeting you in Chicago. This guy killed three women and then five more disappeared without a trace."

"No bodies were ever found for the five?"

"Not yet. But, of course, they're assumed dead. Remember, let the police do their jobs and keep a low profile, but do whatever's necessary to stop this guy."

Marcus nodded. When he had first been recruited, the Director had made it seem that their only desirable outcome was to kill the men they hunted, but sometimes it worked out fine to just help where they could and let the police take the killers down. He hoped that he wouldn't have to do any killing on this trip.

The Director started toward the door but added, "I want you to get at least a day's rest before jumping into this case. The police can start laying the groundwork, and you'll be there in plenty of time. We need you at one hundred percent. Is that clear?"

"Absolutely, crystal clear. One hundred and ten percent."

The Director's eyes narrowed slightly, but he didn't comment further. As he closed Marcus's door, he said, "Godspeed and good hunting."

Marcus walked back toward his desk and cleared off a spot for the file. There was a thumb drive in a plastic baggy attached to the cover page. He slipped it out and plugged it into his MacBook Air. He wondered why the Director still brought him paper files. Since taking over, he had transitioned his entire team to digital. He opened the case files and dropped them into a secure email for Andrew and the other members of the team. Then he brought up pictures of the women that the Anarchist had killed a year and a half ago and the girl from the previous night. The images were candid shots of happy smiling faces. He imagined some of these pictures probably adorned missing-persons reports posted around the Chicago area. These women had once had families. They had once had hopes and dreams, wants and desires. But everything they were and would ever be had been stolen from them. He studied the eyes. He memorized the faces.

After a few moments in silence, he retrieved the cell phone from his pocket and dialed Andrew. "I just sent you an email."

Silence stretched on the other end of the line. "We're going out again already?"

"No rest for the wicked. I want to be on the road in a few hours. Start gathering our things."

Andrew sighed. "You're the boss."

Marcus hung up and then punched a key on his computer keyboard to bring up the case files. He felt for the pills in his pocket and stared down at the bottle. Then he dropped it into his desk drawer and shut it away. Innocent lives hung in the balance, and he had a lot of reading to do before they headed out for Chicago.

INSIDE THE WORKSHOP in his garage, Harrison Schofield routed his Internet access through three proxy servers. He was relatively certain that the police would never be able to trace anything back to him. The cameras had no access logs, and he had taken precautions to mask his digital identity. He had installed a wireless range extender in a set of trees behind his home and had connected to the unsecured wireless network of one of his neighbors. Even if they could trace him back to the source IP address, they would end up at his neighbor's house, not his. As always, he had considered all the possibilities, calculated all the variables. At least, he hoped he had.

Being sure that he was fairly anonymous, he accessed the feed for the cameras and cycled through the different views. There she was, Jessie Olague, the next sacrifice. She was going through her nightly routine. A routine that he had been studying for over six months.

She was playing music, and although he couldn't hear it, he could feel the beat through the rhythm of her body. The subtle bobbing of her head. The gentle sway of her hips. She seemed so happy, so at peace with the world around her. He wondered how she managed to feel that way. Through his research, he had learned everything about Jessie Olague.

Her parents had been drug addicts. Child welfare had stepped in, and she had spent the remainder of her youth bouncing from foster home to foster home. She had no children. Repeated ovarian cysts had scarred her reproductive organs beyond repair and made her infertile. Her husband was an abusive drunk when he was actually home. Luckily for her, the husband worked nights, and she rarely saw him. They met only in passing, but even those moments were tense and potentially violent. Jessie had only a few close friends and worked a dead-end job at a local coffee shop in the mall, where Schofield had first taken notice of her.

Despite all this, she was rarely without a smile. She volunteered at a local soup kitchen every Sunday and at an animal shelter on the second Tuesday of every month. She seemed to brighten every room she entered. Jessie Olague had a good soul.

Schofield wanted what she had. He needed it.

That kind of joy and contentment was so elusive and rare. He had been born without a soul. But soon he would steal a piece of hers. He would feel what she felt. He would taste her happiness and make it his own.

SCHOFIELD PARKED IN the alley behind Jessie Olague's home and slipped the black balaclava over his head, leaving only his eyes and mouth exposed. He scanned the area one last time and then stepped from his vehicle. There was no hesitation in his stride. He had visualized and choreographed his every movement. *Slip past the garage, follow the walkway, bend down to retrieve the key to the back door hidden beneath a pot containing a withered Cajun hibiscus that Jessie should have brought inside for the winter, up the steps to the sliding glass door, insert the key, twist, slide the door gently to the side, step into the house, slide the door shut.*

He scanned the interior of her kitchen. It was odd seeing the room from this angle and in full color. He had become accustomed to the grainy black and white of the video feed. Red and white Americana decorations adorned the walls and countertops of the kitchen and the connected dining room. A meager Christmas tree—bedecked with homemade ornaments—sat in the living room beside the front window. The blinds were drawn but light from a passing car seeped through the cracks and ran along the ceiling. He listened for movement but heard nothing beyond the creaks and groans of a house in winter.

His eyes closed, and he took in the scent of the house. She had been burning a candle. The sweet smell of butterscotch still floated through the air.

Schofield stepped through the living room and up the stairs toward Jessie's bedroom. The second and fifth steps had developed nasty creaks with age. He avoided those altogether, skipping over them and stepping straight to the third and sixth steps. At the top of the stairs, he clung to the side wall in the shadows and made his way down the hall to the door at the end.

The door would be locked from the inside by a common chain latch. He took out and unfolded a wire tool with a magnet on the end that could easily bypass the simple lock. He pulled open the door just a centimeter and slipped the wire through the crack at the top of the frame. Then he positioned the magnet to catch the slide and gently eased it free. He kept hold of the latch, not letting it fall, as he crept inside the bedroom.

With cautious and quiet steps, Schofield moved to the side of the bed.

He stood over Jessie for a moment and watched her sleep. She wore a long T-shirt and flannel pajama bottoms. The gray donkey from Winnie the Pooh adorned the front of the shirt. A stray strand of hair had fallen across her cheek and mouth. He resisted the urge to brush it away.

Moving to the foot of the bed, he gently raised the covers to expose her bare feet. From a pocket of his jacket, he slipped out the Lidocaine, a powerful topical anesthetic, and applied it to the area between her toes. He watched for another few minutes as he waited for the Lidocaine to deaden the skin sufficiently. Then he inserted and emptied a syringe filled with a cocktail of Demerol, Valmid, and Valium into the deadened section of flesh.

Schofield checked his watch and waited another few minutes. After which, he stepped to the side of the bed and brushed away the strand of hair. She didn't move. He bent down and kissed her on the cheek.

"I'm sorry, Jessie. I wish it didn't have to be this way."

MAGGIE CARLISLE STEPPED down the metal stairs into the garage bay. A single roll-up door opened to the outside world but the large open bay contained their unit's entire vehicle pool—a black GMC Yukon, a cream panel van, a white Ford Escape Hybrid, a silver Buick LaCrosse, and a 1969 Chevrolet Camaro Z28. It was black with red racing stripes and all the trimmings and served as Marcus's personal vehicle. She often wondered if Marcus had conned the Director into buying it for him like some kind of signing bonus.

The walls around the vehicles were faded brick. The floor had once been smooth concrete but had cracked and split in certain spots to the point where they had been forced to bust it free and replace whole sections with gravel. Some type of vegetation had taken root in one corner and climbed up the brick.

Above her head sat the nerve center for their unit that housed the offices and training areas. The building, an old textile-manufacturing facility, had sat empty for over ten years. It had been scheduled for demolition. To say that the accommodations were modest was an understatement, but Marcus had found the place and had fallen in love with it. At least it was in a good location. The brick building sat nestled within a group of trees on a dead-end road near Rose Hill, Virginia. Which placed them only a short drive from I-395 that could take them north over the George Mason Memorial Bridge and into the heart of Washington DC in a little under half an hour.

Maggie reached the bottom of the rusty metal stairs and

stormed across the garage bay toward the Yukon. The doors of the black SUV stood open, and Marcus and Andrew were piling the vehicle up with equipment. She could hear them bickering.

Andrew opened up the top of an ammo box and said, "Why in the hell do we need this much firepower?"

Marcus's reply echoed across the cracked and patched floor. "It's the condom principle."

"Huh?"

"You know, I'd rather have one and not need it, than need one and not have it."

"We have two fully auto KRISS Super Vs and 5,000 rounds of .45 ACP ammo. Plus multiple sidearms. What are you expecting, zombie apocalypse?"

"You never know. But the next time we go close-quarters, I want the firepower on our side."

"I'm coming with you," Maggie said as soon as she reached them. Marcus dropped a duffel bag back to the gravel and turned toward her. His eyes were unreadable behind a pair of dark Oakley sunglasses. "I need you to stay here, Maggie. We may come up with additional leads that we'll need you to investigate outside the Chicago area."

She looked to Andrew for support, but he only raised his eyebrows and shrugged his shoulders in a way that told her she was on her own. "Dammit, Marcus. You can't do this to me. This is the third case where you've stuck me on the sidelines doing paperwork. Ever since Harrisburg you've been coddling me like I'm some kind of child who needs babysitting. I made a simple mistake that could have happened to any of us. I don't deserve to be benched over it."

"A simple mistake? You disobeyed my orders, and you were almost killed. But that's beside the point—it's not why you're hanging back. We may need you here. End of discussion."

She reached out and grabbed his arm. She whispered, "Is this because of what's been happening between us? I'm a professional. I would never allow our personal relationship to affect my performance."

Marcus closed his eyes for a second and then said, "It has nothing to do with that, either. I really just need you here. Okay?"

Maggie sensed some emotion in his voice. Fear. Shame. Regret. But regret over what? Was he sorry for the way he was handling their relationship or that they had a relationship at all? She didn't know how to respond, and so she said nothing.

Heavy footsteps slapped the concrete at her back, and she turned to see Stan Macallan, their unit's technology guru, approaching. Stan said to Marcus, "I emailed you those statistics and files you wanted on Chicago."

Marcus nodded. "Thanks." To Maggie, he said, "I'll call you tomorrow morning with an update on the case."

Andrew had finished loading the Yukon and raised the door to the garage. He gave Maggie a little wave as he climbed behind the wheel. Marcus glanced at the SUV and back to her. It looked as if there was something more he wanted to say, but as usual, he held his tongue. With a nod, he walked over to the Yukon and climbed inside.

As Maggie watched the big black vehicle pull away from the building and down a dirt path dotted with alternating patches of grass and gravel, she wondered why the man she loved didn't reciprocate her feelings. And if he did, why did he push her away?

SPECIAL AGENT VICTORIA VASQUES thanked the pale-faced young man at the Starbucks drive-through for her coffee and pulled the gray Crown Victoria out into traffic on Route 30. The Jackson's Grove PD crime techs had already cleared the second abduction scene, and the woman's husband was down at the station answering questions. She wanted to get another look without all the distractions, and tonight would be her best opportunity. It was only a short drive across Lincoln Highway and down Division Street to reach the young woman's house on Hickory.

The Chicago Metropolitan Area consumed over ten thousand square miles of land and had a population of 9.8 million people. The suburbs stretched out as an interconnected series of towns and villages, each almost filled with wall-to-wall houses and businesses. All of them had their own quaint little names and self-contained police departments with jurisdictions defined by street names rather than geography. The actual city of Chicago was the epicenter, but it was all Chicagoland.

As Vasques traveled through the peaceful suburban neighborhood, she couldn't help but consider how the residents would never expect such a thing to happen here. No one ever did. But she knew that the Anarchist could live in any one of the houses she passed, a wolf nestled unseen among the sheep.

She followed the path the killer would have taken and pulled into the alley behind the cream two-story house. From the passenger seat, her little Yorkie puppy yapped and hopped onto her lap. The pink dog tag on its collar jingled like a bell when it moved. It sniffed her face and licked her on the nose. She recoiled and patted it lightly on its head, still not used to its affections. Her brother, Robbie, had given her the dog as an early Christmas present, commenting that if she was never going to find a man she should at least have a dog. Luckily, she had an elderly neighbor who could care for it while she was away at work. Robbie was impulsive. He never considered things like that.

"Okay. That's great," she said as the little dog's tongue lapped at her cheeks. She pressed its head down, away from her face. "Okay, enough. I've got work to do. If you crap in this car while I'm gone, I'll buy a big snake and feed you to it."

She looked at the back of the house and thought of the missing woman, Jessie Olague. The poor girl was still out there somewhere at that very moment. Terrified, alone, waiting for someone to save her, wondering what would happen if no one came, brooding on the fact that her own death might be approaching.

A cigarette craving attacked Vasques as it usually did when she was stressed. She popped in another stick of gum and chomped on it frantically. She had picked a hell of a time to quit smoking.

As she worked on the piece of gum, she noticed something strange about the house. The lights were still on in several of the rooms. The crime-scene techs surely would have turned off all the lights when they left, and the husband was still at the station.

She reached for her phone and dialed Belacourt's number. "Hey, Trevor. I figured you'd be questioning the husband."

The tinny voice on the other end of the line said, "We're taking a break. Letting him get it together. He's pretty torn up about the whole thing."

"So you don't think there's any chance of him being involved?"

"Too early to say for sure. But if he is, he's trying for an Oscar. So what's up at your end?"

"Do you have any units still at the house?"

"The Olague house? No, they buttoned it up a couple hours back." She was afraid that she was just being paranoid, but it was better to be safe than sorry. "The lights are still on."

"I guess they might have forgotten to turn them off. It was still daylight when they left, but those guys are obviously pretty detail-oriented individuals. Tell you what, you stay put, and I'll send over a couple units to give you backup."

"Okay. Thanks."

Vasques ended the call and then watched as another light flipped on in the home's second story. Her hand flew to her .45 caliber handgun, and she stepped out of the Crown Vic, leaving a yipping Yorkie behind.

Someone was inside the house, and she didn't have time to wait for backup.

13

VASQUES MADE HER way into the house through the sliding glass door and stopped to listen. She heard movement on the second floor and headed toward the stairs, taking aim at the railing above her head. Her weight automatically shifted forward, and her arms locked straight out. Her heart rate pulsed, and her index finger twitched against the trigger guard of her .45 caliber Sig Sauer 1911. Situations like this never seemed to get any easier.

She crept up the stairs and cursed them as they cracked and popped beneath her feet. At the top, she paused again to listen. Footsteps sounded from the victim's bedroom, the same room where the killer had left his signature.

This could be him. Killers often returned to the scene of a crime in one way or another in order to relive the events of the crime or re-enact their fantasy. The Anarchist could be less than twenty feet away.

Breathing in deeply, she pressed forward down the hall and nudged the bedroom door open with her right foot. Inside the room, she saw a man in a gray button-down shirt and khakis staring at the pictures resting on Jessie Olague's oak dresser. He was turned away from her.

In a calm but firm voice, Vasques said, "Put your hands on your head."

He complied and raised his arms slowly. But something wasn't right. Too late, she sensed a presence behind her.

She spun toward the second intruder, but he was already on top of her. She caught only a flash of him from the shadows as he lunged forward. Black hooded sweatshirt, leather jacket, blue jeans.

He caught her gun hand in a strong fist, and with frightening precision, he twisted her wrist and wrenched the weapon from her grasp. Before she could react, he thrust out a palm into her breastbone, driving her through the doorway of the bedroom.

As she fought to regain her balance, she immediately regretted not waiting for backup.

From behind her, she heard the man in the khakis say, "I think it's your turn to put your hands up."

The man in the hallway stepped into the light of the bedroom and aimed her own weapon at her chest. He was slightly larger than average size, maybe six foot one, and had dark brown hair. His clothes fit loosely, but she could see the ridges and contours of firm muscles hiding within the folds of cloth and leather. He had bright, intelligent eyes, but cracks of red cut through the whites. She wondered if she'd stumbled onto some kind of robbery. Maybe these guys had heard what had happened and didn't expect anyone to be coming home anytime soon. Society was full of parasites like that, waiting in the wings to take advantage of someone else's pain.

Vasques raised her hands and placed them against the sides of her head.

The man holding her gun surprised her by ejecting the magazine and jacking back the slide to remove the shell loaded into the chamber. He caught the ejected bullet, slid it back into the magazine, and tossed it along with the .45 onto Jessie Olague's bed. Without a word, he reached into his front pocket and held up an ID that read *Department of Justice, Special Agent Marcus Williams.*

Her hands immediately dropped from her head, and she jammed a finger into his chest. "What the hell are you doing here? This is a crime scene. You never go to a crime scene without first contacting the agency conducting the investigation. Of all the stupid things to do. I could've killed the both of you."

Williams actually rolled his eyes. Vasques wanted to kick him squarely in the balls. That would have wiped that smug look off his face. "I'm sure we'll all lose sleep over it," he said.

"Who do you think you are? Since when does Justice investigate cases like this? You have no right even to be here."

Agent Williams stepped forward, closing the distance between them to inches. "We're special investigators ordered here by Thomas Caldwell himself. You've heard of him, right? Attorney General of the US. Highest-ranking law-enforcement officer in the country."

"I don't care who sent you. That doesn't give you the right to bypass the proper channels and ignore protocol."

Willams's eyes narrowed to slits. "There's a woman's life on the line. I don't have time to stand here and listen to you blow smoke. You can take your proper channels and protocols and ram them straight up your—"

The man in the khakis cut into the conversation and stepped between them. "Okay, well, I'm Special Agent Andrew Garrison, and we're very sorry that we didn't follow protocol. We were coming through this area and wanted to save some time, but you're right, we should have called ahead." Williams rolled his eyes again and stepped away. Garrison shot him an irritated look. "We've been sent here to consult on the investigation. I think we might have gotten off on the wrong foot, but same team and all, so no reason we can't start fresh. How would that be? And I don't believe we got your name."

She started to tell Garrison that they didn't need any help, but she knew government bureaucracies well enough to know that it wouldn't do any good to shut them out. If they really had been sent by the AG, then these two were about as well connected as anyone could be. "Fine. Special Agent Victoria Vasques, FBI. What were you doing here, anyway?"

Williams said, "I wanted to get a look at the crime scene without all the distractions."

She remembered her own motives for coming there and then realized that Belacourt had called in other officers. She swore as she grabbed for her phone and canceled the backup units. Then she gestured toward the hallway and said, "Since we're already here, I guess I might as well give you the grand tour."

14

ACKERMAN PUNCHED A key on the laptop to bring up the command-line interface. Then he activated the back-door Trojan that would give him access to a workstation located within the office of the Director of the Shepherd Organization. The Trojan was a small program embedded within the actual operating system of the host machine and, according to his expert, it was virtually undetectable. He had used his special skills to kidnap the sister of a renowned hacker and force the man's cooperation. The hacker's skills had proven well worth his trouble. Ackerman had always found it easy to get what he wanted when he was willing to cause pain or take life to achieve his goal. And he was an expert in pain.

He pulled up the active case files for Marcus's unit and began to read about this man the media had dubbed *The Anarchist*. The more he read, the more impressed he became. He admired the Anarchist's work. This fellow knew about the hunger. Ackerman could tell that for sure.

He closed the laptop and gathered his things. Chicago. He could easily be there by morning.

His gaze found the clock on the nightstand, and his mind calculated the travel time for any police units in the area. The cheap hotel room had wi-fi included with the price of a night's rental. He had routed his activity through remote nodes and proxy servers as his hacker friend had shown him—mainly through those located in foreign and less than friendly countries like Belarus, nations that would be unlikely to cooperate with US government investigations. But, as an extra precaution, he never stayed in the location where he accessed the files. He got in and out quickly like a ghost in the machine, as though he had never even been there. Then he simply slipped away into the night. They had tried to track him through his calls to Marcus, but he was too careful for that. And he was too careful to be caught by his computer access as well.

The walls of the hotel room were black and white. Pictures had been hanging there when he had first entered but he had removed them all. Ackerman had spent his childhood in a tiny cell being tortured by his father. After that, he had spent several more years in mental institutions and prisons. He had become accustomed to a lack of possessions and decorations, and it made him feel strangely uneasy to sleep in a room with pictures hanging on the walls. In fact, he preferred a room without furniture of any kind, and he often slept on the floor.

He considered putting the pictures back but decided against it. He needed to get on the road. Marcus would soon be needing his special brand of help.

15

VASQUES WATCHED AGENT Williams with suspicion as his stare crawled over every inch of the crime scene. He seemed to be lingering on and absorbing every minute detail. She checked her watch and tried to fight down her growing anxiety. She said, "The killer's very careful. He leaves virtually no evidence behind."

"Everywhere you go, you take something with you, and you leave something behind. Locard's Exchange Principle," Williams said.

Vasques replied, "I had that class, too. Of course he's left behind traces. Unfortunately, this guy hasn't left behind anything to tell us where to find him. He's left shoe prints, size ten and a half, but he changes the shoes after every scene. The shoes he wears are as common as you can get. They can be picked up at any Walmart. We've found talcum powder on the door handles."

"Latex gloves."

"Right. No hair samples or skin cells that we've found. No fingerprints. He drugs the women so there's no struggle and no blood left behind. He—"

Agent Williams held up a hand to stop her and said, "I've read all this in the files. I really just need you to be quiet. I'll let you know if I have any questions."

His rudeness and audacity struck Vasques speechless. She fought for words. "What exactly is your specialty at the Department of Justice, *Special* Agent Williams?"

His mouth curled into a lopsided grin. "Call me Marcus. And that's classified."

He stepped past her and headed toward the back door. She was dumbfounded. She turned to the other agent, the one who had introduced himself as Andrew Garrison. She gave him an *is-he-always-like-this?* look, to which Garrison answered with an awkward *sorry-about-my-partner* shrug.

She followed Williams out the sliding glass door, furious that she had to babysit these idiots instead of catching a killer.

16

MARCUS EXITED THE Olague house and made his way through the backyard. The snowfall crunched beneath his feet, and the cold irritated his cheeks. He reached the alley and released a deep breath. It hung in the air as a puff of white vapor. His eyes closed, and he tried to shut out all the distractions and center himself. Somewhere in the distance, he heard Vasques complaining to Andrew and Andrew playing the role of the diplomat, but he ignored them.

He reached down inside and felt the hunger churning in his gut. It waited for him down in the depths, in the dark place, and he called it to the surface.

When his eyes opened, he was ready. He looked at the house with new awareness.

From his vantage point, he could see into part of the kitchen and dining room but not clearly enough to know when Jessie Olague had gone to bed. They had left the lights on. He could see many of them burning in the windows, but from the alley, he couldn't see her bedroom window on the far side of the house. Maybe from the front? No, a large hard maple tree blocked the view from there.

The killer would want to see her. That was part of the game, part of the excitement. To violate her privacy. Watch her and then own her, possess her.

The alleyway was on a slant. Maybe farther up it? Marcus walked up the slight incline and turned round. From here, he would have had a better view of the kitchen and some of the other rooms if he'd used binoculars. Marcus flipped on his flashlight and scanned the ground, looking for anything out of place—cigarette butts, candy-bar wrapper, coffee cup. But no such luck.

It still didn't feel right. This woman hadn't been chosen at random. She'd been selected for a reason, and every aspect of the crime was planned out carefully. He would want to see her, Marcus thought again. Maybe even know her, or at least feel as though he did.

"What the hell is he doing? It's freezing out here," Vasques said to Andrew.

Marcus ignored her and moved back to his original position. He would have wanted to know the lay of the land in order to ensure that he wasn't seen as he approached the house. He was very careful. Every movement calculated, analyzed. Marcus made a mental note that the killer might work with numbers or variables, but he knew that was pure conjecture at this point.

As he examined the area—the alley, the position of the Olague house, viewpoints from the homes of neighbors, fences, trees, obstructions—the killer knew that there would be no way to make sure that no one saw him or his vehicle. He took them in the night, so most of the neighbors would be sleeping, but that couldn't be guaranteed. Too many variables, not a risk he would take.

He would wear a mask or hood, obscure his face and hair in some way. And he would have taken precautions to make sure that his vehicle was untraceable.

Marcus moved toward the house, following the path the killer would have taken, until he reached the back porch and the sliding glass door. The porch was just an elevated concrete slab with an awning over the top. It provided no cover from watching eyes. A credit card wouldn't work in a sliding glass door. He could pick the lock—as Marcus and Andrew had done earlier—but that would leave him very exposed. If someone was observing, he would want his entry to seem casual, not like a burglary. Picking the lock was risky, especially if the back-porch light had been left on. It would've been best to have a key.

"No signs of forced entry, right?"

"Oh, so you're talking to me now?" Agent Vasques said.

Marcus shot her a withering glance and waited. After a moment she gave up on the staring contest and replied, "No forced entry."

He nodded. Then he felt round the door but found no box for a hidden key. His gaze traveled across the small porch. There were a few potted plants scattered around. There was also an area on the outside of the porch filled with small rocks of assorted colors and dried-up flowers covered in snow. Red landscaping bricks surrounded the sectioned-out area and separated the rock from the grass. A key could have been hidden beneath any of the bricks, but that would have made getting to it more difficult. It would have been filthy, covered in dirt, surrounded by bugs and worms.

He walked over to the potted plants and started tilting them over. Beneath the third pot sat a small black box with white letters on it spelling out the words *Hide-a-Key*.

"Has this been dusted for prints? Maybe we'd get lucky. Maybe he forgot to put on the gloves until after he had the key." Marcus doubted it, but everyone made mistakes.

Vasques said, "They might have checked it already, but I'll find out for sure."

Marcus pulled open the back door and stepped inside. He took in the red and white kitchen, the dining room, the living room. He absorbed the smells, the sounds. A few typical pops and groans. A faint trace of something in the air. Butterscotch. A candle showing signs of recent use sat nearby on an old oak hutch. The plain white label on its face read *Maple Valley Candles*.

He followed the path through the living room and up the stairs to the bedrooms. The stairs creaked loudly beneath his feet. He tested each step to find which ones made noise.

He wondered if the killer would have known this as well. Was he that good?

At the top of the stairs, Marcus moved to Jessie's bedroom and imagined her sleeping peacefully in the bed. The files and notes he had read climbed to the front of his mind. The killer drugged them to make sure there was no struggle. Marcus imagined inserting the syringe, scooping her into his arms, and humming softly to keep her feeling calm and safe.

But how did I know for sure that she would be asleep? he thought. The Anarchist was too attentive to every detail to leave that to chance. If he opened the door and she was reading a book or had worries weighing on her mind that kept her from getting to sleep, there would be a violent struggle. She would fight him. She would scratch and bite. She would run, throw things at him. But that had never happened at any of the abduction scenes.

More questions came to mind. How did he know her husband wouldn't be home? How did he know that no one would be stopping by to disturb them? What time did she go to bed? What time did she have to be at work in the morning?

The answer was simple. The killer knew those things because he had studied her. He knew all her habits and routines. He was a highly organized offender. Calculating, leaving nothing to chance.

But it still seemed as if he was missing something.

How did I know for sure that she would be asleep?

Marcus's gaze centered on the three-foot-tall red capital letter A within a circle written in spray paint on the wall of the bedroom. It was the killer's signature, his calling card, and it had earned him his nickname. *The Anarchist.*

Marcus imagined carrying the girl through the doorway, down the hall, down the stairs, to the back porch. At that point, he would once again have had to move exposed through the backyard.

"Have there been any witnesses at all?"

"We put the time of all the abductions and killings at

around three in the morning. Most people are asleep. We did have one guy on the previous set of murders that went out for a smoke and saw a car pulling down the alley. It was a dead end. The best one was from the scene of the last girl's abduction. A woman saw a guy park in the alley and approach the house. But she didn't think anything of it at the time, so she couldn't give us many details beyond what we already know."

"I'd like to talk to her myself."

Vasques pressed two fingers against her temple and rubbed. Then she took a piece of gum from her pocket and shoved it into her mouth, adding it to at least two other pieces already there. "Whatever," she said. "I'll arrange it. Are we done here? I'm going to turn off the lights and lock up."

Marcus glanced around the room and then nodded. "Yeah, we're done."

As he stepped into the cold on the back porch, he fought down a wave of despair. He had learned a few things, gained a few insights. But it wasn't much. The Anarchist was a pro, and Marcus had a terrible feeling that there was no way to stop him before more innocent people died.

17

ELEANOR ADARE SCHOFIELD bent down and kissed her husband good-night. He squeezed her hand and rubbed it against his cheek. "Love you. Don't stay up too late," she said. She worked the early-morning shift as a nurse at Oak Forest Hospital. She was in bed early most every night.

"Love you too," Harrison Schofield said as he watched Eleanor ascend the open staircase leading to the second floor of their beautiful home.

The dark wooden floors were a custom job based upon vintage designs. They featured a perimeter apron made from strips of oak in a log-cabin pattern inlaid with narrower strips of walnut with a square-knot pattern in each corner. Schofield had found the design on the Internet and had learned that inlays and intricate patterns became popular after the Industrial Revolution when wood flooring became cheaper to manufacture. The house itself was four thousand, six hundred, and fifty-six square feet, not counting the partially finished basement. Five spacious bedrooms. Three full bathrooms. Dark granite countertops. The master bath contained a whirlpool tub and a large and luxurious walk-in shower with multiple showerheads that caressed his body from all angles. He and his wife both had walk-in closets the size of many people's apartments. The ceilings were twelve feet high in the normal rooms, but many of the others had cathedral ceilings. The outside of the house sat on two lots and was clad in red brick dotted with diamonds of white brick.

It was their dream home. It was perfect in every way. And yet it wasn't enough.

He hated himself for not being happy in this life, but nothing seemed to fill the numb hollow feeling that had infected his heart like a cancer. He felt so anesthetized, so empty, so worthless.

A few years previously, Eleanor had found him a psychiatrist with a ratty gray beard, and he had agreed to a few visits. After a few months of sessions, the therapist had told Schofield that further testing was needed but he might be suffering from a reduced hedonic capacity or an impairment of his ability to gain pleasure from enjoyable experiences. The doctor with the gray beard had gone on to say that this was coupled with a knockout combination of mild depression and Avoidant Personality Disorder. He had explained that this accounted for Schofield's feelings of inadequacy, extreme sensitivity to negative evaluation, and avoidance of social interaction.

But Schofield knew it was much more than that. He had ended the sessions shortly thereafter. A psychiatrist couldn't help him. There was no treatment for what he had.

He couldn't feel joy because he had been born without a soul. Still, he loved his family, and he wanted to be better for them.

They deserved better. They deserved a whole person, and there was only one way to accomplish that.

Schofield pressed the power button on the remote and the large flat-screen television blinked out with a digital chime. He sat alone in the dark for the next hour, planning out the rest of his evening. Then he walked up the stairs and checked on his wife and children. They were all sleeping peacefully in their beds.

It was time for him to go to work.

He made his way to the garage connected to his workshop and opened the trunk of his Toyota Camry. Jessie Olague was still asleep. He had dosed her periodically throughout the day based upon her height, weight, and body-fat percentage in order to ensure that there would be no complications that evening.

He stroked a strand of brown hair away from her face. Jessie reminded him of one of the girls from the compound in the woods where he had grown up. That was what had attracted his attention when he had first seen her working at the coffee shop in the mall. She looked so much like the adult version of the girl he had known all those years ago. The girl's name was Mary Kathryn, and he had once had a secret crush on her.

A vision of the other children screaming and burning flashed through his mind. Their eyes were held open in terror as they stared into the center of the circle at him.

Schofield swallowed hard and pushed away thoughts of the past. He took one last long look at Jessie, and then he closed the trunk. It was time for another sacrifice.

TAKING AIM AT the target, Maggie placed six 9 mm rounds into the center circle of the black silhouette's chest. Breathing hard and seething with frustration, she ejected the magazine and slammed home another. This time she unloaded all fifteen rounds in quick succession into two tight circles, one in the chest and one in the head.

She blew a strand of light blond hair from her eyes and dropped the ear-protection headset over a nail on the side of the firing stall. Then she expertly broke down the Glock 19 by holding back the slide with her right hand and pulling down on the slide releases on both sides of the gun. She pushed the spring forward and pulled it out, repeated this with the barrel. She sprayed down, brushed out and oiled all the components, and reassembled the weapon.

As she exited the firing range, she flipped the lights on and off three times and proceeded down a long hallway to the second door on the right. The bathroom contained an old white sink with exposed pipes and an American Standard toilet. She moved to the sink, washed her hands with antibacterial soap, rinsed, and repeated the process twice more. As she stepped back toward the hall, she quickly flipped the lights on and off three times, creating a strobe effect.

The end of the hall opened into a large room that had once served as a sorting area for the old textile plant. The room now contained an odd combination of brick walls crumbling from decay and rusty red support pillars sitting beside some of the most advanced computer equipment that money could buy. The various server racks and workstations rested inside a large cage. Maggie remembered their resident tech genius, Stan Macallan, mentioning something about it being a Faraday cage that guarded against electromagnetic-pulse attacks. Network and power cables snaked across the floor in a tangled mess. Along with the computer equipment, the cage also contained an eighty-two-inch television, two black leather couches, a coffee table, and a PlayStation 3. The big television displayed the pause screen of a game, and a game controller flashed bright red on the coffee table.

Stan sat at one of the workstations, pounding away at its keyboard in quick staccato blasts. The big hacker wasn't at all what she had expected after hearing about his career highlights. Stan had a PhD from MIT and had started a small software firm that had been purchased by Google for a lucrative stock-and-cash package. Maggie wasn't sure what had happened to him after that.

Within the Shepherd Organization, they had an unwritten "don't ask, don't tell" policy concerning their sordid pasts. They all understood that they had been selected to join the group because of a trauma or incident that gave them a unique perspective. They were all damaged goods. She had learned that Andrew had once had a wife and a daughter and the Director had once been a profiler with the FBI's Behavioral Analysis Unit.

And then, of course, there was her own story involving her younger brother and a serial killer known as *The Taker*. She cringed, thinking of how her brother's killer was still out there, still at large. But she knew virtually nothing about Stan's dark secrets except that she had never seen him leave the building.

Stan also didn't resemble what she'd expect from someone with a PhD. He was six-foot-three and weighed two hundred and seventy pounds. Tattoos ran down his arms, and a reddish-blond beard stretched from his chin to the center of his stomach. A half-empty bottle of twenty-year-old Scotch and a plastic cup sat next to him on the formica surface of the desk.

Flipping a chair around backward, Maggie sat next to him and said, "What are you working on?"

His stare didn't leave the computer screen. "Marcus thinks the Anarchist may not have been dormant during the past year and a half. He thinks maybe he just altered his MO or changed cities. So I'm scouring the cyber landscape for any connections."

"Have you found anything?"

"Nada. What are *you* working on?"

Maggie filled the plastic cup with a double shot of Scotch and downed the whole thing. "You're looking at it."

Stan stared at her, his mouth hanging open. "I don't think I've been more attracted to a woman in my entire life. Would you mind taking off your shirt and doing that again?"

She punched him in the shoulder and poured another glass.

Stan checked the time and said, "I take it Marcus hasn't called you yet."

"No, he hasn't."

"It's still early."

She said nothing but tipped back the glass of Scotch.

Stan continued. "You know, I agree with you. I think it's a load of crap that he made you stay behind. What do you think Marcus would do if he were in the same situation?"

Maggie laughed. "Marcus would tell his superior where to stick it and do whatever he thought was right." The smile faded from her lips. That was exactly what *she* needed to do.

Stan swiveled his chair toward her and said, "If it were me, I'd be off like a prom dress." He grabbed a piece of paper sitting on the opposite side of the computer monitor and held it out to her. "I took the liberty of booking you on the next flight out of DCA heading to O'Hare. Here's your boarding pass. You better get packing."

19

HARRISON SCHOFIELD SAT down for breakfast beside his three children: two girls and one boy, ranging in ages from five to fifteen. His oldest daughter, Alison, placed a plate heaped with pancakes into the center of the dark granite island. He and the kids ate breakfast together every morning at the island in the middle of their kitchen. They had an elegant dining room, but it seemed so formal and impersonal. He and the kids typically ate cereal or Pop-Tarts for breakfast, but Alison had been taking a cooking class at school and had insisted that she prepare them a real breakfast at least once a week.

He knew that he should have felt a surge of pride and pleasure at her responsible and caring nature. After all, his firstborn child was becoming a young woman. But he felt very little, only the same dull ache that permeated every other moment of his existence.

Despite this, he went out of his way to make sure that his children couldn't gauge his true feelings. He sniffed the air and put on a false smile. "It smells wonderful, Alison. I'm very proud of you. You did a great job."

She sat down and winked at him. "You know me, most awesome daughter of the year and all."

He grinned back at her and gave her a loving squeeze on the shoulder. His fork shot out to the plate of pancakes and stabbed the first of the heap.

"Daddy," his five-year-old, Melanie, said. "We need to pray first."

"Of course, dear. Would you lead us, please?"

They joined hands, and in a tiny high-pitched voice, Melanie said, "Thank you for the world so sweet. Thank you for the food we eat. Thank you for the birds that sing. Thank you, God, for everything." She pronounced the *th* sound as just *t*, making "thank" into "tank" and "everything" into "every ting."

Schofield barely noticed. His mind had traveled back in time to prayers that he had recited during his childhood. The prayers had been taught to him by a man he knew only as The Prophet while he'd been living in the commune of a satanic cult known as the Disciples of Anarchy.

He thought of the other children within the cult.

He thought of their screams. He thought of them burning alive. "Daddy?" Melanie said.

He snapped back to the present and said, "Yes, honey?"

"I need the syrup."

"Sure, babe." He slid the bottle toward her and leaned over to kiss her on the top of the head. She smiled up at him. Her two front teeth were missing. He smiled back at his beautiful little girl and thought of how much he loved his wife and kids. Although he could rarely feel joy, he could feel other things such as love, loyalty, and attachment. It would hurt them terribly to discover how much of a monster he truly was, but he only wanted to make them happy and feel happiness himself. Visions of his children spitting on him and calling him a freak cascaded before his eyes. He imagined their angelic faces curled into snarls as they stoned him to death.

Schofield thought of Jessie Olague burning and bleeding to death during the previous evening, and he knew that he would deserve such a fate. He had earned every stone.

20

As Allen Brubaker approached the door to the hotel room and raised his hand to knock, he noticed a tiny device mounted at about knee height on the wall of the niche holding the door frame. The device resembled a circular Band-Aid and blended well with the cream color of the hallway walls. It would have been invisible to the untrained eye, but Allen's were well-trained, at least when he wore his glasses. The little Band-Aid was actually a motion detector that sent an SMS text message to a cell phone or computer if the field around the door was broken. He imagined that Marcus had investigated the typical hours of the housekeeping staff so that he could ignore the maid's attempts at cleaning the room. A do-not-disturb sign also hung around the door handle.

The kid was really getting paranoid, even for Marcus.

Allen shook his head and again raised his hand to knock, but his fist never reached the door. A voice at his back startled him as it said, "Who goes there?"

He raised his hands and turned slowly. "I am nothing, but truth is everything."

"Put your hands down. You're embarrassing yourself." Marcus smiled. "So who said that, Professor? Quote from Shakespeare?"

Allen—a history and literature aficionado—replied, "Actually, it was Abraham Lincoln."

"I think I've heard of him. Beard, big hat."

Allen chuckled and gave Marcus a slap on the back. "That's the fellow." He had accompanied Marcus during his first few months as a Shepherd, and they had grown quite close. He had become accustomed to Marcus's smart-ass comments and impressed by his skills as an investigator. But the kid still had a lot to learn. "Are you going to invite me in?"

"We're over here, Professor." Marcus pointed to the adjacent room. "That room's just a decoy. I got that one under my name and put this one under Henry Jones, Jr."

Good Lord, Allen thought again. The kid really is getting paranoid.

As he stepped through the entryway into the adjacent room, he greeted Andrew and admired their accommodations. It was a two-room suite with a front room containing a pull-out couch, two chairs, a mini-fridge, and a flat-screen television. But the boys had shoved the cabinet containing the flat-screen TV into the corner against the wall and replaced it with a state-of-the-art touch-screen display board. Marcus had talked to him about getting one of these shortly after joining the group. The screen was a foldable paper-thin active-matrix organic LED display mounted on a pair of glass shields and silicone rubber—which was a hyper-elastic material that could endure a huge strain from stretching. The technology had been first developed by Samsung but was still in the prototype stages. Allen knew the Director had connections through DARPA—the DOD's Defense Advanced Research Projects Agency—but he had never seen the need to use such technologies in his investigations.

"What happened to my old corkboard?"

Marcus shrugged. "I had Stan burn it. Welcome to the future, Professor."

Allen let a low growl escape from the back of his throat but then said, "Show me what you have so far."

"Well, you've read the files, so you're up to speed on most of it. But a few things have been bothering me. First of all, how does the killer know for sure that the victims are sleeping when he enters the house? This guy is a calculator, not a fighter. I just don't see how he's never had any kind of a struggle. Second, why does he take them one night and kill them the next?"

Andrew said, "Maybe he wants to keep them for a while, like a collector. He gets off on possessing them, controlling them."

Marcus chewed on his lower lip as his eyes scanned the various pieces of evidence listed on the display board. His hand reached up and repositioned a couple of the items. "Maybe."

Andrew rolled his eyes. "Whenever you say *maybe,* you really mean *I don't think so.*"

Marcus nodded. "Maybe."

Andrew looked to Allen for support, but he just grinned. It was good to see that not everything had changed in his absence.

Marcus continued. "Something else. The eyes. Why does he need their eyes to be held open? He makes it so that it's impossible for them to look away."

"Because he wants them to watch, to see him. Could be that he feels it's the only time when anyone actually sees him for who he truly is."

Marcus gave Andrew a large lopsided grin. "Maybe." Andrew's eyes shot daggers in return.

"Marcus, what do you think about the satanic-ritual connection?" Allen said.

"Despite public perception, there are almost no cases of people being murdered in actual satanic rituals. Of course there are the rare delusional individuals who claim that the devil made them commit murder, but that's really no different from saying that your dog or Elvis made you do it. It's just another delusion. Still, it's not outside the realm of possibility for it to be a true satanic cult. But even if there is a cult connection, judging by the consistency of the crime scenes, handwriting analysis on the symbols, and footprints found at the scenes, it's safe to say that we're dealing with one offender actually committing the crimes. I had Stan working on the cult angle."

Marcus tapped an icon in the lower right-hand corner of the screen, and a window containing a circular loading symbol expanded from the bottom of the display. After a few seconds, Stan's face appeared. "Go for Kung-Fu Master Stan."

"What have you found on the cult connection?"

"The symbols don't match anything I could find, and there's no documented ritual that the killer is following."

"What about the Circle A?"

"Right. It's the symbol for anarchy, which earned the killer his nickname in the press after some cop must have leaked a photo of the calling card. The flatfoot probably took the wife and kids to St. Lucia or Aspen or maybe Disney with the money he got from that one. Or maybe the mistress. Ran off with her. That makes for a much better story."

"Let's stay on task here, Stan."

"Gotcha, boss. When I dug deeper, I found a source that says the Circle A can represent the Antichrist as the ultimate bringer of anarchy and the apocalypse."

Marcus stopped him there. "Okay, I want you to hack into the database of every hospital, psychologist, and therapist in the Chicago area and find any references to the Circle A or anyone believing themselves to be the Antichrist or doing the work of the Antichrist. Also, check for any connections between the Circle A and any satanic groups or individuals. Then I want you to find me an insider who would be willing to talk with us. Someone with their finger on the pulse of the subculture."

Stan was quiet for a moment. The picture of him on the screen blinked rapidly, and his face scrunched up. "Boss, do you have any idea how many psychologists and therapists there must be in the Chicago area?"

Marcus didn't hesitate. He crossed his arms over his chest and said, "Two thousand, four hundred and ninety."

"How the hell do you know that?"

"It was on the stats sheets that I had you prepare for me."

"But how could you possibly remember that?"

Marcus thought about it for a moment. "I actually don't memorize the numbers. I take a mental snapshot of each page and then store the image away in my head. Then I can refer back to it as needed. Just like storing digital pictures in a folder on a computer."

"Scientists should study your brain, boss."

"They wouldn't like what they'd find there." Marcus glanced at the time on his phone. "Okay, Stan, you've got some work to do, and we're heading out to a briefing with the Jackson's Grove PD."

Stan gave a sarcastic little salute and then killed the connection. Allen said, "We're going to a briefing?"

Marcus rearranged some of the pieces of evidence on the screen again, and Andrew said, "Yeah, an FBI agent named Vasques invited us last night."

"The Director told me you had a bit of a run-in with the Bureau."

"You could say that. Her and Marcus really hit it off."

Marcus's gaze didn't leave the board, and he didn't rise to the bait. "None of the actual murders have crossed state lines, and they've all occurred within the same jurisdiction. Typically, the scenes of killings and dump sites for serial murderers follow consistent spatial patterns, although those patterns are different for each offender. They each have a comfort zone, just like any of us, that surrounds their home base, usually where they live or work. But, statistically, their comfort zones also grow over time as they hone their craft. Not this guy. He's stretched to all corners of this jurisdiction, but has never left it. Makes me wonder if he's doing it on purpose for some reason. It also means that the FBI has no real jurisdiction on this case."

Allen snapped his fingers, and the boys turned to him. He wagged a finger at them. "Vasques. I knew that name sounded familiar. Two detectives named Vasques and Belacourt were the leads on the case when we worked it during the last series of murders."

Andrew said, "But we never actually got involved with the police during that case. We didn't start working it until the very last, right before those five women went missing and the killer went dark. By then it was too late to accomplish much."

"I never met them, but I make it a point to do some background work on the lead detectives in any case that I'm working on. Vasques was a good cop. His work was solid. I actually called in about six months after the case went cold to see if they'd come up with any new leads. I discovered that he'd been killed in a fire. The Anarchist was the last case he worked."

"That makes sense," Marcus said. "It seemed to me like our Vasques might have had a personal connection to the case. I think she's suspicious of our involvement. And she had a bit of a stick up her ass."

Andrew stared in disbelief at Marcus. "Are you serious? It's no wonder she's suspicious of us. You were being a complete jerk to her."

"I was not."

"Yes, you were."

Allen raised both hands to stop them. "Boys, it doesn't matter now. Let's just stay out of her way and keep a low profile."

Andrew chuckled. "That's not one of Marcus's strong points."

Marcus pointed a finger at Andrew and said, "Watch yourself. You're starting to piss me off with all that. I can play nice as well as anybody."

Andrew shook his head. "Okay. Whatever."

Marcus checked the time on his phone again. "We better get going. We don't want to be late for the briefing."

21

"WHERE'S YOUR BROTHER? We need to get going," Harrison Schofield said to his oldest daughter, Alison.

"I think he's in the backyard."

Schofield held up the boy's Spider-Man backpack. "He may need this."

Alison sighed with frustration and said, "I can't take care of everything, Dad."

He held up his hands in surrender. "Easy, teenager. I mean you no harm."

She stuck out her tongue, and he gave her a little wink. "Hey, Dad. Are you going to see Grandma today?"

A flash of shame passed over him, and he felt his stomach churn into knots as he thought of his mother. Still, no matter what she had done, no matter the pain she had caused, she was the woman that had given birth to him. A part of him loved her despite it all. Another part hated her and could never forgive her. "Why do you ask?"

"I heard you and Mom talking about it. I was…well, just wondering if maybe I could come along. I'm old enough to handle it."

"Honey, I don't think *I'm* old enough to handle it. But I tell you what, we'll see how she's doing today. If it goes well, you can come on the next trip."

"Thanks, Dad."

He finished making lunch for the two younger kids—peanut butter and jelly and apple slices for Melanie and a ham-and-cheese Lunchable for Ben—and packed them into their

Dora the Explorer and X-Men lunch boxes. Alison, unlike her siblings, was too cool to bring cold lunch.

As he hurried the girls out the door to the backyard, he heard his son laughing. But a jolt of fear shot through him when he heard a man's voice. He rushed forward and rounded the corner. He found them standing in the open patch of grass that spanned the distance between his home and that of his neighbor. Ben stood in the snow, wearing a puffy blue coat. A football flew from his right hand. It sailed through the air and was snatched down by an old man with long white hair and a close-cropped white beard.

Ben noticed him and said, "Dad, Mr. O'Malley came over to play catch with me."

Schofield's next-door neighbor tossed the ball back to Ben and said, "The boy's got a wicked arm, Harrison." O'Malley's words flowed out in a thick Irish brogue. "He'll be playing in the NBA before we know it."

Ben laughed, his head tipping back as his little body shook with delight. "That's basketball, Mr. O'Malley. Football is the NFL."

O'Malley laughed with the boy, and Schofield felt a stab of jealousy and anger at how naturally and easily their laughter blended together, like two old friends sharing a joke at his expense. O'Malley said, "Sorry about that, my boy. The only sport I keep up with is soccer. But I did play rugby when I was at University."

"I play soccer, but I've never even heard of rug bees."

"Oh, it's a splendid game. I'll teach it to you when the weather's better."

"Did you hear that, Dad? Mr. O'Malley's going to teach me how to play rug bees."

Schofield patted his son on the head and said, "That's great, Ben. But we need to get to school, and Mr. O'Malley's a busy man." As he spoke, he tripped over some of the words and tried not to make eye contact with his neighbor.

Ben waved at the white-haired old man as he headed for the garage. "Bye, Mr. O'Malley. Have a good day."

"You too, my boy."

Schofield seethed with rage at the old man's intrusion into his life, his time with the kids, but he kept the feelings bottled deep inside. He turned without a word and started after his son. At his back, the old man said, "Harrison, I wanted to thank you for loaning me that snow-blower contraption."

Schofield raised a hand in acknowledgment but didn't turn. He hated the old man. Hated the sound of his voice. That ridiculous accent.

The old man continued. "I'm done with it now, so I'll just be sticking it back in your garage."

Schofield wheeled around. "Fine, just leave it outside the door."

"Oh, this is a good neighborhood, but it could still get stolen if it's just sitting out like that. Maybe I'll ask Ben to help me with it when he gets home from school. He's a good kid. He likes to help."

"No, we're...busy. The garage is fine." Schofield quickly shuffled off to join the kids before the old man could hit him with anything else.

He could see through the window in the garage door that the kids were already piled into the Camry. Each breath he took was quick and shaky, and his hands trembled in the cold. He placed a palm on the side of the garage to steady himself. He felt queasy.

He hated that old man. Even the sound of his voice made Schofield cringe. Most of all, he hated that the old man had a habit of injecting himself into his family's lives. He thought that perhaps, one day, he'd have the courage to do something about it.

22

THE JACKSON'S GROVE Police Department was a one-story redbrick structure surrounded by bare trees and bordered by a large swath of undeveloped land. Ackerman watched Marcus and the others pull off Route 50 and into the parking lot of the small police precinct. An enormous radio tower jutted into the air over the building, and the lobby and entranceway running through the center of the structure was encased all in glass on its front and ceiling. It reminded him more of something you'd see at a shopping mall. A blue and beige sign announced *Jackson's Grove Village Center.* Squad cars lined the parking lot.

As he drove past, the killer thought of how destiny, by the hand of some higher power, had led him to this place. He had once believed that everyone was just wandering through the darkness alone. No God, no devil, just men. He had thought of human beings as nothing more than animals that had deluded themselves with the concepts of religion and life after death.

But now, as he looked back on the events of his life, he no longer saw merely random chaos, pain, and death. He saw purpose. He saw meaning. All of that pain had been to mold him, to sharpen him into a finely crafted weapon, an instrument of fate. And it was still molding him, shaping him, changing him. All people were the sum of their collected experiences, and his suffering had made him strong. Just as the events of Marcus's life had shaped him.

And soon Marcus would truly understand the inner workings of fate. The puzzle pieces would snap into place, and all would become clear. Marcus would look at the world through different eyes. And fate had chosen Ackerman to be the catalyst of this epiphany, just as Marcus had been for him.

He was reminded of a quote he had absorbed somewhere along the way: *A person often meets his destiny on the road he took to avoid it.*

That was Marcus. He would try to fight fate at every twist and turn, but the destination would still be the same. Fate would win in the end.

Ackerman twisted the blade of his fifteen-inch survival knife and watched the light reflect off the stainless steel. As he admired the weapon, he wondered if he'd first have to remove some of the distractions in Marcus's life before he could realize his true potential.

23

SITTING ON AN uncomfortable gray folding chair in the back of the briefing room, Marcus watched as Detective Sergeant Trevor Belacourt stepped up to a small podium at the head of the room and called for everyone's attention. A whiteboard occupied the wall at the detective's back. It was lit by a projector suspended from the ceiling by silver chains. The room had bare cream-colored block walls and windows looking out onto a patch of rural land. A big folding table packed with doughnuts, coffee, and various creams and sugars sat against one wall. A mixture of uniformed officers and men and women wearing khakis and white shirts and suits filled the room. Maybe thirty people in all. They ceased their conversations and began to take their seats. The whole place had an institutional smell like some community-college classroom—traces of lemon-scented cleaning fluids, coffee, and fumes from erasable markers. He noticed Vasques sitting quietly in the front row.

Leaning over to Allen, Marcus whispered, "I read that Jackson's Grove is a member of the South Suburban Major Crimes Task Force. Are some of these guys detectives from other precincts in the area?"

Allen just nodded and pointed toward Belacourt, who had begun to speak. The balding commander of the Jackson's Grove detective division presented the details of the case, directing the gathered officers to the packets each had received upon entering the briefing room. He explained that, since he had worked the Anarchist case before, he would be investigating alongside the lead detective, Marlon Stupak, on it. He instructed his men to coordinate everything with one of them. Stupak stood and gave the room a wave. He was a thin black man with a perfectly shaved head and an overly coifed goatee. His suit looked a little too clean and expensive to Marcus.

Belacourt said, "We are also honored to have Special Agent Victoria Vasques consulting on this case with us." Vasques stood, looked out over the officers, and nodded curtly, all business.

"As you may know," Belacourt continued, "a woman named Jessie Olague was abducted two nights ago. If our killer holds to his pattern, then she may already be dead."

Marcus flipped open his packet and thumbed through the information. Belacourt proceeded to discuss the department's efforts to stop the killer, but Marcus had little interest in patrol routes and information that he already knew. However, the packet did contain one item that he had yet to read. A profile of the killer.

The document described the Anarchist as a highly organized offender and a white male between the ages of thirty-five and fifty. With that much, and some of the other conjectures, he could agree. But, as his eyes continued down the page, he became increasingly dismayed at the profile's content. It made several leaps of judgment that he felt were flat-out wrong. It stated that the killer was probably single, though socially adequate and charming in his own way, but also a loner who didn't like people. It went on to say that he was a narcissist and a psychopath incapable of feeling any remorse for his crimes. He would have problems with women and blame them and others for the issues in his life.

The profile had all the right terminology, but it lacked the proper insight. And it could have been leading the police in the wrong directions. Depending on how much stock they put in it, a profile like this could cause investigators to ignore potential suspects and send them spiraling down a road that would lead to the deaths of more innocent people.

Belacourt was discussing the victim demographics when Marcus raised his hand and waved it back and forth to draw the cop's attention. Beside him, Andrew whispered, "What are you doing? Put your hand down."

Marcus ignored him. He was sure that Belacourt had seen him but had diverted his gaze. He persisted with even more exaggerated movements. Finally, Belacourt said, "Yes, in the back, do you have something to add?"

Marcus stood and said, "Yes, I do. I'm Special Agent Marcus Williams with the Department of Justice. I just wanted to let you know that this profile"—he held up the packet—"isn't worth the paper it's written on. If you follow this, you'll never catch this guy."

Allen whispered, "Sit down, Marcus."

Belacourt cocked his head to the side and said, "Really, Agent Williams. Why don't you enlighten us?"

"This profile makes some great leaps that could potentially be sending the investigation in the wrong direction. First of all, there's no indication of the killer being a loner. In fact, I believe the killer may be married or living with someone."

Belacourt laughed. "Thank you, agent. But—"

Marcus cut him off and plowed forward. "He takes the victims one night and then holds them somewhere throughout the next day, waiting until the next evening to kill them. This suggests to me that he doesn't have time to do everything properly on the first night because he needs to get home before he's missed. He might have a wife who works a night shift like Jessie Olague's husband did."

"We'll take that under—"

"Also, he's likely not charming or very socially adequate. It would be much easier to abduct a woman from the street or charm them into his vehicle like Ted Bundy did, but this guy doesn't. He immobilizes them within their own homes without the slightest confrontation, which requires a great deal of work and planning. Then this profile says that the killer is a psychopath, which he isn't. He hates himself for what he's doing, but he can't stop for some reason."

"Thank you, Agent Williams, we'll take—"

"Look at the care that the killer has taken with the victims."

"Care? He drinks their blood, forces their eyes open, and burns them alive."

"Yes, but only after he's cut their femoral arteries, which is unnecessary. I think he does that because, true or not, he feels that he's sparing them prolonged suffering. A psychopath would take pleasure in controlling the women and causing them pain. This guy drugs them in such a way that if he didn't wake them up they wouldn't even remember the incident. In his own twisted way, he doesn't want them to suffer more than necessary. He's mission-based. He kills to gain something other than pleasure."

Belacourt stood there for a moment and then said in his nasal voice, "Is that it? Can we move on now?"

"Actually, no. The profile also doesn't mention anything about a profession or vehicle. I would say that this killer works with numbers or variables in some way. Risk management, insurance, bank, financial, systems analysis. Definitely something white-collar. And he drives either a Toyota Camry, Honda Accord, Toyota Corolla, Honda Civic, Nissan Altima, or Ford Fusion. Those are the top-selling cars of the year."

Belacourt chuckled. "So that's really just a guess based on statistical probability. We can look up stats online, too."

"Sure you can, and so can our killer. That's why he drives one of those vehicles. He wants to blend in. He doesn't leave anything to chance. He would have analyzed the data and chosen a car that had the highest probability of blending with others on the road. That's the way he thinks."

"Thank you, Agent Williams, for your insight. But it seems to me that the current profile seems more accurate. So, moving on, we—"

"Who put that profile together? It reads like it was written by a cadet. It surely didn't come from the BAU."

Allen grabbed his arm. "You need to sit down now."

Belacourt's nostrils flared, and his mouth formed into an angry slit. The man had endured enough interruptions. "That's quite enough. If you attempt to hijack this briefing one more time, I'll have you removed."

Marcus dropped into his seat and seethed at the dismissal. Andrew opened his packet to the page containing the profile and pointed to a box in the lower-right corner. It read: *Prepared by FBI Special Agent Victoria Vasques*. Marcus closed his eyes and rubbed furiously at his temples. He had forgotten his migraine medicine at the hotel.

"Smooth," Andrew commented.

Allen leaned over and said, "Do you know the meaning of the word discretion?"

HARRISON SCHOFIELD AND his wife, Eleanor, pulled through the security gate and into the parking lot of the Will County Mental Health Center. The hospital had changed its name in 1975 to be more politically correct. Prior to that, it had been known as the Will County Home for the Criminally Insane.

Schofield took a deep breath and looked around the grounds of the so-called hospital. It didn't resemble any other hospital he had ever seen. It reminded him more of a prison. The home consisted of a large single-story building faced with red brick and surrounded by a twenty-foot barbed-wire fence that curled inward to make it nearly impossible to climb. Snow covered the ground, and shards of ice clung to the bare hard maple and oak trees that dotted the landscape. As he stepped from the car, he smelled a combination of diesel and sewage-tainted water wafting through the air. The sewage flow of the Chicago River and Ship and Sanitary Canal found their way into the Des Plaines River south of where he now stood, and if the wind was just right, industrial run-off mixed with the flow from the canal to make a perfect storm of noxious odors. It seemed to him that he always visited his mother on windy days.

He and Eleanor walked into the visitor area, and a security man buzzed them inside. The big black guard sat behind an inch of Lexan polycarbonate. He slid a clipboard through a waist-high slot. As he filled out the proper paperwork and signed in on the guest registry, Schofield noticed that the guard had abnormally small hands for his size.

"Do you need a locker key?" the guard said.

"No, thank you. My wife is waiting here."

"Okay, I'll let you know when the patient is ready to be seen." Schofield walked over to the row of linked orange visitor chairs and sat next to Eleanor. He emptied his pockets and gave her the contents.

"Are you sure that you don't want me to come in with you?" she said.

"I'm sure. You really didn't have to take time off work to come with me. I could've done this alone."

"You could have. But you shouldn't have to. I know how hard this is for you. Are you sure that you're okay?"

"I'm fine."

"I love you, Harrison. I'm here for you no matter what. You can tell me anything."

He knew that he should have felt some kind of warmth or surge of happiness at hearing those words, but unfortunately he felt nothing. He squeezed her hand and raised it to his lips. "Thank you."

After a moment, the guard called, "Schofield?"

He thought it strange that the guard went through the same motions even though he was the only visitor on the list. As he stood, his wife commented, "If she's doing better, maybe next time we can bring the kids."

He smiled back at her. "I'm sure she'd like that."

THE NARROW VISITOR room was one of many holding areas in a long hallway. A Hispanic orderly dressed all in white opened the windowed door for Schofield. The man had a tattoo of a python running up the left side of his neck. Inside, the walls of the visitor room were yellowed with age, and his mother sat in a metal chair at the far end of a gray rectangular table. She looked good. She was a beautiful woman with long black hair and rosy cheeks. She had given birth to Schofield when she'd been only thirteen and could easily have passed for his wife or sister rather than his mother.

He sat down across from her at the long table. The light

from a barred window at her back fell over her shoulders and reflected off her black hair. She gave him an angry look and then turned away in disgust.

"Hello, Mother," he said. "Merry Christmas."

She spat at him. "Why do you come here? You filthy little maggot. You're an abomination."

He swallowed hard and fought to remain calm. "I hear that you're doing well. You look healthy."

She turned away and refused to acknowledge him. He looked at the window in the door to see if the orderly was watching, but the tattooed man was nowhere to be seen. "No one's listening, Mother. Don't you think that it's time you told me who my father really is?"

Her face curled into a snarl. "You know who he is. That demon raped me and impregnated me with his vile seed."

Schofield closed his eyes and tried not to let her see him cry. He had listened to this for as long as he could remember. His mother, who had always been mentally unbalanced and had run away from home, had been twelve years old when she became pregnant with him. At the time, she had been taken in as a member of a cult led by a man that called himself the Prophet. The group was comprised of others like her—runaways, miscreants, the mentally unstable. When she became pregnant, she told the other cult members that Satan himself had come to her in a dream and implanted her with the seed of the Antichrist. She attempted suicide during her second trimester, but the Prophet stopped her.

From the moment of his birth, Schofield had been a revered outcast. The other children were afraid of him. They refused to play with him and resented his special status. They called him names when the adults weren't listening. Freak. Monster. Devil. They hated him, but he only wanted them to be his friends, to treat him as a member of the group.

But worse than any of them was his own mother. She hated him with a passion and intensity that he never understood. She tried to murder him on many occasions throughout his youth, and if not for the intervention of the Prophet, he would never have grown to see adulthood.

"So are they treating you well here, Mother? Do they have a Christmas tree? Do you exchange gifts?"

Her lips trembled with rage, but she wouldn't meet his gaze or respond. He sighed and stood up. "Merry Christmas, Mother. Eleanor and the kids wish you the same. The kids would like to see you."

The angry look on her face melted away, and her eyes grew large like those of an expectant child. When she spoke, her voice was filled with a breathless anticipation. "Will you bring them? I'd love to see them."

He looked out the window and thought for a moment. "I'll only bring them here if you behave yourself. You don't have to love me. I don't blame you for that. You're right. You've always been right, and I understand that now. I am an abomination. But I won't let you speak to me like you did today in front of my kids."

"I promise. Please, bring them."

"I'll consider it."

With that, he pounded on the glass. The tattooed orderly opened the door and escorted him toward the exit. As they moved down the long white hallway, Schofield tried to focus on the white tile floor and the glowing reflections of the fluorescent lighting instead of on his mother and the past. Deep mouthfuls of air filled his lungs over and over. It took all his strength and focus to keep from hyperventilating or throwing up.

25

VASQUES FUMED AS Belacourt concluded the briefing and dismissed the officers. She had been utterly humiliated, but she refused to let Williams get under her skin. She needed to maintain her composure. She needed to maintain control.

The room was getting warm from all the bodies, and she had to get some air. But Agent Garrison stepped in front of her as she moved toward the door. He gave her that awkward what-can-you-do smile and said, "Agent Vasques, we were hoping to meet with you about the case. Maybe review some of the evidence together. Question the witness."

She wanted to bust his teeth out. These men had publicly disgraced her, and now they wanted to waste more of her time. But it would give her the chance to give Williams a piece of her mind. The corners of her mouth curled into a faux smile that took all her willpower to maintain. "Sure. I have some work to do at the Chicago field office. You can meet me there in an hour." She handed Garrison one of her cards. "The address is there on the card. It's on West Roosevelt Road. Park in the garage across the street."

Garrison seemed a bit surprised at her easy acceptance of their request. "Great. Thank you. We'll see you there."

She pushed out of the building and reached her Crown Vic. She popped in four pieces of gum, chomped them furiously, and gripped the steering wheel until her fingers ached. Her phone had been on vibrate during the briefing, and she had felt a few text messages buzz through. With great effort, she tore her fingers from the steering wheel and ripped the phone from her jacket pocket. The first text was from a friend at the Bureau.

Checked out your new buddies from the DOJ. Williams is listed as working there, but he doesn't seem to exist at all beyond that. Like he's been erased.

She sat there a moment watching the traffic fly past on Route 50 and let her mind wander through the implications of this new information. The Bureau had some of the best diggers in the world, and if her friend couldn't access Williams's background, that meant that it was classified at the highest levels.

The more Vasques thought about what had happened in the briefing, the more she realized that Williams was right. His points were valid, and her assessments were flawed. It was really Belacourt's fault. Her father's old partner disliked the Bureau and didn't want to deal with anyone there other than her. He had forced her into putting together a profile for him. It wasn't something she enjoyed or for which she had much of an aptitude. That was why she had dropped out of the BAU and had pursued a career investigating human-trafficking cases instead.

A single question kept floating to the surface of her thoughts. *Who the hell are these guys?*

She had no idea, but she was damn sure going to find out.

26

THE CHICAGO FBI field office sat off to itself along Roosevelt Road on a lot enclosed by white pillars and a black rod-iron fence. It was as long as it was tall, and a grid of mirrored windows covered its entire front. Vasques's office was on the fourth floor against the south wall, overlooking a room full of agents working away at cubicles.

She ushered the three men from the DOJ inside and shut her door. The office had no windows and was fairly private, but she still reminded herself to keep her voice down and remain calm. Gesturing at a pair of visitor chairs, she stepped around her desk and sat down. The older man, who had introduced himself as Brubaker, and Williams sat in the chairs. She had only two, so Garrison remained standing. Brubaker and Garrison wore identical black suits, white shirts, and black ties. But Agent Williams wore a gray silk shirt undone to the second button, no tie, with a black T-shirt underneath. She already knew he was the maverick of the group, but even his attire, perhaps subconsciously, suggested some small defiance of authority. She had known rogues like him during her tenure with the Bureau, and in her experience, they often got people hurt or killed.

"Okay, gentlemen. Why don't we cut the crap, and you tell me who you really are."

Brubaker looked at Williams and something passed between them, but she couldn't be sure what it was. Williams said, "We haven't lied to you. We're part of a group within the DOJ that specializes in this type of case. We're all on the same team. All we want is to catch this guy and make sure that he doesn't hurt anyone else."

Williams looked at Brubaker again, and the older man raised his eyebrows and tilted his head toward her. Williams continued. "I also want to say how sorry I am for what happened in the briefing. If I had known that you prepared the profile, I would have handled it differently."

She considered this. Thought about letting him off the hook but decided against it. "Why would we want your help? What do you bring to the table?"

His eyes went distant for a second, and his hand reached toward the spot where his tie would have been. He rubbed at the spot on his chest. Finally, he said, "I notice things."

Silence stretched within the room. "That's it?" Vasques laughed. "You notice things. I'm afraid you're going to have to do better than that."

Williams closed his eyes and started pointing around the room. "Your trash can is small and black, wire mesh. It's filled with some papers but mostly junk-food wrappers. A half-eaten box of McDonald's fries, a wrapper from Subway, Snickers-bar wrapper, from what I could see. You've got a vent in the far-right corner of the room, up high. It's missing a screw and squeaks a little. So does your chair, which is actually a different model from all those we passed on the way in. I assume you brought it from home. It looked like it has better lumbar support. You have fourteen awards and diplomas hanging on the left wall in two rows of seven. The third one in the second row still has part of the price tag showing on the frame where you apparently gave up on scraping it off. There are three gray filing cabinets in the left corner with five drawers each. There are twelve pictures in black frames sitting on top of the cabinets."

His eyelids opened, and his gaze found hers. His eyes were beautiful and bright, stunning yet piercing. She noticed that the eyes were different colors. Half bluish green and half brown. He said, "Those things are just the obvious ones, though. All on the surface. They're not just objects. Each has a story to tell about you."

Without glancing away from her, Williams pointed to the pictures in the corner. "Closest one to us is a picture of Belacourt and a man I assume to be your father. It was taken at the same precinct we just came from. Next one to the right is of you at your college graduation with your dad and brother. You're wearing a cap and gown. Your dad's wearing a gray suit with a red tie. Your brother, a guess based on resemblance, is wearing a blue sweater and a wool jacket. I can see that you went to Duke University from the chapel in the background. It's pretty distinctive. Also, there are no pictures of your mother anywhere. So I can infer that you were raised by your father and your mother died when you were very young. But then again, that doesn't quite fit. She didn't die. If she had, you'd probably still have a photo of her. I'm guessing she abandoned you and your brother. Maybe she couldn't handle being a mother and having a cop as a husband. You're single with no kids. Easy to tell that since you have no pictures of family other than your father and brother."

Vasques's breathing had become shallow and forced. She wanted him to stop but couldn't find the words.

"You're on temporary assignment to help with this case, and you once received training from the Behavioral Analysis Unit. But you dropped out. That's why the profile contained all the right terminology, but not the right kind of insight and assessment that you can only gain from working real cases in the field. You're a workaholic, and you don't know what to do with yourself when you're not here. All those takeout boxes, and there are also tiny stains on your desk blotter. Looks like barbecue sauce or steak sauce, maybe. You eat a lot of meals in this office. There's also a few smudges there that look like makeup and lipstick. You must have fallen asleep and planted your face there on the desk."

Brubaker said, "I think she's heard enough, Marcus."

But Williams ignored the older agent. "You just quit smoking. You've been chewing on your lower lip, and every time I've seen you, you have at least two pieces of gum jammed in your mouth. The awards and diplomas also tell me that you're somewhat insecure about your position in the Bureau. You probably have every shooting trophy and commendation you've ever received on display. Then there's your gun. Bureau typically issues Glock 22s or 23s, maybe even a 19 chambered for 9 mm since it has a smaller frame and fits a woman's hand better. Or you could carry a Sig P226 or P220. But you're packing a custom Sig Sauer 1911 chambered for .45 ACP. It's the biggest model they make. It's like you're trying to prove something to yourself or those around you. Telling everyone that you're tough enough to handle anything. We've come a long way in terms of equality, but I'm sure there are still plenty of hurdles for a woman in the Bureau."

"Okay, Marcus. You've made your point," Garrison said from the corner of the room.

"Not sure if I have. There is one more thing. If I had to guess, I'd say that you dropped out of profiling around the same time that your father died. You told everyone that was the reason, but the truth was that you didn't like trying to get inside the heads of killers. Some people just aren't built for it. Plus, I can tell you're a hands-on type of person. You like being in the field. Kicking down doors, taking down bad guys, saving the day. You get to see the faces of the people you help. But a profiler spends most of his or her time in a basement at Quantico living inside the minds of some of the world's most deranged individuals. Still, it was quite an honor to be selected. There are only around thirty actual profilers out of 13,864 special agents in the Bureau. Your dad must have been really proud. Maybe that's why you only quit after he was gone. Didn't want to disappoint him. But, ultimately, it wasn't a life that you wanted. You were afraid that to admit the truth to anyone would some-how show weakness."

Williams continued to stare deep into her eyes, and Vasques felt the odd sensation that he was looking straight into her soul. Her heart throbbed against the walls of her rib-cage. She felt naked and helpless. She swallowed hard and said, "I see what you mean about noticing things. I'm sure that will come in handy during the investigation. Garrison mentioned that you wanted to talk to the witness."

"That's right."

"Okay, meet me downstairs in the lobby in five minutes."

She stood up quickly, still flustered. Her cheeks were on fire. The air was hot. Her composure was cracked and bro-ken, but she fought to maintain control. She slipped past the three men and out of her office, leaving them to find their own way out. The way to the bathroom wound around the corner past some additional offices and cubicles. She shuf-fled inside the women's restroom and found an open stall.

After slamming the stall door and sitting down on the toilet, she tried to breathe deeply and wrestle her emotions under control. But she couldn't. Williams had discovered things about her that no other living person knew. He had laid her bare and touched on subjects she never discussed with anyone. She felt as if he was the only person in the world that had truly seen who she was. And that made her feel frightened and ashamed.

With her face buried in her hands, Special Agent Victoria Vasques began to cry.

27

THE MASSIVE WHITE parking structure directly across West Roosevelt Road from the Chicago FBI field office was six levels high, counting the roof. They had found a spot for the Yukon on the far west end of the fourth level. Marcus had volunteered to drive, and Vasques had agreed a bit too quickly. He had expected her to put up an argument, not for any real reason, just as a display of independence and authority. To his surprise, her frosty attitude had melted significantly. His little display had apparently made an impression.

They all made small talk on the walk over to the garage. Allen was asking Vasques her impressions of Duke University. His son, Charlie, was hoping for a basketball scholarship there in the fall. Marcus was half listening to them and half analyzing every detail of their surroundings when his phone vibrated in his pocket. He didn't recognize the number and knew what that usually meant. It was Ackerman.

Marcus had changed his number twice when the killer first started to make near-daily calls, but, somehow, Ackerman always learned the new number. At his request, Stan had searched through all their computer systems and had found nothing. Marcus couldn't imagine why anyone within the organization would provide such information to the killer. It had to be the computers. He made a mental note to have Stan double-check everything once again, including all their cell phones, laptops, and servers.

After several failed attempts and more wasted resources, they had given up on trying to trace the calls back to the killer. Ackerman always used remote nodes with disposable cell phones or payphones. They could trace the calls back, but he never stayed in the same spot long enough to catch him there. He was careful and cautious, and Marcus suspected that he had been masking his appearance whenever he was in public. The killer had learned how to blend in over the years. Ackerman's use of technology did suggest, however, that he was receiving help from someone skilled in electronics and computer systems. It wasn't much, but it was a lead.

The others moved on up the ramp, and Marcus slowed his pace to put a little distance between them. "Speak."

"Marcus, it's good to hear your voice." He didn't respond.

"Are you enjoying your time in the Windy City?"

His jaw clenched. How did Ackerman always know so much about their operations? "What do you want?"

"You sound even more on edge than usual, Marcus. Have you been sleeping? That pesky insomnia. And the migraines. We really need to do something about those. I need you at your best."

"I'm touched by your concern."

"You should be. I'm the best friend you'll ever have, Marcus. No one will ever love you the way that I do. And you need to be on top of your game if you want to take down the Anarchist. I've been reading about our new playmate and, quite frankly, I'm impressed."

A Chevy Malibu skidded around the corner ahead of them, taking the curve a bit too fast. The vehicle's tires screeched as the driver nearly collided with a Chrysler 300 that was trying to back out. The driver of the Malibu laid on his horn and shook a fist at the woman behind the wheel of the Chrysler, even though it was hardly her fault.

Ackerman continued on the other end of the line. "This Anarchist. He's the real deal. He understands the hunger. He's like us, Marcus."

"We're nothing alike."

Ackerman chuckled. "You can lie to everyone else. You

can even lie to yourself to a certain extent. But you can't lie to me. I know all too well about the demon running around inside of you, trying to break free."

The killer's words had fallen to the back of Marcus's mind. Something had just happened. He had heard something. His subconscious had picked up on it, but it took him a moment to realize the significance.

His eyes went wide.

His pulse rate soared, and he could hear the blood pumping faster through his veins.

But he couldn't look or sound surprised. He couldn't let Ackerman know what he had heard.

When the driver of the Malibu had skidded around the corner and then laid on his horn, Marcus had heard the sound not only echoing through the parking garage but also coming through from the other end of the line. *Ackerman's* end.

And that could mean only one thing.

ACKERMAN WATCHED THE group move up the ramp toward their vehicle through a pair of Bushnell Fusion 1600 ARC binoculars. He sat low in the front seat of a silver Dodge Avenger about fifteen cars up the row from their Yukon. He wanted to be able to see Marcus's face as they spoke. He wanted it to be as if they were there together, speaking in person. Soon they would be.

But as some idiot took the curve of the garage moving entirely too fast and nearly caused an accident, Ackerman knew that Marcus was aware of his presence.

Marcus had tried to conceal his shock, but a hesitation as he walked and a tensing of his shoulders gave him away. When Ackerman thought about it, he supposed that he would have been disappointed if Marcus hadn't realized.

His plan was only to observe and follow. That way he could spot possible opportunities where his assistance could prove valuable to the investigation into the Anarchist. Being spotted and forcing a confrontation wasn't part of the plan. But he had learned long ago how to adapt and overcome. Situations like this were fluid and unpredictable. A person needed to be prepared to react to unforeseen circumstances and deal with unintended consequences.

Luckily, he'd had the foresight to reverse into the parking spot so that he could make a quick escape. Those few extra seconds could make all the difference.

Ackerman sat up, turned the key in the ignition, and threw the Avenger into drive.

MARCUS COULD FEEL Ackerman's stare slithering over him. But how to warn the others without alerting the killer? Vasques, Allen, and Andrew were ten feet ahead with their backs to him. Vasques's shoes clicked against the pavement, the sound reminding him of a ticking clock.

Thirty feet up the ramp, the engine of a silver sedan roared to life. It could have been just another working stiff on their way to lunch, or it could have been a sadistic murderer. His mind searched for the right move, offense or defense, react or attack. The killer was watching. If he assumed Ackerman was the sedan's driver, he could be blowing the best shot he'd had at the killer in months. There was no way to judge Ackerman's location based on the noises he had heard over the phone. Sound carried in strange ways.

The car was facing forward in the parking spot. For a quick exit?

That was the way Ackerman would have parked, the way Marcus would have in the same situation. A second's hesitation could mean the difference between stopping the killer once and for all or failing again and letting him slip away. It could also mean the difference between life and death for him or his colleagues.

A predator is most dangerous when cornered, and he had no idea how Ackerman would react if faced with the possibility of capture. The killer wouldn't go quietly; he knew that much for sure.

He made his decision and sprinted up the ramp toward the others, closing the distance as quickly as possible.

The tires of the silver sedan squealed, and it jolted forward.

He saw Vasques's head jerk toward the noise. Her black hair, pulled back in a ponytail, whipped around her neck with the sharp movement.

The sedan shot down the ramp. The others, having no idea how close they were to one of the country's most prolific serial murderers, didn't sense the danger until it was too late to react.

Vasques moved to the side of the ramp near the line of parked cars. She stood against the trunk of a black Ford Focus. There was no way for her to truly know the danger she was in.

Marcus's feet pounded up the ramp.

He had only a split second to react. His right arm shot toward Allen, shoving him away. Then Marcus wrapped his left arm around Vasques's waist and rolled them both onto the trunk of the Ford.

The sedan smashed into the back of the Ford in the spot where Vasques had been standing a second before. Sparks shot into the air. He could feel pinpricks of heat landing on his skin. The Ford kicked sideways and smashed into the vehicle beside it. He pulled Vasques in tight as they were thrown from the trunk and smashed onto the pavement.

Ackerman rocketed down the ramp, screeching around a tight corner.

In one fluid movement, Marcus untangled himself from the dumbfounded FBI agent, pulled his gun, and sprinted after the killer.

The metallic taste of blood filled his mouth. His face had smashed into the concrete during the fall. The smell of burnt rubber and exhaust clung to the inside of his nostrils.

"Get the car!" he yelled.

He knew he'd never catch Ackerman on foot. But the killer would be forced to follow the ramps down through the structure. Marcus needed to move vertically, not laterally. He looked over the edge of the ramp. The level below showed through the gap in the layered structure, over the top of a three-foot concrete barrier.

He slipped his gun back into its shoulder holster and his feet carried him toward the edge. And then over it. He didn't have time to consider his actions or hesitate. *React, don't think.*

Knees bent, he landed against the roof of a white car on the next level. His gaze swept the area. There was the silver sedan. Ackerman made the turn, spiraling downward.

Marcus grabbed the edge again and swung down.

The roof of another mid-size car awaited. The impact jolted him, but he pulled his Sig Sauer and aimed at Ackerman's vehicle. The silver sedan fishtailed sideways, almost striking a support pillar as Ackerman guided it around the turn to the next level.

Marcus cursed and shoved his pistol back inside his coat. He was getting closer with every drop, gaining on the killer. But he was almost out of ramp.

He dove toward the edge and swung through the gap.

This time, however, the spot below was empty. There was no car's roof to break his fall. He dropped a full twelve feet to the concrete. He tried to bend his knees and roll, but he still felt the impact in his bones. His ankle twisted below him. Pain lanced through his leg. He stumbled forward, pulling out the gun.

He would only have one shot at this. He moved into the path of the oncoming sedan and took aim. Ackerman's head was visible behind the windshield, the fluorescent lights burning overhead illuminating the calm face.

Marcus's finger found the trigger, and he squeezed. The gun bucked, and the sound of the blast, amplified by the structure's interior, reverberated throughout it. His finger twitched back repeatedly, unleashing a stream of hot metal toward the front of the sedan.

He could see Ackerman ducking down inside the vehicle

as the windshield splintered out in spiderweb cracks. But
Marcus didn't let up.

On a normal day, he carried either a 9mm P226 Platinum
Elite or a Diamond Plated P220 chambered for .45 caliber.
The .45 had more stopping and takedown power, but it also
only held ten rounds in the magazine and one in the chamber while the 9mm held fifteen in the magazine and one
in the chamber. Today, he had opted for stopping power,
so he counted off ten shots. Then, with the calm precision
of a maneuver that had been practiced over and over and
while he still had a bullet in the chamber, he ejected the
clip and slammed another home. The blasts from the gun
didn't skip a beat.

But the car was still coming. Faster and faster. The distance between them growing to nothing.

He had time to fire three more rounds from the new clip
before Ackerman was on top of him.

Waiting until the last second, Marcus dove away from
the path of the onrushing vehicle, narrowly avoiding being
crushed beneath the tires and the unforgiving weight of the
sedan.

While still on the ground, he turned toward Ackerman
and fired again, trying to hit the tires. But the sedan careened
forward and smashed through the gate to the garage, reaching the public streets of the city.

Yelling a primal scream, Marcus was back on his feet.
His ankle protested with every step, but he ignored the pain
as he sprinted after Ackerman, onto the street and down
Roosevelt Road.

30

VASQUES SHOVED ANDREW away from the driver's door of the big black SUV. "I'm driving," she said.

He didn't argue, and it was a good thing. This day had been a roller coaster, and she wasn't in the mood to discuss this with a committee. Being humiliated, psychoanalyzed, and nearly run down had a funny way of putting her in a pissed-off mood. But this time she knew exactly what she was going to do about it, even if she still had no clue as to what had just happened or who had tried to kill her.

She slammed the Yukon into reverse and jammed down the accelerator even before Andrew had closed his door. The Yukon barreled down the ramp, bottoming out and spitting sparks as she took the turns at breakneck speed. She tossed a cell phone into the back seat at Andrew as she pulled out onto Roosevelt Road.

"Speed dial 3. Tell them we're in pursuit of a suspect wanted for the attempted murder of a federal agent and get us some backup."

As he fumbled for the phone and dialed, Andrew said, "I'll just tell them we're in pursuit of Francis Ackerman. They'll send the National Guard."

"Ackerman? How do you know that?"

The killer topped the most-wanted lists, and his exploits had grown to be the stuff of legend, especially after his escape from a burning hospital in Colorado Springs. Somehow, he had managed to stay under the radar and evade capture since then. Many within the law-enforcement community believed that the only explanation was that he had fled the country.

"It's a long story for another time," Allen said from the passenger seat. Then he pointed at the road ahead of them. "There's Marcus!"

Agent Williams sprinted down the road ahead of them, hugging the center line and barely managing to avoid being hit. She screeched to a halt beside him. "Get in!"

Williams hopped into the back seat and pointed down Roosevelt Road. His words were punctuated by gasps of air. "He just turned ahead. We're going to lose him."

"The hell we are," Vasques said under her breath. This was her town, and Ackerman had just made a major mistake. The killer had turned down Wood Street. Unfortunately for him, a crew was filming a scene for some movie at a statue in front of the University of Illinois Medical Center located on the corner of Wood and Taylor. They were going to close the streets and block traffic for the whole afternoon.

She jerked the wheel and turned onto Damen Avenue. The tires squealed in protest, and the big top-heavy SUV listed to the side. An angry commuter in the opposite lane pounded his horn as he slammed on the brakes to avoid crashing into them.

"Do you know what you're doing?" Williams said. She ignored him and continued north down Damen until she whipped the vehicle right onto Taylor.

Ackerman was trapped. He had nowhere to go but straight into their path.

Vasques slammed down the accelerator again and held the wheel in a vise grip. "Take a look," she said. The silver car that had nearly run her over was heading straight for them. The car swerved around a red S-10 pickup truck and then nothing separated them but a couple of football fields of gray pavement.

"What are you doing?" Williams said again from the back.

Once more she didn't answer, kept accelerating. This wasn't the first time she had played chicken.

"You can't."

The street was a narrow two-lane patch of road bordered by parked cars. Both of their vehicles hugged the center, straddling the yellow lines. Ackerman was in a mid-size Dodge sedan. Vasques was driving a full-size extended SUV. She was twice his size. He would swerve or stop the vehicle and try to escape on foot. He had to. Anything else would be suicide.

"He won't swerve!" Williams bellowed.

As Vasques watched the smaller sedan from the raised vantage point inside the cab of the Yukon, she knew Williams was right. In fact, Ackerman too was accelerating.

31

REALIZING THAT SHE had made the grave mistake of playing chicken with a deranged psychopath, Vasques jerked the wheel to the side. But Ackerman still clung to the center of the road, and there wasn't enough space for both of them. He was only a hundred feet ahead and closing.

She waited until the last second and then slammed on her brakes and jerked the wheel hard, smashing into a little Chevy parked along the street. Then Ackerman was on top of her. Sparks shot from both sides of the Yukon as Ackerman slid along their left side and the Chevy slammed against their right.

The killer didn't even slow down as he continued east down Taylor Street. Vasques tried to keep her vehicle under control and pull away from the collision, but the dual impacts had thrown her into a tailspin. The Yukon swung in a circle down the center of the road and crashed into a light pole directly in front of a squat brick building marked with three crosses and the words *Children of Peace School*. Luckily, the students were on Christmas break.

Her head shot away from the headrest and struck the windshield. She tasted blood, and her ears rang like someone had jammed an alarm clock inside her skull. She pressed her hands against her forehead and tried to get her bearings. Something wet and warm trickled down her forearm. She heard someone asking if she was okay, but the voice sounded distant.

After a few long seconds, her vision cleared, and she dropped the lever on the steering console into reverse, pulling away from the pole. Ackerman was still only a few beats ahead of them. They still had a chance.

Vasques scanned Taylor Avenue, but the silver Dodge sedan was gone. Ackerman must have taken the next turn, and he wouldn't have headed back toward the FBI building, so he must have turned north down Damen Avenue. She slammed the pedal to the floor and took the next turn right. Damen was a four-lane road divided by a four-foot concrete median and bordered by tall black lampposts ornately designed to look like something from nineteenth-century England. Several vehicles dotted the road ahead, but no silver Dodge. Along the left side of the road, on the corner, she caught sight of a group of people at a black covered bus stop gesturing east down Polk Street. Reasoning that the people were most likely commenting about a car that had just skidded by at high speed, she took the turn onto Polk. The pale green and tan campus of John H. Stroger Jr. Hospital loomed off to her left. They were entering the heart of Chicago's medical district.

Farther down Polk, she caught sight of Ackerman weaving in and out of traffic. From the back seat, Williams said, "There he is!"

Vasques thought she heard sirens heading their way, but they needed to maintain visual contact. A siren of her own would have helped. The traffic was extra thick on Polk, and she nearly collided with a red minivan as she swerved into oncoming traffic to pass a slow-moving car. But then she got stuck behind a FedEx delivery truck as oncoming traffic and parked cars boxed her in on each side. The truck also blocked her view of the sedan. The intersections of Wolcott and Wood flew past, but before reaching Paulina she saw Ackerman's vehicle parked along the right side of the road in front of a long row of multicolored newspaper dispensers. The driver's door hung open. The raised platform for the Pink Line of CTA Rapid Transit sat only a few feet away.

The Yukon skidded to a stop. "He must be trying to get

away on the train," Vasques said as she leaped from the SUV and sprinted toward the glass front of the station's entrance.

At her back, Brubaker called after her. "Vasques, wait! He wouldn't have taken the train. We could just call ahead and have officers waiting for him at the next station."

She hesitated in front of the station doors and glanced toward Paulina Street. A man wearing a blue stocking cap and a Chicago Bears jacket was securing a bright green ten-speed bike to a rack in front of the transit station. "Hey, you!" The man glanced up. "Did you see a guy get out of that car?"

The Bears fan nodded and pointed north. "Yeah, he went that way."

32

ALLEN BRUBAKER FELT like his lungs were being crushed in a vise. The air was cold and thin, and he wasn't in nearly as good shape as he had once been. Still, he urged his legs to pump along with the others, who were at least twenty-five years his junior. The sound of their feet slapping the sidewalk and his own shallow breathing were the only noises he could hear. They sprinted north in the direction the man with the bike had pointed and were rewarded with a glimpse of Ackerman ducking into a large building up the street.

Allen's eyes weren't as good as they used to be, either, but he was fairly certain that he saw Ackerman clutching his left shoulder. Apparently, one of Marcus's rounds had struck home, but it also hadn't been enough to slow the killer down too much.

As they drew closer, Allen's gaze traveled up the strange-looking building that Ackerman had entered. From his vantage point, it was the color of light sand with one central section touching the ground while the first levels of two adjoining wings were exposed and supported by square pillars. It reminded him vaguely of some sort of space station. A dark gray awning jutting out over the entrance bore the words *Johnston R. Bowman Health Center*.

They pushed inside and glanced around the small lobby. A dark-skinned security guard with a gray Fu Manchu mustache sat behind an information desk. Vasques flashed her ID and said, "Did you see a guy in a dark coat come through here holding his shoulder?"

"Yeah, I told him the emergency entrance is all the way

on the other side of the hospital, but he didn't listen. He just jumped in the elevator."

"Are there any other exits?"

"There's a walkway that connects to the Academic Center on three." All stares fixed on the lights above the elevator. They indicated it had stopped on the third floor.

"Dammit," Vasques said. "The Rush University Campus is a maze. If he makes it into the Academic Center we might lose him."

"Plus it's full of people," Andrew added.

"Okay," Marcus said as he moved toward the exit. "Vasques and I will try to cut him off from the Academic building before he makes it across the walkway. Andrew, you and Allen take the elevator up after him and come at him from behind. We'll try to box him in."

Vasques followed Marcus out, and as she did, she raised her cell phone to her ear. Allen overhead her calling in reinforcements as she rushed from the building. The ding of the elevator sounded at his back, and the doors slid open.

Andrew stepped inside and stopped them closing with his palm. "Come on, Allen."

Allen took a step toward the elevator but then hesitated. Something didn't seem right. Off in the far corner was the door to the fire stairs. Maybe Ackerman was trying to double back on them? "I'm going to take the stairs and make sure that he doesn't try to sneak past us that way."

Nodding, Andrew slid his hand away from the doors' sensor, and they slid shut. Allen moved off toward the emergency door and pushed inside. The metal stairs climbed skyward, and he bounded up them two at a time.

By the time he hit the door to the second floor, his lungs were burning, and a wave of dizziness swept over him. He gasped in large gulps of air but pushed forward. In the recent months of his retirement, Allen had often looked back fondly on his time with the Shepherd Organization. The thrill of the hunt. The knowledge that he was making a difference.

Saving lives. Being a tool for justice and righteousness. The human mind had a funny way of romanticizing the past, and as he ascended the stairs, he realized that all too well. Now he recalled what it was truly like to be a Shepherd. It was adrenaline-filled, for sure, but it also meant fear. In fact, he now remembered that, in most cases, it was actually ninety-five percent terror and only five percent exhilaration.

As Allen fought for air, he wondered why in the hell he had volunteered to take the stairs.

But then, finally, he crested the last flight and came to the third-floor landing. As he reached out for the door handle, it seemed to twist on its own and swing toward him. The progression of time seemed to slow down and speed up simultaneously.

His hand flew to the Beretta holstered beneath his left arm. Ackerman's face appeared in the doorway.

Allen gripped the weapon and pulled it free.

Before he could bring his gun to bear on the killer, Ackerman rushed forward and slammed against him, his hand clamping onto Allen's right wrist. Ackerman forced Allen back against the white railing. Allen swung his left fist into Ackerman's side, but the killer smashed his forehead into the bridge of his opponent's nose.

Allen felt something crack, and his vision blurred. A disorienting and nauseating deluge of pain thundered through his skull.

Then his whole world dropped out from beneath him, and he tumbled backward over the railing.

THE WAITING AREA at the Rush University Medical Center had both a modern and a retro feel. Marcus sat on a strange curvy couch that snaked across one entire wall of the room. It was brightly colored with red, yellow, orange, and brown stripes. Windows overlooking the city filled the entire wall at his back, letting sunlight invade the space. The whole place seemed too cheery for his tastes. The walls were bright yellow. Chairs were mint green. He wondered whatever had happened to hospital white. The only aspect of the room that matched his mood was the carpet checkered with shades of gray.

He pressed his palms against his temples, trying to push back the pounding in his skull. Andrew paced back and forth in front of a business center in the middle of the room. The door opened and the sounds of the hospital slipped inside. They both looked quickly toward the entrance, expecting a doctor with news of Allen's condition. But it wasn't the doctor; it was Vasques.

She walked over and sat next to Marcus on the Technicolor couch. Her right hand held a tray filled with cups of coffee. Andrew took one with a nod of thanks.

As Marcus reached for a cup, he said, "Ackerman?"

She sighed. "They think he stole an ambulance and slipped through the perimeter. He's gone, but we have an APB out. We'll find him."

Marcus shook his head. "No, you won't. He's lived most of his life on the run, learning every trick. He's a chameleon when he wants to be."

Vasques swallowed hard. "I'm sorry about Agent Brubaker. I know that I had only just met him, but he seemed like a wonderful man. Were you two close?"

"We *are* close," Marcus snapped. "I'm sorry. I didn't mean to…"

He waved his hand dismissively. "It's fine. You didn't mean anything by it. I'm just on edge. I've only known Allen for a little over a year. He actually helped recruit me into our organization, and then he took me under his wing and showed me the ropes. My parents were killed when I was little, but in a lot of ways, Allen reminds me of my father. Dad was a detective with the NYPD. That's where I started out, too. Anyway, when I was learning from Allen, it was almost like I had a little piece of my dad back. He's a good friend."

They sat in silence for a few moments, and then Marcus's phone vibrated in his pocket. He pulled it out, and the anger swelled up like a volcano inside his chest. He gritted his teeth, fought the urge to throw the phone across the room, and switched it off.

"Who was that?"

"It was him."

"You mean Ackerman?"

He said nothing. He shut his eyes and leaned his head back against the couch.

"Who *are* you guys?" Vasques said. "I don't know too many people on Charlie Manson's speed dial."

Marcus swallowed hard and let out a long breath. "Ackerman was sort of my first case within our organization. He became obsessed with me. Thinks I'm the yin to his yang. He claims that our destinies are linked. Since he got away he's been following our investigations somehow and actually trying to help with them. In his own sick way."

"So he's following you around?"

"I don't know. I guess."

"How does he know about your cases?"

"I don't know."

"What *do* you know?"

"I know that Ackerman is an expert in pain." He reached up and rubbed the bridge of his nose, thinking of the pain that the killer had caused him. Maybe that was truly why Ackerman had latched on to him. To kill him slowly, a little piece of his soul at a time. "Have you heard his story...what he went through as a boy?"

"Just that his father tortured him. I am familiar with his more recent exploits. There was a lot of buzz about that hospital fire in Colorado Springs and Ackerman's escape."

Memories of that night cascaded through Marcus's mind like a tsunami.

Flames calling out for him, longing to devour him. Ackerman's fists slamming against his rib cage. Hanging from the edge of the building, the killer looking down on him. Falling through the flame-damaged roof. The fire surrounding him, closing in. And then Ackerman saving his life, carrying him from the inferno to safety.

That was the night he had faced his darkest demons and deepest secrets and came through the flames alive, but not unscathed. It was on that night that his dreams of a normal life had died. Trying to push away the memories, he continued with his story. "Ackerman's father was a nut-job psychologist who wanted to gain some insight into the minds of serial killers by subjecting his son to every traumatic experience ever documented in the lives of the world's most deranged men."

Vasques nodded. "Okay, I do remember this. He kept the kid in a little cell and taped all the experiments. The boys at the BAU treat those tapes like they're some kind of sacred religious texts. The Ackerman Tapes, they call them. Like they're the Dead Sea Scrolls or something. You've heard the conspiracy theory, right?"

"No," Marcus said.

"What do you mean?"

She turned in her seat as though she was about to share an extra-juicy piece of gossip. "Ackerman's daddy taped every move the kid made. Everything he did to him and made him do. But one of the eggheads was watching the tapes and realized that there is a two-week period of time with nothing. No experiments. No video of any kind."

"I've watched most of the tapes myself, but I've never paid attention to the dates and times. Maybe something interrupted him?"

She shrugged. "You're probably right. But I guess we'll never know." Marcus opened his mouth to ask if there were any theories, but thoughts of Ackerman were pushed to the back of his mind when a petite Asian woman in a white coat walked into the room. He shot to his feet.

"Is he alive?"

The doctor nodded. "He'll live, but we still don't know how bad the damage will be. He's broken several bones, but our main concern is that he's suffered significant damage to his spine." She hesitated and looked to the floor. "It's too soon to know if he'll ever walk again."

Marcus looked away as tears filled his eyes. He thought of Allen's family—his son, Charlie, his daughter, Amy, and his wife, Loren. They were good people and had taken him in as one of their own, a surrogate uncle or son. Allen had finally retired and escaped this life. He had came through all those years of hunting unscathed, and now when he could finally devote himself entirely to his loved ones, he might have to do so from a wheelchair. It wasn't fair. This would devastate them.

Marcus could never imagine putting anyone through that. He didn't understand how Loren or Allen could deal with the pressures of family and the work of a Shepherd. Two different worlds. Worlds that would never be compatible.

The doctor added, "He's conscious and stable right now. You can speak to him briefly, if you wish. But only for a moment and then he needs to rest."

Marcus's head bobbed from pure reflex. The doctor led the way down a hall of grays, blues, and whites. The strange antiseptic smell of a hospital clung to everything, but they had tried to mask it with something floral. Allen's room wasn't far away. It was filled with different shades of blue. A sink was off to the right. A recliner and a love seat sat along the wall in front of a window. Allen lay in the hospital bed in the center of the room, connected to all manner of tubes and machines that buzzed, whirred, and beeped.

They approached, and Allen's eyes turned in their direction. Marcus swallowed hard and squeezed Allen's hand. "You scared us, Professor. You must be getting soft in your old age. Five years ago it would've been Ackerman in that bed."

A ghost of a smile crept onto Allen's lips, but he looked frail and weak. When he spoke, his voice was only a whisper, and they had to lean close to hear. "'Of all the wonders that I yet have heard, it seems to me most strange that men should fear; Seeing that death, a necessary end, will come when it will come.'"

Marcus chuckled. But Vasques had a strange look on her face. "Shakespeare," he explained.

"Don't worry about me. I don't want you sitting around here coddling me with your thumbs up your asses." Allen coughed, and pain showed on his face. "Get out there, boys, and catch me a killer."

Thinking of Ackerman and the Anarchist, Marcus said, "How about two?"

"Even better."

34

AFTER DIALING MARCUS for the fifth time and still receiving no answer, Ackerman threw the disposable pay-as-you-go cell phone across the dingy little room. It shattered against the wall, the pieces raining down over the two dead bodies that had been shoved into the corner. The men had been scumbag drug dealers peddling a chemical escape to anyone with the cash. Ackerman didn't understand drugs. What did normal people need to escape from? Why burn up your precious brain cells and your intellect along with them for a cheap high? He would have given anything to be like the people he passed on the streets every day, to be normal, to escape from the monster in the mirror. But fate had chosen a different path for him. He accepted that. But others longed for an escape from the normalcy and monotony that he craved. It was human nature, he supposed, the grass always being greener on the other side.

He pounded his fist on the 1970s-style table decorated with different-colored boomerang shapes. Why wasn't Marcus answering? He was clearly upset about his friend. But the least he could do was give Ackerman a chance to explain. He hadn't meant to harm anyone, hadn't meant for Allen to fall. It had all just been a terrible accident. He had even grabbed for the old man as he'd tumbled over the railing.

Not that he really cared whether or not Brubaker lived or died, but he *did* care about Marcus. Their tenuous relationship was about to go through a major upheaval. His plan would be put into action soon. The incident with Allen shouldn't affect that, but he didn't like leaving things to chance, either.

The entire incident had been his fault. He had screwed up in the parking garage. He had been sloppy. The call to Marcus should have taken place while they were on the road. It wasn't a mistake he would make again.

The smell of the small house located in Englewood, one of Chicago's most notorious neighborhoods, was beginning to truly bother Ackerman. The decomposition of the bodies—which he needed to dispose of soon—contributed to this, but it wasn't the main factor. That was a smell that he had become accustomed to, even comforted by. But the filth that the two degenerates had been living in was a different matter. Not even Marcus could possibly fault him for the disposal of this human garbage.

He reached out with his left hand for another unopened phone resting on the table, and pain lanced through his shoulder. He touched the ragged bullet hole, and his fingers came back bloody. With thoughts of Marcus plaguing him, he had almost forgotten about his injury. Luckily, the big .45 caliber bullet had pierced straight through the meat on the edge of his shoulder as he had ducked down. It was all skin and muscle damage, barely more than a grazing flesh wound. A minor annoyance. Still, it needed to be tended to in order to stop the bleeding.

Ackerman stood and moved to the kitchen of the dilapidated little house. As he flipped on the lights, cockroaches scattered. Dirty dishes and moldy food dotted the counters, and trash covered the yellowed linoleum. A musty, fungal smell mixed with a smoky taint burned his nostrils. The space disgusted him. He wished he could revive the two drug dealers and kill them again. But he had lived in far worse, and it had never really bothered him before. It must have simply been his anger over being ignored by Marcus that was coloring his attitude.

An ashtray filled with ground-out cigarettes sat atop a

lime-green table. A dark purple book of matches rested beside it. He ripped off his shirt, but as he glanced around the noxious little kitchen, he couldn't see anywhere he really wanted to lay it down. He decided to drape it over the back of one of the kitchen chairs and opened the pack of matches. It was nearly full. He tore out the whole contents and rolled them into a round bundle. Then he struck one of the matches and used it to start the others burning.

The matches in his right hand found their way up to the bullet wound, and Ackerman jammed the flaming wad inside the hole in his flesh. The more pleasant smell of sizzling meat overpowered the other aromas in the house. His teeth ground together, and he lost himself in the ecstasy of the pain. Over the course of his life and the experiments conducted upon him by his father, the pain had actually become a comfort to him. It centered him. Cleared his mind and gave him focus. He was strangely at peace in his pain, and he imagined it to be comparable to the feeling that a normal person would experience when returning home for the holidays after a prolonged absence.

His gaze fell on the cover of the book of matches. The address and name of a bar adorned its front in a plain, utilitarian script. *The Alibi Lounge.* Judging by the address, the bar wasn't too far away. He considered this and decided that a little walk might do him some good.

But first, he put on a clean black polo shirt and chinos, opened up a new phone, and tried Marcus again. No answer. This time he resisted the urge to throw the phone against the wall. The anger at how easily Marcus could dismiss and ignore him burned and roiled through his guts. Ackerman's hunger grew in the darkest part of his soul.

Maybe he'd find some interesting playmates at the Alibi Lounge.

35

MARGOT WHITTEN LIVED in a yellow split-level with brown shutters. Two large maples bordered a short blacktop drive. Next door was another split-level that was identical except for its color and landscaping. It had once been the home of a woman named Sandra Lutrell—the first of the Anarchist's latest victims. Margot had witnessed a man in the alley that night.

As they pulled up in front of Margot's home, Vasques received a phone call. Judging by her reactions, Marcus knew the news wasn't good.

"They found Jessie Olague's body," she said. "This time he did the deed in an empty house on the south side of town. Same as the others. Maybe we should put this off and head over there instead?"

Marcus considered it for a moment but replied, "It's your call, but I'd let the cops do their jobs and process the scene. We can head over after we talk to Mrs. Whitten."

Vasques nodded, and the three of them walked up the snow-covered sidewalk to the front door of the split-level. Margot had been expecting them, and she quickly opened the door and ushered them in from the cold. Vasques made the introductions, and she and Andrew sat down around a glass coffee table on a white floral-patterned couch. Margot sat on the edge of a tan recliner while Marcus remained standing and examined the room.

A glass display case filled with Elvis memorabilia sat along one wall of the living room. The knick-knacks and souvenirs weren't of any real value, but Margot had amassed quite a collection. A little table next to the display case held a phone with a lifelike Elvis figure in a gold jacket mounted on top.

"I've seen these," Marcus said, gesturing to the phone. "He dances when you get a call, right?"

Margot smiled shyly and scrunched up her nose. She had short white hair and was well built. Not fat, but thick. "And it plays *Blue Suede Shoes*."

"You've got a nice collection. I'm a collector myself. Movie memorabilia, mostly. But I like yours better. Mine's all stuff that I've bought on the Internet. But I can tell that every item in this case has a story behind it. That's what really makes a good collection. Not just the stuff, but the memories that go with it."

"Thank you," Margot said. "It's a hobby. You know, I was there at his last concert."

"June 26, 1977. Indianapolis."

Margot's eyes lit up. "That's right. I'll never forget it. I got to hear the last song he ever played on stage. *Can't Help Falling in Love*."

Marcus walked over and sat down on the love seat next to Margot. "Can you tell us about that night, Mrs. Whitten?"

"The concert?"

He grinned. "No, ma'am. The night you saw the man in the alley."

"Oh, right." Her expression turned somber. "I want to help in any way I can. Sandra was a very nice young woman. I still can't believe…I'm sorry. I really don't remember much."

"That's okay. Anything you can recall could help."

"Well, I work as a garbage woman so I keep pretty odd hours. I typically wake up between two and three in the morning. Then I'll fix myself some breakfast, watch some TV before work. Anyway, that morning I saw a man park in the alley behind Sandra's house."

"Do you remember anything about the man? Anything

distinctive?" Marcus wasn't taking any notes. He'd never needed to.

"Pretty average size. He was dressed all in black or dark blue, but I couldn't see his face. I was suspicious at first, but he knew right where she kept her key. I figured he was just some new boyfriend." Tears filled her eyes. "How else could he know about her key? He just didn't act like he was out of place. But I..." She looked away, and the tears rolled down her cheeks.

Marcus leaned forward and placed a hand on her shoulder. "It wasn't your fault. I know there's nothing I can say to really convince you of that. Guilt's funny that way, but—trust me—you couldn't have known. That man is the bad guy, not you. He's the one to blame for this. The only one. But if you can remember anything else about him and help us find him, I promise I'll make sure he never hurts anyone else."

"I'm sorry. I just...I did look at his license plate, but I didn't write anything down. It started with an M or N, but I can't really remember."

"What did the car look like? Did you recognize the model?" Andrew asked from the couch.

"It was dark. Like I told the others, I just don't know."

Marcus decided to change tactics. "Let me ask you this, Margot. What were you doing at the moment when you saw him?"

"I was making breakfast."

"Cooking?"

"Yeah, I was frying a couple eggs. Why?"

"This may seem strange, but would you mind cooking some eggs for me? I'd like you to try and re-enact exactly what you were doing when you saw him. Most people don't realize it, but smell has a powerful bond to memory. Sometimes doing the same thing, the same smells and sounds, will help you to remember things that you didn't even realize you had seen."

"Anything to help."

Margot's kitchen also served as her dining room. The whole room was white with red accents. White cabinets, red handles, red countertop. White table, red chairs. Red and white knick-knacks on white shelves. White curtains with red dots.

The room made Marcus feel like he was drowning in blood, but he supposed that wasn't the reaction a normal person would feel. To most people, red was just a color.

Margot took a skillet from a white cabinet and cracked two eggs. "Just go through everything as you normally would. Exactly like you did that night. Try to imagine that you're back there in that moment, watching him pull up and get out of the car. Try to recall every detail."

Her brow furrowed in concentration. She closed her eyes, opened them, and closed them again. "Okay, the guy pulls up. The car's dark, blue or black maybe. I don't know."

"Don't force it. Take your time."

She sighed and was quiet for a long moment. Then she added, "The brake lights slanted inward and down, and there was a silver emblem above the license plate."

Silence stretched out again. The smell of sizzling grease wafted up from the stove. Marcus didn't rush her.

Margot suddenly turned her head quickly toward him and got very animated and excited. She was almost bouncing. "I remember. I remember. The license plate was MJA 4… and then maybe a 59 or a 69. But I'm not sure about those last two digits. Does that help?"

"You did great. That's more than enough for us to track the plate."

ACKERMAN SAT DOWN on a black leather stool in front of the bar at the Alibi Lounge. Chips and channels, marks of age, grooved the bar's surface, which was in need of a coat of polish. The place was small and narrow with a few booths and tables, a pool table, and a dartboard along one wall. The bar and rows of liquor bottles rested along the opposite side. A haze of smoke infected the air, even though smoking in a bar was illegal in Illinois.

"I'll take a shot of Jack Daniel's," he said to the bartender.

She was abnormally tall, with freckles and a long puckered face. A front tooth was chipped and jagged. She looked Ackerman up and down, and he knew what she was thinking. He was too clean-cut for this place. But she didn't say a word. She just dropped a shot glass onto the bar and filled it up.

Ackerman had called Marcus again during his walk to the bar. Still no answer.

He slammed back the shot and tapped the bar to indicate that he wanted another. She tipped the bottle and let more of the brown liquid flow into his glass. She still didn't speak. It wasn't the type of place where the patrons expected conversation.

A beautiful young woman sat two stools down from him, leaning her elbows atop the bar and flipping the cap from a bottle of Bud Light between her fingers. She sported a black long-sleeve shirt displaying the picture of a heavy-metal band. Long dark hair flowed over her shoulders and hid one side of her face.

Ackerman gave her his best movie-star smile. She blushed, and a grin almost formed on her lips but then disappeared. Her gaze darted back to the pool table as if to see if someone there was watching. He glanced in that direction and found an enormous biker with a shaved head and unkempt goatee who was wearing a black Harley shirt. A tattoo of an eagle stretched across the back of the biker's neck. The man's partner had dark skin and short dreadlocks. Another pair of goons matching in appearance and attitude were watching the game from a small table nearby.

He looked back at the woman on the bar stool. Her lip was pierced, and he could see the tip of a tattoo jutting out from beneath the sleeve of her shirt. Tattoos and piercings were typically a turn-off for him, but in her case, the unnecessary adornments were unable to mask the beauty beneath. And something about her—the eyes, cheekbones, facial structure—reminded him of his mother. She glanced in his direction, again noticing his attention, but she turned away quickly. As she did, her black hair swept away from the left side of her face, leaving it exposed for the first time. A large purple bruise that she had tried to cover with makeup ran down her cheek.

Ackerman smiled. Apparently, fate had led him to the right place at the right time, as always.

He moved over to the stool directly beside her and said, "Hey, bartender, I'll take a Budweiser and another Bud Light for the lady." The tall woman behind the bar didn't move or speak. Her gaze shifted slowly from him, to the dark-haired beauty, to the bald biker. Ackerman's gaze burrowed into the bartender, and after a moment, she reached down into a cooler and pulled out two bottles. She placed them on the bar and then walked away.

The dark-haired beauty kept looking over her shoulder, but apparently, she didn't want to cause a scene or draw her boyfriend's attention by refusing the drink. Instead, she whispered, "Thanks for the drink, but you need to back off.

If that guy over there sees you flirting with me, there'll be trouble for both of us."

"I appreciate your concern, but I don't scare easily."

"You should. He's not a nice man."

"Then why are you with him?"

She wouldn't make eye contact, and her breathing had become short and ragged. "Listen, just stay away from me."

Ackerman thought about the situation for a moment. Then he said, "So you're afraid of this guy, and he treats you like a piece of property. He hits you. Probably abuses you mentally as well. Calls you names. Makes you feel like you're inferior, broken, that no one would ever love you. Despite all this, you stay with him. Are you really that afraid of this man? You think he'd kill you before he let you leave? Maybe he's told you as much. Or do you actually believe the things he tells you? Do you honestly believe that you couldn't do better?"

She swallowed hard, and a tear rolled down her cheek. "Please, just…"

"I tell you what," he whispered. "Let's play a little game. Rules are simple. I'll let you choose. If you really want, I'll pay my tab and walk out that door. You can go back to your life, continue on like nothing ever happened here. But after tonight, it will be a prison of your own choosing. Because I'm offering you deliverance. I'm giving you a way out."

"What are you talking about?"

"So that's option number one. You keep going down the road you're on. Wherever it leads. Option number two is that I make sure that he will never hurt you again. That choice has consequences as well. Ones that you'll have to live with. You'll feel responsible, guilty, ashamed even. But you will be free."

"Why are you doing this?"

"Why not? Sometimes fate intervenes when you least expect it. It has a funny way of turning your world upside down and setting you on the right path. I'm just the instrument of your course correction. Like I said, it's simple. If you say no, I'll leave. But if you say yes, fate will intervene on your behalf."

She was quiet for a long moment. Her hands shook against the sweating bottle of beer, and her breathing was fast but rhythmic. Each breath a fall and a crescendo, fall and crescendo. She turned and studied him, probably trying to gauge the validity of his offer. She looked away again. More tears fell. But then she whispered, "Yes."

37

BELACOURT AND STUPAK had already arrived at Glasgow Jewelers when Marcus pulled up to the curb. The store occupied the corner of a tan-colored building bordered by redbrick town houses. Art deco windows lined the store's entrance that was carved into a triangular recessed niche. A blue Toyota Camry with the license plate *MJA 459* sat in front of the store. The name on the car's registration was Raymond Glasgow, the owner of the small shop.

Vasques stepped out of the vehicle and said, "Are you coming in?"

Marcus glanced at the shop and the car. "No, I'll let the professionals handle it."

She gave him a look. "You did a good job with that witness. I owe you dinner if this turns out to be the right guy."

"I'll take you up on that."

She shut the door without further comment and crossed the street. The two cops exited their red Chevy Impala and joined Vasques, who held open the door for them. Marcus leaned his head back against the seat and closed his eyes, trying to get a moment's rest.

From the back seat, Andrew said, "Okay, show and tell. Why isn't this him?"

"You'll find out in a few minutes."

Andrew muttered something, but Marcus tried not to hear. He tried to shut out the world for just a few seconds. He only needed a moment to rest his eyes and recharge. Just as he was about to doze off for the first time in two days, Andrew said, "How long has it been since you've slept? You know being overly tired is as bad as being drunk. It's going to affect your judgment."

Marcus sighed. "I already have one shrink. I don't need another."

"Come on. I'm your best friend. Hell, I'm damn near your *only* friend. What's been bothering you so much lately? Bottling all that up inside isn't healthy."

"Who are you, Dr. Phil? You want to help me? Then shut up and let me rest a minute."

Andrew grumbled under his breath. "Fine. I'll just keep my mouth shut. Won't hear a peep from me. Not a word. You can just crash and burn. Doesn't matter to me one way or the other. How dare I try to help?"

"Would you shut up!"

"Fine. Whatever."

Marcus tried to close his eyes and rest, but his mind wouldn't allow it. His head kept filling with a collage of a million unrelated thoughts, a million images flying through his brain at high speed— Ackerman, the missing time on the tapes, the Anarchist, burnt bodies, eyes held open, a filthy mattress on the floor, a trembling girl, the bullet hole in Ty Phillips's forehead, smiling faces, blood, pain, the night his parents were murdered, the voice in the darkness.

After a few minutes, Vasques tapped on his window, and he pulled up on the switch to roll it down. "Airtight alibi," she said. "He was at a jewelers' convention in San Diego. His flight came in yesterday morning. We'll check it out, but I don't think he's lying. He claims that his wife drove him to the airport, and his car's been sitting here since he left last week. We're going to get a forensics team on the car to see if the Anarchist stole it and used it to kidnap Sandra Lutrell."

"I figured the Anarchist would be too careful for us to get him off a plate number. And I bet your forensics team won't find anything in the car, but tell them to check the plate itself."

"You think he switched them?"

"That's what I'd do."

Vasques reached up and massaged her neck. "Then we got nothing," she said.

Andrew leaned forward from the back seat and commented, "Not necessarily. If a cop ran the plate and it came back as the wrong type of car, it could lead to him getting caught."

"So he drives the same car as Glasgow," Vasques said. "That's good. We'll put together a list of every person who drives a Toyota Camry in the Chicago area. It'll be a big list, but maybe we'll find something to cross-check it with." She looked at Marcus and pursed her lips as if considering something. "That also means that you were right in your assessment of what kind of car the killer drives. If memory serves, a Camry was the first one you listed."

"Yeah, well, I'm not going to break my arm patting myself on the back. All it really tells us is that this guy is smart, methodical, and can do a Google search. I'm not sure that we're any closer to catching him...or stopping him from killing again."

38

ACKERMAN SPUN ROUND on his bar stool and walked straight over to the big bald biker. He tapped a massive shoulder, and the man turned, looking down at him with a furrowed brow. The biker outweighed him by at least a hundred and fifty pounds and stood seven inches taller.

The bigger they are, he thought.

"What the hell do you want?" the big man said. His voice was a low grumble. He gave Ackerman a look that the killer supposed had been practiced and honed by years of back-alley brawls. The look in the biker's eyes announced him as a force to be reckoned with: indestructible, frightening, powerful. It was a good look.

Ackerman smiled back. He knew the type. The man's size, bulk, and attitude had helped him to avoid more fights than he had ever started or participated in. The biker was little more than an overgrown bully, and behind the bravado he saw something present in the heart of every bully he had ever met: fear.

"Are you the one that gave the beautiful young lady over there that nasty bruise?"

The biker looked him up and down and laughed to his friends. He set his bottle of beer down on the side of the pool table. "Are you serious? You some kind of knight in shining armor?"

"Far from it."

The biker growled out another throaty laugh. "I'll do whatever I want to her, and it's nobody's business but mine. That answer your question?" A meaty paw shot out and pushed against Ackerman's shoulder. The killer stumbled back but then returned to his previous position in front of the big man, his smile not faltering.

With a snarl, the biker said, "Did you come in here just to get your face smashed in? If so, you came to the right place."

Ackerman replied, "I just came here to blow off some steam."

His hand shot out and grabbed the bald biker's bottle from its resting place atop the big Brunswick table. He smashed it against the edge, and the bottom half of the bottle shattered. He lunged forward with the bottle stretched out.

The big biker was ready for the move and reacted quickly. Too bad for him that it was only a feint.

As the biker moved out of the path of the blow, all his weight shifted to his right leg. Ackerman's foot shot out and collided with the inside of the man's right kneecap. The joint buckled, and the big man dropped to one knee.

Ackerman slammed the man's bald head against the side of the pool table and stabbed the jagged edge of the bottle into his left eye.

The big man wailed in agony and clutched his face. He fell the rest of the way to the ground and rolled around the floor of the bar. Screaming, cursing, spitting.

The black man with the dreadlocks just looked at his fallen comrade in wide-eyed panic. When he saw Ackerman staring at him, he dropped his pool cue and raised both hands in surrender.

"Don't move!" said a woman's voice at Ackerman's back.

He turned to find the bartender holding an old black Smith and Wesson 9mm pistol. She had come around the side of the bar and stood a few feet away. Still mindful of the biker's friends, he cocked his head to the side and examined her weapon. He took a step toward her.

"Stop!" she screamed, shaking the gun at him.

"There's a layer of dust on your gun. How long has it been sitting back there under the bar, unused?"

She didn't answer.

"You see, the smarter move would have been to stick a revolver back there. Maybe a .357 magnum. That 9 mm has a clip, and if it's been sitting back there loaded, the spring within the clip has been under constant pressure. Eventually, the spring will go bad. The shells won't jack up into the chamber correctly. It'll jam up on you or not fire at all."

Slowly, he took another step forward.

"Are you willing to take the chance of that gun not firing or maybe even blowing up on you? Plus, you have to ask yourself if you really have what it takes to kill a man."

"Just get out of here," the tall woman said in a whisper. "Just leave."

"I will. In a moment. But first, you need to make a choice." Ackerman held out his hand, palm up. "You can either put that gun in my hand and get back behind the bar, or I'll come take it and break your neck."

She stood frozen. Time stretched out. But then she dropped the gun into his palm and scurried away. "Good choice," he said.

He turned back to the bald biker and his friends. The big man had pulled himself up to his knees, still clutching the left side of his face. Blood ran out from beneath his fingers and dripped down his forearm to the floor.

Ackerman raised the 9mm to the man's head and fired. Flame shot from the muzzle, and the big man dropped back to the floor, never to get up again.

As he twisted the Smith and Wesson in his hand and examined it, Ackerman raised his eyebrows and said, "Guess it fired after all."

39

THE PLACE WHERE Jessie Olague had taken her final breath was a tri-level on Jackson's Grove's south side with an orange brick and blue siding front and a private yard bordered by a wooded area filled with maples and oaks. According to the realtor, the house had been sitting vacant for the past six months with no serious offers. It was unlikely that interest would increase now that a young woman's screams had filled the building's corridors.

As they pulled up to the scene that was still surrounded by squad cars and barricades, Marcus first watched the crowd. Killers often visited their crime scenes pretending to be a bystander, but the Jackson's Grove PD had been taking detailed photos at every scene and had drawn no correlation.

He then examined the area and asked himself a series of questions that would shed light on the offender. How familiar did the Anarchist need to be with the surroundings? What were the best points of ingress? Would the neighbors have heard anything or seen the car? The closest house on the left was also for sale, and trees bordered the right side of the tri-level. It wasn't likely that they'd get lucky with any witnesses here, but he knew that the police would be canvassing the surrounding neighborhood to be sure.

Having seen nothing outside to shed new light on the case, Marcus, Vasques, and Andrew entered the house through the back door, the same entrance the killer would have used, and walked through to the crime scene. The place buzzed with the activity of crime-scene techs, photographers, and investigators. Tape measures were extended and cameras flashed. The rooms were freshly painted beige with light blue and brown-accent walls. The whole place reeked of burnt flesh and smoke.

Jessie Olague had been tied to a specially designed chair in the center of the house's den. The fire had consumed most of her body, leaving only a charred husk. The chair had metal plates welded to the bottom of its frame and a high back that secured her head in place. The plates were screwed to the floor to keep the chair from moving. The Anarchist had done similar things at all the scenes, and Marcus guessed that the killer had set it all up before he'd brought the girl here and the actual killing took place.

Marcus hung back, letting the techs do their jobs and examining the killer's stage for the murder. It matched the others perfectly. Strange symbols drawn in red paint covered all four walls, a mixture of satanic emblems and cryptic runes.

Jessie Olague's body drew his gaze even though staring at the remains of the poor woman was the last thing he wanted to do. He'd seen many dead bodies during his years in law enforcement, and he'd never forgotten a single one. He could remember all the victims' names and instantly recall the scenes of their deaths in vivid detail. There were many times in his line of work where an eidetic or photographic memory was a blessing, but also many times when it was a curse.

He'd smelled the odor of burnt flesh and charred bodies before at a few car crashes during his stint as a NYPD patrol officer and a few other times at murder scenes when he'd been a detective. The scent hadn't been anything like he had expected. He had foolishly assumed that it would smell like a pot roast left in the oven for too long, just another cooked piece of meat. There were hints of that, yet it was also very different.

A body contained all manner of things that were normally never cooked. Livestock were bled and butchered, their organs and blood removed. But that hadn't been the case with

Jessie Olague. Her iron-rich blood added a metallic component to the smell. The keratin in her hair contained large amounts of cysteine, a sulfur-containing amino acid, adding its distinctive odor. Burning skin created a charcoal-like stink. When exposed to flame, cerebrospinal fluid generated a musky, sweet perfume.

The mixture of conflicting fragrant and putrid aromas wasn't something that he would ever forget. And he knew from experience that it would cling to the inside of his nostrils for days.

"My God," Vasques said at his side, covering her mouth and looking away from the body. "How could someone do that to another human being?"

Marcus didn't answer. He understood the darkness inside necessary to take life in such a way, but it wasn't something that could easily be explained or comprehended, even by those who had felt its power. Instead, in almost a whisper, he said, "What have you found out about the symbols?"

"Not much. We've contacted some experts, but as far we can tell it's a mixture of satanic symbology and gibberish." Vasques referred to her notebook, flipping through several pages, but she had to pause for a moment and cover her nose. She looked pale, and Marcus wondered if she was going to be sick. He should have warned her about the smell. One of the techs or cops might have had some Vicks ointment that she could have rubbed on the skin beneath her nose.

But, after a brief hesitation, she found the information and said, "The characters appear to be a mixture of Cypriot, a language used on the island of Cyprus from 1500 BCE to 300 BCE, and Glagolitic, used in Eastern Europe between the ninth and twelfth centuries CE."

He shook his head and breathed out harshly in frustration. What could possibly be the correlation between the murders and these strange symbols and writings? It was the only part of the crime scenes that didn't make sense to him. This killer was smart and organized. Why use random symbols and strange scripts that didn't have any meaning or connection? He wondered if the killer believed that the symbols had been given to him from some supernatural source.

"The accelerant?" Andrew said.

"Same as the others. Aliphatic petroleum solvent, commonly known as lighter fluid. Available at nearly any hardware, department, or grocery store."

Marcus squeezed his eyes shut. His head pounded and throbbed as though someone had buried a hatchet deep into the center of his brain. The migraines again. He needed painkillers and caffeine, and all he'd eaten that day was a Twinkie first thing in the morning.

Entering the den through another door, Belacourt and Stupak approached them. Belacourt shot him a look of distaste and said, "Now that you've seen his handiwork, big shot, you still think this guy's not a psychopath?"

Marcus groaned. He didn't like where this was heading, and there was something about Belacourt's voice and derisive tone that made his head pound even harder. "Psychopathy is a personality disorder. One which he doesn't have. If I thought you could read, I'd direct you to some books on the subject."

Belacourt laughed, but there was only anger in his eyes. "You think you're so slick, don't you? So much better and smarter than all of us simple-minded detectives. I'm going to save us all some time and energy and just be straight with you. We don't need you here. We don't want you here. If this guy sticks to his pattern, he's going to take another girl tonight, and I need Agent Vasques, someone who actually knows what she's doing, in the trenches working this case. Not babysitting you."

Vasques spoke up and said, "That's way out of line. Agent Williams has—"

"Has contributed nothing to this investigation. He used

an old trick to get a useless piece of info out of a witness. What did that accomplish other than wasting our time and resources?"

Belacourt stepped close and poked a finger into Marcus's chest. Even through the smell of the dead body he could detect the stink of cigarettes and onions on the cop's breath. "I'll tell you something else. That fiasco today with you chasing after some guy that you claim was Francis Ackerman and shooting your gun all over the place, that kind of loose-cannon act is not going to fly in my town. I don't know who you are or what you're really into, but I am going to find out. What I do know, just from what I've seen and heard since this morning, is that you think you're some kind of investigative genius. But you're not. You're just some stupid kid that a bureaucrat back east gave a badge to. You're probably somebody's nephew who wanted to play cops and robbers so they made up a position to stick you in."

Vasques started to come to his defense, but Marcus raised a hand to stop her. He preferred to fight his own battles. He glanced down at the finger stabbing into his chest and then met Belacourt's eyes. "I have a lot of respect for cops. I'm third-generation myself. So out of consideration for that badge on your belt, I'm going to give you one warning. If you ever jab one of those fat sausages that you call fingers into my chest again, I will break it off and use my investigative genius to find a place to stick it."

Belacourt's lip twitched in a snarl of contempt, and he looked as if he was ready to throw a punch. Marcus hoped that he would.

Stupak put a hand on his superior's shoulder and said, "Come on. Just let it go. Let's worry about catching this guy."

Belacourt's gaze drilled into Marcus. Through gritted teeth, the cop said, "Get out of my crime scene, boy, before I take off my belt and give you a spanking."

Marcus smiled. "I don't know how it works around here,

but where I'm from you have to buy a guy dinner first before you start trying the kinky stuff."

Belacourt just shook his head slowly from side to side. "You've wasted enough of my time. You're not worth another second." Then the cop turned and stormed from the room.

Vasques said, "You're not good at making friends, are you?"

With a little chuckle, Andrew added, "Thank you. That's what I've been trying to tell him."

SCHOFIELD STARED OUT across the crowd assembled inside the Tinley Park middle-school gymnasium. The happy smiling faces etched with joy. The normal people. Children laughed. A dark-haired grandmother bounced an infant on her knee. The parents of one of the players jumped in the air after their son hit the second of two free throws. Such simple pleasures, yet they eluded him. None of them understood how lucky they were to have been given the gift of happiness.

His son, Ben, sat on the end of the bench, rubbing his shoe against the red gym floor and staring at it intently. Concern overwhelmed Schofield's thoughts. Something was wrong with the boy. There had been a change in him. Two years ago he had been a star player, but now he seemed so distracted. A good father would be able to get to the bottom of it and help the boy overcome whatever it was that distressed him. The dark cloud pushed down harder against Schofield as he thought of how many ways he had failed the people he loved. He felt the black hand of sadness pushing him down, crushing him, bleeding him dry.

"Harrison? Are you okay?"

He looked at his wife and put on his best smile of reassurance. He felt so lucky to have her. During college, he had sat in the back of all his classes and avoided the other students like the plague. But their math teacher had asked him to tutor Eleanor and, much to his surprise, she had actually shown an interest in him. And it wasn't even that she chose to overlook his many flaws. She saw them and accepted them. He loved her for that.

"I'm fine. But, Eleanor, you know how much I love you, right?" She gave him a strange look, her eyebrows arching and her neck cocking to the side. "Are you sure you're okay? You're not dying or anything?"

He laughed, but it was all for show. "Can't a man just tell his wife how much she means to him without any ulterior motive?"

"I guess so," she said, but there wasn't much confidence behind the words. "I love you, too. But you can talk to me if anything's ever bothering you."

"I know, but I'm fine. Really. You know how I am about crowds and people. It just makes me uncomfortable. But speaking of things bothering people, do you know what's going on with Ben? Is he having problems at school?"

Eleanor shrugged. "I don't know. I hope he's just going through a phase, but he won't talk to me about it. He's his father's son," she said, with a sideways glance.

Schofield ignored the jibe and continued absently to watch the kids of his son's team run up and down the court. Back and forth, back and forth. Going through the motions.

But then, across the glistening floor of the gymnasium, sitting two rows up in the opposite team's bleachers, he saw her. Melissa Lighthaus—the woman he had chosen to be the next sacrifice. But why was she there? He knew everything about this woman from the brand of shampoo she used to the last thing she did every night before she crawled into bed. She had no children. She had a sister with two kids, but they lived in Arkansas. There was no reason for her to be there.

He felt his chest tightening as if the world was closing in on him. Yellow spots dripped across his vision, and he felt dizzy and nauseous.

She shouldn't be there. It didn't make sense. The variables didn't add up.

He couldn't breathe. He felt like someone was holding him underwater.

Growing cold, drowning, his arms flailing, the bloodred water. He was no longer in the gym. A memory from his childhood had fought its way to the surface of his mind.

It was an unusually cold day in August. He remembered because he'd only had shorts and a T-shirt to wear. They were staying in a hotel room with an orange bedspread. He remembered that, but he couldn't remember his age. Memories were funny that way. His mother had called him into the bathroom with her. She lay naked in the tub, her hair flowing around her. She had sung a quiet lullaby to him or maybe to herself. Then she slit her wrists. He watched her do this and cringed away from the tub. Tears ran down his cheeks, but he didn't truly understand the depth of what she was attempting.

She had waited a moment for the blood to leak from her body and then called him closer. He leaned over the edge of the tub, and she grabbed him and held him against her chest under the water. He kicked and fought, but her grip and her resolve were like iron. The water streamed through his eyes and mouth, his mother's blood flowing down his throat and filling his lungs, a metallic taste on his tongue. He remembered thrashing as he tried to push away and the softness of her skin beneath his fingers. He remembered her arms hugging him tightly around the chest. The warmth of the water covered him like a blanket, encasing him in a comforting cocoon, changing him, preparing him for the next world. Then things became blurry, but he remembered a distinct feeling of peace. This was what he had always wanted, for his mother to hold him and make him feel safe and loved. And in that moment, he somehow knew that she did love him, and she was trying to protect him. But then the Prophet had heard the noise and had burst into the bathroom, saving them both from the brink of death.

Now back in the gym, years later, he wished that his mother had succeeded on that cold day in August.

"I need some air," Schofield said as he stumbled down the steps of the bleachers. He pushed his way through the door of the gym and found the bathroom. He threw up in the sink and then stared at his reflection in the mirror. He saw the demon inside staring back at him. If the Prophet was right and he truly was the son of Satan, the harbinger of the apocalypse, then he needed to be stopped. His children deserved to be free of him. His wife and kids were all that mattered, and there wouldn't be room for them in the Prophet's new world.

As if in a daze, he made his way through the belly of the school building. The halls were empty and lit only by ambient light. The stuttering rhythm of his footfalls smacked against the tiles. The whole place reeked of pine-scented cleaning chemicals. Before he realized that he had a destination, he had searched and found access to the building's roof.

Schofield made his way across the blacktop surface, past vents and heating and cooling units spewing exhaust, to the building's edge. The wind ruffled his hair. The air was freezing. The snow-shrouded ground called to him, ready to embrace him like his mother had on that cold day from his memories. He stepped up onto the raised lip of the roof. His arms stretched out at his sides, and one leg dangled over the edge. All he needed to do was take one step. One step, and the nightmare would be over. The demon would be dead, and the world would be a brighter place.

But what if the fall didn't kill him? How would he explain what had happened? There was no way for it to have been an accident.

As he considered this, he realized that it didn't really matter. Either way, the fall would stop the final ritual. The world would continue on even after the darkest night. It would stop him from hurting anyone else. One step and the Prophet's plans would be vanquished.

His thoughts turned to the Prophet, the rituals, the darkest night. Something didn't add up. How had he not seen it before? Did he really follow the Prophet that blindly?

The darkest night was three days away, but that evening

he had planned to secure the first of the five sacrifices needed for the final ritual. Did the Prophet plan for him to take more than one girl a night? If so, the old man hadn't shared his plans, and Schofield wasn't prepared.

Then, suddenly, things became clear.

A terrible thought struck him and burned through his heart with the ferocity of a thousand suns. He stepped back from the edge and fell to his knees. His arms wrapped around his chest, and he rocked back and forth. His body trembled with fear and shame.

He suspected he knew where the Prophet planned to acquire the final three sacrifices. And it changed everything.

MAGGIE PULLED HER luggage from the trunk of the bright green taxicab and paid the driver. It had been a long day. Her flight had been delayed, and her rental car had blown a tire on the way to the hotel. She had spent an hour waiting for the rental company to get her a cab. The representative had claimed that they would deliver her a new car directly to the hotel, but she suspected that wouldn't get done without another hour on the phone. And now she would have to face Marcus.

He would be furious that she had disobeyed his orders, but she didn't care. She was going to assist on this case whether he wanted her help or not. She checked in at the front desk. The lobby was jammed with people and there was a long wait for assistance. Luckily, she had Stan in her corner, and he had already booked her a room just down the hall from Marcus and Andrew.

She made her way upstairs, dropped off her luggage, and then knocked on Marcus's door. After a short wait, Andrew answered. The top two buttons of his starched white shirt were undone, and his black tie hung loosely around his neck. He held a slice of pizza in his left hand. Judging from the lack of the typical warm pizza aroma, it was a leftover from a previous meal.

"Maggie?" he said, an expression of genuine surprise on his face. She raised her eyebrows. "You going to invite me in?"

"Umm, yeah. Come on in."

Maggie entered the outer room of the suite and looked

at the display board showing all the evidence that they had gathered so far. The board was truly a marvel. She definitely didn't miss Allen's old corkboard, but she did miss his calm and thoughtful leadership.

"What are you doing here, Mags?" Andrew said.

She took a deep breath and ignored the question. "How are things going with the case?"

He sighed. "I actually just got off talking with Stan. He's dug up a couple new leads for us to follow."

"Good. Then what are we waiting for? Where's Marcus?" Andrew's gaze darted around the room as if he was searching for something. He opened his mouth and closed it again. Then, after another pause, he finally replied, "He's having dinner down in the hotel restaurant with an FBI agent who's also consulting on the case."

Maggie's eyes narrowed. "Why are you acting so funny?"

He shrugged his shoulders almost as high as his eyebrows. "I don't know what you're talking about."

"Okay. I think I'll join them."

"Well, umm, I—"

"What?"

"Nothing. I'm just sure he'll be thrilled to see you."

42

VASQUES TOOK A sip of her wine and tried to stretch some of the tension from her shoulders. The day had been a roller coaster, and she needed a moment to unwind. She stared across the table at the man examining a cream and purple menu. His beautiful strangely colored eyes scanned each item, but she also noticed those same eyes gazing swiftly around the room, scanning the scene in micro-glances, taking it all in. He had rolled the sleeves of his gray silk shirt up to his elbows, exposing the tightly wrapped cords of muscle on his forearms. He must work out, Vasques thought, and she wondered if the rest of his body looked as good.

It was strange how she had started her day passionately hating this man and ready to run him out of town, and now she was ready to...

Easy, girl. One step at a time.

The waiter took their orders and filled their glasses. The place wasn't exactly five-star, but it was nice and quiet, a good place to enjoy a late dinner and go over the particulars of the case or whatever else might come up. Marcus leaned against the back of the booth and casually rested his right arm along the top of his seat. "So why the FBI?"

"It seemed like the place where I could make the biggest impact, do the most good. Why the DOJ? It seems like you'd be a good candidate for the BAU. I didn't even know there was a unit at Justice investigating serial murder."

"We're small, very specialized. Only work...special cases."

"Ones that are extra-bad?"

"I guess you could say that. Ninety-nine-point-nine per-cent of the time, regular law enforcement are good at what they do. They don't need a guy like me. But sometimes, ex-treme cases need extreme...tactics."

"They need a guy who notices stuff." Marcus shrugged. "Among other things."

"You like what you do?"

His face went serious, and he took a long sip of his cof-fee. "Sometimes destiny doesn't care whether or not you like the path it sticks you on."

Vasques nodded. She had seen firsthand what happened to some agents at the BAU. It wasn't uncommon for the mon-sters to get inside a person's head and follow them home. Marcus had chosen a booth in the back of the restaurant with his back to the wall. Still, his body language was that of someone who was hyperalert, as if he was expecting an attack at any moment. Yet he didn't come across as a ner-vous type. He wasn't tense. He seemed perfectly calm, as if it was merely second nature to him. Her dad had been that way as well, but not nearly to this extent. She had once seen the same look in the eyes of a friend's husband who was a special-operations soldier and had just returned from a war zone.

"What do you see?" she said.

"I don't know what you mean."

"You keep glancing around the room. What do you see?"

He held her gaze with those piercing green and brown eyes. "Everything. I see everything."

"You can't turn it off, can you?"

"It's exhausting, really. Every piece of clothing, every gesture, every movement. All stored away and analyzed. And it goes beyond that. I also can't help breaking objects down in my head. Analyzing their parts. I guess the best way to explain it is to think of it like TV screens. Me sitting across from you is one screen, but then imagine if there was a TV sitting next to me. And the remote's broken. It keeps flipping through the channels over and over."

"That would definitely be annoying."

"Now imagine that it's not one TV. It's a whole wall of them like you'd see in the control booth of a news program or maybe one of those big sports betting places out in Vegas with a thirty-foot wall of TVs. That's why I love movies and books. When I'm sitting in a movie theater, it's not so much that they all turn off, but it is like someone clicks the mute button. It's the only time that I can escape from me."

"You don't like yourself?"

"Who does?"

"Like you?"

He smiled. "Who likes *themselves*? Anyway, now you know why I say that it's a curse, not a gift."

"I can see what you mean about that being exhausting, but I can also see how it could help in an investigation."

The waiter walked by and refilled her wine glass. Marcus added, "The problem is that I'm really not that smart. I'm not some brilliant Sherlock Holmes. I have all the info in there, but that doesn't mean that I can always make sense of it or even realize what's significant." Her eyes went distant as she considered something. There was one fact of the case that wasn't contained in any of the reports. Only she, Belacourt, and Stupak knew of it. "In all the reports you've looked through for this case, you haven't read the name Anthony C, have you?"

He looked down and to the left, pausing like a computer accessing its hard drives. "No, nothing comes to mind. Why?"

"After my father died, I found a note on his desk at home that read *Anthony C—The Anarchist?*"

"You think he was on to something." He looked down again and added, "There's nobody on the suspect list with that name or alias."

"I know. It could be nothing, and it's hard to get much

from just a last initial. It could have been an informant, a suspect, a lead, anything. I did have them check the list of Camry owners, but nothing there either."

"Well, I'll file it away in my head. Right next to the crime-scene photos and that awful smell of Belacourt's aftershave."

Vasques laughed and put on her best smile. "It is pretty bad." Marcus mirrored her playful grin.

But then his face fell and his eyes went wide. She turned to see what he was looking at and noticed a beautiful young blond woman approaching them. She was wearing jeans and a tight leather jacket. Vasques could see the gun beneath the woman's coat and the badge clipped to her belt. The woman grabbed a chair from a nearby table, and turning it around backward, she pulled it up next to their booth and sat down.

The newcomer glared at Marcus and said, "I hope I'm not interrupting anything."

43

MAGGIE FORCED A smile onto her face, but she was shaking so badly and felt so overwhelmed with rage that the gesture was impossible to hold. Marcus sat dumbfounded for a moment, apparently unsure of what to say or how to react. She had caught him red-handed. His betrayal crept inside her heart and made her feel cold all over.

"Aren't you going to introduce me to your friend, Marcus?"

He glanced between them and finally said, "Maggie, this is Special Agent Vasques with the FBI. She's working on this case with us. And Vasques, this is Special Agent Carlisle. She works out of my unit at the DOJ."

Maggie looked at Vasques, sizing up the competition. The dark-haired agent was quite beautiful with a tanned complexion the color of light caramel, high cheekbones, and large brown eyes. She resisted the urge to punch the woman in the face. It wasn't Vasques's fault that Marcus had stabbed her in the back.

"Pleasure to meet you," Maggie said in a clipped tone, and they shook hands.

Vasques's thoughts were written across her face. The FBI agent could tell that something was going on here, and she said, "You know, I'm sure you want to get Agent Carlisle caught up to speed, and I want to check in with Belacourt. So I think I'm going to head on out."

"Okay, I'll give you a ride back to your office."

As Vasques grabbed her purse and slid from the booth, she said, "Don't worry about it. I'll just catch a cab."

Marcus opened his mouth to protest, but Maggie gave him a fierce look. His words died in his throat. They sat silently for a few moments, just staring at each other. Maggie broke the silence first. "Now I see why you didn't want me to come along."

"Oh please, Maggie. I don't know what you're suggesting, but you're way out of line."

"You know damn well what was going on here."

"I do know one thing. I have an agent under my command that's disobeyed my direct orders. Just like she did in Harrisburg. What do you think I should do about that?"

She couldn't contain herself any longer. She spun from her chair and slapped his coffee cup off the table and into his lap. Then she stormed out of the restaurant. She felt like falling to her knees and crying, screaming, breaking things. How could she have been so stupid and blind?

She heard Marcus calling after her, but she didn't want to see him at that moment. She wasn't sure if she ever wanted to see him again.

His hand wrapped around her bicep, but she ripped free of his grasp. "Don't touch me!"

"Dammit, Maggie! What the hell has gotten into you? You're acting crazy."

"So now *I'm* crazy, huh? I suppose that's why you don't want me with you on investigations. Because I'm so nuts."

"Don't put words in my mouth. I said you're *acting* crazy. There's a difference."

"Don't worry about it. Doesn't matter, anyway." She rammed her fist against the elevator call button. "Maybe, if you hurry, you can still catch your girlfriend."

He breathed out with a low growl and cracked his neck to the side. She recognized the gesture. He did it, whether consciously or unconsciously, every time he was getting ready for a fight. "Maggie, let's just calm down and talk about this."

"I don't have anything to say."

"Then shut up and listen! There's nothing going on. And even if there was, it's really none of your business."

Her eyes went wide. She couldn't believe what she was hearing. First, he betrayed her, and then he acted like they'd never had anything going between them to start with. Not knowing what else to say, she just slapped him across the face. The elevator dinged behind her, and its doors slid open. Maggie stepped inside and pounded the button to close the doors again and shut out the rest of the world.

44

WHEN MARCUS ENTERED the hotel room, Andrew was standing in front of the display board, looking at images of some type of small office building. He turned at his partner's approach and said, "Did Maggie find you?"

Marcus slapped his leather jacket down onto the room's couch and shot Andrew a contemptuous look. "Oh, she found me. By the way, thanks for the heads-up. Nice to know you've got my back."

"Why? What happened?" Andrew looked him up and down. "Are you wet?"

Marcus dropped onto the couch as though his legs could no longer support his weight. He rubbed his temples and growled in the back of his throat. "To be honest, I have no idea what just happened. Maggie, who I had ordered to stay behind, shows up, causes a scene, dumps coffee on me, slaps me. The way she was acting, I suppose I'm lucky she didn't shoot me."

"Really? Did she have any reason to be upset?"

"Don't you start too. Number one, we were just having dinner. Number two, Maggie and I called things off a while back. We should never have got involved. It was a mistake."

Andrew sat down on the small mahogany coffee table in front of the couch. "You don't really believe that. Besides, to hear her tell it, the two of you are just on a break while you get your head together."

"Is that what she told you?"

"What did you tell her?"

"When?"

"When you called it off."

Marcus thought about the incident in Harrisburg. They had been investigating a string of shootings where the killer was targeting young mothers. Maggie had gone to check out a lead that paid off with a name and address. He ordered her to wait, but she decided to question the guy on her own. The killer shot her in the shoulder with a little Davis .32 ACP pistol right there on his own front porch. It was a cheap gun that had a reputation for jamming up, and true to form, a shell casing stove-piped just as he was about to shoot her in the head. It had given her just enough time to get out her backup weapon and take the killer down. But she had almost died that day. It had only been pure dumb luck that had kept her alive.

Marcus realized then that he could never have any semblance of a normal life. Anyone that he loved was in danger because of his line of work. He had always wanted a family of his own. Emily Morgan would probably have said that it stemmed from a subconscious desire to replace the family he had lost, and maybe she would have been right. Either way, fate had other plans for him.

It was only a few days after Harrisburg when he had ended their relationship. He had told Maggie that the stress of the job was too hard and he needed some time to…

"Oh crap. I can see how she might have gotten that impression."

"Why would you want to break up with her, anyway? Maggie's incredible. I don't know what she sees in you."

"Thanks, wingman. I'm glad that I can always count on you."

"I'm just saying."

"You say too much."

Andrew added, "You don't say enough. You keep it all bottled up inside. So are you going to tell me?"

Marcus sighed and reached for a cup of day-old cold coffee sitting on an end table. He choked back the contents with a cough and a wince. "After what happened in Harrisburg, I just couldn't imagine doing what we do and trying to have a real relationship or a family. It's just not worth the risk. You know what they call a brave man with a family?"

Andrew shook his head. "No."

"They call him a coward."

Andrew laughed. "So what's your plan? Are you going to be a warrior monk devoted to a higher cause?" He groaned and tapped his fist on the coffee table. "You just…"

"Spit it out," Marcus said.

"You're so smart and yet sometimes you are so dumb. You can't refuse to enjoy life out of fear that something bad may happen. If you do that, something bad already *has* happened."

"You don't understand. Everyone that I've ever cared about has been taken from me. I don't want to worry about anyone anymore."

Andrew bit down on his lower lip as his eyes took on a watery sheen. Then he leaned in close and whispered, "You don't think I understand? I'd give anything, *anything,* to have my little girl back. But even as bad as it hurts, if I had to choose, I would much rather have known her and lost her than never to have had her at all."

Marcus swallowed hard and clenched his eyes shut. Andrew was right. *He was an asshole.* "Andrew, listen, I'm sorry to have—"

Andrew stood up and walked back to the display board. "Forget it. Just get over here and take a look at this. Stan's found a lead on the Anarchist."

45

Marcus punched the icon to connect with Stan, and after a moment of watching the loading indicator spin, Stan's bearded face appeared on the screen. "Hey there, boss. How's it hanging?"

Stan's head and chest filled a three-foot section of the screen. His long sandy blond beard stretched down his chest, cutting a path between a tattoo of Popeye on one pectoral and Super Mario smashing through a block on the other side. Marcus cocked his head and said, "Stan, tell me you're wearing pants."

"There's nobody else here. Don't hate me because I'm beautiful." With a shake of his head, Marcus ignored the remark and continued, "Andrew said you found something."

"Right," Stan said. "I was trying to figure out a way to narrow down the list of psychologists and therapists, so I contacted an old friend that works for the NSA to get her thoughts. She works in an offshoot of the Echelon Project. You know, Big Brother kind of stuff. They have a monitoring system in place that tracks all email and phone traffic in the country. But it's not all read or stored. Only items containing flagged keywords are investigated. So my friend tells me that they actually monitor for certain religious keywords, watching out for extremists. Stuff like Jihad, Great Satan, Apocalypse, Cleansing Fire. That kind of thing. I'm not sure exactly how the algorithm works, but I assume it's more complicated than just pulling out those words, otherwise they'd be sorting through false positives well after the world goes boom. It's a pretty slick set-up. This chick is the real deal, boss. And, good lordy, she is uber-hot. Back at MIT, she used to—"

"What did she find, Stan?" Marcus interrupted.

"There was an email flagged from a therapist asking a colleague for some advice about a patient that he thought was really dangerous. It had a lot of those naughty keywords in it as the doc describes the patient. And then…you ready for it? Gimme a drum roll."

Marcus waited for the pay-off, but Stan actually seemed to be waiting for him to give a drum roll. He raised his eyebrows, and Stan said, "Fine. You're no fun. As I was saying, this patient believes himself to be the Antichrist."

"Okay, that could be our guy. You have an address? We'll pay him a visit."

"That's the problem. This therapist is like a caveman. He still keeps his records on paper." Stan raised his eyebrows and bobbed his head. "I know, right, craziness."

Marcus thought about it for a moment and then replied, "Send me the address and any details you have about the building. Security, blueprints, anything you can find. What about my satanism expert? Did you track somebody down?"

"Of course I did. Found a dude named Ellery Rowland. You've got a meeting with him later this evening. I'll text you the details."

Andrew said, "How are we going to check out the therapist lead and meet with this guy at the same time? It would sure be nice if we had another agent here in town to help us out."

Marcus groaned, but he knew that Andrew was right. They needed to use every resource at their disposal, and he refused to allow his personal issues to interfere with an investigation. "Fine. Stan, contact Maggie and have her meet with Ellery Rowland."

"Why can't *you* ask her, boss? You two not speaking?" The big man chuckled in a throaty staccato rhythm. "Sounds juicy. Come on. Gimme the details."

"Goodbye, Stan," Marcus said, killing the connection.

He checked the time on his phone. The staff from a therapist's office would surely have all gone home for the evening. If the Anarchist followed his pattern, and there was no reason to think that he wouldn't, he'd abduct another woman within a few hours. Another dead girl, another grieving family. More pain, blood, and tears. Unless they could find him first.

He turned to Andrew and said, "Are you ready to do a little breaking and entering?"

46

It took some time for Stan to hack into the database of the
security company employed to keep watch over the therapist's office, but it had been well worth the wait. They had
all the info they needed to make sure that they could get in
and out of the building without any complications. So after
changing their clothes and gathering the necessary supplies,
Marcus and Andrew headed out toward the psychologist's
office on Chicago's South Side.

Andrew drove the Yukon while Marcus sat in the passenger seat and tried to close his eyes and rest for a few minutes.
He was out of his migraine medicine, but he'd swallowed a
handful of extra-strength Tylenol before leaving. The pills
had helped to quell the throbbing in his skull, but they did
little to shut out the other images and thoughts that kept his
mind burning through a constant stream of data. And that
day had contained more than its fair share of unpleasant data
to be processed. First, he had made an ass out of himself
at the briefing and had humiliated Vasques. At least he had
been able to recover from that one. He hadn't been so lucky
in his confrontations with Belacourt and Maggie. And then
there was Ackerman.

When Ackerman's calls had first begun, Marcus had
thought that the killer was taunting him, trying to prove
his superiority. But now he realized that Ackerman really
just wanted a friend. A part of him pitied the killer for the
terrible things that had been done to him and for his dis-
torted perceptions of the world and right and wrong, but in
the back of his mind, Marcus knew that either he was going

to kill Ackerman or Ackerman was going to kill him. He cringed, thinking of the number of opportunities that the killer might have passed up. The bottom line was that if Ackerman wanted him or anyone he cared about to die, there was little that he could do to protect himself or his friends.

And where was Ackerman getting his information?

All those situations, questions, and worries, combined with the details of the Anarchist case, created a constant twisting vortex of information that assaulted his mind every time he closed his eyes.

Frustrated, dejected, and exhausted, he watched the buildings, lights, and pavement flow past. He wished that he could block out the barrage of data—sounds of the city, people, vehicles, groans and creaks of the Yukon, sloshing of the tires through the snow pack on the road, Andrew's breathing, the hum of the heater, a rattle in the dashboard. His mind broke the dashboard and heating system apart. Analyzing how the components fitted together, their inter-connections, their weak spots. A three-dimensional blue-print appeared in his head, spinning, twisting.

He resisted the urge to pound his fists against his skull. He was so tired. He thought of a ranch he had spent some time on in Asherton, Texas. It had been so calm there. Not as many distractions. It had been the last time his mind had felt even slightly at ease. But Asherton was also where he had met Francis Ackerman and where his indoctrination into the Shepherd Organization had begun.

"Do you think we should stop by the hospital and check on Allen?" Andrew said.

"I don't know." Marcus wanted to make sure that Allen was okay, but he also assumed that the Brubaker family had arrived in force by now. It was his fault that Allen was confined to that bed. His fault that his mentor might never walk again. Ackerman had been after *him*, and Allen had just stepped into the cross fire. He wasn't ready to look into the eyes of Allen's wife and children and see the pain and fear that he had caused. "He should rest tonight. We'll stop in and see him tomorrow."

Andrew changed lanes, and Marcus's gaze wandered to the rearview mirror. He suddenly sat forward in his seat. "Take your next left," he said in a tight, urgent tone.

"Okay. What's up?" Andrew said.

"Three cars back. White Ford Taurus. I've seen it three times today."

"Are you sure?"

"Last time I spotted it, I memorized the license plate. I'm sure."

Andrew took the left turn onto a side street. The Taurus turned as well, but it kept a good distance back. Andrew said, "How do you want to play it?"

"Take the next sharp right you see that's hidden by a building. Hug the right-hand sidewalk and slow down just enough for me to hop out. Then make sure that you get stopped at the next light."

"Okay. Get ready."

Marcus prepared himself as Andrew took the next turn and followed his instructions. Marcus stepped from the vehicle onto the sidewalk as soon as the Taurus was out of sight. Andrew barely slowed. Marcus pulled the hood of his sweatshirt up and blended in with the other pedestrians. At that hour, foot traffic was sparse, but the Taurus's driver wouldn't be looking for him on the sidewalk anyway.

He kept his stride casual, quick and purposeful but not hurried. From the corner of his eye, he saw the Taurus slip past. Andrew sat ahead of him at the next red light. It was a four-lane road, and a red Jeep with a soft top waited directly behind Andrew. Next in line was the Taurus.

Glancing around at the passersby and not seeing anyone close, Marcus decided to make his move. His right hand slipped beneath his leather jacket and pulled the Sig Sauer P220 from its holster. With his left, he whipped out a spring-assisted knife. It was a quality weapon designed for quick one-handed access and had a Tungsten DLC coated blade and a grip with fiberglass inserts. The bottom of the knife was also equipped with a seat-belt cutter and a glass-breaker, a sharp metal cone designed to provide rapid entry for first responders in emergency situations. He used the tool now as he rushed up to the passenger window of the Taurus. In a swift and violent movement, he swung his left arm and the tip of the glass breaker against the window. The result was an explosion of glass shards bursting into the vehicle and a startled yell from the man inside.

Marcus wasted no time in unlocking the door and slipping into the passenger seat with his gun pointed at the vehicle's occupant. The light turned green. "Drive," he said.

47

SCHOFIELD WATCHED AS Melissa Lighthaus slumbered peacefully. Her skin was smooth like silk and the color of home-churned butter. Her arm was draped over the side of the bed. She wore an oversized white men's T-shirt.

The whole scene reminded him of a painting by Henry Fuseli entitled *The Nightmare*. He had seen the disturbing piece at the Detroit Institute of Arts while on a business trip, and it had stuck with him. The painting depicted a young woman asleep in bed and clothed all in white. Her long hair cascaded down, mirroring a set of red blankets that were also disheveled, giving the impression that she had been tossing and turning. A small demon sat upon her chest with its legs curled up. It was half-shrouded in shadow and had its hand resting on its chin as if in thought. Its grotesque countenance and piercing eyes faced outward, toward the viewer. According to folklore, the crouching monster was an incubus, a representative of the devil that would come to women in the night and engage in sexual relations with them. The wall behind the creature showed its shadow, suggesting that it existed not only in the mind of the dreamer but had substance within the real world.

But if Melissa was the woman in white, that made Schofield the incubus. A monster born of nightmares charged with sowing the seed of the devil. A grotesque and evil creation. The thought filled him with sadness, but he resisted the urge to cry.

He walked back to the foot of the bed and prepared his instruments. But just as he was slipping back the covers from the woman's feet, a car alarm sounded from just beyond her window. The keening wail pierced the walls of her bedroom and filled the space with an air of urgency and panic.

His eyes went wide, and reacting on instinct, he dropped out of sight at the foot of her bed. The bed frame shook slightly against his back as the covers stirred. She had sat up.

Schofield's heart thundered, and his fingers snaked around the grip of the P22 Walther .22LR caliber pistol mounted with a Gemtech Outback IID sound suppressor that he carried in case of glitches such as this.

It was too early. He never should have attempted to operate at this hour. The risks were greater. The variables racked with inconsistencies.

But he needed what Melissa had. She possessed a beautiful and caring soul. One that he envied in every way. Most of all, she had strength. She had been abused in her life, first by a drunken father and then by a controlling husband, but she had come through it all intact. He would need her strength for the confrontation he knew was coming, when he would face his own abuser. And her work hours had dictated moving up his timetable.

He waited. If her feet touched the floor, he would have to kill her right then and there. No choice. He visualized his movements, choreographing how he would react.

A groan of the boards beneath her feet. He pushes off the floor with his left hand, getting to his knees, aims the gun with his right. The angle would be bad. He'd be shooting across his body, but there wouldn't be time to adjust his position before she spotted him. He squeezes the trigger. The pistol pops with a muffled retort. He keeps firing until she's down. She may fall back into the lamp, making a loud crash, but it doesn't matter. But what if he missed? What if the first bullet caught her in the shoulder, and she had the presence of mind to run? Maybe he could force her to inject herself with the drugs? But wouldn't flight be her first instinct? What if she made it out of the house? Across the yard, to the neighbor, to a phone, calling the police...

Variables, outcomes, assessments, risks.

His lungs cried out for air, but he hadn't even realized he was holding his breath. The bed vibrated again, and his grip tensed around the gun. But she didn't get up. She was going back to sleep.

Gently, he allowed himself to breathe. Then he waited.

48

THE INTERIOR OF the Taurus was slate gray with black and wood-grain accents. It reeked of burnt coffee and fast food. On the radio, Lennon and McCartney sang about *A Hard Day's Night*. Two extra-large cups of generic gas-station coffee, one filled with candy-bar wrappers and one full of liquid, rested in the cup-holders of the center console. The man behind the wheel wore jeans and a black and white Chicago White Sox jersey beneath a puffy brown North Face coat. He was in his early thirties with a shaved head and acne-scarred cheeks covered by two days of brown stubble. And he was big. Not fat, but large and muscular. Marcus guessed by the way the man's big frame was crammed inside the Taurus that he was at least six-foot-five and probably two hundred and seventy-five pounds.

The driver said, "Listen, buddy, I—"

"Shut up. Pull over into that lot."

The man complied, flipped up his turn signal, and pulled into the nearly vacant lot of an office building. The big man threw the Taurus into park and said, "Okay, I'm going to reach for my wallet. I'm a cop. Just take it easy. Don't shoot me."

Slowly, he took out and displayed a faded brown leather wallet containing a Jackson's Grove PD badge and an ID stating his name was Erik Jansen. Marcus reluctantly placed the Sig Sauer back into his shoulder holster. But he kept the knife in his left hand near the center console and knew that he could have the blade buried to the hilt in the guy's throat before he could draw any weapon.

"Why have you been following us?"

Jansen raised his hands in surrender. "I'm just doing my job. Belacourt told me to keep an eye on you."

"I didn't see you at the briefing this morning."

"I didn't come in until this afternoon."

"Call him."

"Who? You mean Belacourt?"

"No, I mean Papa Smurf."

"Come on, man. Let's just forget about this. He'll be pissed."

"Not my problem. Make the call."

Jansen reluctantly grabbed for his phone and dialed, his face a mask of frustration. Marcus could hear the ringing on the other end of the line. When a voice came on, he snatched the phone away from Jansen's ear.

"Don't you think you have better uses for your resources than following us?" he said.

The other end was silent for a moment, but then Belacourt's voice came over the airwaves. Surprise still resonated in his tone, but he covered it well. "I wish I did. Unfortunately, I can't force you to leave, and you won't take the hint."

Marcus didn't get this guy. In his experience, local law enforcement usually had no huge problems cooperating with federal agencies. Sure, there were pissing contests and times when someone got their toes stepped on, but nothing like this. Nothing with this much ferocity and venom. "Why do you care so much about me? We're all on the same team. All I want to do is stop this guy."

"Let's get something straight. You are *not* on my team. You are nothing but a distraction and a hindrance to this investigation. I know your type. I could tell what you were from the first second I saw you. You're nothing but a—"

Marcus hung up the phone and cursed under his breath. Belacourt was nothing but a brick wall of closed-minded ignorance. If the Anarchist was going down, it would be without the cop's help. To Jansen, he said, "I know it's not your fault that your CO is an asshole, but trust me, there are more important things you could be doing right now rather than following me." As he stepped outside, he added, "Besides, you need to get that window and tire fixed."

"Tire? Oh come on…"

Marcus buried the blade of his knife in the front tire of the Taurus and then walked over to where Andrew was waiting to pick him up. At his back, Jansen called, "Was all that really necessary?"

49

HAVING ADMINISTERED THE drugs and wrapped Melissa in a black blanket, Schofield scanned the backyard and the path to his waiting vehicle. There were no signs of life, but his view was obstructed by a detached garage, a white fence with cracked and flaking paint, and a row of snow-encrusted lilac bushes. A pole light on a neighbor's garage lit the alley, so he couldn't hide within the darkness. He couldn't be sure that his route was clear of complications.

It's too early. Too many people still out and about.

But he had little choice. He had to take the risk, so he punched the button on his keychain to automatically open the trunk of the Camry. Taking a deep breath, he scooped Melissa up. Out the door, across the yard, hugging the wall of the garage, staying out of the light, dumping her into the trunk, closing the lid.

It was done. He had made it.

A little snarl and a yap sounded behind him. He turned around slowly.

Twenty feet away at the edge of the alley, a middle-aged man in blue Adidas windbreaker pants and a thick brown winter coat stood holding the leash of a little orange Pomeranian. The man's coat was entirely too small for his frame and looked like it was made for a woman, as if he had simply grabbed the first jacket he had seen before taking the dog out to the bathroom. The Pomeranian couldn't seem to make up its mind on how to react to the newcomer. It snarled and showed its teeth, but its tail was wagging.

The two men just stared at each other.

Time seemed to stand still. Neither of them moved.

But then the man with the dog took a furtive step backward. Schofield tried to speak, but the words came out jumbled and his voice sounded an octave higher than normal.

"I, ummm, we, it's…not what it…"

Schofield realized that he was dressed all in black, was wearing a black balaclava, and had just dropped a body-shaped bundle into his trunk. There would be no explaining it away. No reasoning with this man. No excuses could be made, and he lacked the capacity for such subterfuge anyway.

He raised the P22 Walther and fired three times into the man's chest. The dog yapped out a string of high-pitched barks, and the man screamed for help. The smell of gunpowder filled the night air, and stuffing from the interior of the man's coat floated in the breeze. The man rolled onto his front and tried to crawl away.

Moving purely on instinct now, Schofield rushed forward and kicked the man over and onto his back. Stains of blood streaked across the snow, and a trail of ruddy brown liquid flowed down the man's chin. When he opened his mouth, his teeth were red. "Please," the man forced out in a wheeze. One of the bullets must have punctured a lung.

"Look in my eyes!" Schofield said.

The man fixed him with a disbelieving stare as if he couldn't comprehend that this was truly happening, that his life was truly over.

Schofield fired twice into the man's forehead and once more into his chest.

The little dog still yapped and growled ferociously at his back. Its retractable leash trailed behind it as it ran back and forth from one side of the alley to the other, the plastic handle scraping and bumping over the rocks.

He aimed the pistol at the Pomeranian and said, "Be quiet!"

The little dog's incessant yipping pierced his ears like

needles. His finger tensed over the trigger. He willed himself to fire, to stop the noise. The neighbors would hear. The dog was drawing unwanted attention. It had to be silenced.

But he couldn't kill the poor little animal. He groaned and chased it around the alley, eventually catching its leash beneath his foot. Scooping the dog up, he spoke to it in a calm and comforting voice while he stroked his fingers through its orange fur. Its tail wagged furiously from side to side, and it licked his face.

"Okay, okay," Schofield said, with a laugh. "You have a new family now."

50

Dark brown brick and a row of shrubs and small flowering trees stripped bare by the cold bordered the office for the Northern Oaks Psychiatric Group. Out front, four bronze statues of children danced in a circle on a raised and illuminated concrete pad. The address was displayed prominently on the building's right corner, written in two-foot-tall white letters. The office of Dr. Henry Burkhart occupied the southeast corner of a building that rested within a large group of medical offices. Marcus knew that it was the kind of place that would contain all sorts of prescription drugs and expensive equipment, a prime target for junkies and thieves, which meant that it was undoubtedly patrolled by uniformed security. Stan had hacked the security company's records and obtained the alarm code, but he wouldn't be able to help with the human factor.

They parked down a block in the lot of a Presbyterian church and made their way across the well-manicured church grounds toward their target, then up a concrete walkway, past the four bronze statues playing ring-around-the-rosie, and to the glass doors of the psychiatric office. Andrew picked the lock while Marcus kept watch. Within a minute, they were in the building. Andrew tapped in the code on a panel to the left side of the door, and they headed off to find their prize.

They passed through a waiting area scattered with magazines and children's toys and into a long corridor stretching to the end of the building. Lighting their path with adjustable spot-to-flood flashlights, they checked the labels for

each door until they found one marked *Records Room*. Inside, they discovered rows upon rows of blue and white
shelving stacked full of multicolored folders. Marcus had
no doubt that some gray-haired nurse who had managed
this office for the past fifteen years would have no problem
making sense of the color-coded filing system and locating
the proper patient records, but he wondered if he and Andrew would manage the task before the staff showed up for
work in the morning.

His fingers shifted to his temple and rubbed gently. He
wished they had brought coffee.

Andrew groaned at his side and said, "We should have
met with the devil worshiper."

"I hope Maggie does okay with him. Maybe I should have
briefed her on what to ask."

"Marcus, you…" Andrew's voice trailed off. "Say what's
on your mind. You always do."

"You're a perfectionist and a control freak, and you've got
a bad habit of thinking that you have to do everything yourself or it won't get done right. Or you dictate exactly how it
should be done. Sooner or later, you've got to trust people.
She may not handle it the same way that you would, but
she'll get the job done." Andrew stared around at the rows of
files. "But I still say we should have made her do this crap."

"That's okay. I'm sure her little rendezvous will be about
as much fun."

51

MAGGIE FOLLOWED HALSTED Street past a string of restaurants of various types and nationalities—Thai, Italian, Mexican, BBQ. It was a nice street. Dotted among the hole-in-the-wall restaurants and small locally owned businesses were several new apartment buildings and town houses. The cars parked out front were new and fairly expensive, not top of the heap but far from bottom of the barrel.

Ahead, she saw a building of light-colored brick with a bright orange awning. Black letters stenciled over the orange read *Kingston Mines*, then in slightly smaller type *Live Blues Music 7 Nights A Week Till 4 a.m.* She found a place to park a block up in front of a small corner grocer and followed the sound of blues guitars back to the bar. After paying the cover charge, she slipped inside. The room was larger than she had expected. The ceiling tiles were orange and white. College kids lined the bar along the right side and the tables in the center. There was a stage backed with slatted wood paneling and doors that seemed to lead nowhere. Instruments filled it, but no band. The music came from an adjoining room containing another stage.

She had been told that Ellery Rowland would meet her in the back of whichever room the music was in. She stepped around the corner into the second room. Three big black men and one short white woman with graying hair were on the stage. The white woman was on lead guitar and vocals. Maggie was no blues connoisseur, but she knew the woman could play, despite looking a bit out of place. The tables were long and narrow and reminded her of the ball returns in an old bowling alley. There had been one near Maggie's home when she'd been a kid. It had been closed down for years, but she and her friends had broken in on more than one occasion.

She stepped up into another section filled with the narrow tables and shiny black and chrome stools. Murals depicting scenes reminiscent of old-time speakeasies covered the walls, and she couldn't tell if they were painted on or some kind of wallpaper. There was only one person in the far back of the room. He sat next to three vintage arcade games—Pac-Man, Galaga, and an old Atari racing game. He was an unusually handsome man dressed in a light purple-and-white-striped shirt beneath a dark blue suit with subtle purple pinstripes. He had long brown hair and a prominent widow's peak. He looked out of place among the college kids and their jeans and Abercrombie and Fitch.

"Are you Ellery Rowland?"

"The one and only," he said, raising his voice over the music. He had a slight English accent. "You must be Special Agent Carlisle. The man on the phone should have just told me to look for the most beautiful woman in the place. I would've spotted you straight away."

Maggie felt herself blushing but resisted the urge to giggle like some obnoxious schoolgirl.

He gestured for her to sit down. "Would you like something to eat? They have some great Cajun food. I especially recommend the jalapeño and cheddar cornbread."

She had noticed the smell of grease, and although she was a bit hungry, she said, "No, thank you."

As she removed her leather jacket and draped it over an empty stool, the waitress approached. "Drinks?"

"Ladies first," Rowland said, gesturing with an upturned palm. "Tanqueray and tonic."

"Make that two. I didn't think federal agents were supposed to drink on duty?"

"We're not your typical federal agents. Besides, I'm always on duty."

"This is a good place to let your hair down."

"I can see that. It's a nice place. And you're not quite what I was expecting."

He laughed and threw back his head. It was a good laugh, honest and full of charm. "You probably expected to meet me at some type of gothic rave pumping dark techno music. With me all decked out in makeup and piercings."

"Yeah, that's about right."

"I'm not surprised. There's a lot of misconceptions and confusion about modern satanism."

"Enlighten me."

"Okay, first of all, there are several different types of modern satanic groups. The LaVeyan satanists and several other types that make up the majority actually don't believe in the devil. There are no elements of what you would consider devil worship within the Church of Satan. Such practices are looked upon as being Christian heresies. They don't accept the dualistic Christian worldview of God versus the devil, so they obviously aren't choosing to side with any supernatural being. These satanists don't believe in the supernatural at all, good or evil."

"So why call themselves satanists at all? Wouldn't they be atheists?"

"In a way, but they see themselves as their own god. Satan is just a symbol of man living as his prideful, carnal nature dictates."

"Okay, but you said there are several types."

"Right, there are also groups of theistic satanists that *do* believe in an actual supernatural entity. The different Luciferian groups are an example of this type. Many of them don't even consider themselves satanists because they argue that Lucifer is a positive figure while Satan is a negative and evil figure. Some consider Lucifer to be the Christian fallen angel. Others believe him to be an elder god who pre-dates Christianity. They take a stance that Lucifer is depicted as a mythic figure or symbol who represents admirable qualities—knowledge, independence, pride, mastery of self. He's seen as the lightbearer, the bringer of knowledge and truth. A being of both fire, representing light, and air, representing wisdom. He's characterized by sunlight, wind, and fire."

The waitress arrived with their drinks. Rowland gave the shorthaired brunette a wink and said, "Thanks, love." Then he continued on with the lecture. "So, Lucifer's the lightbearer, but in acknowledgment of the dual nature of wisdom and knowledge, that it can be used for good or evil, Lucifer is also represented to a lesser degree by the more traditional qualities of darkness. But these qualities are viewed not only as admirable, but highly desirable. In many ways, these satanists want to become Lucifer. However, in no way does this entail performing obscure demonic rituals to empower oneself. It's more of a conscious effort toward self-improvement through learning and effort."

The constant barrage of fried-food smells was making Maggie feel even hungrier, and she noticed the patrons at a table near them carry out a large cookie sheet filled with potato skins, jalapeño poppers, and loaded cheese fries. In between songs, a raspy-voiced man she assumed to be the manager or owner introduced the band and talked up their latest CD.

She said, "You make all this sound very mainstream and New Agey. Like the devil is some kind of self-help guru."

Rowland shrugged. "Take it like you want, but satanism is definitely becoming more mainstream and breaking into the light of day. In fact, satanism is now allowed in Britain's Royal Navy, despite much opposition from Christians. And in 2005, the US Supreme Court debated about protecting the religious rights of prison inmates who are satanists."

"Okay, to each his own, and you paint a nice rosy picture. But what about satanic rituals involving human sacrifice and worshiping the Christian idea of the devil as the ruler of hell?"

His mood darkened a bit, his tone growing more serious. "Most of what you're talking about is kids being stupid. Just looking for an excuse to vandalize property and piss off their parents. But the real deal is out there. Just like Christians or Muslims, we have our zealots. There are extreme sects that would fall within the clichéd definition of what a satanist should be, but they're denounced and rejected by true satanists."

"Listen, I'm not here to argue about religion or attack your beliefs. I'm here to catch a killer. Do you have any information that can help me do that or not?"

Rowland downed the rest of his drink, caught the waitress's eye, and tapped the top of his glass. "I've heard talk. There are some groups operating in the Chicago area, but I'm not familiar with any of them. But I know someone who probably is. If this Anarchist bloke has ever been part of a larger group, this guy would know something about it. He'd have heard something."

"Where do I find him?"

"Before I tell you, I want you to promise not to go see him alone. In fact, it's probably better if you send one of your male counterparts."

"I can take care of myself."

Slowly, he looked Maggie up and down. "I'm sure you can, but this guy hates women. I don't know the full story, but he's been to prison. He's a scary kind of guy." Rowland took a pen from his suit pocket and scrawled down a name and address on a napkin.

She picked it up and said, "Is this name for real?"

He shrugged. "That's what he goes by. So, now that we've gotten all that out of the way, I've seen your mouth watering over there. Why don't you let me buy you dinner? You won't regret it." There was a clear invitation in his eyes for more than dinner.

Maggie smiled shyly and said, "You never told me what kind of satanist *you* are."

The corners of Rowland's mouth curled up in a devilish grin. "I'm one of those who follows my carnal desires."

52

"I THINK I FOUND HIM," Andrew said from the floor, a stack of files with brightly labeled tabs surrounding him. "And we've got an address."

"Okay, just take the whole file. Let's pay him a visit."

After replacing the various folders exactly as they had found them, they moved back down the hall, but then Marcus stopped and listened. At first, he didn't fully comprehend what had changed, just that something was wrong. He held his breath and took in the sounds of the building and the city beyond. A furnace running. Dog barking. Cars zooming past on the Dixie Highway. And an engine idling somewhere close by, just outside the building's walls, the sound vibrating against its front glass.

"I don't think I locked the front door behind us," Marcus said. "If they're following SOP and are by-the-book kind of guys, the guards will check every door to make sure that they're locked properly."

"Maybe we can lock it before they make it up there."

In reply, Marcus pushed through the double doors into the waiting area of the therapist's office.

A flashlight beam struck him in the face, blinding him. A guard called out, "Don't move!"

But Marcus didn't listen. He recovered from the momentary surprise and rushed forward.

The beam of the flashlight jumped and stuttered around the room as the guard went for the taser on his belt.

A kids' sand table covered with little metal boats and cars rested between Marcus and the guard. Kids could use a magnet attached to the surface with a piece of red thread to push the miniature vehicles around. A nice little science lesson. As he swept across the room, Marcus grabbed one edge of the small table and turned it on end. Still with one hand, he flipped it spinning in the guard's direction.

The man's left arm shot up to shield himself from the blow. The guard was young and in good shape, not some fat and balding reject from the police academy.

By the time Marcus had hurdled a row of purple imitation-leather chairs and reached the guard, the man had a Taser X26 in his hand and was taking aim.

Marcus's left forearm collided with the guard's wrist as he ducked away. The taser discharged. Small barbed darts connected to a long coil of wires, designed to cause neuromuscular incapacitation, shot across the room.

He brought an elbow hurtling toward the guard's left temple. The blow collided with the man's skull, and Marcus drove the impact home, throwing his full weight and momentum into the strike.

It was a good solid blow, the kind that ended confrontations before they even began. The guard struck the dark brown Berber carpet just as his partner came through the doorway. The second man already had his taser drawn. But he was also close, less than five feet away.

Marcus continued forward but raised his hands and shouted, "Wait! Police!"

If it had been him, even years before he had joined the Shepherd Organization, he'd have shot first and asked questions later. Hell, he probably would have shot first if he'd been pointing a .44 Magnum, let alone a less-than-lethal alternative like the taser. The rent-a-cop, however, didn't have those instincts. He hesitated for only a split second, but it was enough.

Marcus grabbed the man's wrist and wrenched his arm back, twisting the taser from his grasp and aiming it at his chest. Shock contorted the man's face, and he said, "Wait! No!"

Marcus, however, didn't hesitate. Five seconds of pulsing current later, and the guard was incapacitated and writhing on the ground.

53

THE STREET HADN'T been plowed yet, and Marcus could feel his tires slipping on the snow and ice. Luckily, the Yukon could tear through almost anything. The scene around him was the same as it would have been on any of a million other streets—new homes jammed together with small yards and little privacy, some houses indistinguishable from those next to them, probably mass-produced by the same company. Some of the drives had been cleared, maybe by some young entrepreneur, but most hadn't. The sidewalks were invisible beneath their covering of snow. Large flakes floated lazily through the air. He had heard the weatherman predict over ten inches in the next three days. The trees that weren't stripped bare were pregnant with snow, and the cars lining the road were tucked in beneath a blanket of white. The cold had pushed everyone indoors and into bed. Only a few lights burned in the houses and none of the cars had been cleaned or used recently. Marcus and Andrew's destination was the third house on the left. A car sat in the driveway, covered with snow just like the rest. He couldn't see if it was a Camry beneath the thick white shroud but it had the proper size and shape.

Marcus pulled past and around the block, took in the surrounding area. There was an alley in the back. The snow there was compacted much worse than it was in the street. No garage in the back for another getaway vehicle, just a small shed for tools and a lawnmower. Route 43 was a block away. He could see the lights and hear the traffic there over the silence of the immediate neighborhood.

His cell phone vibrated against the cup holder in the center console. The display burst to life, and the name *Victoria Vasques* showed on the screen. "Hey, sorry about earlier," he said, after sliding his finger across the phone's touchscreen to accept the call.

"Don't worry about it. It worked out. I headed over to the Jackson's Grove precinct. While I was there, a call came in about a shooting in an alleyway. It turned out to be the Anarchist. He's taken another woman and killed some poor bastard walking his dog in the wrong place at the wrong time. I'm heading over there now. I thought you might want to tag along."

"Okay, text me the address. I'm in the middle of something right now, but I'll try to come after."

"Anything I should know about?"

"No, just DOJ stuff."

"More highly classified, you-could-tell-me-but-you'd-have-to-kill-me kind of stuff ?"

"Something like that."

"Hmm…"

"Did he shoot the guy walking his dog?"

"Yeah, I think so."

"He's collected his brass at every other scene where he's used a gun, but maybe he forgot this time. It would be real hard to do in an alley like that, especially in the snow. See if you can find the shell casings. Most people don't think to wear gloves when loading their gun."

"I'm sure the crime scene guys are on it. They know their jobs," Vasques said.

"I've been told I need to work on trusting people."

"That's good advice."

"It's not as easy as it sounds. Keep me posted if you find anything."

"Okay, maybe I'll see you in a bit," she said as they clicked off. Marcus suspected that if they did find the casings it would turn out that the Anarchist was in the minority and had probably worn gloves when handling his ammo. But the killer had to make a mistake at some point. They always did. The Anarchist was human just like everyone else. The problem was that cops were just as human, and they had to catch the mistake when it occurred. He needed to be at that scene, but it would be pointless if they had just driven past the Anarchist's home.

But the car bothered him. It had been covered with snow when they'd passed. He wondered how long ago the killing had occurred and how long it would take for snow to cover the car.

"How do you want to approach this guy?" Andrew said from the passenger seat.

"We'll try to talk to him first. See how he reacts. See if he matches the profile. But I'm going to drop you off at the alley, just in case he tries to run out the back."

"Great. I get to stand out in the snow and freezing cold in some nutball's backyard."

"We live a glamorous lifestyle," Marcus said as he pulled the Yukon up next to the end of the alley.

Andrew jumped out, still mumbling something under his breath. Marcus smiled. He had never had a brother, and Andrew was as close as he would ever get. He drove the Yukon around the block and pulled in behind the snow-covered car in the man's driveway.

As Marcus stepped out, the snow crunched beneath his feet and came over the top of his tennis shoes. He wished that he had invested in a good pair of boots, but it was too late now. His socks were already soaked from his last walk in the snow, and his feet were freezing.

He pressed the doorbell, but nothing happened. Knocking instead, he heard movement inside, and a light came on. He tried to glimpse the interior through the glass in the front door, but thick blue curtains covered all the doors and windows. After a moment, the door cracked open and a groggy man peeked out, wearing red flannel pants and a white T-shirt that was yellowed from age and sweat. His gaze was wary, darting around the small porch, and he left the chain lock in place. His hair was long and had an oily sheen. The stink of body odor crept out from behind the door.

"What do you want?"

"Rudy Kolenda?"

"Yeah, what's this about?"

"Sorry for disturbing you at such a late hour, sir." Marcus raised his ID. The man squinted at it, and Marcus pushed it closer. "I'm from the Department of Justice. I'm just here to ask you a couple of quick questions, and then I'll let you get back to sleep."

The man shook his head in confusion. When he spoke, his voice was thick, as though his tongue was too big for his mouth. "Questions about what?"

"About a string of abductions and murders that have been taking place in the Chicago area."

The man was quiet for a long moment. Then he said, "Just a second." He shut the door again.

Marcus stamped his feet against the cold and blew into his hands. He expected the man to be unlatching the chain or maybe slipping on a coat to step outside. A guy like this could have drugs sitting out on a coffee table and would never willingly usher an officer of the law into his home.

There was some rustling and shuffling on the other side of the door. Then there was a sound that Marcus recognized immediately. The sound of a shotgun being pumped back.

He dove away from the door just as it exploded outward. Fire and flame. The heat of the blast searing his skin. Pieces of wood and fiberglass filling the air. Ears ringing. Heart pounding. He landed in a rose bush and rolled away, the thorns clawing at his face and hands.

Purely on instinct, he pulled the Sig Sauer pistol from his shoulder rig.

Then the greasy-haired man in the yellowed T-shirt threw open the door and raised the shotgun to fire again.

54

MARCUS ROLLED AWAY as the shotgun boomed again. Snow and black dirt twisted up and into the air a few feet to his left. Without really aiming, he opened fire with his P220 pistol. Ten .45 ACP rounds tore into the ruined frame of the house's front door. He dropped the mag and popped in another, but Rudy Kolenda was already gone.

Weapon at the ready, Marcus approached the house. Kolenda was probably heading for the back door, and Andrew would have heard the shots and been ready for him at the rear of the building. But Marcus wasn't taking any chances. He did it by the numbers, scrutinizing the rooms from cover and checking all the corners.

The inside of the house was disgusting. The walls might have been white at one time, but now the drywall was yellowed down to the studs. The whole place stank of cigarette smoke, sweat, and moldy food. Stacks of newspapers, plates of half-eaten meals, candy wrappers, and piles of dirty clothes nearly blocked out the dull orange carpet. A brown and white couch sat in the living room. Long slashes exposed the couch's innards. Cigarette burns scarred its arms. The bedroom was just a mattress on the floor surrounded by dirty clothes, loose change, and pornography. The only clean spot contained a square mirror covered by a pipe and small white rocks of methamphetamine. Dirty dishes covered the kitchen counters and table. Drawers and cabinets had been opened but never pushed back shut, exposing overturned boxes of food.

Marcus reached the back door. "Andrew?"

His partner stepped around the corner, a .40 caliber Glock 22 in his hand. Marcus said, "Did he get past you?"

"No way. He didn't come out the back."

Marcus swore under his breath. The only door he had ignored had opened onto a set of bare wood stairs that descended to the house's basement. He hadn't expected Kolenda to trap himself down there, but maybe he had more firepower stashed below. Or another way out. "Did you see an egress window or a cellar door out there?" he whispered.

"Nothing like that."

"Okay, cover the basement door. I'm going to do another quick sweep of the upstairs. I don't want to give him our backs."

He proceeded into each room as if he hadn't already checked it. The search of the small house only took a few seconds. All clear. He rejoined Andrew at the top of the stairs. Nodding, Marcus pushed the door inward as Andrew covered him and shone his flashlight down into the murky depths of the basement. They were silent for a moment, listening. Nothing from below.

Andrew stepped toward the stairs, but Marcus stopped him with an outstretched arm. "Did you hear that?" Marcus moved back to the bedroom and heard it again.

Just a creak of the house as it contracted in the cold?

The house was silent except for the hum of the furnace and the distant drone of cars out on Route 43.

But there it was again.

This time he tracked it back to its source. It wasn't coming from below, but from above. *The attic.*

Andrew started to open his mouth to speak, but Marcus placed a single finger against his own lips and the gesture silenced him. Marcus crept slowly over to the bedroom closet and looked up. The closet was missing the expected clothing rod and instead contained a faded mahogany bookshelf. The shelving could be used as foot and handholds to reach an access panel set into the ceiling.

He found an umbrella on the floor, and steadying himself with a hand on the top of the door frame, he climbed up onto the third shelf. He just needed to extend his reach enough to push open the panel. Guiding the umbrella toward the ceiling, he pressed the panel inward.

A sound like thunder reverberated from above. A shotgun blast destroyed the access panel and shredded the top of the umbrella. Marcus fell back down and rolled away from the closet as three more shots tore through the ceiling and into the bookshelf. Drywall dust and fibers of pink insulation filled the air like a sandstorm. He responded by raising the P220 pistol and placing several shots of his own into the ceiling.

The dust and pink insulation floated down on him, causing his skin to itch and burn as he got back onto his feet and listened.

Silence answered him.

Then another blast, but this one more distant. Not directed at them.

Andrew said, "What's he doing?"

At first, Marcus had no idea. But then he cursed and said, "He must have blown out a vent or something. He's trying to get out through the roof. Head outside and try to cut him off!"

Andrew took off around the corner, and Marcus scrambled up the bookshelf and into the attic. The space was empty except for exposed beams and insulation below and exposed rafters and OSB sheeting above. A ragged hole had been torn in the side of the wall ahead of him where a circular vent had once hung. On his hands and knees, he moved forward and through the hole. An old TV antenna clung to the side of the building, and he used it to help him descend to the ground.

He caught a glimpse of a shadowy form hurrying away through the alley. The sound of frantic footfalls crunched in the new fallen snow. Once on the ground, he took off in pursuit. Andrew came around the side of the building, hard on his heels.

The air was freezing and heavy in his lungs, but Marcus willed his legs to pump faster and faster. He was gaining on Kolenda, the greasy-haired man encumbered by the shotgun he still clutched in his right hand.

Kolenda wheeled around and opened fire, but he was too far away and didn't take the time to aim. The blast tore into a wooden fence beside a red-brick home. Marcus didn't slow down.

Dropping the shotgun, Kolenda stumbled through the snow. Tripping through backyards, fumbling his way over side streets. A Beretta came up from his waistband, and he fired again. His shots were wild and undisciplined, but Marcus feared that one of the stray bullets would find a nearby house. The man was screaming. But the angry shouts contained only primal sounds of anger, nothing coherent.

Kolenda was nearly at Route 43. From there he could try to grab a car or stumble into one of the many businesses lining that road and take hostages.

Marcus wanted him alive.

He took cover behind a light pole and sighted in low. The .45 boomed, and one of Kolenda's legs buckled. The man wailed in pain and anger, but he wasn't down. He stumbled the last few feet into the four-lane traffic of Route 43.

Cars came to screeching halts, sliding into each other on the slush-filled road. The sounds of squealing tires, protesting brake pads, and twisting metal assailed the roadway. One of the cars, a red Ford Festiva, slammed into Kolenda and sent him sliding across the ground. He rolled through the icy brown slurry covering the road, but somehow he kept hold of the Beretta. The crystal meth had given him extra strength. He probably hadn't even felt the impact.

Marcus took aim. "Drop the gun! You've got nowhere to go." Kolenda laughed. His eyes were wild. He radiated an air of madness. He was either truly insane or so hopped up on drugs that he had lost his faculties. Maybe a bit of both.

"Don't do it!"

Blood was on Kolenda's teeth as he smiled and raised the Beretta.

Marcus fired three times. Each round struck its intended target. One in the brain, two in the chest. Kolenda fell back into the dirty sludge of the roadway, his blood adding its own taint to the mix.

55

MARCUS CALLED IN the incident, although he was sure that people in the neighborhood had already reported the shots. Two black-and-whites arrived from the local PD within a few minutes. Andrew flashed his credentials and respectfully directed the cops to cover the body and secure the perimeter. They had only a short time before word of the incident leaked out to the detectives and Belacourt and his crew from the Major Crimes Task Force showed their faces. Marcus wanted to get a look at Kolenda's basement, and he wasn't in the mood to fight his way past Belacourt and his cronies in order to do so.

Returning to Kolenda's filth-ridden home, Marcus descended the stairs. The bare boards creaked beneath his weight. The air was cool and moist, but he also detected the smell of mold and a strange chemical musk. The basement had a concrete floor, but it was covered with a layer of dirt, probably the legacy of a previous flooding. Red metal jacks supported the floor above. A furnace and a large blue and white water heater sat in one corner, but most of the space was open and unused. The only partition was a makeshift wall of old mismatched wood paneling. The door was just another section of paneling with hinges mounted on one edge. But a padlock secured the opening.

Marcus gripped the padlock and yanked. The wood was thin and brittle, and the screws of the lock plate pulled away easily from the wall. The homemade door swung open with a moan. Its lower half grated over the concrete floor and caught at the halfway point. But the opening was more than big enough for Marcus to slip through.

Inside, he found an old wooden table. A screwdriver and two butcher knives sat atop it. Dried blood was caked on all three. If he had to guess, he would have said it was chicken blood or that of a stray cat that Kolenda had used as a sacrifice. But it could just as easily have been human. The far wall contained a mixture of strange satanic-looking symbols and jumbled, incoherent writings, but none seemed to match those from the previous crime scenes. The strangest aspect of the room was the countless sheets of thin book pages hanging from the rafters above on lengths of fishing line. Marcus looked closely at one of the pages. It had been torn from the Book of Revelation. Several passages had been furiously underlined in red ink.

He recalled Kolenda's medical records that they had borrowed from the dead man's former psychiatrist's office. The files stated that Kolenda was paranoid and delusional. Add crystal meth to that equation, and you got a deadly combination. But something still wasn't right.

Judging by the look on his partner's face, Marcus guessed that Andrew had come to the same conclusion. Andrew said, "It's not him, is it?"

"I don't think so. Our guy is a highly organized offender. This place is a mess. And Kolenda lives alone. I still think the Anarchist has a family. Kolenda was definitely a nutjob. He's just not our nutjob."

They searched through the basement for a few more moments but then heard the sound of someone heavy and out of breath descending the stairs. "You down here, Williams?"

Marcus rolled his eyes. He had hoped to avoid Detective Sergeant Belacourt, but that would have been too easy. "Over here."

Belacourt slipped through the makeshift door and took in the scene. Stupak was close behind him. The thin black man was perfectly groomed and wearing a suit more suitable for a high-priced attorney. Belacourt was sweating like a pig, streams of perspiration running down his forehead and collecting in his hair. Marcus wondered how anyone could break a sweat in such cold weather. Maybe the detective had the flu or a penchant for certain substances, legal or illegal, himself?

The detective shook his head and rubbed at his mustache. "Second time today that you've discharged your weapon in public. Congratulations. You know, I've got cops that have been on the force for over twenty years and the only times that they've fired a weapon on duty is when they've had to put down an injured animal hit by a car."

"Good for them."

"Maybe you can help me out. I've been trying to decide whether trouble follows you around or if you go looking for it."

"Just lucky, I guess."

"You're a real smart-ass, you know that?" Belacourt stepped close, within a foot of Marcus. The cop's eyes were full of an abnormal amount of hatred. His breath smelled of cigar smoke and meatballs.

Marcus didn't shy away. Instead, he smiled. "I'd rather be a smartass than a dumb-ass like you."

"Stay the hell out of my investigation! I won't say it again."

"That's good. I'd hate to have to keep ignoring you. You might develop a complex." Belacourt shoved him.

It wasn't really a violent or powerful shove. It was the act of someone who couldn't come up with anything intelligent to say and was not really meant to start a fight. Marcus knew that. He could have ignored it. He could have turned the other cheek and walked away. He had nothing to prove, nothing to gain.

But he also was sick of the cop's crap, dead tired, and sore all over. Plus he had a thousand thorns piercing into his brain that needed his attention more than some suburban detective staking out his territory. The thorns needed to be pulled before he could rest. Maggie. Ackerman. Missing tapes. The Anarchist. The abducted women, maybe still alive out there somewhere, scared and alone. The night his parents died.

He didn't need anything more to worry about, but at every turn, there was Belacourt, complicating things, aching to butt heads with him.

Marcus moved before he realized what he was doing. It was as if he had momentarily stepped outside himself and had taken on the role of spectator rather than active participant. His right hand clamped over Belacourt's left fist, and he squeezed hard. Belacourt's face contorted into a mask of agony, but Marcus didn't stop there. Before anyone else in the room could react, he twisted Belacourt's arm behind his back and slammed him against the concrete wall.

Marcus screamed at the cop, but it didn't sound like his own voice. It was deep and frightening. It frightened even him. "Who do you think you're playing with!"

Then he felt other arms wrapping around his back and more screaming. They pulled him away from the detective. He didn't resist. He let them drag him to the dirty ground. Someone shoved his cheek down against the concrete, the grit there grinding against his face like sandpaper. The sound of shuffling feet, more people coming down the stairs.

He heard Belacourt yelling. "Cuff him! I'm pressing charges!" Then someone slapped on the restraints. Marcus closed his eyes. He really didn't need this right now.

As THEY WERE getting ready for school, Melanie Schofield grabbed her father's hand and dragged him out of the kitchen to the dining room table. She had assembled a paper lunch bag, cotton balls, construction paper, crayons, and scissors. She looked up at him with her large green eyes, curly brown hair cascading down the shoulders of her pink shirt, and said, "I'm sorry, Daddy." She was on the verge of tears.

"Why are you sorry, baby?"

She stuck out her bottom lip. "I was supposed to make this Santa Claus picture with you last night, but I forgot. The teacher's gonna be mad. We're supposed to hang them up on the wall today for the parents to see when they walk into the gym for the Christmas play. But I forgot, and now I'm gonna be the only one without a Santa picture."

"Honey, don't worry." Harrison Schofield bent down and placed a hand on her shoulder. He smiled warmly as he checked his watch. "I bet we've got time to finish it before we leave. And if not, then we'll take your brother and sister to school and then Daddy will call work and tell them that I'm going to be late, that I've got more important business to take care of. It will all work out. Trust me."

Melanie grinned, showing her missing front teeth. "Thanks, Daddy."

"Oh, no. You're not getting off that easy." He tapped a spot on his cheek, and she strained up on her tiptoes and kissed him. "Who's your best buddy?"

"Daddy is."

"And who's the awesomest, most super-cool dad in the whole wide world?"

She rolled her eyes and giggled. "You are, Daddy!"

"Okay. Do you have everything we need?"

Melanie puckered her lips and bent a finger against the side of her cheek as if in deep contemplation. "We need black construction paper and a glue stick."

"Check. You get started. I'll grab them and be right back." Schofield walked across the intricately designed hardwood floors to a spare bedroom that his wife, Eleanor, used for scrapbooking and the occasional art project with the kids. The newest member of their family, the little Pomeranian, skittered around his feet and followed him inside the room. Each of the children had their own set of plastic drawers beneath a long countertop. He checked Melanie's drawers first. On top were a few unfinished projects she had started with her mother. Beneath those, there were stacks of multicolored construction paper, straws, craft sticks, feathers, beads, pieces of foam, little googly eyes, yarn, glitter. And then in the bottom he found a glue stick. One item down, but he didn't see any black construction paper.

Pulling open the next drawer down, the one marked with Benjamin's name, he sifted through more supplies and pulled up a stack of construction paper. What he saw wedged underneath made his heart break.

They were drawings. Pictures of animals and people in pain, dying, dead. They were dark and frightening, yet intricate and created with loving skill. Blood and fear were common themes among them. Some showed knives; some showed fire.

Schofield dropped to his knees and wept. He had suspected, but now he knew. His curse had been passed down. Just like his father before him, Benjamin had been born without a soul.

57

THE JACKSON'S GROVE police station had six holding cells. Three were empty, and three were occupied. Marcus sat against the wall of the second one on the right. The room was small and narrow. White block walls, no windows except for the one blocked off by a shutter in the metal cell door. There was a gray metal cot bolted to the floor with an almost non-existent mattress and a thin blanket sitting on top. The toilet was small and stainless steel. It was connected to a sink that doubled as a drinking fountain. Two metal buttons were set in the wall above the sink, one to provide water to flush and one to supply drinking and washing water.

Marcus had closed his eyes and had actually slept for a whole hour. He woke feeling somewhat rejuvenated and considered that maybe he should get locked up more often. Then he had stared at the block wall and reviewed the case. He accessed his mind as though it was a computer terminal. The block wall fell away and became invisible as pictures flashed through his mind's eye. Crime scenes, victimology, everything he'd seen, everything he'd read, everything he'd felt. It was all in there. The killer was in there. Along with how to catch him. Marcus just had to be smart enough to figure it out.

The door to the cell slid open. He smelled Vasques's perfume before he saw her. The flowery scent was soft yet crisp and had an air of the exotic like something from the rainforest. It suited her well. He didn't stand or look in her direction. She sat down next to him on the cot.

"What were you thinking?"

"I wasn't thinking. I was just reacting. Somebody pushes me, I push back. Somebody spits in my face, I bury my fist in theirs. It may be stupid, but it's the way I was raised."

"That's your excuse?"

"No excuse. Just an explanation. I screwed up. I don't know what happened."

"I do. You broke seven bones in a cop's hand and dislocated his shoulder. Luckily, they were able to pop that back in. He wants to press charges."

Marcus said nothing. There was nothing to say. "I've talked him out of it."

He swiveled to face her. "I sense a 'but' coming."

Vasques sighed. "He's been looking for an excuse to push you out, and now you've given him one. The charges only get dropped if you drop the case."

"Where's Belacourt now?"

She checked her watch. "Probably on the treadmill. The locker room and a small gym are in the basement across from the evidence lock-up."

"He runs?"

"Twice a day, every day. At the same times, religiously. Seven o'clock before work and twelve-thirty during lunch. Even with a broken hand."

"You can't push me out now."

"Give me one good reason why."

He smiled. "Okay, but it might be easier if I just show you."

58

JESSIE OLAGUE'S BEDROOM hadn't changed since the last time that Marcus had seen it. Her husband must have not returned to the house. Maybe he never would. The bed was still unmade, the covers pulled back. Jessie's scent was still in the air but only faintly. Vasques's perfume was blocking it out. The killer's calling card still covered the wall like a brand.

Marcus supposed that eventually someone would buy the house and erase the last traces of its previous occupants. But, in his experience, houses had memories. The walls remembered even if the people forgot. Certain rooms would always carry echoes or vibrations of what they had seen. The evil done within left stains and a cold hollowness behind. Houses were like men's souls in that way.

"I've been trying to figure out how the killer knew so much about the women and their homes."

Andrew sat down on the bed. Vasques remained in the doorway and said, "That's easy. He'd been in here before and checked the place out. He watched them. Knew their routines."

"Absolutely, but never did any of the neighbors report seeing anyone strange in the neighborhood. Not a single report out of all the cases."

"That's not impossible. It's not even far-fetched."

Andrew said, "But this guy wouldn't leave that to chance. He doesn't leave *anything* to chance."

With a grin and a nod, Marcus said, "Exactly. He'd have found a way to blend in and hide in plain sight. Pretend to be a meter reader, road worker, plumber, electric company, something like that. People see a guy in uniform with a clip-board and they don't give him a second thought."

"Okay," Vasques said, "but how does that help us?"

"It doesn't, really—not by itself. But then I started won-dering if it would be enough for him just to be in the house. Or would he want more?"

Vasques pulled a pack of gum from her pants pocket and popped a piece in her mouth. She held out the pack, silently offering some to the others. Marcus shook his head and paced the room. Andrew grabbed a piece.

"The eyes. You're thinking about the eyes," she said as she chomped the gum.

"Yeah, but I can't wrap my head around it completely. It's like a name that's right there on the tip of my tongue. I get the feeling that he wants to consume them in some way, possess something that they have. The eyes are the key. He's mission-oriented. He wants something from them. Not just anyone. These women were chosen. They're special."

"But why? We haven't found any strong correlation be-tween the victims. No pattern."

"I don't know. But he would want to know these women before he kills them. To *really* know them, intimately."

Andrew said, "You think he knew them socially? Most of them worked in public places. Restaurants, coffee shops."

"No, too surface. It wouldn't be enough." Marcus ges-tured toward the door frame near where Vasques stood. "When we were here before, I noticed that chain lock on the door. It seemed a little out of place to me. But as I thought about the scene, I remembered something from Jessie's file. Someone broke in a week ago and stole a DVD player. They filed a report, but it wasn't enough to turn in to the insur-ance."

"Stupak followed up on that," Vasques said. "He thought it might have been a front for the killer, but the same guy got caught two days later down the street. He was a junkie.

Didn't even wear gloves. The prints matched for this robbery as well."

"Right, but the lock looks new. So I got to thinking, maybe she put the lock on after the break-in."

Andrew added, "If you're right, then the killer was in here within the past week. And that night, he brought a tool specifically to open the door without waking up the girl."

"That brings up something else that's been bothering me. He doesn't like to take chances. I see the biggest risk factor here being the women themselves. How does he know for sure that they're asleep? He doesn't want a confrontation, and he's never gotten one. Also, highly organized offenders like our guy are often curious about the investigations. More than a few of these guys have been caught because they couldn't resist standing in the crowd outside the scenes of their crimes." Vasques shook her head. "We've been checking for that. Besides, this is all very intriguing conjecture, but I don't see where you're headed. How is this going to help us catch this guy?"

Marcus smiled. "I realized it when I thought back on our confrontation with Kolenda. The way that he hid from us in the attic. Most killers go after a very specific type of victim. But our guy has even crossed racial lines, which is almost unheard of in this type of case. Like I said, something connects these women in his mind. But there's also something more obvious that every single one of them has in common."

Andrew chuckled. "They all have attics."

"Exactly."

Vasques's eyebrows formed into a V. She wasn't getting it, and Marcus decided that it would be easier to just show her. He walked back into the hallway and found the attic access. It was a small square in the ceiling, no elaborate pull-down or hidden stairs, just a simple hole cut into the drywall.

"Wait here."

He remembered seeing a small collapsible stepladder in the laundry room. He retrieved it and carried it up the stairs.

Within a moment, it was unfolded, and he was climbing into the attic. The air was freezing, and when he breathed it came out in a visible puff. Blown-in insulation, which looked like something a rat would make a nest in, filled the space between the rafters. There was little headroom, and he crawled forward on hands and knees. Vasques poked her head up into the hole behind him.

It only took a few seconds to find what he was looking for. It was burrowed down into the insulation. He pulled it up, exposing a wire that snaked off to another point in the attic.

"What the hell is that?" Vasques said.

He removed the cord from the back of the device, pulled it free from its mount, stuffed it in his pocket, and scooted backward toward the hole. "I'm coming down."

Once he was back on the ground, he showed them the small camera that he had retrieved from the attic.

"Dammit," Vasques said. "We won't be able to use that in court. Chain of custody hasn't been maintained."

Marcus almost laughed. He wasn't worried about compiling evidence for a court case. He doubted whether the Anarchist would live long enough to stand trial, but he couldn't tell Vasques that. "Let's worry about finding the guy first. This is a state-of-the-art surveillance device. The killer probably has the whole house wired and set to transmit to a remote system somewhere. He may even have been using the house's own wireless network. He watched these women, and then he watched the cops as they checked out the scene."

"How did the Anarchist know that they wouldn't use the attic or find the cameras?"

Marcus shrugged. "It's a risk, but a manageable one. How many people with an access panel like that actually use their attic? And if they do, how many just stick a couple of boxes right next to the access panel? Who breaks out a ladder and goes crawling around up there?"

"You mentioned him blending in," Andrew said. "Maybe he works for some kind of electronics or security company."

"That's a good lead. We may be able to track the equipment back to a buyer or wholesaler."

Vasques winced and said, "We won't be able to follow anything back. Just like the car. He would want the cameras to be untraceable, in case someone found them."

"You're both missing the obvious," Marcus said. All eyes turned to him. "There could be several women out there right now with a bunch of cameras sitting in their attics. We can warn them. Involve the media. Go on the news and tell women to check for the cameras and call the police if they find them."

"That won't help us catch him."

"It may keep another woman from getting hurt. Plus, we may be able to trace back a live feed. And it could make him get sloppy."

"What if the women he's targeted don't watch the news?"

"It's still our best shot right now. And he might not see it on the news, either. We could get lucky."

Vasques thought for a moment and then said, "Okay, I'll make some calls."

Marcus and Andrew headed back out to their car. Vasques had driven separately. While Marcus had been sitting in a holding cell, Maggie had informed Andrew of the details of her meeting with Ellery Rowland. She had found them another good lead to check out on Chicago's north side, though it was far from time to pop the champagne and celebrate. Still, for the first time in this investigation, Marcus felt like they were making headway. It was a good feeling.

Then his phone rang, and the feeling faded.

59

STARING OUT THE window of a newly acquired arctic-white Saturn Astra, Ackerman watched Marcus walking toward the Yukon and staring down at the cell phone. The fingers of his left hand clenched around his own phone.

Pick up the damn thing, Marcus.

He could feel the rage welling up again. The knife in his right hand dug furrows into the dashboard of the Saturn. But then Marcus's voice replaced the ringtone.

"What do you want?"

The relief washed over Ackerman like a cleansing flood. "I'm sorry about Allen. I didn't mean to hurt him. It was unfortunate."

Marcus was silent for a moment, his heavy breathing pulsing over the phone's speaker. "It doesn't matter. Don't you get that? It doesn't change anything. If I ever get the chance, I'm still going to kill you." Ackerman closed his eyes and thought of how everything would be changing soon. They were coming to the end of one era and the beginning of another. As soon as his plan was complete, Marcus would see the world very differently. Ackerman was reminded of the story of Paul the Apostle. Paul had been devoted to the persecution of Jesus's early followers, but on the road to Damascus, fate had drastically changed the course of Paul's life. The sinner became the saint. And it would be the same for him and Marcus.

"I've never lied to you, Marcus. Unlike everyone else in your life."

"What is that supposed to mean?"

"Have you ever asked your friend the Director why I was specifically chosen for your recruitment?"

Marcus was silent.

"We're connected, Marcus. You know that I'm right. A part of you feels it. Our destinies are linked and have been for a very, very long time. But don't worry. You'll understand everything soon enough."

60

MAGGIE HAD SLEPT in that morning after having a late night and a few too many drinks at Kingston Mines with Ellery Rowland. She had woken up just in time to catch the tail end of the Continental breakfast and had grabbed a stale muffin and some orange juice. Afterward, she had found the hotel's fitness center and had tried to work off some of her anger toward Marcus. It hadn't helped.

She showered for exactly eight minutes and then started on her daily morning routine. Wash hands three times with soap. Brush teeth, stroking each section forty-two times back and forty-two times forward. Gargle with mouthwash for one minute and forty-seven seconds. Brush through hair, twenty-seven times on each side. Right, back, left, top. Trim fingernails and toenails into perfect symmetry. Always working from thumb or toe outward. Right hand, left hand, right foot, left foot.

She had just finished up and was setting out her clothes for the day when she heard a knock on the door. The peephole revealed Marcus standing in the hallway, holding two cups of Starbucks coffee. She took a deep breath, centering herself, and then opened the door.

"Good morning," she said, trying to keep her tone even and neutral.

"Morning, Mags. I was wondering if you'd accept a peace offering." He held out the coffee. "Two packets of Stevia that I had to pick up special from a local grocer and two creams. I even lined up the markings on the packets before opening them, just for you."

She tried not to show much of a reaction, but she knew that this was as much of an apology as she could ever have hoped for. Marcus wasn't good with relationships, and he was even worse at saying he was sorry. She noticed that he had dark patches beneath his sunken eyes. "You look terrible," she said.

"Thanks. You look great."

She felt her cheeks flush, and she quickly snatched the coffee from his hand. "Come on in."

"I can't. Andrew told me about your meeting with Rowland. We're heading over to check out this Crowley guy that he gave you the address for. I thought maybe you'd like to come along." She smiled. This was perfect. "I'd like to, but I'd just be a third wheel anyway. And I have lunch plans."

The shock in his eyes was priceless. "With who?"

"Ellery Rowland is taking me out to a restaurant called Everest. I hear it's a really nice place."

"You mean the devil-worshiper guy?"

"That's right. And he actually doesn't *worship* the devil. He doesn't even *believe* in the devil."

Marcus laughed. "I'm sure. He just lives the way the devil would want him to. That reminds me of a line from *The Usual Suspects*. Kevin Spacey's character says, 'The greatest trick the devil ever pulled was convincing the world he didn't exist.'"

"It doesn't matter. We really hit it off last night. I'll give you a call when I get back. Good luck."

As Maggie started to close the door, she heard him saying, "Wait a second. You—" But she ignored him and let the door swing shut in his face. She leaned her back against the wall for a moment and let her breathing slow. She wondered if she had ever felt a greater sense of satisfaction in her life.

61

THE CORPORATE HEADQUARTERS of Schofield Security Associates sat on a corner lot nestled among shopping plazas, chain stores, and fast-food restaurants just across the Indiana border in a town named Highland. It was only forty minutes from downtown Chicago, fifteen from the Gary/Chicago International Airport, and ten from Briar Ridge Country Club, where Schofield's grandfather liked to play golf. When the site was chosen, they had been one of only a few companies in the area, but the urban landscape had expanded around them. It was a massive slate-gray metal-and-glass-covered structure. One end of the building was rounded like a sports stadium and had always vaguely reminded Harrison Schofield of the ancient Roman Colosseum. His grandfather, Raymond Schofield, had paid an architectural firm from Los Angeles an exorbitant amount of money to design the monstrosity. As Chief Financial Officer, Harrison had been opposed to the project from the start, but it had been his grandfather's dream.

Raymond Schofield had founded SSA in the 1970s and had built it into a world-renowned consulting organization with operations covering ninety cities in thirty states and employing over seventeen thousand workers. They provided security for every type of industry and situation including financial, manufacturing and industrial, retail, and residential.

Schofield pulled the Camry up to the security gate and swiped his ID card. The white automated reinforced fencing slid open to allow him to pass. The parking garage occupied two underground levels below the rounded side of the building and was used only by SSA personnel.

He parked in his designated spot and shut off the car's engine. The company had its own motor pool and a fleet of vans used by on-the-ground installation teams. A man named Rick Mortimer was in charge of the maintenance and assignment of the company vehicles. Mortimer's office, positioned next to the elevator, had an open window where employees could drop off or pick up keys for their assigned vehicles. As Schofield stepped from the Camry, he could feel Mortimer's stare drilling into his back.

Heading toward the elevator, he passed the window to Mortimer's office. Mortimer was handsome with a full head of perfectly coifed salt-and-pepper hair and chiseled features. If someone had replaced the blue and white coveralls and name tag with a tailored suit and a power tie, Mortimer could have passed for a Presidential candidate. But that morning, he wore a scowl.

Schofield smiled in at the older man and said, "Is everything okay?" But he tried not to make eye contact.

"I don't know. You tell me."

"Umm, I'm…not sure what you mean?" Schofield felt himself shrinking away and fought the urge to run.

"I guess I've just been wondering why you've been using one of my vans. And someone stole a set of our coveralls and a name tag. You wouldn't know anything about that, would you?"

He was on the verge of hyperventilation now. The concrete walls of the garage were caving in around him. "I haven't…I just… Well, maybe once."

Schofield had once watched a Discovery Channel program with his kids on the fight-or-flight instinct. He had identified most with the opossum. When it saw danger, it played dead, ignoring the threat and hoping for it to go away.

Choosing flight rather than fight, he shuffled away from the window and tapped furiously on the button for the elevator. It dinged, and the doors slid open. In a sharp and quick rhythm, his finger pressed against the button inside to close the doors. From the garage, he was fairly certain that he heard Mortimer's voice say, "Freak." He agreed. He was a freak. But maybe he wouldn't always be one.

He got off on the third floor and walked past rows of cubicles and along corridors lined with glass-fronted offices. This was always the worst part of his day. He had tried to convince his grandfather to allow him to work remotely from home, but Raymond had felt that social interaction would do Schofield some good. His grandfather didn't understand, couldn't understand. Trying not to make eye contact with anyone and hoping he could avoid drawing attention to himself, he made it to his office after having had to give only a few nods to various co-workers and his secretary.

Closing the door behind him and dropping his black leather briefcase on the floor, he released a deep breath and bent forward with his hands on his knees. Luckily, his grandfather had agreed to give him a private office and his own bathroom. Work started at nine, but he usually arrived at least an hour late in the mornings to avoid the foot traffic and make sure that everyone else was already pounding away at their desks. The evening was easier. He could wait until the others had gone and avoid them entirely.

As he tried to calm his heart rate and breathing, he walked around the spacious office. It was all white and chrome and glass in what the interior designers had called modern art deco. The only items that he had supplied were the photos and awards that lined the shelves along one wall. The photographs were mostly recent pictures of his family. Only two were from his childhood. One was of his mother. The other was a nature shot taken from a bluff near the cult's compound in Wisconsin. It was filled mostly with trees. Maples, ashes, junipers, balsam firs. But it also showed a rocky slope and a small creek. It had been his special place.

Sneaking away from the compound as a curious child,

he had spent a lot of time at that spot. He had imagined the woods as his own little kingdom where he could escape from people, their stares, their mumbled words behind his back. It was the site of his first kill. The place where he had taken his first soul and discovered the strength that it gave him.

Another boy who had always been especially cruel to and jealous of him had followed Schofield into the woods. The boy teased him and pushed him down. They struggled and rolled around in the dirt of the forest floor. Then the boy's struggling ceased. His head had struck a rock and the back of his skull had caved in. Schofield sat atop the boy, staring into his eyes as his life drained away.

The Prophet had been proud of him.

A knock on his office door drew his attention back to the present. His grandfather came in. Raymond was tall and muscular with white hair and a thick beard. He cast a powerful shadow. His voice was deep and commanding. "Hello, my boy," Raymond said warmly as he stepped inside and slapped Harrison on the back. His grandfather had always been good to him. After all, his mother was Raymond's only child, and Harrison his only grandchild.

Raymond stood next to Schofield in front of the wall of photos. Picking up one of the shooting trophies displayed there, he said, "We should go to the range sometime, maybe at lunch. I've got a new Remington twelve-gauge that I've barely touched. Or maybe just cut out and do a full-blown hunting trip. We could take Benjamin with us."

His boy's dark dreams of death filled his head. "I'm sure he'd love that."

"Good. I'll start checking into it. We could do Wyoming this time, or would you rather head back to Canada?"

"Either way."

A pregnant silence filled the room. Schofield could sense a question on Raymond's mind. Finally, his grandfather said, "Where were you yesterday?"

Schofield said nothing, and Raymond added, "How is she?" His voice was soft, and sadness filled his eyes.

"About the same."

"I think it's wonderful the way that you still care for her and visit, despite all she's put you through. I can't imagine. You have a good heart, Harrison. I should go more myself, but it's just…"

"Difficult."

"Yes. I'm so sorry for all that happened to you when you were a boy. If I…" Raymond placed a hand on Schofield's shoulder and looked down at the black and white photo of his mother hidden among the others. She wasn't smiling. Her eyes were distant and sad. "Your mother was always unstable as a girl. Still, it was the darkest period of my life when she ran away. But it was also the happiest day of my life when you came back to live with me."

Raymond cleared his throat and checked his watch. "I'm late for a meeting, but I'd rather be going on a hunting trip. I'll make the arrangements. Maybe we could take Ben to the range this weekend to get him ready."

"That would be great."

As Schofield watched his grandfather leave, he knew that he should have felt great joy at Raymond's words. But he felt nothing, just an anxious, hollow pain. He looked out the window and thought of his past—his mother, the compound, the Prophet—and his future—Eleanor, Alison, Melanie, and Benjamin. His grandfather's words came back to him. *You have a good heart, Harrison.* But he didn't. The evil twisted and clawed through his heart like a cancer, and he couldn't stop it, couldn't deny it. He had betrayed everything and everyone he loved.

In a sudden fit of anger, he swept all the papers from the top of his desk. Annual reports, earnings statements, stock profiles. They all struck the floor and scattered everywhere. He stared down at the mess and sighed. Feeling foolish, he started to re-organize the documents back into neat stacks.

CROWLEY'S OCCULT BOOKS was on Chicago's north side, not far from I-94. Across the street was a tall white apartment building and a small, fenced-in park with no playground equipment and three gnarled trees. The bookstore shared the street with a liquor store, nail salon, and a pastry and coffee shop. Brightly colored awnings, names and numbers scrawled in three-foot letters, and neon signs marked each. All except for the bookstore. Only a small sign hung in the front window of the red brick building. It read *Rare and Antique Artifacts—Serious inquiries by active spiritualists, occultists, and shamans only.*

Marcus rolled his eyes. "What kind of a name is Vassago Crowley?"

"The made-up kind," Andrew said. "Stan told me that Vassago is the name of some demon and Crowley probably came from Aleister Crowley."

"The guy from the Ozzy Osbourne song?"

It was Andrew's turn to roll his eyes. "Fake IDs?"

"Yeah. I think we'll be from the FBI today."

They pushed through the front door of the shop, and the ding of a doorbell announced their presence. The interior smelled of incense.

The sound of a string quartet came from speakers mounted in the ceiling. The store was filled with rows of books but also contained a myriad of candles, jars filled with strange substances, skulls, talismans, and symbols. The sales counter rested along the back wall. A blond-haired man in his early fifties stood behind it. He was leaning forward with his elbows on the glass and thumbing through an old leather-bound tome. Without raising his eyes from the book, he said, "What do you want?" Judging by his accent, he was from Australia or maybe New Zealand.

Marcus hated him from the first second he laid eyes on him. "Vassago Crowley?"

Crowley stared at them over his glasses and then returned to his book. "Sod off."

"Sir, we're from the FBI."

"You here to arrest me?"

"No."

"You have a warrant?"

"We don't need a warrant. We're just here to ask you a few questions."

"Oh well, in that case, sod off, like I said. I don't know anything. If you come back tomorrow, I'll know even less then."

"We're trying to catch a killer and have reason to believe that you have information to help with the investigation. We won't take up much of your time."

The front door dinged again, and a heavyset old man with a thick reddish brown beard stepped inside. He was stooped and limping. He had a bulbous nose that looked like it had been broken a few times, and long brown hair hung down over half of his wrinkled face. The man barely acknowledged them as he headed off toward a stack of books along one wall.

"I've got a customer. And I don't know anything. I can't help you." Andrew said, "Come on. Let's just go."

But Marcus could feel his anger bubbling to the surface. He cracked his neck and slammed a hand down on the counter. "People's lives are at stake here. We just want to ask you a few questions."

"Okay, you can ask me one question. Ask me if I give a squirt of piss about those people's lives. Go ahead. Ask me."

Marcus's teeth ground hard against one another. He counted backward from five, then he said, "Sir, please, just—"

"If you're not going to arrest me, then get out. I'm not answering any questions without a lawyer. Is that clear enough for you?"

Marcus smiled. "Crystal."

Then his open palm shot out and slammed into Crowley's throat. The man's glasses flew from his head as his neck whipped back. Marcus grabbed him by the hair and slammed his head forward onto the glass of the counter. It splintered out in a spiderweb of cracks. He continued to press Crowley's head down against the glass and pulled his Sig Sauer pistol. The barrel twisted against the side of Crowley's face.

"Tell me about the Anarchist!"

"I don't know anything!"

He cocked back the hammer on the Sig Sauer. "Tell me!" Andrew's fingers curled around Marcus's left bicep. His voice was calm yet firm and insistent. "Come on, Marcus. We're done here." Marcus's hand shook, and he dug the pistol harder into Crowley's cheek. He bit down on his lip. "Marcus! Enough!"

He wrenched the gun away from Crowley's head and turned for the door. The guy with the red beard knew when to mind his own business and tried not to make eye contact. Marcus didn't blame him. As he jerked open the front door, the bell dinged again, and he heard Crowley screaming. "I'm pressing charges, you bloody psychopath!"

Resisting the urge to turn back, he headed straight for the Yukon.

"Give me the keys!" Andrew said. "And get in the damn truck. I'm sure the police will be on their way soon, and you've beaten up enough cops today."

63

ACKERMAN WAS WORRIED about Marcus. The little display of violence that he had just witnessed had been completely uncalled for. Not that Ackerman was ever opposed to violence, but Marcus's reaction was sloppy and lacked calculation. It served no purpose and was out of character. Marcus was slipping up. He needed help. Just a little push in the right direction.

The killer reached up and scratched at his red beard. This was one of his least favorite disguises, but it was also very effective. He had covered the area where his nose, forehead, and eyes intersected with a latex prosthetic and had added wrinkles to his forehead and around his eyes. Then he had applied several coats of stage make-up to ensure that everything blended and looked natural. That was the most time-consuming step, but to be properly effective he needed to do even more. His clothes were padded to make him look heavier. Most simple facial-recognition software would probably have been fooled by the fake nose, but if thermal IR cameras were employed, they would pick out the differences in skin temperature and detect the use of a prosthetic. And the fake beard was completely useless against the software. The solution was simple yet elegant. The majority of recognition software relied heavily on analysis of the eyes and needed symmetry to be effective. The hair of the long brown wig hung over the right half of his face and specifically his right eye. In his tests, there was less than a three percent chance of his being detected.

He scanned through the book in his hand. From what he

could gather, it discussed divination and magic in ancient Egypt. Once Marcus and Andrew had pulled away from the curb, he slid the book back onto the shelf where he had found it. Then he approached the counter.

Crowley was still cursing and examining his face in the mirror of a small bathroom marked *Employees Only* just behind the counter. He caught sight of Ackerman and pointed a finger at him. "What do you want?"

Ackerman smiled as he laid a large revolver on the counter. It was a Taurus Judge loaded with Winchester PDX1 .410 home-defense shotgun shells. Each shell contained three copper-plated defense discs and twelve copper-plated pellets in order to ensure maximum stopping power. The Judge covered the epicenter of the web of cracks and blood where Marcus had slammed Crowley's head only a few moments before.

"I want to play a little game," he said. "Let's call this one *The Whole Truth*."

64

ANDREW JERKED THE Yukon into a parking lot between a small Mexican restaurant and a dilapidated, graffiti-covered building. It might have once been a convenience or liquor store. Marcus couldn't tell for sure. There was fire damage on the roof, and the windows were boarded up. As they pulled in, a couple of gangbangers heading for the Mexican restaurant gave them a look as though they were in the wrong place. *Carry On Wayward Son* by Kansas was on the radio, but Andrew switched it off.

"I like that song," Marcus said.

Andrew's breathing was quick and agitated as he seethed in the driver's seat. After a moment's silence, he said, "What is going on with you? I can't keep doing this."

"What do you want me to say? I just feel like I'm on edge all the time. I can't sleep. I can't breathe. I feel like my head's going to explode. I'm losing control of everything."

"Then suck it up and get a grip on yourself. I'm sick of babysitting you."

Silence stretched in the car. The wind was picking up. It blew the snow from the top of the run-down building and dropped it onto their windshield. Andrew said, "What's really bothering you? The truth."

Marcus released a deep breath. "How many people do you think I've killed?"

"You know, one time when I was in high school, this veteran came in to speak to our history class. He had fought in Vietnam, and we were doing a unit on the war. He told us about his experiences and then opened it up for questions. Being a stupid kid, I asked him if he had ever killed anyone while he was over there. His answer has stuck with me to this day. He told me that he would rather focus on the people that he had saved. And that's exactly what you need to do. You can't let guilt consume you for no good reason."

"It's not that simple."

"Yeah, it is. You're just making it complicated."

"You don't understand."

"Enlighten me."

Marcus watched the snowflakes roll lazily over the windshield. People walked by with their collars and hoods pulled up against the wind. He watched them as they passed and wondered where each of them was going. Their worlds seemed so alien to him. What did the normal people do? What did they feel?

"I don't feel guilty about killing any of them, Andrew. Not at all. In fact, there's a part of me that liked it. There's a part of me that's no different than Ackerman. And with every squeeze of that trigger, it gets just a little easier. My heart grows a little colder. The world gets a little darker. And I worry that one day I'll cross some threshold and something in my head will just snap. It's in me, clawing to get out. And it's getting worse."

INSIDE THE WORKSHOP behind his home, Schofield paced back and forth across the concrete floor. His mind was a tornado of conflicting emotions. He considered turning himself in. He contemplated suicide. He thought of his mother. Maybe she had been right all along. Maybe he had been damned from birth. Maybe he truly was an abomination. The world would probably have been a better place if she'd succeeded in killing him before he reached adulthood.

He sat down at a small wooden desk that he had purchased from an auction at an old church. At one time, it might have been the pastor's. It had heavy oak drawers with locks on them. Schofield retrieved his laptop from the third drawer down and brought up the camera feed from the home of the woman he had chosen to be the next sacrifice. She was standing at her stove, preparing a meal. She poured something into a boiling pot of water. He couldn't make it out from his vantage point, but it looked liked pasta.

He needed her, and he was supposed to take her that evening. But if he gave her to the Prophet and his suspicions were correct...

The thought was too terrible to even be considered. He closed the laptop and sat at the desk staring out the window for a few moments. The day had been overcast, and now the sun was abandoning the world.

He stood to head back into the house, but something caught his eye as he looked out the window. Their property bordered a small wooded area, and a white-haired man stood just before the edge of the treeline where the manicured lawn gave way to weeds. He was talking with someone. Schofield moved closer to the window to get a better look and realized that the second person was his son, Benjamin.

Rushing out of the shed, he quickly closed the distance between himself and his son. Benjamin wouldn't look him in the eyes. "What's going on here?"

His neighbor ran a hand through his long white hair and replied with the thick Irish brogue that always grated on Schofield's nerves. "Hello, Harrison. I was just talking with young Ben about something that I found out in the woods. But now that you're here, I'll let you handle it."

As he walked away, the old man slapped Schofield on the shoulder. Schofield's angry stare burned holes in his neighbor's back. Someday he would be strong enough to deal with the old man once and for all.

Benjamin still wouldn't look at him, so he squatted down to eye level and said softly, "You can tell me anything, buddy. What is it?"

"Promise you won't be mad?"

"I promise. You're not in trouble."

Benjamin pointed down at a shoebox that sat on the snowy ground next to one of the closest trees. It was a black and brown Nike box made from thick cardboard. Its lid was connected to the sides and could be folded up like a hinge. The box was closed.

"What's that, buddy?"

Tears formed in Ben's eyes. He looked away and didn't speak. Schofield stepped toward the box and stared down at it. The wind picked up, and he shivered in the cold breeze. He was only wearing a light University of Illinois sweatshirt and jeans, and hadn't expected to be standing out in the snow. With the toe of his shoe, he flipped open the top of the shoebox.

He was shocked at what he found inside, but then he considered that he should have been expecting this. Blood coated the box's interior. The mutilated and dissected body of a small animal rested at its center. It might once have been a cat, but he couldn't say for sure because of the extent of the disfigurement. He had performed similar acts upon small animals that he had captured near the compound when he'd been a child.

Schofield looked back at Benjamin, and as the wave of sadness crested, it nearly carried him off his feet. He swallowed hard. The kids had never seen him cry. Ben's face was wet with tears. In a small and brittle voice, he said, "I'm sorry, Daddy. Mr. O'Malley said…"

He grabbed the boy and lifted him from the snow-covered ground, squeezing him against his chest in a loving embrace. Ben cried against his shoulder. "It doesn't matter, Benjamin. There's nothing you could ever do that would make me love you any less."

"Are you going to tell Mom?" Ben said, his face still buried against his father's sweatshirt.

"No. This will be our little secret."

Schofield squeezed the boy tighter. The cold breeze whipped against them, but he didn't ever want to let go. He had always wondered what he would have done had he been in his mother's position. And now he knew. No matter what any of his children did, he could never hurt them. They were his world, all that mattered, and it gave him all the more reason to find a way to fill his own hollow soul and be the best father that he could be.

They stood that way for a long few minutes, but then his wife's voice called out from the back door of the house. "Boys, are you out here? Supper's ready." Her voice was growing closer as she spoke.

He put Ben down quickly, wiped the tears from his son's cheeks, and nudged the top of the shoebox closed. "Go inside and get ready for dinner, Ben. Remember, our little secret."

Ben ran off just as Eleanor came around the corner of Schofield's workshop. The boy ran right past her and up to the house. Eleanor had a thin yellow cardigan pulled up around her shoulders. Her arms were tucked tight against her chest, and she was shivering from the cold. "Everything okay?"

"Fine."

"What did Mr. O'Malley want?"

Schofield's gaze drifted over to the old man's house. It wasn't nearly as extravagant as theirs. It was a smaller single-story ranch covered with beige brick. It had a large glass sun room built onto the back, and a door on the side where the old man could walk directly over to their house and stick his nose into their business.

"I don't want the kids to be around Mr. O'Malley anymore."

"What? Why? He's such a nice man, and the kids think of him as a grandpa."

"I don't like him."

"He's just a lonely old man."

"You don't know him."

"Did something happen?"

He resisted looking down at the shoebox. "No, everything's fine. I'll be inside in just a few minutes."

She didn't seem convinced but said, "Okay, it's chicken stir-fry. Your favorite."

"I just have one thing to take care of, and then I'll be right in. Don't wait for me."

Schofield watched his wife walk all the way back into the house, and then he headed for the garage. Once inside, he grabbed a shovel with a long fiberglass handle and a spaded end. The ground was probably frozen and would be difficult to dig. Luckily, he wouldn't have to go too deep to dispose of his son's handiwork.

MAGGIE'S LUNCH DATE with Ellery Rowland had gone exceedingly well. Everest was an elegant French restaurant on the fortieth floor of the Chicago Stock Exchange. Bronze sculptures created by the acclaimed Swiss artist Ivo Soldini adorned each table, and paintings by the Chicago artist Adam Siegel lined the walls. She had ordered hazelnut-crusted skate wing with brown-butter caper emulsion. She wasn't quite sure what any of that meant, but it had been the first item on the menu beneath the heading *Main Course.* The restaurant was normally closed for lunch, but Ellery was a personal friend of the chef. The whole thing had made her feel strangely like Julia Roberts in *Pretty Woman.* Rowland had been both charming and intriguing, but for some reason she couldn't help thinking about Marcus.

We always want what we can't have, she supposed.

After leaving Rowland, she had returned to the hotel and started in again on compiling evidence and reports. Her afternoon as a princess was over, and it was time to get back to work. She had just opened a digital report detailing the life of Sandra Lutrell, the first victim of the Anarchist's current spree, when someone knocked on her door. It was the last person she was expecting.

Vasques wore a cordial smile as she said, "Hello, Agent Carlisle. Have you seen Marcus? He's not in his room and not answering his cell phone. I thought maybe he was here with you."

Maggie kept her expression flat. She noted the way that Vasques had only asked for Marcus and not Andrew and had referred to him by his first name, not as Agent Williams. "They're not here right now, but they're on their way back."

"Okay, well, just tell Marcus I came by, in case I miss him. I think I'll just hang out in the lobby and wait."

Fighting back an eye roll, Maggie said, "You can wait here. They shouldn't be long."

"Are you sure? I don't want to impose."

"It's fine. I'm just reviewing some evidence from the case."

As Vasques stepped inside, Maggie could tell that the other woman was taking everything in. She glanced at the makeup and toiletry supplies laid across the black marble of the bathroom countertop. They were all perfectly organized in symmetric rows. Maggie always got a room with two beds, one for sleeping and one for organization. The articles of her clothing were folded in neat stacks atop the second bed. Vasques looked at them with a raised eyebrow. Maggie wanted to tell Vasques that she had invited her to wait in the room, not come in and psychoanalyze her host, but she bit her tongue.

Grasping for something to say, Maggie asked, "Your father worked this case, right? During the last series of murders?"

Vasques nodded. "I think he was getting close to something, but he died before he could see it through."

"I'm sorry."

"He was a good cop and a good dad. It was just a stupid accident."

"Car crash?"

"Fire. He fell asleep smoking."

"I'm sorry."

"You said that already."

"I meant it. Have you had any hits on the hidden cameras?"

"Not yet, but it's still early."

The silence stretched out, and Maggie couldn't remember feeling as awkward since her first real date in seventh grade.

It was Vasques's turn to grasp at straws. The FBI Special Agent sat down on the corner of the bed and said, "How did you get into this line of work?"

Maggie wasn't sure how to respond. No one within the Shepherd Organization had ever asked her such a question, and she had never dreamed of volunteering the information. Don't ask, don't tell. Each member of the team had some skeleton buried in the basement that was best left undisturbed. She considered lying but supposed there was no real harm in sharing a few nuggets from her past.

She sat down on the bed, propped a pillow against the headboard, and leaned back. "My younger brother was abducted by a serial killer known as 'The Taker'. I was supposed to be watching him at the time. I learned about law enforcement while I tried to track the bastard down. Then this job found me."

"Wow, now *I'm* sorry."

"It was a long time ago."

"Did they ever catch the guy?"

"No."

"What about your brother?"

Now she remembered why none of them ever talked about things like this. "They never found him, either."

"I'm sorry."

"You said that already."

Vasques gave a little smile. "How long have you been working with Marcus?"

"We've been together for a little over a year."

Vasques raised her eyebrows, and Maggie realized that her phrasing left room for interpretation. "Oh, it's not like that. It sort of was for a while."

"But not anymore?"

"No, not anymore."

As Vasques nodded slowly, Maggie saw the hint of a

girlish little grin at the corners of the FBI Special Agent's mouth. Even though she had no real right to do so, she wanted to knock Vasques across the room. She pictured it. Elbow to the temple. Maybe bash her face in with the butt of her gun. She knew plenty of ways to dispose of a body.

But Maggie didn't do any of those things. She just sat there, bobbing her head like an idiot.

67

THERE WAS A knock on the door of Maggie's hotel room. Vasques was glad. She had run out of things to say as the direction the conversation was taking had become more and more awkward.

"I'll get it," she said.

Andrew stood on the other side of the door. He looked deflated somehow, and there was a sadness in his eyes that hadn't been there earlier. "Umm, hello, Agent Vasques."

"I was looking for Marcus."

"He's back in our room."

"Okay, thanks."

As she slipped past him into the hallway, Andrew said, "He really needs to get some rest while he can."

"Absolutely, I just wanted to run something by him. I'll be quick." Vasques didn't give him a chance to object. She just swung the door shut and headed for the elevator. The hallway had textured walls the color of a Georgia peach, and the carpet's red swirl pattern gave her vertigo. Or maybe it was just the situation she was rushing into. She felt sweaty and a little sick to her stomach.

While sitting on the edge of Maggie's bed, she had come to a decision. In her professional life, being passive and overly cautious could get people hurt or killed. But so could jumping in head first with your eyes closed. Despite that, she had no problem reacting to life-and-death situations. Within a split second, her body and mind would spring into action. It was second nature.

So why did she find it so damn hard to make decisions concerning her personal life?

In the past, Vasques had never allowed herself to be spontaneous or adventurous when it came to emotion. But as she had sat there thinking of the enigmatic new man in her life, she'd decided that now was as good a time as any to start.

68

THE ALERT MESSAGE from the tiny motion detector that Marcus had placed by the door to his hotel room vibrated against his chest. The room was dark, and his face was buried in a pillow. Still, he wasn't sleeping. He assumed that it was probably Andrew who had triggered the device, but he also wouldn't let himself be killed by a lazy assumption. The gun beneath his pillow was a snub-nosed .357 Magnum Taurus revolver. It was compact and made from a lightweight polymer, but it also packed a punch and kicked like a mule. Most importantly, it required a heavy ten-pound double-action trigger pull, which meant that there was virtually no chance of it discharging accidentally. Marcus found that particular trait to be very important for a gun that rested next to his head every night.

Rolling from the bed with the .357 in his hand, he paused and listened. No one had entered or knocked. He cocked back the gun's hammer, changing the ten-pound pull into a mere 2.5 pound squeeze. Someone from the hotel would have knocked already, and the list of people who knew which room he was actually staying in was short. Andrew, who wanted him to rest. Maggie, who either didn't know they were back or knew from Andrew that he was trying to sleep. Allen, who was still in the hospital. Stan, who was back in DC. Or Vasques.

He dialed her number, and she answered on the second ring. "Are you outside my room?"

"How did you know that?"

"I didn't hear you knock."

"Because I hadn't knocked yet. Come let me in. I've got something to show you."

Marcus slipped the gun into the back of his pants and headed for the door. Checking through the peephole first, just in case, he let her in. "Has something happened? The camera thing pan out?"

"No, I just thought you might want some company."

For the first time since he had met her, she seemed almost timid. It cast a softness on her features and an innocence in her eyes that only added to her beauty. He shut the door behind her, and before he realized what was happening, she had pushed him back against the wall and pressed her lips against his.

He didn't fight it. The kiss was intense and full of a longing hunger. His arms slipped around her back, pulling her close. He could feel the firmness of her body as she rubbed against him. The exotic flower scent of her perfume was stronger than ever. He ran a hand through her long, dark hair, and she went for his belt.

"A bit fast, isn't it?" he said breathlessly.

"I'm tired of being cautious. Tired of waiting. Just go with it." Vasques pushed him back onto the black leather couch and straddled him. The gun dug into his back, but he ignored it. She pulled off her shirt, revealing a lacy black bra. The sight of it surprised him; he had expected something more utilitarian from her.

Bending down, she kissed him again with even greater ferocity. Her long dark hair fell over his face and chest. He closed his eyes and ran his fingers through it. But in his mind, all he could see was Maggie's face. He thought of her on the lunch date with Ellery Rowland, and jealousy overwhelmed him.

And then Vasques's phone rang. She growled and looked at the screen. "It's Belacourt. I have to take this."

Marcus could only hear her side of the conversation, but it was enough to know that something had happened. She hung up and said, "A woman in Orland Park found cameras in her attic."

"Call him back."

"Why?"

"Don't let him send anyone inside the house and make sure that she doesn't mess around with those cameras."

"She may have already."

"Or she may have freaked out and called the cops first."

"You think he'll still show up there?"

"He may not have watched the news or seen her calling the cops. It's worth a shot."

Vasques hit redial as she dismounted Marcus and looked around for her shirt. He knew that he should have felt disappointed that the call had interrupted them. But instead he was strangely relieved.

69

ACKERMAN STOOD BACK and admired his handiwork. As a general rule of thumb, he preferred to keep his games simple, but as he stared at the device he had built he knew it would prove to be worth the extra effort. Everything was now in place, and it was time to begin the evening's entertainment.

He waved the smelling salts beneath Crowley's nose, and the man came slowly awake. "What? Where am I? What is this!"

Ackerman reveled in the fear on Crowley's face. It had been too long since he had truly indulged himself, and Crowley was the perfect playmate. Marcus might even thank him for this one.

The man sat naked atop the device with his hands bound behind his back. Leather shackles adorned with hooks dangled from both his ankles. Ackerman had built the torture device from specifications used during the Spanish Inquisition. He had been unable to procure an original, but his version would work just as well. The apparatus consisted of a tall vertical board topped with a sharp V-shaped wedge. While Crowley had been unconscious Ackerman had carefully positioned him with his legs straddling the wedge.

Crowley's eyes jerked from side to side, taking in his surroundings. Since the device required tall ceilings, Ackerman had originally planned to conduct the interrogation within an abandoned school building near the repurposed crack house he had been staying in. He had even driven to Crowley's shop with the device loaded into the back of a stolen delivery truck with that purpose in mind. But after a quick search of the back room of Crowley's store, his plans had quickly changed. It was so thoughtful of Mr. Crowley to have provided his very own soundproof torture chamber. The ceilings in the consumer end of Crowley's shop were around twenty feet high. The ceilings within the torture chamber matched those of the bookstore, except that noise-absorbent foam blocks lined ceilings and walls alike. Cameras hung around the room at different angles. Some high, some low. There had also been a small bed, a child's bed, that Ackerman had pushed into the corner.

"You're a bad man, Mr. Crowley."

"Screw you. Who do you think you are? Get me down from here!" Crowley was trying to keep up his bravado, but Ackerman could see it quickly crumbling.

"What could you have possibly used this room for? Did you bring little boys here, Mr. Crowley? You are a registered sex offender. I hear that's how your tastes run. The charge for which you were sent to prison."

The high-speed rhythm of Crowley's breathing reminded Ackerman of a washing machine spinning on high. "I don't know what you're talking about."

"I'm not here to judge you. Personally, I think that anyone who molests a child should have their lungs cut out. But I live in a glass house, so I won't be throwing stones at you for your sins. I'm not here to seek revenge or force atonement. I just need answers."

"Fine. Get me down. I'll tell you anything."

"I'm sure a man like yourself, someone who dabbles in the darker side of life and is somewhat a student of history, would be familiar with the Spanish Inquisition."

"Whatever, mate! Please, just let me down."

"This device was used by the Church's Inquisitors during that time period and also by the Spanish and British armies. My father made me read about several methods of torture when I was a boy, but this one in particular has always fascinated me. The Spaniards had such vivid and twisted imaginations. I've been dying to try it out. Bring back an oldie but a goodie, so to speak. It's called the Spanish Donkey."

Apparently deciding to change his tactics from pleading to ordering, Crowley screamed, "I said get me down, you freak!"

Ackerman's father's words filled the killer's ears—*You're a monster... We're going to play a little game, Francis*—but he ignored both voices, the one from the present and the one from the past. "The Spanish Donkey is widely regarded as one of the most brutal and painful forms of torture that the wicked mind of man has ever devised. When it was employed, there were many instances of men and women being torn completely in half. Can you imagine how intense the agony must have been? Feeling yourself being slowly eviscerated, knowing that the more you fought, the deeper the wedge would penetrate. Even if the accused survived the interrogation, almost without fail they died from infection. Of course, back then, they performed these actions one right after another. Little concern was paid to cleaning the apparatus before each new rider."

"You don't have to do this. I get the point, mate. I'm sufficiently freaked. I'll tell you anything you want to know."

"Please shut up now. You're spoiling the moment. Where was I? Oh yes, the way the Donkey works is that I'll ask you questions, and if I don't like the answers, I'll add weight to your feet. The sharp edge of the Donkey will cut into you. And I'm afraid that, by the very nature of the device, the initial consequence will be a slow castration."

"Please! Let me down!"

"What would be the fun in that? Consider it a science experiment. You're a tough guy, Crowley. Let's measure what it takes to transform a real tough guy into a little girl."

Crowley screamed and tried to struggle off the wedge. The sharp edge dug into him as he fought. He threw all his weight to the side, apparently trying to tip himself over. But

Ackerman's hand shot out and wrapped around Crowley's ankle, holding him in place.

"Afraid it's not that easy. But that does remind me: this was usually at least a two-man operation, but I'll be making do with one. So when I add weight to one side, I'll have to move quickly to the other to distribute the weights equally. I'm worried that the extra fluctuations and discrepancies will speed the process, but I guess we'll just see what happens. So let's play."

Ackerman had purchased two 255-pound sets of rubberized Olympic weights and several yards of black nylon rope. While Crowley had been unconscious, he had threaded the rope through the holes in the weights in order to connect them to the hooks dangling from Crowley's ankles. The original Inquisitors had used cannonballs, but this would work just as well. He hoped that he had acquired enough weights. After all, he hadn't the foggiest idea of how many pounds of pressure would be required to split a man in half.

Crowley continued to struggle but only succeeded in causing himself additional pain. Ackerman started off slow, adding only five pounds to each ankle. He continued until the wedge began to draw blood. Crowley howled in agony, but Ackerman knew that very little permanent damage had been done so far.

"What do you know about the Anarchist, Mr. Crowley?"

"Get me down!" Crowley said, sobbing.

"Out of curiosity, does a satanist such as yourself ask God for help in moments such as this or do you believe your dark prince will save you?"

"Please!"

Ackerman added more weight. "The Anarchist?"

When Crowley spoke, his frenzied words came in a breathless flurry. "I don't know who he is, but he was a member of a cult founded by a guy who went by the name Prophet. Said the devil spoke to him. His name was Conlan. They had some hidden compound up in Wisconsin. Thought they were going to kick-start the apocalypse with a kid they claimed was the Antichrist."

"What was the kid's name?"

"I don't know!"

"Where's Conlan now?"

"I don't know. He's gone underground. When he had the compound, he was actively recruiting. But there was some incident there, and he dropped off the map."

"Did he try to recruit you?"

"Yes! Please!"

"Where's the compound?"

"I only went once. It was on some guy's farm—up in Wisconsin, like I said. Jefferson County."

"What was the guy's name?"

"I don't know!"

Ackerman added more weight, and Crowley shrieked as the wedge sliced into his body. Tears and sweat made his skin glisten, and the fluids rained down on Ackerman as Crowley writhed and whipped his head around in pain.

"Please," Crowley cried. "I think it had Bowman or Beaman on the mailbox, something like that."

The killer considered this. It was a good lead. Marcus could check the property records in Jefferson County. Maybe find the compound. Maybe find Conlan. It was enough to get Marcus moving in the right direction, and Ackerman didn't want to do all the work for him.

"Very good, Mr. Crowley. I believe you." He retrieved a small notepad with a blood-red cover from his back pocket. After flipping to the first page, he wrote something down and tore out the sheet. Scribbled on the next and tore it out as well. He placed the notebook back into his pocket and stuck out his hands like a magician preparing for a trick. Each hand contained one of the torn sheets of paper. "Since you've answered my questions, I'll give you a fifty-fifty chance of escaping with your life. One of these papers contains the word *Life*. On the other, I've written *Death*. Pick one."

Crowley sobbed and mumbled something unintelligible.

"It's not complicated. Every day we make decisions that influence our life and the lives of others. People choose to have one more drink, stray across the center line, and collide with another vehicle. They choose to abuse their children, do drugs, go to prison for tax fraud. But even simple and seemingly insignificant choices can change everything. Think of a man who called in sick for work or missed his train on September 11, 2001. All I'm doing here is pulling back the curtain and showing you how fragile life truly is. Now choose."

"No, I can't!"

"That in itself is a choice, but you won't like the outcome." Crowley continued to sob for a long moment, but then got himself under control just long enough to say, "Right."

Ackerman opened his right fist and read what was on the small piece of paper. "Too bad. It's not your lucky day, Crowley."

"No! Please!"

"I've seen a lot of things in my life. Had many fascinating and beautiful experiences and also felt a thousand years' worth of pain. But I've never seen a man torn in half. Since you've been honest with me, I'll return the favor. There's no need to second guess yourself or your choice. I cheated and wrote *Death* on both papers."

Crowley screamed. And Ackerman added more weight.

70

SITTING IN VASQUES'S gray Crown Victoria twenty-three miles southwest of downtown Chicago, Marcus drummed his fingers against the passenger-side dashboard and sipped a Starbucks coffee. A local classic-rock station was playing Led Zeppelin over the radio—Robert Plant singing *When the Levee Breaks*. The target's house had mint-green siding and black shutters. It was perfectly average, not old not new, not poor but not rich. The street was quiet, and they hadn't seen much traffic. It was the kind of street that Marcus and his friends would have used for stickball when he was a kid back in Brooklyn—suburban, calm, isolated. Small flurries of snow floated lightly through the air and landed on the windshield. The snow would restrict visibility and obstruct their surveillance of the target's residence if it got any worse.

Fast-food boxes littered the passenger-side floor of the Crown Vic, and Marcus had to shove them back against the seat to make room for his feet. The scent of grease left behind in the empty containers merged with the smell of their coffees, overpowering Vasques's exotic floral perfume. But Marcus could still taste her on his lips. The car was cold and dark. Both of their coats were pulled up around their necks, but they couldn't risk showing any signs of life in the vehicle by turning on its lights or heating—the condensation on its windows would be a giveaway.

"Where's Belacourt?" he said.

Vasques took a swig of her coffee and replied, "Watching the alley up on the next block."

"Does he know I'm still here?"

"Nope."

"What's he going to do if he sees me?"

"Not sure. Smoke will probably come out of his ears. An aneurysm may be involved. But let me worry about that."

The Led Zeppelin song faded out on the radio, and the DJ ran through a list of news items. He mentioned the predicted snowstorm scheduled to hit the area, and then started talking about the upcoming winter solstice. Marcus grabbed the dial and turned up the volume.

"...and due to the lunar eclipse, this year's winter solstice will not only be the longest night, but also the darkest. And not just the darkest of this year, it's predicted to be the longest, darkest night of the past five hundred years."

Marcus said, "That's it. Whatever the Anarchist is planning will happen that night."

"You sure?"

"Darkest night in five hundred years. What better time to perform some kind of apocalyptic ritual?"

"But that's two days away, and he's only taken one victim that he hasn't killed. His pattern was two killed in four days and then five abducted over the next five days."

"Things change. Maybe he plans to escalate things. Or perhaps he's already taken three that we don't know about."

"Let's hope not."

"I can feel it. That's what he's working toward, and two days from now he'll have five sacrifices ready for his ritual. Unless we can stop him."

Vasques's police-band radio squawked to life, and Belacourt's voice came over the airwaves. "We've got a dark blue mid-size approaching the house. It could be a Camry. Everyone hold positions until I give the go, but this could be our guy."

71

WHILE SITTING OUTSIDE the home of the next sacrifice, a woman named Liz Hamilton, Schofield used one of the neighbors' unsecured wireless networks and accessed the camera feed inside the house. He watched as Liz slept peacefully, the covers rising and falling at slow, consistent intervals. Liz was an early to bed, early to rise kind of person.

Closing the laptop, he observed the falling snow and tried to work up the courage to do what had to be done. He had to know the Prophet's plans for the final ritual, and he could no longer delay the inevitable. He dialed the number from memory, and after three rings, the Prophet's slow and soothing Southern voice came over the phone.

"Do you have the girl, Harrison?"

Schofield's voice failed him. His tongue felt fat and useless in his mouth.

"Harrison? Are you there, boy? Did you get my message from earlier?"

"I'm here, Prophet. And I did receive your message."

"So you've stayed away?"

"Yes, sir. Just as you instructed…Sir, I…I was wondering about the final ritual."

"Just do as you're told. Don't concern yourself beyond that. I've made all the arrangements."

"That's what I'm afraid of. I need to know who the final three sacrifices are. I need—"

"How dare you question me! I speak for the Father. By questioning me, you are questioning him. We each have our roles to play. You focus on preparing yourself for the ascension, and let me handle the details."

Schofield bit down on his lip, and his whole body shook. He could almost feel the whip tearing into his back, ripping the flesh. The Prophet naked and screaming in some strange tongue. But he'd only been a boy then. A boy with a hollow soul. Now he was a man and had taken the strength of others.

He summoned all the strength and courage of his victims and said, "That's not good enough. Tell me! Who do you plan to use as the sacrifices?"

The Prophet was quiet. His slow breathing and the hiss of static filled the line. "I think you already know."

"They're not part of this. I'll never let you near them."

"You'll do as you're told."

"I won't let you hurt my family!"

"Why do you think I sent you back to live with your grandfather and lead a normal life?" The Prophet laughed. "You've honestly never considered it until now, have you? I gave my permission for you to have a family. They're mine. Your children only live because I allowed it. And why do you think that is?"

Schofield was quiet. Tears rolled down his cheeks.

"I allowed it because they provide what's been missing from the other rituals. When you were a boy, we made sacrifices, but they didn't really mean anything to you. It was the same last year. They weren't your sacrifices. It wasn't your choice. Your heart wasn't ready. It wasn't dark enough, hard enough. The last ritual was only to prepare for the darkest night. Everything we've worked for has been leading to this. The darkest night in five hundred years. Now you are ready. When you choose to sacrifice your own children to the Father, you will ascend to the throne. You will be the true Antichrist. This world will be no more, and a better one will be born from the ashes."

The fear and doubt flooded over Schofield, but he wiped away his tears and said, "No. I won't allow any harm to come to them. I'm tired of doing what you tell me to do. I'm not your puppet. I'm not that little boy anymore."

"You'll do as you're told!"

Schofield hung up the phone. Anger, fear, and confusion swirled inside his mind. The maelstrom threatened to tear him apart from within. It felt as though the pillars holding up his fragile world were crumbling, and the sky was falling down upon him. He was losing control and had no idea how to stop the downward spiral.

He looked toward the home of Liz Hamilton. He needed her strength. His confidence and power had grown with every kill, and if he wanted to protect his family and stop the Prophet, he would need all the souls he could get.

It was time for another sacrifice.

72

THE SUSPECT WAS just sitting in his car. Marcus could tell that it was a man, but little else could be discerned through the increasing snowfall. It appeared that the man had a cell phone to his ear. "It's not a Camry," he said.

Vasques lowered her binoculars and said, "It could definitely pass for one in the dark."

"Maybe."

Marcus's phone vibrated in his pocket. The display showed an unknown number, and he knew exactly what that meant. It had to be Ackerman. He pressed the power button on top of the phone to deny the call and avoid further distractions.

"Who was it?"

"Not important."

"Does he call you a lot?"

"All the damn time."

Belacourt's voice came over the radio, cutting their conversation short. "Okay, all units move in. We want him alive."

Marcus had overheard Vasques debating with Belacourt about how to handle any strange vehicles. She had persisted in her belief that they should allow the killer to approach the house and catch him in the act. She was worried that capturing the wrong person could alert the real killer to their presence. Belacourt had argued that they had no officers in the house, for fear of them being seen by the cameras, and they hadn't had time to loop the feed. He had been worried about the woman's safety. Marcus knew that they were both wrong and both right. Although, in this situation anyway, he agreed with Belacourt. Of course, he never would have told Vasques that.

The man in the car had put down the cell phone and was staring at some small device that he was cradling against the steering wheel. The bright LED display of the device lit the man's features with an eerie glow. It could have been some type of remote video monitoring system.

Marcus watched as the police units converged on the dark blue sedan. Four SWAT team members in full body armor approached unseen alongside a neighbor's house. Then three of the unmarked vehicles drove up, waiting to hit the lights until they were right on top of the suspect vehicle. The cars skidded to a halt and blocked the target vehicle in on all sides. Coordinating with the vehicles, the SWAT team scrambled through the snow and surrounded the sedan. The officers in the cars had their guns drawn and covered the suspect. The whole thing took only a few seconds, and the suspect was secure.

The man was wearing jeans and a button-down dress shirt with some type of logo on the left-hand pocket. He wasn't dressed all in black or even dressed appropriately to go trudging through the snow.

Vasques swore under her breath. "It's not him."

"No, just a guy who parked on the wrong street. I'm betting that was a GPS unit that he was looking at. He's lost."

"Dammit, if the Anarchist was out there watching, he's definitely gone now."

Marcus took another long swig of coffee and said, "He's not here. We're in the wrong place."

73

SCHOFIELD HEARD SOFT music playing inside Liz Hamilton's bedroom. It was some type of acoustic coffee-house rock. Her living room smelled like a forest. A beautiful Fraser Fir Christmas tree covered with decorative orbs and lights and topped by an angel blocked the home's front window. It was a healthy and fragrant tree. An expensive one that seemed out of place in the modest single-bedroom home. He looked up at the angel perched near the ceiling. Its eyes seemed to follow him accusingly.

The door to the bedroom lay only a few feet away, and the animal part of his brain was exhilarated by the proximity and by what he was about to do. He had no plans to drug this woman and deliver her to the Prophet. He had no plans to shoot this one. This time, he would demonstrate his newfound strength by overpowering her and consuming her soul. He was about to force the type of confrontation that he had previously worked so hard to avoid, and in prospect, the act felt strangely liberating. It would give him confidence that he would finally be able to face the Prophet. It would prove that he was indeed stronger than he had ever been.

Knowing that if he thought too long about it then the unknown variables and risks would prove too dissuasive, he acted quickly and rashly. He kicked in the door. The lock plate cracked easily from the frame, and the door swung inward.

The light from the living room flooded into the bedroom and lit Liz Hamilton's face. The noise and light caused her to spring up, instantly alert. She looked directly at him. Her shrill cry filled the bedroom and made him hesitate for just a split second. But it provided enough time for Liz to roll from her bed and lunge into the attached master bathroom. She slammed the door in his face.

He stepped back to kick it in, but then he realized her plan. He knew the layout of her house as well as she did. The bathroom connected to a small laundry room that in turn opened back into the kitchen. She wasn't locking herself in the bathroom. She was heading for the back door off the kitchen.

Trying to block her escape, Schofield turned back and ran through the ruined door of the bedroom, past the Fraser Fir in the living room, and into the home's kitchen.

He slid around the corner on the dark linoleum. The kitchen lights were dark, but a window above the sink provided access for ambient illumination. He could see Liz's dark shape in the shadows. The thrill of the hunt had his adrenaline pumping. He felt alive. She grabbed for something on the counter and lunged forward.

With a speed born of pure animal instinct, he pulled to the side and barely avoided taking the knife in the center of his abdomen. It sliced through his black jacket. He was not normally a fighter, but that didn't mean that he lacked the ability to defend himself. He slapped the knife from her hand and lunged for her throat.

His weight overpowered her, and they fell to the ground, his hands crushing her larynx. Liz tried to scream, but it died in her throat as a harsh choking rasp. Her fingers clawed up at him.

A light burst through the window in the back door. His stare shot in that direction—he was half expecting to see a policeman aiming a gun and a Maglite through the glass. But there was nothing there. It must have been another car driving through the alley. Luckily, he had pulled his Camry far enough into Liz's yard to allow the car to pass.

Schofield heard a noise and looked back down in time to

see Liz pull a nearby drawer completely out of the cabinet
and slam it against his head.

Falling backward away from her, he landed flat on his
back on the dark linoleum. He reached to his head and found
it bloody and aching. The sudden pain brought a moment of
clarity, and he wondered what he had been thinking. Had
he wanted to be caught this time?

The sound of her footfalls scurried toward the bathroom,
and he pulled himself up from the floor.

Stumbling after her in pursuit, he grabbed the handle of
the bathroom door and shook it. Locked. The doors were
cheap hollow-cores, and he kicked it in easily. She had already moved through the other door and into the bedroom.

She looked back and screamed again as he rushed from
the shadows. He tackled her down onto the bed and pounded
his fists against her. Another scream filled the air, and it
took him a moment to realize that it was coming from deep
in his own throat.

She pulled away and tried to crawl across the bed, but
he grabbed her legs and wrenched her back beneath him.

His hands found her neck again, and he squeezed even
tighter than before. The light from the living room shone
over her face, which was turning purple as she fought for
air. She clawed at his hands, scratching against his gloves.
Then she swiped at his neck, and her nails dug into the skin
on the side of his throat.

He screamed again and shook her, pressing her farther
down into the folds of the blankets and mattress. His fingers
were like a vise, and he could see the strength leaving her.

She was a blond just like his oldest daughter, Alison. He
had never noticed the resemblance before, but he saw it now.
He thought of his wife and children and what the Prophet
would do if he found them.

He regretted having to hurt this woman. He regretted
being forced to kill them all. He had never wanted any of
this. But if he had to choose between the sacrificed women

and his family, the decision was simple. He had always gone along with the Prophet before for fear that the older man would hurt his wife and children, but it had also made him stronger. That was the Prophet's mistake. The killings had filled Schofield's hollow heart and given him the strength to fight back. A strength that he had never known before.

Liz's arms continued to flop ineffectually against him for a few more seconds, but then they fell limp. He looked deep into her eyes as she lost her grip on this world and slipped away.

He caught her soul, her life force, and drank it in.

He debated on whether to leave a signature, but he supposed that it didn't really matter. Prison wasn't an option for him. If the police tied him to one murder, that would be more than sufficient to destroy his life. So he removed a small folding knife from his pocket and carved the Circle A into her forehead. Then he slit her wrists and used her blood to smear a large Circle A on the wall. He rubbed some more blood into his mouth and felt more of her power enter him.

The house was a mess, debris from the confrontation and other evidence everywhere. This was exactly what Schofield had always tried to avoid. His fingers found the gash on his neck, and he looked down at Liz's hands. His DNA would be there for sure and maybe in other places in the house from the wound on his head.

And they had also made a lot of noise. A neighbor might have called the police. They could be on their way at that moment. They could be approaching the house, closing in on him.

Pulling his silenced pistol, Schofield checked out the windows and then stepped into the backyard. He didn't see anyone looking out their windows, but that didn't mean that they hadn't called the police and retreated to the safety of their homes. He needed to be quick.

Inside Liz's garage he found a pair of hedge clippers. Then he went back inside and, after dropping the garden tool onto her bed, retrieved a gallon of bleach from the laundry room. Starting in the kitchen, he dumped the bleach anywhere he thought he might have dripped blood. After following the trail back to the bedroom with the bleach, he soaked the body and the sheets. Then he looked down at the woman's fingers. Knowing what had to be done, he picked up the hedge clippers.

74

SITTING IN THE basement of his antiques shop, the Prophet prepared to confer with his master about the complications arising from Schofield's defiance. He placed three pieces of blotter paper treated with lysergic acid diethylamide—or LSD—into his mouth. Most hits of acid obtained on the street contained a mere one hundred micrograms or less per hit, but in order to break down the walls of this reality and contact the other side, the Prophet employed a dose containing four milligrams. He had no fear of overdose, since no documented human deaths had ever been caused directly from the use of LSD. The only downside of the drug for him was that regular use caused a rapid tolerance buildup due to the down-regulation of 5-HT2A receptors in the brain. Luckily, his tolerance would diminish after several days without use, so there was little fear of his lines of communication with the Father ever being severed.

The drug could be absorbed either sublingually by holding it in the mouth or in the stomach if it was swallowed. But sublingual absorption led to a faster onset of the drug's effects. The Prophet needed answers now, so he held the pieces of blotter paper in his mouth for several moments, chewing them and rubbing them on his tongue, before swallowing.

He stood up from the old wooden table and walked across the cold concrete floor to the sturdy cage that held the girl. He was naked and each step sent lovely tendrils of sensation up through his body. Schofield had said the girl's name was Melissa Lighthaus, but the Prophet didn't care about her name. She was just another dumb animal, a piece of livestock, to be used and thrown away. She was merely another one of the slaves that would soon die in *The Great Fire*.

He had soundproofed the block walls of the old basement in order to contain the screams of the women it held. This was especially necessary since the old basement actually extended farther out than the building's upper floors. The sidewalk was directly above the cage. The thought of the other slaves passing over her without any knowledge excited the Prophet. He had shared this information with her to add to her despair. So many people, so close. Yet no one could help her.

The effects of his medicine were taking hold, and *the sight* would be upon him soon. Reality was already changing around him, breaking down. What none of the slaves realized was that hell wasn't in another place. It was all around them at all times. But on the darkest night, when the ritual was complete, the barriers placed around this world that kept the Father out would be no more. It would be such a glorious day when the walls crumbled. When hell and Earth would finally become one. Mankind was approaching the next momentous and inevitable step in its evolution. Soon, *The Work* would be complete, and he would step out from among the slaves and sit at the right hand of the true god.

But until that day came, he enjoyed being underground. It made him feel more connected to the Father by being separate from the world of the slaves.

The girl cowered in the corner of the cage. Her skin seemed to glow. Her eyes were bright purple orbs shining out from inside her skull. Her stink permeated the air from the bucket he had placed in one corner of the cage for her to use as a bathroom. But soon the smell would no longer be a bother. He could taste the metallic tinge of the medicine on his tongue as the other side began to bleed through. The padded walls were breathing around him. Eyes watched him from the dark corners of the basement. The shadows were alive, pregnant with the dark ones. The concrete had melted and now it rippled beneath him. His feet were sticking to it and sinking into it, and it took great power to pull them free and move across the room.

The basement was a large open space supported by concrete pillars. In its center, there was a large black pentagram painted onto the floor. Tall mirrors lined up with each of the symbol's five points. A black metal stool rested within the pentagram's center. The Prophet entered the sacred circle, sat on the stool, and waited.

The shadows along the outer perimeter of the circle changed forms. Oily black figures swirled all around him now, the dark ones. His thoughts curved in on themselves as he broke through to the other side of reality. Strange shapes crawled across the concrete. His reflection in the mirrors disappeared, and a smoky darkness swam on the other side of the glass.

"Father, Schofield has betrayed us. He has rejected *The Work* and rebelled against us both. I need guidance. The darkest night is so close." He closed his eyes and waited for the Father to show him the way. Strange colored patterns swirled behind his eyelids like a vivid kaleidoscope that transcended time and space.

Then a face emerged from the ocean of colors.

The Prophet opened his eyes and spoke into the darkness. "The boy is of the bloodline, and we've been preparing for this day. Still, I don't know if he's ready. But it's not my place to question your will, Father. The boy *will* be the new Chosen. The true Antichrist."

75

VASQUES WALKED THROUGH Liz Hamilton's home as if in a daze. The whole place smelled of bleach and showed obvious signs of a struggle. Crime-scene techs were pouring in and unpacking their equipment. The scene was still fresh.

Less than an hour before her arrival, a neighbor had reported some strange noises coming from Ms. Hamilton's home. Two officers had been dispatched and had found the body. After that, there had been little point in watching the other woman's house, but they still left a few officers and the four members of SWAT, just in case. Belacourt stood near the body, conferring with Stupak and another of the detectives from the Major Crimes Task Force. Belacourt's clothes were wrinkled and worn, while Stupak looked like an investment banker with his expensive suit, perfectly shaved black head, and sculpted goatee.

As she took in the scene, Vasques couldn't comprehend that this could have been the same man. The carnage and violence were completely out of character for the Anarchist.

Belacourt walked over and said, "What do you think?"

"It doesn't make any sense."

"I agree," Belacourt said, stroking his mustache. "This has to be the work of a copycat."

"Have you checked the attic for cameras?"

"Not yet, but we will."

"You should get a handwriting guy to analyze the writing on the wall and the victim's forehead. If we find the same cameras and the handwriting matches, then we'll know for sure that this was him."

"I just don't understand this one," Belacourt said. "For God's sake, he cut her fingers off with a pair of hedge clippers. If this was the Anarchist, then he's getting sloppy. Losing his damn mind. But that will make him easier to catch."

Vasques bent over the body and looked into Liz Hamilton's eyes. "It may, but it could also make things infinitely worse. If this was him, then he's definitely escalating, becoming even more dangerous. I've got a bad feeling that there's going to be a lot more bloodshed before this is over."

76

MARCUS LEANED BACK against the headrest of the Crown Vic and growled to himself. He looked toward the front of Liz Hamilton's house. It was old and small, but well kept. Apartments that looked government-subsidized lined the opposite side of the street. Officers had set up a perimeter, but the apartments had emptied as the neighbors fought for a good view. It was like some kind of macabre block party. They could probably see as much as he could, which wasn't much. There was a fresh crime scene and a dead woman in that house, and his own stupidity had made it so that he couldn't visit it. He wasn't sure how Belacourt would react at seeing that he was still in town, and he didn't need the extra complications. He couldn't afford another wasted night in jail. As much as he hated to, he would have to trust Vasques's assessment of the scene.

He was tired and felt useless, but there was more than just the case weighing on his mind. Ackerman's words from earlier that morning kept repeating in his head. Could the killer have been telling the truth? Was there a reason why Ackerman had been chosen for his recruitment? It wouldn't be the first time that the Director had lied to him or deliberately withheld things from him.

Grabbing for his phone, Marcus dialed Emily Morgan. It took six rings for her to answer, and when she did, she sounded groggy. "Hello?" The word was punctuated with a yawn.

"I'm sorry for waking you."

"Don't be, it's what I'm here for. What's going on?"

"Do you know anything that you haven't told me?"

"I'm not sure what you mean."

"Have you ever seen my file?"

She was silent for a moment but then said, "I don't have access. Only the Director is allowed to view personnel files. I've requested to see them, but he won't allow it."

Ackerman's words came back to him again. *I've never lied to you, Marcus. Unlike everyone else in your life.*

"How are you supposed to treat us from a psychiatric standpoint if you're kept in the dark about our pasts?"

"I've asked the same thing, but the Director feels that I should only know what you want me to know."

"What about the things that we don't even know ourselves?" he said.

"Like what?"

"Ackerman told me that he and I were connected and that there's a reason why he was chosen for my recruitment. Something that the Director's keeping from me."

"Do you have any ideas?"

"In the sessions where you were helping me remember the night my parents died, I kept hearing that voice in the darkness that comforted me while they were screaming downstairs."

Emily yawned again over the phone, and Marcus remembered that it was actually an hour later in DC. "We had talked about that. Many researchers refer to it as the Angel Effect and believe that when people have a traumatic or near-death experience, their subconscious minds manifest a comforting voice or figure to help their brains deal with the situation." She hesitated for a moment. "Then again, I do believe in God and angels. So it wouldn't surprise me if you did have a guardian angel watching over you that night."

"Yeah, maybe I did."

Emily started to say something more, but Marcus's phone showed another call coming through. It was Maggie. "Emily, I need to go. I'll call you tomorrow."

He clicked over to Maggie and said, "What's happening?"

A hint of fear permeated Maggie's voice, evident in the tremor of her speech and the shallowness of her breathing. "I just got a call from Ackerman."

Marcus jerked up in his seat. The killer had never involved another member of the team in such a way. "Are you okay?"

"I'm fine. He wanted me to give you a message immediately. He said that he has important information for you about the case and that I should tell you to answer your damn phone."

As if on cue, the unknown number appeared on the screen. *Speak of the devil.* "He's calling now."

"Call me back."

This time, Marcus accepted the call and said, "I don't need your help."

Ackerman laughed. "That's highly debatable. Does this mean that you don't want to hear what I learned from your friend Crowley?"

Marcus's fingers clenched around the phone, and his teeth ground against each other. He didn't want Ackerman's help, but innocent people's lives were on the line. He wondered if, by accepting the information, he was condoning the methods used to obtain it.

"Are you still there, Marcus?"

"What did you do with Crowley?"

"I wouldn't worry about him. Did you know he was a pedophile?"

Marcus noted Ackerman's use of the past tense. "Is he dead?"

"If I were you, I would worry more about the Anarchist and saving those poor, innocent women. Leave Crowley to rot."

Marcus closed his eyes and thought of the monster he could feel himself becoming. There had been a time when he would have taken the moral high road, a time when there were values that he held above all else. The world had once seemed so black and white, good and evil. But now everything was cold and gray. The lines between right and wrong had blurred to the point that he no longer understood on which side he stood.

"Tell me what you've learned."

77

SCHOFIELD PULLED OVER along the road on an overpass cross-ing above I-80. His tires bumped over the rumble strips until the vehicle came to rest. The coppery taste of blood was still fresh in his mouth. It collided in his mind with the scent of the Fraser Fir in Liz Hamilton's living room and combined into some strange metallic amalgam that made him feel queasy. He looked over at the plastic bag sitting on the pas-senger seat, and the nauseous swirl in the pit of his stomach could no longer be contained. He threw open the door and vomited alongside the roadway.

He looked over the edge at the cars zooming past on the interstate and considered jumping. Even if the fall didn't kill him, surely an unsuspecting motorist would. In that moment, he knew that the life he had wanted could never be his. The analysis and calculation of variables had always come easy to him. He supposed that he should have predicted this in-evitable outcome, but he had never wanted to believe that it would all crumble down. He just wanted to be a whole per-son for his family, but now his actions had placed them in grave danger. He needed to be strong for them.

Making his decision, one that would change everything forever, he dialed his wife's number. She answered after several rings. "Hello?"

"Eleanor, listen to me very carefully."

"Harrison?"

"Yes, honey. I need you to trust me right now and not question me. Just do exactly as I say."

"You're scaring me."

"You should be scared. Get the kids and get out of the house right now. Just throw on some clothes and go. Go to a motel."

"What? Where?"

"There's a place called the Belmont Motel in Brookfield. Check in under the name Patricia Raymond, and pay cash. Leave your cell phones at the house. I'll call you tomorrow at the motel."

"Tell me what's going on." The fear and doubt in her voice broke his heart.

"There's no time. Just do exactly as I said. I'm going to get enough money for us to get away from the city."

"Are you in some kind of trouble?"

"You have to trust me. We're all in very serious danger."

"Okay."

"I love you all so much…and I'm sorry." He hung up without waiting for her reply, for fear that she would not reciprocate his feelings.

His gaze traveled back to the plastic bag on the passenger seat. He needed to find a place to dispose of the fingers.

78

KEISHA SCHUYLER SHOULD have been the next Jackie Joyner-Kersee. Her face should have appeared on Wheaties boxes and Nike ads. She had been able to run the fifty-meter hurdles in 6.69 seconds, nearly beating the US record. And she was getting better and better. Although she had been born pigeon-toed to the point of it being a handicap, when she ran the crookedness of her body corrected itself. In fact, on the track was the only time anything felt natural to her.

A knee injury and a bout with prescription-drug and alcohol addiction had stolen all her hopes and dreams, leaving her an empty shell of a human being. Her continued addictions cost her another good career and landed her in rehab. But that was also where she had met Greg, her sponsor and future husband.

Now, with Greg's help, her life was finally getting back on track.

Keisha checked the time. With a yawn, she said, "Come on, baby. It's really late. We need to get to bed."

Greg grumbled and said, "We're on vacation, remember."

"That's right. And I don't want to sleep the whole time. We need to be on the road by four at the latest."

"Okay, you win," Greg said as he shut off the movie.

They had both taken the next week off from work and were leaving the following afternoon after Keisha's stepdaughter, Rhaelyn, came home from school. They were headed to Seattle. Keisha's parents had moved there three years ago, and she had yet to see their new house. So they had decided to head out for a visit.

She stood up from the couch, her knee protesting at the movement. The pain was always worse during the winter. She smiled at her husband and gave him a little wink. He leaned in and kissed her. Greg was such a caring and handsome man with his large frame, dark black hair, and big brown eyes. And he could even cook.

Life had finally settled into a comfortable and secure rhythm. And for the first time in a long time, everything seemed to be going Keisha's way.

79

THE PROPHET'S ANGER was a bright red. He could see the pulses of color radiating from his hands and arms as he gripped the steering wheel of the white Ford Taurus. He had just left the Schofield residence. It sat empty and in shambles. The family had been warned. Another betrayal at the hands of the former *Chosen*, but he would find them. With the Father on his side, he was invincible.

But while he worked out a way to track down Eleanor and the children, he also knew that he needed to acquire another of the slaves for use in the ritual. He needed five. One for each point of the pentagram.

Unlike Schofield, whose eccentricities when choosing the sacrifice had always been an annoyance but one that he had indulged, the Prophet didn't care to know the ignorant piece of meat before abducting her. He didn't feel the need for any type of dramatics beyond the ritual. No Circle A signatures scrawled on the walls. Just another meaningless slave to be sacrificed to the Father. Nothing more, nothing less. The dark ones would lead him to the next sacrifice, as it should have been all along.

He popped another piece of blotter paper treated with LSD into his mouth, to ensure that he could see the world as it truly was without the hindrance of the mortal coil. He sat there for a few moments. The snow falling all around him was lit from within like the small bioluminescent creatures living in the darkest parts of the ocean. The air was heavy as if it had become a liquid, and it smelled like rage. The suburban street swelled and contracted around him. It wasn't that the houses had necessarily changed. It was more that they were alive, that they were breathing.

Then a section of the shadows coalesced into an oily amorphous figure. The figured moved away from him leaving tracer lines of black behind. The Prophet placed the Taurus into drive and then tried his best to keep the vehicle between the glowing and undulating lines on the road as he pursued the dark one down the street.

80

Keisha Schuyler padded across the dark burgundy carpet and flipped down the lock for the sliding glass door that led to the patio at the side of their home. Her hand stretched up beneath the dark brown curtain on the door's left-hand side to flip off the patio light, but she froze in place. She hesitated for a second, and then she screamed.

There was a man approaching her back door. He was dressed all in black, and the look on his face told her all she needed to know. His eyes were wide and angry, and his face was haggard.

She stumbled back from the door and tripped over the cedar coffee table. The sound of her husband's footfalls pounded down the stairs. "Greg!" she yelled. But the words had barely left her throat when the man in black grabbed a chair from their patio set and threw it through the glass. Shards exploded into the living room, and the chair twisted in the air and slammed into the cedar table near where she had fallen.

The man kicked out the remaining glass and stepped inside. Keisha back-pedaled on her hands and rear. Her bad knee shot pains down her leg, but the adrenaline overpowered the discomfort.

Greg ran through the archway into the living room. He held up a baseball bat, ready to swing on the intruder.

The man's face showed no change, just the same wide-eyed stare. His eyes seemed distant. Then he raised his arm, and Keisha noticed the large revolver for the first time.

She opened her mouth to yell for Greg to run, but before

she could utter the words the big pistol spat fire. Greg's left leg flew out from beneath him, and he slammed down face-first onto the burgundy carpet.

The noise of the gunshot left her ears ringing even from several feet away. Everything felt so surreal, like something happening to someone else in a movie.

Greg's screams echoed off the walls, and he tried to crawl away.

But the man in black stepped casually over to him and fired again.

Greg's body jerked violently from the bullet's massive impact, but then he lay perfectly still.

Keisha bolted for the stairs and her stepdaughter's second-floor bedroom, but another blast into the wall in front of her made her stumble back from the steps.

"Don't move. Get down on your knees." The man's slow Southern drawl surprised her. It was the type of voice she might have expected from a plantation owner living two hundred years ago. Not a country accent, but more that of a Southern aristocrat or professor.

"Please! Take whatever you—"

"Be quiet. I want you alive, but that doesn't mean that I can't put a hole in you. Maybe somewhere especially painful and debilitating. Like the kneecap. With a cannon like this, it's liable to blow your leg clean off."

The tears ran down Keisha's cheeks, and she stifled a whimper as she fell to her knees. The man in black stepped forward and placed the barrel of the big gun against her forehead. It was still hot from his past three shots and burned her skin. But she dared not flinch. Her whole body trembled, and she closed her eyes, certain that her life was now over. Her only hope was that her stepdaughter had heard the noises and would find a hiding place rather than coming to help.

She heard a muffled thump in front of her and opened her eyes. A pair of handcuffs and a syringe rested on the carpet. "Inject that into your arm and then put on the handcuffs. Arms behind your back."

"Please, I—"

The man cocked back the revolver's hammer. It was a sharp sound that grated across her eardrum. "You have three seconds to decide whether you want that needle in your arm or a bullet in your brain." As she picked up and plunged the needle, she thought of her stepdaughter. She had complied more for the girl's sake than her own. If Greg's killer had Keisha, he wouldn't need to search the rest of the house, and Rhaelyn might have a chance.

She locked the handcuffs around her wrists. The man in black pulled her up from the ground and shoved her past the dead body of the only man she had ever loved and toward the door.

81

AFTER ACKERMAN'S CALL, Marcus had contacted Maggie and asked her to pick him up in the Yukon. They needed to take a little trip up north, and he wanted some time alone with her to talk about what had been going on between them. Then he had called Stan and relayed to him what Ackerman had learned from Crowley. They needed a possible location for the cult's former compound and more information on the man called Conlan, who apparently went by the name of The Prophet.

He had also sent Andrew and Vasques over to investigate Crowley's shop and see if the man could still be alive. The call had come back quickly that Crowley was dead. But he hadn't been simply murdered, he had been nearly cut in half. Andrew had seemed extremely shaken by what he had seen, and that was saying something coming from a man who worked around the macabre on a daily basis. Marcus couldn't help but feel responsible for Crowley's death, but he couldn't quite make himself feel sorry about it. Crowley had been found in a torture room of his own design, and they had also found tapes of the man abusing young boys. If anyone had deserved such an encounter with Ackerman, it was Vassago Crowley. And in some deep animal part of Marcus's mind, he wished that he could have extracted the information himself.

Knowing that the compound was somewhere in Wisconsin's Jefferson County, he had taken I-290 up to Route 53 and then across to Route 12. Along the way, they had passed through all manner of terrain, from suburban to rural to forest. They would be in Jefferson County within a couple of hours, just before sunrise. With luck, Stan would have a location for them by then.

Maggie had been silent for most of the drive, and Marcus couldn't quite find the words to express his feelings. He drummed his fingers against the steering wheel and said the first thing that came to mind. "What's the deal with you and this Rowland guy?"

"Why? Are you jealous?"

"We're not teenagers, Maggie."

"Only teenagers can be jealous?"

"I'm just saying that he doesn't seem like a good fit for you."

"You haven't even met the guy."

"I know the type. Rowland shouldn't even call himself a satanist. People like that should just be honest and say that they're selfish. How could you be interested in a guy who thinks that people should be their own god and only be concerned with their own desires and what makes them happy?"

She turned in the passenger seat to face him. The leather squeaked beneath her, and the movement stirred the scent of her perfume into the air. It was both sweet and fragrant, like orchids mixed with honey.

"Explain this to me," Maggie said, "because I'm a bit confused. You're not jealous because another guy asked me out: you're simply worried about my soul."

"Never mind. Forget I said anything."

"I'm just trying to understand where you're coming from." Marcus said nothing, and the silence stretched out.

After a few moments, she said, "Do you love me or not?"

The bluntness of the question shocked Marcus and made him hesitate. He wasn't sure how to respond to something like that.

Apparently taking his silence as a negative, Maggie said, "I guess that's my answer."

"It's not as simple as all that."

"Yes, it is. Either you do or you don't."

"It doesn't matter either way. You just don't understand that. What did you think would happen? That we'd get married, have kids, and bring them along on cases? There was a time when all that I wanted was to be normal. Settle down with you and start a family. But I can't do that, because I'm not normal. I'm just as broken as the men we hunt."

"I can't quit the Shepherd Organization, if that's what you want," she said.

"I don't know what I want. But I know now that I can't run from what I am."

A long, cold silence accompanied them down Route 12 past houses and businesses and bare trees. They were all vague shapes at the dark edges of the headlights' beam. The snowfall had tapered off as they drove, and the snowplows were out in force. They had already seen three of them along the way. But Marcus had heard that the worst of the storm was still on its way.

THEY DROVE IN silence until they reached the northernmost edge of Jefferson County, but Stan still hadn't called back with the information they needed. Marcus decided to fill up the Yukon, and if Stan hadn't called by the time they pulled from the pump, he'd make a call of his own.

He pulled the Yukon up to the third pump of four at a small red and white Citgo station with a separate car wash in back. He hadn't caught the name of the town, but the gas station appeared to be the hub of village commerce.

Stamping his feet and blowing on his hands to combat the chill in the air, he watched the numbers on the pump tick past the sixty-dollar mark. Then his phone rang.

"What did you find, Stan? We're flying blind up here."

"Okay, I've learned quite a bit about our new friend Conlan. Full name Anthony Mason Conlan."

"Wait. His first name is Anthony?"

"Does that mean something to you?"

"Yeah, it does. It means that Vasques's dad has been a step ahead of us this whole time. After he died, she found a note on his desk that referred to *Anthony C.* He must have been onto something."

"If he knew about Conlan, then he definitely was. This dude is an A-number-1 nutball. When he was a boy, a doctor tried to diagnose him with a mild form of schizophrenia, but Conlan's rich daddy wouldn't hear of it. So the kid grows up and joins the military. He became a lieutenant in the army and volunteered for some experiments conducted in the late 1960s and early 1970s. It was codenamed Project

Kaleidoscope. They were dosing the grunts with LSD, synthetic marijuana, and two dozen other psychoactive drugs. All to develop chemical weapons that could incapacitate enemy soldiers. Very illegal."

Marcus said, "Sounds a lot like the MK-ULTRA project the CIA had going."

"Yeah, right along the same lines. But in 1981, a study was conducted that claimed the participants of the experiments suffered no long-term effects. Conlan wasn't involved in the study because he had dropped off the grid by then."

"There has to be more to it than that."

"I'm getting there, boss. You gotta let me roll it all out for you nice and sweet. So, anyway, I dug deeper into the actual classified journals of the head researcher. A dude by the name of Dr. Ted Uhrig. And Dr. Teddy had a lot to say about our man Conlan. Apparently, during the experiments, the nutball freaked out and claimed to have been receiving messages from the devil himself. So fast forward a few years, and Conlan had started his first cult at his father's plantation in Georgia. Then daddy kicks the bucket—under suspicious circumstances—and leaves a small fortune to his only son, who has now started to go by the name of *The Prophet*."

A man in a beat-up Chevy truck pulled up behind Marcus at the pump and honked his horn. Marcus replied with a form of sign language that he had learned at a young age back in Brooklyn. It involved liberal use of the middle finger.

"Where's Conlan now?" he said into the phone.

"Completely off the grid. If he's alive, then he must be using a false identity."

"Okay, keep looking. What about the location of the compound?"

"I found several landowners named Bowman or Beaman in Jefferson County, but I cross-referenced topography and the time period. Came up with one old guy named Otis. Which sounds like a dog's name to me, or maybe a cow's, but I suppose it was probably more common back in the day. Anyway, you got lucky. The old man still lives there. I'm texting you the address and directions."

83

MARCUS HAD TO guess at where Otis Beaman's drive actually ran. It was just an old dirt lane that had been completely covered over with snow. Luckily, the Yukon was a powerful four-wheel drive and could push through just about anything. The farm itself sat on a hundred and twenty acres nestled back in the trees. They passed a few fields that probably would have been pregnant with corn during the summer but now sat barren and empty. The lane followed an old fence made from three rows of wooden beams, but the fence had rotted and fallen apart in many sections.

Outbuildings and an old barn and silo dotted the property. The barn's snow-capped roof was sagging in from the weight. It had once been a grand structure with several lean-tos jutting off from its sides. It had probably started off red but now it was the color of dark soil and old rust. The house itself was built in a modest Cape Cod style—one and a half stories with a steep pitched roof and end gables. It had been added onto a few times throughout the years, but now the old white siding was crumbling and nearly stripped of paint. Rusty machinery and implements littered the grounds, and an old orange International Harvester Scout truck sat in the driveway. It was a small and boxy type of vehicle that Marcus couldn't recall ever seeing out on the road.

They plowed their way up through the driveway and stepped out into the snow. It came up to Marcus's shins and fell over the top of his tennis shoes and jeans. The air was sweet and pure but also freezing. The snowfall had stopped but the temperature had fallen as they'd traveled farther north.

The sun was still young in the sky, but farmers were usually early to bed and early to rise. And Marcus didn't really care if they woke the old man or not. The doorbell didn't work, but a moment's worth of banging brought Otis Beaman to the door. His face was thin and wrinkled. He had wispy gray hair and a Wilford Brimley mustache.

But he was also tall, and he struck Marcus as a guy who had once been formidable even if he had been ravaged by the years.

"Otis Beaman?"

"Yes." Beaman's voice was quiet, but gravelly.

Marcus flashed an FBI badge, since people often responded better to those credentials. The Bureau was a well-known law-enforcement body. When he flashed his DOJ creds, people thought he was there to collect back taxes or something equally absurd, and explaining took unnecessary time. "We're here to ask you a few questions about a man named Anthony Conlan."

A strange look passed over the old man's lined face. *Shame? Sadness?* With a nod, Beaman seemed to come to a decision. "Come on in."

Everything in the house seemed old and worn. The brown patterned carpet was thin and well-used. A dusty upright piano sat in a corner beneath family photos, some of them black and white. There was a curio cabinet filled with knick-knacks and antiques and a nineteen-inch console television along one wall facing a couch. The couch had a floral pattern, but the design had been worn off the center cushion.

Beaman pulled in a white high-backed vinyl chair from the kitchen table and directed them to sit on the couch. "I'm surprised it took so long for someone to come asking about Conlan. I expected you years ago. I've thought many times about what I would say."

"Why don't you just start at the beginning, Mr. Beaman?"

"You have to understand that at the time the bank was preparing to foreclose on my farm. It was a tough year, and I had three kids and a wife to think of. When Conlan first came to me, I thought my prayers had been answered, that God had provided me with the means to save my farm. But now I know that it was a test. Matthew 16:26: 'For what is a man profited, if he shall gain the whole world, and lose his own soul?'"

Beaman fell silent, his eyes distant. Marcus said, "What did Conlan want?"

"He said that he wanted the use of a remote piece of land on my property. Said that he was the leader of a small religious group that wanted to avoid persecution for their beliefs. He offered me a fat load of money to allow them to build some kind of bunker up there and keep it quiet. I asked around a bit, and he had approached others in the area as well. Some of them were considering it."

"So you agreed?"

"That land was good for nothing to me. Just timber. I prayed about it for two days, and I had the distinct feeling that God was telling me to turn him down. But I didn't listen. The letters from the bank kept coming and telling me something different. I didn't like it. Guy seemed off to me. But I had my pride and a family to consider. So I agreed, took the money. Sold my soul to the devil for a damn farm."

"What were they doing up there?"

"I don't know. It was part of the deal that I never tell anyone about it or meddle in their business. They built their bunker and lived out there for over two years. Never heard a peep from them. No problems at all. They had one big fellow with crooked teeth who was the only one that ever left the woods. He would go into town and get supplies. I think he was driving around the whole day, buying small amounts from several different grocery stores so that it wouldn't seem suspicious. Then one day his old van pulled out, and he had others with him. I was out doing chores, and I saw Conlan's face in the passenger seat. Didn't think much of it. None of my business. But they never came back."

Tears formed in Beaman's eyes, and his gaze fell to the brown patterned carpet. Maggie said, "Did you ever go out to the compound?"

Beaman nodded. "I knew that they couldn't have all their people in that van. I didn't know how many were out there, but I knew there were families. Eventually, I went to check."

The old man went silent, but neither of them prodded him to continue. After a moment, he spoke in a quivering voice. "I'll never forget that smell. I'm a farmer. I been around death plenty of times, but this was different. This was evil. And I knew that I had damned myself. All for Conlan's fat load of money. I sealed up the entrance and never looked back. Even told my wife that I didn't find anything."

Beaman covered his face with the gnarled old hands of a farmer.

Marcus leaned forward and placed a hand on the old man's shoulder. "Whatever happened out there would have just happened somewhere else. You made a mistake, but this is your chance to set it right." Beaman met his gaze, and Marcus added, "We need to see that compound."

AFTER NEARLY AN hour of searching for the correct spot and tromping through the snow in boots borrowed from the old man, they finally found the bunker's entrance. Beaman had brought along a shovel, and Marcus dug the entrance clear of snow and dirt. The rusted metal doors were only a few feet beneath the surface. It reminded Marcus of the door to a cellar, except that in this case there was no house above it.

Marcus looked around the area. It sat on a slight hill, but there were no outward signs of the bunker. "I don't see any intake or exhaust pipes."

"I cut those off and filled them in," Beaman replied.

"That means the air might not be very good and there's nowhere for our carbon dioxide to go. We'll leave the doors open and only stay down a few minutes. But if you start feeling strange or light-headed, we get out immediately."

Maggie and Beaman nodded.

Using the end of the shovel, Marcus pried open the doors. He expected to find a set of stairs but instead there was an old metal ladder bolted into the concrete blocks. The shaft was as wide as the cellar doors and descended into darkness. The ladder did make more sense; stairs would have taken up a lot of space. He shone the Maglite down into the hole. The floor looked stable enough.

"I'll go first."

Marcus stepped down onto the first rung of the ladder and tested its strength. It seemed sturdy, so he began his descent. Along the way, he noticed that the bunker's top seemed to be constructed of wooden support beams topped with corrugated metal. He reached the bottom and tested the wooden floor. It was made from thick sheets of plywood, but no carpet or other material covered it. There were only a few rugs and blankets scattered about. The plywood creaked under his weight but gave no indication that it would cave in.

"Come on down."

As the sound of feet on the metal rungs echoed off the bunker's walls, Marcus examined the space. The right wall was constructed from gray concrete blocks. A blackboard hung from it. There was a large circular rug sitting in front of a stool near the blackboard. *A schoolroom?* The wall at his back that held the ladder was also made from concrete blocks, but the walls on the left and at the back of the room were interior partitions covered by dark wood-grain paneling. Marcus guessed that the room was fifteen feet wide and thirty long. The back half contained old particle-board folding tables, chairs, and bookshelves. Some of the tables still had cups and plates and opened books on them. The air was stale and musty.

Maggie's flashlight beam danced around the space, revealing the same sights. She said, "I bet they used plans for an old fallout shelter and just expanded the dimensions."

"Could be. They could also have skimped on some of the materials from bomb-shelter plans, since their goal really wasn't to survive a nuclear blast."

Three cheap hollow-core doors lined the left-hand wall. Marcus walked over, pulled open one of the doors, and shone his light around the room on the other side. He supposed it was a bedroom, but the bare utilitarian space reminded him more of a monastic cell. He stepped inside. There was a triangular-shaped piece of wood that acted as a desk mounted in the left corner. A gray folding chair sat in front of it. The right wall contained a home-made set of bunk beds. There were several sets of deteriorated clothing stacked in one corner. The neutral-colored garments looked similar to prison jumpsuits.

From the doorway, Maggie said, "Could you imagine living like this?"

"I've seen worse," he replied, thinking of the tapes of Ackerman as a boy. He stepped back into the first room. "I'm going to see what's behind that door on the end. You check these other two bedrooms." Marcus moved across the room, past the makeshift classroom, past the tables and chairs and bookshelves. He shone his flashlight on the spines of a few of the books. He saw names that he recognized from his research on the case—Anton LaVey, the iconic founder of the Church of Satan, and Aleister Crowley—and then other names he recognized, such as Ayn Rand.

The door on the end, like the ones for the bedrooms, had no lock. He moved inside and found what appeared to be some type of communal dining area. This room was darker than the previous one, since there was no ambient light coming through the opened cellar doors. There was a wood-burning stove connected to a pipe that led up into the ceiling and an old-time icebox in the corner. Shelves filled with canned goods and jars covered the back wall. There was enough food there to feed several people for at least a couple of months. More doors lined the left wall as they had in the first room. Marcus made a cursory search of each, but they were all the same and filled with nothing but the bare essentials for human existence. The only anomaly was that the back wall of the last bedroom had bulged inward and dirt had seeped in, probably from the intrusion of a tree's root system.

Returning to the first room, he asked Maggie, "Did you find anything?"

"Just this. It was on one of the desks in the corner." She held out a stack of old dot-matrix printer paper, the kind that had perforated edges and rolled from the printer in a long interconnected strip.

He shone the light onto the pages and read a few lines. It seemed to be some type of satanic manifesto. It described the world with terms like *The Father*, *The Slaves*, *The Disciples*, *The Work*, *The Great Fire*, and *The Chosen*. Marcus had done some basic research on cults and had found that most of them developed their own special vocabularies and terms. Controlling words and encouraging black-and-white thinking helped the leaders to control the thoughts of the members.

Quickly flipping through the pages, he also found mention of ceremonies like those from the Anarchist crime scenes.

He shone his light around the space again, knowing that there had to be more to the compound than this. And then he saw it in the corner.

There was another hole, covered by a trapdoor, near where they had climbed down. The trapdoor had a small brass handle screwed to one edge. Marcus pulled it open and found a ladder that descended to a second underground story.

Shining his flashlight up into the faces of the others, he said, "Let's see how deep this rabbit hole goes."

85

THERE WAS SOMETHING different about the bunker's second level. Marcus tried to tell himself that it was merely psychological. It just felt darker because they were farther from the cellar doors. It just felt colder because they were moving farther away from the sun. In reality, the temperature at this depth should have been a fairly consistent fifty-two degrees, and for all practical purposes, darkness was the same whether you were in your own bedroom with the lights off or at the bottom of the ocean. It was all in his head, but he couldn't shake the feeling that in this place the cold penetrated deeper and the darkness was somehow thicker.

The room was the same size as the one above, but it felt more like the sanctuary of a church, with chairs organized to face a central speaker. Strange symbols similar to those from the crime scenes covered the walls and floors. It was definitely a place of worship. The left-hand wall here only contained one door, and this one looked sturdier than the others. Marcus shone his light on the door's knob and found the hole for a key. This door, unlike the others, had a lock.

"I think we just found Conlan's room," he said.

He stepped forward and twisted the knob. It was locked. He directed Beaman and Maggie to stand back, and then he kicked the door. It flew inward with a sound of splintering lumber.

This room and the ones above were a study in contrasts. Not that the bedroom was something you'd find in a mansion, but it was also anything but utilitarian. Rugs covered almost the whole length of the floor. A large and ornate oak desk sat in the center, littered with pens and paper and a small plastic container. A padded rolling chair sat behind it. Books and bookshelves covered the back wall. A king-sized bed was at one end. There was an armoire and a night-stand next to the bed.

Marcus stepped up to the desk and opened the sealed plastic container resting on its surface. It contained plastic baggies filled with tin foil. He opened one of the bags and unwrapped the foil. Small squares of yellow blotter paper had been crammed inside. He pictured Conlan dispensing the blotter papers onto the tongues of his flock like a priest giving out Communion wafers.

He showed the foil's contents to Maggie and commented, "LSD."

Maggie growled in disgust and said, "I bet this creep was sleeping with every member of their group. Bastard had the nerve to live down here like a king while women and children were living in conditions harsher than most prisons."

Marcus didn't comment, and Beaman hadn't spoken a word since they'd descended the ladder. "Are you both feeling okay? No dizziness or disorientation?" Marcus asked.

"No, I'm good," Maggie said. "Beaman?"

"Fine," the old man said in a barely audible whisper.

They all walked back into the main room of the second floor, and Marcus shone his light down to the far end of the chamber. He stepped toward the door there, but he had a bad feeling about what they'd find on the other side.

He expected to find death, but what he saw shocked even him.

86

THE ROOM WAS the biggest open space in the bunker. Marcus estimated that it was thirty feet wide by thirty feet long. The walls had been completely covered from floor to ceiling with mirrors. A massive black pentagram covered the floor. At each of the symbol's five points rested a chair. Each chair contained the small burnt body of a child. Their hands had been bound behind their backs. Their heads were tilted at odd angles. Agony was etched onto their charred features.

Maggie covered her mouth and looked away. Beaman stumbled back into the previous room. Marcus could hear his whispered prayer clearly in the silence of the bunker.

He shone his flashlight around the rest of the room and found more bodies stacked in the corner like a pile of garbage. Adults. Five women, three men. The parents of the murdered children.

Stepping closer, he made a quick visual examination of the bodies. He wished that Andrew had been there to tell them an exact cause of death. With the level of decay, it was difficult for him to determine much about how they had died.

Maggie said, "I bet they tried to stop Conlan when they found out that he planned to…"

She didn't finish her sentence, and she didn't have to. Marcus guessed that Conlan had been a very charismatic and persuasive man. After all, he had convinced several families to move into a hidden underground bunker. But apparently his brainwashing techniques hadn't been effective enough to convince these people to sacrifice their own children. But Conlan wouldn't have cared about them, anyway. He had been prepared for their objections and had dealt with them. Poisoning would have been the easiest way. Marcus pictured all of them sitting down for a meal. Maybe laughing. Maybe even happy in their simple lives. And then they were gone.

He turned back to the pentagram. When he had first looked at it, his eyes had been immediately drawn to the burnt bodies on the symbol's periphery. Now he saw there was also a small stool at its very center. And it was empty.

Stepping to the core of the dark annulus, Marcus sat down on the stool. His eyes swept around to the faces of the children. They were all looking in at him. Their eyes accusing him.

"This is where the Anarchist sat," he whispered.

"Oh my God," Maggie said. "He sat there and watched all the other kids burn to death. His friends."

The room was silent.

As Marcus looked around the circle, he wondered what he would be like if he had been subjected to even a fraction of the pain and suffering that men like Ackerman and the Anarchist had endured.

He sat there for what felt like a very long time, but finally he said, "We should go. We'll get some fresh air and then come back down. See if we can find any other clues."

Maggie nodded, and they stepped back into the previous chamber, leaving the death and pain behind. Maggie placed a reassuring hand on Beaman's shoulder and ushered the old man forward.

But then Marcus heard a strange sound, like the quiet rumble of a distant shower or faucet running. And he smelled something as well. He sniffed the air.

Then everything clicked, and he ran toward the ladder. He scrambled up it. He could hear Maggie and Beaman saying something, but he didn't have time to listen.

His body was halfway through the trapdoor opening when he looked up toward the cellar doors and the other ladder that led outside. The figure standing there was lit from behind, but the man was also leaning down into the opening. What looked like a sixty-four-ounce bottle of Kingsford lighter fluid was turned upside down in his hands. The contents of the bottle flowed down the ladder and pooled on the floor.

Marcus looked up into the man's face. Their eyes met.

Then the man lit the stream of liquid. Fire exploded down the ladder, and the cellar doors swung shut.

87

As THE FLAMES burst to life, Marcus released his hold on the ladder and dropped back down to the second floor of the bunker. His leg slammed into the concrete as he landed. Pain shot up through his ankle, and he dropped to the ground.

Maggie grabbed him by the shoulders and pulled him back from the ladder and the opening, where the flames were licking at the air on the floor above. She helped him to his feet. The ankle protested when he put weight on it, but he had more important things to worry about.

Marcus willed the pain away and stepped back toward the ladder. He looked up to the next floor, trying to see if there was still a way out. Flames had begun to devour the plywood and the ladder leading to the surface still burned.

"Dammit!" he shouted.

They weren't getting out that way. With limited oxygen, the fire might burn itself out. But by the time it did, two other things would have happened. First of all, they'd have no oxygen left to breathe. And second, the man who had lit the fire would have already used the shovel they'd left on the surface to re-cover the opening with at least a cubic yard's worth of topsoil. A cubic foot of dirt typically weighed anywhere from ninety to one hundred and twenty pounds. So even if they could reach the cellar doors, there was no way they were going to be able to lift the 2,400 to 3,200 pounds of soil that would separate them from the surface.

Marcus shone his flashlight around the room. There were obviously no windows, nor were there any other entrances or exits. They were trapped.

Beaman was screaming hysterically. "I don't want to burn!" The old man lunged for the ladder, but Marcus hauled him back. Beaman twisted and fought. Marcus released him, and he fell to the concrete.

"You won't make it!"

"What are we going to do!"

Maggie bent down and grabbed hold of him. She tried to quiet him down. "We need to be calm and think. We'll get out of this."

Marcus admired her composure under the current pressure. He thought that maybe he should cut her a bit more slack if they lived through this. He also noted the confident look in her eyes. She had faith in him. Faith that he would figure something out. Faith that he would save them.

The only problem was that he was coming up empty. There was no way out.

He closed his eyes and pictured the structure in his mind. He analyzed it. Broke down its components. Looked for weaknesses. The cellar doors were blocked. The vents and pipes were sealed and were too small anyway.

Maybe they could blow the doors with something. Marcus thought of their handguns and the ammunition they used. Each .45 ACP round contained about seven grains of gunpowder. His gun had a ten-round clip, with one in the chamber. He had two extra magazines and imagined Maggie had the same. Her 9mm rounds would have less gunpowder, but there were also more of them, which would even out. Plus two backup weapons. He estimated they had close to one hundred rounds between them. That was about seven hundred grains of propellant.

Not nearly enough force to blow the door. Plus, how would they get it there through the fire? And they'd have already suffocated by the time they could open all the bullets and empty them of the propellant they contained.

He hadn't seen anything else flammable on this floor or the one above.

Dammit, Marcus. Think. Adapt, improvise, and overcome.

But he was drawing a blank. There was simply no way out. They were going to die down there.

88

THE FLAMES WERE consuming the upper floor of the bunker, and Marcus could already feel his lungs burning from the smoke and lack of oxygen. But he still couldn't find a way to get them out of this mess. They couldn't push their way out. They couldn't blow the door. They couldn't call for help. Even the closest neighbor would never reach them in time. This place would be their tomb.

"I'm sorry, Maggie. There's something that I need to tell you before—"

She stood up and smacked him hard across the face. "Don't you start that crap with me. I know you. You're much too stubborn to give up on anything. Now we're getting out of here."

"I've got nothing! There's no way out."

"There's always a way. Think harder."

The sound of the crackling flames filled the space. Beaman started to hack and cough from the smoke.

"What about Conlan?" Maggie said. "He's paranoid enough to build an underground bunker out in the woods, but he's not paranoid enough to have a back door leading out of the place?"

"You're right. Holy crap, you're absolutely right. I've heard of some cult and militia compounds where they built secret escape tunnels in case they were ever raided by the federal government. Conlan might have built something similar. We just have to find it in time. The two of you check the room with the mirrors. Maybe one of them is on hinges. I'll check Conlan's bedroom."

Ignoring the pain in his ankle, Marcus sprinted toward
the bedroom and shone his flashlight's beam over the walls.
He grabbed high on the bookshelves and pulled, tipping each
one over. The sound of them smashing against the concrete
reverberated off the block walls like cannon blasts. There
was nothing behind them. The light played over the walls,
and he quickly scanned them for any symbols or markings
that would indicate a hidden mechanism of some sort. He
shoved Conlan's bed aside and checked beneath it. There
was nothing there.

Any escape tunnel had to be in the next room. If there
was an escape tunnel.

The smoke was quickly filling both floors now. The trapdoor was gone, and the plywood was caving in near the back
wall. They didn't have much time.

He ran into the room containing the bodies and the pentagram and found Maggie and Beaman working their way
around to each of the mirrors lining the walls. They were
pulling on them, shoving against them, and feeling their
surfaces. Marcus ran to a point in between them and started
doing the same thing, working his way toward Maggie.

But he stopped when Maggie said, "Wait. I think I've
got something."

"What is it?"

"This one's colder than the others."

Marcus ran over to her. "Stand back." He grabbed the
Sig Sauer from his shoulder holster and smashed the butt of
the gun into the mirror. It shattered and the pieces of glass
rained down onto the concrete floor.

And there it was. A small and ragged hole in the earth
just big enough for a man to crawl through. Marcus shone
his light inside. The tunnel traveled up for about fifteen feet
that he could see, but then it curved off.

Something crashed down in the adjacent room. The floor
above was giving way. They needed to move.

"Beaman. You go first."

"I don't like tight spaces."

"Do you like burning to death?"

The old man swallowed hard, made the sign of the cross, and climbed into the hole.

"Okay, Maggie. Your turn."

She smiled. "You're welcome, by the way."

"Yeah, yeah. Later. We're not out yet."

She climbed inside and crawled forward down the tunnel. He allowed her some space, and then he followed. The shaft was cramped, and its floor was just hard dirt and rock. It grated against his forearms and elbows as he crawled and squirmed through the small space. He had never experienced claustrophobia before, but he understood the sensation now. It felt like the entire weight of the world was pressing down on his chest.

Then Maggie stopped her forward progress, and Beaman's voice echoed back. The old man said, "The tunnel's blocked!"

89

A LOUD CRASH echoed down the tunnel from inside the bunker. More of the floor above must have collapsed. But the noise wasn't the only thing following them down the shaft. The smoke rolled in after them as well. It was as though the fire was still reaching out for them, trying to block their escape.

Marcus coughed. His lungs and eyes burned, and he was feeling light-headed. The taste of smoke was heavy in his mouth.

"What do you see?" he yelled up to Beaman.

"It's a wall of mud and sticks, like the tunnel's collapsed!"

He swore and fought for a solution. The cult members had reinforced the tunnel at certain points with 2x4s wedged into the side walls, but encroachment from a tree's root system could have easily caused a cave-in.

Glancing back down the shaft, he noticed a faint orange glow coming from the darkness they had left behind. The fire must have been spreading through more of the compound. Going back wasn't an option.

"Beaman, can you see through the blockage at all?"

"No, it covers the entire tunnel."

Marcus shone his light up beyond Maggie and examined the tunnel. It was slightly larger here. He could try to squeeze past Maggie and Beaman and see if he could dig out the obstruction or muscle his way beyond it. But he dismissed the idea. His shoulders were tight against the side walls, and he barely had room to move. If he tried to squeeze through, they would just get tangled and become stuck.

The tendrils of smoke had reached Beaman and Maggie, and they both coughed and choked as the air turned toxic.

"Wait. Did you say that it's mud and *sticks*?"

"Yeah, all clumped together."

Why would there be a clump of sticks this far beneath the ground?

"Does it look man-made? Like someone put it there on purpose?"

"Could be. Yeah, I think it does."

"Try to push it forward."

Marcus had an idea about what the purpose of the obstruction might be. He hoped his suspicions were correct, otherwise they would all die from smoke inhalation within another few minutes.

"It won't budge."

"Yes, it will. Push with both hands evenly. Like sliding a loose block out of a wall. You can do this."

He could hear the old man straining to push the blockage clear, aged muscles that hadn't been used in years complaining at the unexpected demand. Tears filled Marcus's vision as the noxious fumes attacked his eyes. He hacked and squinted to see through the haze of smoke that was quickly enveloping them.

Then light burst into the end of the tunnel, and Maggie shuffled forward. Marcus squirmed along after her. His head pounded, his lungs ached, and he felt faint. But he pressed ahead, and after a moment he dropped three feet to the ground, landing in the snow next to Maggie beside a small creek. The tunnel terminated beneath a rocky outcropping that overlooked the water. The cult members had used sticks and mud to construct a barrier that would cover the end of the shaft and make sure that no one came across their escape route by accident.

They all took in generous gulps of the cold air and coughed the smoke from their lungs. Marcus flopped his head back into the snow. Right then he wanted nothing more than to sit on that spot and rest.

Beaman asked, "Does this kind of thing happen to you guys a lot?" Marcus nodded. "You get used to it."

Maggie stood and brushed the snow from her clothes. "Somebody tried to kill us back there. Do you think they're still around?"

"I doubt it. They probably sealed off the entrance and got the hell out. And I'm too damn tired to chase after someone right now anyway."

"Who knew we were even here? We weren't followed."

Marcus didn't answer, but he pulled the cell phone from his pocket, turned it off, and removed the battery. His eyes fell closed.

Maggie cursed and said, "Our best lead just went up in smoke, and you're just going to sit there?"

"Pretty much."

"That's great. You picked a hell of a time to give up."

Marcus didn't open his eyes. "Calm down. I just need a minute to think about how I'm going to set up our next move. We need to play this right."

"What are you talking about?"

"I saw the man who set the fire. Got a real good look at him. And it changes everything…because I know the guy."

ANDREW WALKED PAST the guy behind the glass and gave him a nod and a little wave. The man must have recognized him, since he didn't ask any questions or require any ID. The guard buzzed Andrew inside, and he walked down a long beige and white hallway to the stairs.

He had been surprised to hear Marcus's voice on Maggie's phone and even more surprised at what his partner had learned. Marcus had laid out his plan and Andrew's role in it and had then given the time and location where Andrew could find the target.

He peered around a corner to make sure that the target was preoccupied as Marcus had said he would be. Then he entered the locker room and went to work.

91

WHEN MARCUS HAD called and asked if she knew any isolated locations in Jackson's Grove, Vasques had immediately thought of the old Foley Lumber Yard. The place had been out of business for ten years and sat on a secluded lot on the south side of town. True to character, when she had questioned him about why he wanted to know, Marcus had avoided answering, playing his cards close to the chest.

She pulled up to his hotel directly in front of the lobby beneath a large awning made from orange brick, and he stepped out into the cold through a pair of automatic sliding doors. He fell into the passenger seat and said, "Temperature's dropping."

But she didn't have the patience for small talk. "What's this all about?"

"Is he coming?"

"He said he'll be there, but he wasn't happy about it."

"And you kept it quiet that I'm the one who requested it?"

"Yeah."

Marcus leaned back against the seat and closed his eyes. "Are you going to tell me what's going on or not?"

He didn't open his eyes. "Not."

Vasques pressed her foot down harder on the accelerator and squeezed the wheel. A pack of gum sat in the Crown Vic's console, and she popped another piece in her mouth to keep from grinding her teeth. They rode the rest of the way in silence, traveling down Route 30, past the storage yard where Sandra Lutrell had been murdered, turning right on Division Street, past the home where Jessie Olague had been abducted and Vasques had first met Marcus. The Crown Vic bumped over the railroad tracks, and within a few hundred feet, they arrived at the old Foley Lumber Yard.

The lot was usually nothing but dirt and mud, but now the ground was frozen over and covered with snow. She powered the big sedan through a drift and pulled up to the back of the main building where they had arranged the meeting. The city had demolished one of the outbuildings after some kids had started a fire there a few years back, but the main office of the lumber company still stood. It was dusty white and covered with old aluminum sheeting and poorly drawn graffiti. The sides of the building were nothing but awnings where plywood and stacks of lumber of various sizes had been stored. Two long warehouses sat on the back of the lot, but their roofs had collapsed along with most of the side walls. Now they were merely skeletal frames that the weeds laid claim to during the months of summer and spring.

Vasques threw the gear shifter on the steering column up into park and waited. Marcus opened his eyes and said, "Will you do me a favor?"

"I'm doing you one right now, and you still haven't given me anything in return."

"Leave your gun in the car."

"What? Why?"

He started to say something more, but another vehicle pulled into the lot and barreled to a stop, facing them at an angle. It was a metallic-red Chevy Impala that screamed cop car. Belacourt sat there a moment, staring directly at Marcus, but then stepped out of the vehicle. He wore a gray wool coat over a white button-down shirt and khakis. The collar was pulled up around his neck.

Vasques and Marcus stepped from their car and stood near the front wheel wells on either side. The wind whipped over the vacant lot and blew snow from the top of the building down over them. The sun was right overhead but provided little warmth. She could see the sunlight illuminating each wispy puff of their breath.

"What is he still doing here, Vasques? I thought we had a deal," Belacourt said.

"Listen, Trevor, just hear him out. He said this is important. I wouldn't have dragged you out here in the cold if I didn't think it was worth it."

Belacourt shook his head and rested his hands on his hips. "Fine. Get it over with. I'm freezing."

Marcus took a step forward and spoke over the noise of the wind. "Some new information has come to light. It involves both of you, and I felt it would be best if we discussed it privately. Someone you know has been helping the Anarchist."

"That's absurd. I don't have time for more of your—"

"The Anarchist was a member of a cult founded by a man named Anthony Conlan."

Vasques immediately made the connection. The note from her father's desk. He must have really been onto something, maybe even close to catching the Anarchist, when he died. She knew that Marcus would have followed the same train of thought to the same conclusion, but he hadn't shared it with her. Why would he do that?

"Conlan built a compound up in Wisconsin, and they tried to perform some of the same rituals there with a group of kids. The Anarchist would have only been a boy when he watched his friends being burned alive. But I've also determined why all the killings have taken place within this jurisdiction."

Marcus's eyes were locked on Belacourt.

"It was because the killer had inside help…from the police department."

Belacourt raised his arms in a gesture of despair and started back toward his car. "I'm done here. This is ridiculous."

Marcus took another step forward. "Really? Then why

did a guy named Jansen, the same man you had ordered to follow me around, show up at the compound up there and try to kill me and one of my agents?"

Belacourt reached for the car door handle. "This is crazy."

"I checked. Jansen isn't even a cop. Then I asked myself, how did he know where we were? Nobody was following us. At least, not visually." Marcus took the cell phone from his pocket and held it up. "Then I realized. When you arrested me, you activated the GPS tracking on my cell phone. That way you could keep an eye on me without me spotting your man again. I bet if we dug deep enough, Belacourt, we'd find that you have a connection to that compound and to a man the cult members called the Prophet."

"This is absolutely insane!" Belacourt jabbed a meaty finger in Marcus's direction. He wrenched open his Impala's door and stood behind it. "You've gone too far now. When I get back to the station, I'm putting out a warrant for your arrest."

"Why not arrest me now? I'll gladly go back to the station with you. We can tell all your cop friends about how I've already had my people dig into your background. We can tell them about how you were a nineteen-year-old private in the army when you volunteered for Project Kaleidoscope and met a lieutenant named Anthony Conlan. And then we can discuss the gaps in your background that correspond to the time when Conlan had his cult. Or better yet, we can talk about the birth certificate listing you as the father of a little girl born down in Georgia. The girl's name was Tabitha. Her mother was Darcy. I bet your friends at the Major Crimes Task Force would be interested in tracking them down."

Belacourt pulled his gun and pointed it straight at Marcus. It was a big custom Kimber .45 ACP. "Don't you ever mention their names again." Tears formed in the cop's eyes, and his voice trembled.

Vasques couldn't believe this was happening. She had known Belacourt for years. How could any of this be true?

He had been a father, a husband? She'd never even seen him date a woman. The man had been her father's partner right up until his...

She took a step forward, gulping in short gasps of the freezing air. "Trevor, tell me that you didn't have anything to do with Dad's death."

Belacourt swung the gun toward her. "Don't move, Vicky."

"Did you kill him?"

"Not me personally, but I had to tell them that he was getting close. I didn't want any of this. I tried to get away from Conlan, but he said that if I didn't help and they got caught, then he would take me down with them. You don't understand."

Vasques's hands shook at her side, clenching and unclenching, itching to pull her own gun. She visualized it. Pulling the gun, squeezing the trigger, Belacourt's head jerking back, the back of his skull exploding out over the snow. But he had her dead to rights. There was no way she could pull her gun, flip the safety, aim, and squeeze before he fired. All he had to do was pull the trigger. Plus, he stood behind a car door that he could use for cover, and she was completely exposed.

"I understand that you betrayed my father and got him killed."

"I'm sorry, kid. I never wanted you or your father to get hurt. I never wanted anyone to get hurt. But it's too late for that."

Then Belacourt aimed the big .45 at her head and pulled the trigger.

92

ACKERMAN HAD FINALLY taken the time to dispose of the bodies of the two drug dealers. He didn't want their corpses to be found easily. The police would obviously search their former residence for evidence, and then he would have to dispose of more bodies. So he had opened up their chest cavities, cut out their lungs, filled the emptied spaces with rocks, and sewn them shut. The lungs were the organs that caused a body to bloat and float back to the surface. With them removed, the bodies would settle comfortably beneath twenty-five feet of water at the bottom of Lake Calumet.

After tossing the remains of the degenerates from the 130th Street bridge, Ackerman cleaned up the crack house and fashioned a work area in the living room. He had purchased materials and an arc welder from the Lowe's on South Holland Road, and now he had set to the task of building his device.

He popped a flux-coated electrode into the stick welder and turned the handle to clamp it into place. After grounding the machine to the plate of steel and adjusting the current, he flipped down his protective goggles and, as if striking a match, scratched the electrode over the metal's surface to start an arc. The wire's flux coating would prevent oxygen and nitrogen in the atmosphere from touching the weld puddle and would therefore seal it off and temper it as he laid the bead. Once it was secured in place, he checked the LED display and keyboard for proper functionality.

Proud of his handiwork, he attached the bottom and sides

of the small metal box and welded them into place as well.
After all, he didn't want Marcus or a bomb squad to be able
to peek inside and see what tricks he had in store.

93

MARCUS WATCHED AS Belacourt pulled the trigger. Most police officers were damn good shots. And he guessed that Belacourt was above average. Shooting was just like anything else. Practice made perfect, and the Jackson's Grove department had their own small shooting range in the basement beside the evidence lock-up and their gym. That was a rarity for a small suburban department. He had read Belacourt's file, and it listed that he was one of the department's specialized shooting instructors. So the detective had had lots of practice firing the big Kimber pistol. There was no way he would miss at this range. He would go for the head shot, and nobody could survive a good head shot from a .45 caliber.

Of course, none of that really mattered since Marcus had told Andrew to sneak into the locker room and remove the Kimber's firing pin while Belacourt was engaged in his daily treadmill run.

Belacourt squeezed the trigger and was in the process of swinging the gun toward Marcus before he seemed to realize that his weapon hadn't fired. He quickly racked back the slide and squeezed again. Still nothing. So the cop did the only thing he could. He dove into the car, ducked down, and threw it into reverse.

Vasques, recovering from the shock, went for her gun. Marcus screamed, "Hold your fire! We need him alive!" Belacourt's vehicle twisted and jerked in the snow, but he got it turned back around and headed toward the exit from the yard. Vasques dove inside their vehicle, turned the key, and grabbed for the shifter on the steering column. But Marcus's hand shot out and stopped her from putting the vehicle into gear. He was still leaning halfway into the car.

"What are you doing?"

"I'll drive and explain on the way."

Her stare shifted quickly from Marcus to the tracks that Belacourt's Impala had left behind and then back again. Marcus said, "He reacted exactly as I hoped he would. We've got him right where we want him." Vasques took her hand off the shifter, but her bottom lip trembled. He thought for a moment that she was going to go for the shifter again, but then she stepped out of the car and came around to the passenger side. He hopped behind the wheel, and they left the lumber yard behind. He had to gun the accelerator and build up momentum to bust his way through the snow.

"What just happened? I should be dead. We both should."

"Not from Belacourt's gun. I had Andrew remove the firing pin."

"When?"

"During Belacourt's run. You told me that he runs twice a day like clockwork. So I knew exactly where he'd be and when, and I knew that his gun and cell phone would be sitting in his locker at the police station."

"You had this planned?"

"More or less. That's why I wanted to meet somewhere secluded. I wanted to confront him, and then I hoped he'd either give up and want to make a deal or he'd turn on us and run."

"His cell phone. You're tracking it?"

"Andrew installed a little piece of software that we got from the NSA. We can track him and listen in on any calls he makes."

"You put tracking and monitoring software in the phone of a police officer. What you're talking about is completely illegal," she said. "You can turn me in later. If I was Belacourt right now, I'd know that we're probably putting out an all-points on his car and contacting the phone company to track the cell. Which means that he needs help. Hopefully, he calls Conlan."

"So he calls someone else involved, and we let him lead us up the food chain. Why didn't you tell me?"

Marcus said nothing, kept his eyes on the road.

"You thought that I'd kill him if I knew ahead of time."

"Would you have?"

Vasques was quiet for a moment but then whispered, "Probably. What now?"

"We wait for him to make a call."

94

THE PROPHET WATCHED the women tremble in the back corner of their cage. When he had placed them inside, he had stripped them down to their underwear. They were both beautiful. Especially the Schuyler woman: she was an athlete. He could tell by her muscle tone. It was unusual for a woman of her age, and it spoke of aerobics and a strict workout regimen. If only there was more time. He smiled in at them, and the black woman gave him a defiant and angry look. She was strong. He liked that. She cradled the other woman's head against her chest. They had both been crying but were relying on each other for strength. It always amazed him how dire situations could bring total strangers together so quickly.

He chuckled as the women's faces changed. Shrinking, expanding, glowing. But the effect of the LSD was diminishing. The weight of this reality was pulling him back down and chaining his spirit into the mortal coil. The medicine was wearing off. He longed for the moment when this world would be no more, and he would no longer need help from a drug to fly.

A strange noise echoed over the concrete floor, and it took him a moment to realize that it was his phone. "Hello?"

"Prophet, it's Erik."

The Prophet smiled again. It was good to hear the voice of his *Disciple*.

He had known that he would need help to ensure that the darkest night went exactly as planned, so two years ahead of time, he had begun a passive search for a new recruit.

Someone that he could trust to help him complete *The Work*. After all, he had always known that Schofield was weak. And Belacourt had lost his way. The cop had been an unwilling although necessary participant, but he was no longer a true believer. He was no longer one of *The Disciples*. Which saddened the Prophet, since Belacourt and Schofield were the only remaining members of his original flock. But they were also prime examples of the weakness and ignorance of mankind. Even men like them who knew the truth could easily be led astray by the society of the slaves. That was exactly why he had isolated his flock at the compound in Wisconsin.

But then the Father had blessed him with Erik Jansen. He had been a Neo-Nazi and then a Theistic Satanist, whom the Prophet had met in an online discussion forum. A man that the Prophet could trust. A true believer in *The Work*. A new *Disciple*.

"Speak, brother. What troubles you?"

"It's Belacourt. He just called me, screaming. He was very upset. I'm sorry, Prophet, but the agent named Williams survived the fire at your old compound."

The Prophet jerked forward in his chair. "What? How is that possible?"

"I don't know. But he saw me when I set the fire, and it led him back to Belacourt. But that's not the worst of it."

The Prophet stood and paced the room. The concrete floor was freezing beneath his naked feet. "He wants money."

"Yes, sir. He said that you owe it to him. Said that he'd turn himself in and tell the police everything unless you paid. He mentioned that they might give him a deal if he gave them Harrison and the two of us."

The Prophet closed his eyes and watched the colors spin and twirl in strange new shapes. After a moment, he said, "Here's what I want you to do."

95

THEY HAD FOLLOWED Belacourt's signal up through residential areas and then down Route 30 past drug stores, shopping plazas, and fast-food restaurants. Then he abruptly cut north and made a stop in a residential area north of Lindenwood. Marcus guessed that he was stealing another car and ditching the Impala. Then he had made the call. Stan recorded it and then played it back for them. Unfortunately, Belacourt hadn't revealed much other than one name: Harrison. It wasn't much to go on in a city the size of Chicago.

Marcus pulled the car over in a Dunkin' Donuts parking lot while they waited for Belacourt to make his next move. There seemed to be a Dunkin' on every other corner in Chicagoland. Faint worry lines creased Vasques's face. She seemed to be on autopilot while she processed Belacourt's betrayal.

Eventually she said, "Why do you think Belacourt personally asked me to be part of this case?"

"No idea."

"Don't give me that crap. I want an answer."

Marcus rubbed the back of his neck and sighed. "Fine. They didn't want too many investigators involved. The more people, the bigger the chance of someone figuring something out. So almost all the killings took place in Belacourt's jurisdiction. That way he could control the flow of information."

"You're avoiding the question. Why me specifically? He didn't want the feds involved, so he recruited one that he didn't think was smart enough to hurt him. And he was right. I would never have figured any of this out without your help."

He shook his head. "I don't believe any of that. Belacourt just thought you were someone that he could control. I've reviewed your file. You're a damn good agent. You've done fantastic work breaking up human-trafficking rings, and you shouldn't come down hard on yourself because you're not built for profiling serial killers. Belacourt might have seen you transferring from the BAU as a sign of weakness, but I see it as a display of strength. You realized it wasn't a fit, and you figured out what was. Hell, I've tried to run from what I am my whole life."

"Thank you, Marcus."

He scratched at the stubble on his cheek and considered his next words carefully. "This may not be the best time, but there's something else that I want to tell you. About the other night—"

"You don't have to say anything to me. I know. But you probably should say something to Maggie."

He laughed. "Maybe you're not such a bad profiler after all." Vasques smiled back, but he could see sadness in her eyes. He wondered if the Maggie comment was just a self-conscious guess that he had now confirmed. She said, "What about Jansen? Do we know anything about him?"

"We've put out an all-points on him. I had Stan check his background while I was on my way back from Wisconsin. Pretty standard scumbag. Dishonorable discharge from the Marines. Went to Pontiac prison for assault. Started running with the Neo-Nazis, and later he turned to satanism. About two years ago, he dropped completely off the grid. But he's a foot soldier. He's not smart enough to be the Anarchist."

"So we're thinking this Harrison that Belacourt mentioned on the phone is our guy?"

"I think so."

"What about the list of Camry owners? We should check that for the name Harrison."

"Already did. No Harrison."

"When did you do that?"

"In my head. I memorized the list. Your next question is going to be about the spouses, but no go there either. I had Stan add each spouse's name onto the list as well."

"What if it's a company car?"

"I reviewed the list of businesses, too. Nothing that fits."

Marcus's phone rattled in its resting spot in the center console. He slid his finger across the screen to answer the call and then put the device on speaker. "What do we have, Stan?" he said.

"Belacourt just received a call from Jansen," Stan said. "They're meeting behind Jackson's Grove mall in two hours. Belacourt said that he'd be driving a green Honda Civic and would park along the back edge of the parking lot's far corner."

Vasques asked, "Did he say anything else?"

"I can play it for you, but that was pretty much it. Short and to the point."

Marcus slipped the Crown Vic into gear and pulled out onto Route 30, heading in the direction of the mall. This wasn't going as he had hoped. Belacourt hadn't given anything useful away on the phone, and the foot soldier was coming to the meeting instead of the general. Even if they took in both Jansen and Belacourt, there were no guarantees that it would lead to Conlan or the Anarchist. Belacourt might turn state's evidence, but he might not. And if Marcus's suspicions were correct, five women would be ritualistically murdered the next evening, and the clock was ticking. He growled and reached out to disconnect the call, but Vasques caught his hand.

She said, "Wait, Stan, was the list of Toyotas you pulled just for Illinois or did you include Indiana as well?"

"Just Illinois."

"Indiana's only a little over twenty minutes from here."

"Okay, checking now." There was a pause that lasted a few minutes as the phone line filled with nothing but the sound of clicking keys and the whir of computer fans. Then Stan said, "Nothing matching the name Harrison."

Marcus added, "I'm fairly certain that the Anarchist lives within only a few minutes of Jackson's Grove, if not within the city limits."

She shook her head. "What about businesses, Stan?"

"One sec…I think I got something. There's a security company called Schofield Security Associates that owns several Camrys."

Marcus leaned toward the phone, as if closer proximity would make the answers more easily accessible. "That fits, Stan. Can you get a list of employees?"

"I can try, but I'll have to hack their personnel files. Wait a second, I'm on their website now. They list the company officers, and one of them is named Harrison Schofield."

"What's his job?" Marcus said. "Chief Financial Officer."

"That's him. Everything fits. Do you have an address?"

"Hold on to your butts, boys and girls, because our man Schofield lives right there in Jackson's Grove."

Marcus checked the time. A little after two in the afternoon. Schofield should have been at work, but he might already have received a warning from Jansen. They needed to take Schofield down soon or risk the killer escaping. If that happened, they might never find him, and those women would be as good as dead.

Everything was coming together and falling apart at the same time. He knew that Vasques wouldn't let up on Belacourt, and he didn't blame her. If Belacourt was the man responsible for *his* parents' deaths, the monster inside Marcus would have broken free already and killed the cop slow and bloody. Vasques was handling it pretty well, all things considered. But there was no way she would let Belacourt get away.

Andrew was making some calls about Jansen and awaiting further orders, and Maggie was resting up from the

Wisconsin trip. He could call both of them out, but they still didn't have enough bodies. They were spread too thin.

"Stan, call Schofield's office and find out if he's there, but don't tip him off in any way. Then get the local police department out there. Tell them that he's a suspect in a serial-murder case and is to be considered armed and extremely dangerous. Then send me his home address and the address for his office."

Marcus disconnected the call, took a left on a side road, and pulled over. The tires rumbled as he tore through the snow to reach a parking spot next to a packaged liquor store named Cliff's. Advertisements for twenty-dollar thirty-packs of Budweiser and seventeen-dollar bottles of gin hung in the front window.

Before he could speak, Vasques grabbed a handful of his shirt and leaned over the console to stare directly into his face. "I'm going after Belacourt. I won't let him get away with this. And I won't let anyone stand in my way."

Glancing down at her hand, Marcus slipped the Crown Vic into park and said, "Don't be so dramatic. I'm not trying to stop you from taking him down. You can be the one to slap the cuffs on or put him in the ground. I don't care either way. But I'm calling Andrew to pick me up, and then I'm going after the Anarchist. I would suggest that you scramble your FBI friends and use a coordinated effort to arrest Belacourt and Jansen together. But I'll leave that up to you. I'll also send you Stan's contact info. He's at your disposal. Either way, good luck…and be careful."

Without another word, he grabbed his phone and stepped out into the cold.

96

WITH A TAN leather briefcase dangling from his right hand, Harrison Schofield stood in front of a large chrome and glass desk that held a computer and monitor. The woman behind the desk looked at him with questioning yet sympathetic eyes. Her name was Valerie, but everyone called her Val. She was in her mid-forties and had mocha skin and short black hair. Her lips pouted at all times as though she had just tasted something sour and one of her arms hung in a sling, the result of permanent nerve damage from a car accident. She had been like that for as long as Schofield could remember, and when he'd been younger, he had sat in front of his grandfather's office and watched her type proficiently with one hand and a special keyboard. Behind her was a door with large black letters embossed on a gold plaque. It read *Raymond Schofield, President.*

"Hello, Val," he said. "Is he in?"

Schofield already knew the answer to his question before she even opened her mouth. He had known that Raymond was scheduled to meet with a prospective client concerning a lucrative contract to provide security for sports stadiums that the potential customer constructed all over the world. Unfortunately, he hadn't known the details of the meeting and had been forced to monitor the security gate from his office window for the entire afternoon. Then, fifteen minutes ago, he had finally witnessed his grandfather's big Bentley pull through the gate.

"I'm sorry, Mr. Schofield. He just stepped out for a meeting. Can I help you with anything?"

"That's okay. I have some papers for him. I'll leave them on his desk."

He took a step toward the door, but Val said, "You can just leave them here with me."

Once, when Schofield had been a boy, the Prophet had picked him up by the neck and slammed him down flat on his back. The wind had been knocked from his lungs, and he hadn't been able to breathe. He felt the same way in that moment as he fought for words and stammered at the older woman. The silenced .22 caliber pistol felt heavy in his suit jacket's inner pocket. He liked Val. He didn't want to have to kill her.

But then Val stood up from the desk, patted him on the arm, and said, "It's okay, Mr. Schofield. Go on in." She reached out and pulled open the big black door for him.

Once inside and with the door shut, he was able to breathe again. But he didn't have time to truly center himself; he needed to be in and out. There was a massive family photo of Raymond and himself with Eleanor and the kids hanging against the back wall. It was an old cliché to have a safe behind a picture or painting, but it was also the best way to conceal it. The hiding place was more for aesthetics than for security. The safe's protection came from its advanced features: a keypad requiring a fifteen-digit PIN number and a biometric palm reader that monitored ambient skin viscosity and temperature to determine duress.

Luckily, his grandfather had given him the PIN and programmed his handprint. He felt bad for betraying the old man's trust, but he was also confident that if Raymond knew the dire circumstances, he would have given the money freely.

The safe slid open with a whirring of gears and the whoosh of a breaking seal. Val would be expecting him to be back out soon, so Schofield wasted no time in loading his briefcase and suit pockets full of the stacks of money that he found inside the safe.

He closed the briefcase and locked it, but as he stepped back toward the door, he heard the sound of sirens and screeching tires. Rushing to the window, the sight outside nearly stopped his heart. This couldn't be happening now. Not when he was so close to escape. Black and white police cruisers with their light bars shooting out red and blue pulses converged on the office from several directions.

He thought quickly. He had planned for various circumstances such as this and had multiple contingency plans. After all, that was where his aptitude lay. Assessing the risks, calculating the variables.

Moving quickly to the door, he cracked it open and said, "Val, could you come here for a moment? I have something very important to discuss with you."

Schofield wondered if he would have had the courage to do what he was about to do before he'd taken the souls of his last several victims. He didn't think so, but self-preservation was always a strong motivator.

Val stepped inside and shut the door behind her. As she was turning back to face him, he pulled the silenced pistol and jammed it into her face. Her eyes went wide, and she froze in place. He had always heard that your life flashes before your eyes just before death. He wondered if Val was experiencing that now. Did she find happiness or despair in those memories?

Schofield said, "I'm a murderer, Val. The newspapers and television anchors call me the Anarchist. I've killed many, many people. I'm telling you this so that you realize that you don't know me or what I'm capable of. But I know you. I know your family. And if you don't do exactly as I say, I will kill you and every member of your family that I can find."

97

MARCUS WAITED INSIDE Cliff's Liquor Store for Andrew to arrive. The place looked like an old grocery store that had gone out of business. Bottles were stacked haphazardly in an open cooler that had obviously been designed for fresh produce. There was metal shelf after metal shelf full of all types of liquors and different-flavored beers of all brands. Stan had instilled in him a taste for Scotch, and he wondered if downing a bottle of Glenlivet would help with the migraine throbbing at the back of his eyes. An older black man with a Jheri curl eyed him from behind the counter. Marcus wasn't exactly up on the newest trends, but he was fairly certain that the man's haircut had been out of style for over two decades.

His phone vibrated with a text message saying *Here* a moment before Andrew pulled up in the Yukon. He hopped in, and they headed back down Route 30 toward Indiana. The SUV was warm and welcoming and smelled of new leather. Checking his watch, he estimated that they'd be at Schofield's office in twenty minutes.

Glancing toward the back seat, he said, "Where's Maggie?" Andrew's gaze didn't leave the road. "You're not going to like it."

"What?"

"She decided to check out Schofield's house for any sign of the women or a clue to where they may be holding them."

Andrew was right. Marcus didn't like it. But Maggie was her own person and a competent agent. If he was going to lead this team, he would need to trust her and give her some operational leeway. In that moment, the realization struck him that he was exactly the kind of leader that he would never be able to work with. He had a real problem with authority and didn't relish the idea of being a boss. But it wasn't too late to rectify his mistakes.

He dialed Maggie, and she answered without saying hello. "Marcus, I know what I'm doing, and you're not talking me out of anything. You'll just—"

"Whoa, slow down. I wasn't calling to talk you out of it. I trust your judgment."

Total silence filled the other end of the line for a long moment, but then she said, "Thank you."

"Just remember that Schofield may be contained, but Conlan is still out there. Be careful."

"I will."

"Maggie, you know that…"

"What is it?"

"Just keep me posted," Marcus said as he ended the call.

The south suburbs whipped by outside the window. The radio was off; the only sound was from the heat pumping out of the Yukon's vents. Andrew looked at him sideways from the driver's seat. The surprise on his partner's face was clear to see but Andrew didn't say a word.

98

MAGGIE PULLED HER rental car, a light blue Kia Rio, up to the curb in front of the address that Stan had given her. The GPS unit resting on the dark gray dashboard had found Schofield's home easily, but she still checked the address in the device to be sure. The house wasn't at all what she had expected. It was a massive and gorgeous redbrick structure. Professionally landscaped plants and shrubbery, still visible beneath a layer of snow, bordered the house. A stamped concrete walkway that matched the home's brick led up to the front door and then around the side. The sidewalk and the driveway had been recently shoveled.

She parked two houses down and backtracked to Schofield's front door. It was made of heavy oak and was the color of maple syrup. There was no answer when she knocked, and so she made her way around the side of the house to the back. She discovered a large backyard housing an in-ground pool, a covered patio with a built-in grill, and a balcony leading off what she assumed to be the master bathroom. A large building housing another garage and a workshop or pool house rested along the back half of the property. It was covered with the same intricately patterned brick as the house.

Schofield worked for a security company, and it seemed highly unlikely that he wouldn't have top-of-the-line protection for his home. Luckily, Maggie had Stan on her side. He had already broken into SSA's database and extracted the disarm code along with Schofield's personnel file.

After picking the lock, she entered the house and punched the code into a number pad hanging on the wall a few feet from the entryway. The kitchen was all chrome and granite and dark, ornate wood. Elaborate decorative patterns lined the hardwood floors. The house had a new and clean smell mixed with the aroma of French vanilla.

Maggie called out to make sure that no one was home, and then she walked through the ground floor. All the rooms had been beautifully decorated by someone with elegant and expensive tastes, but the house still had a strange feeling of homeyness. There was no doubt that a family lived there, evidenced by little things like colored pictures hanging on the refrigerator and baseball gloves lying discarded on the granite countertop.

There was a large staircase that curled up to the second story from an inviting foyer, but she decided to check for a basement first. If Schofield was hiding something from his wife, that was where Maggie would find it. She doubted that a man living with a wife and children would be able to hide anything right under their noses, but she also knew that people often saw only what they wanted to see.

She had just left the foyer and was walking down a long hallway whose walls were covered with family photos when the doorbell rang. From instinct, she pressed her body against the wall. Hugging the side of the hall but careful not to knock down the photos, she crept back toward the foyer and peeked around the corner. There was a shadowy figure barely visible through the glazed glass of the front door. She could see little else other than that the man was dressed in dark blue or black.

The doorbell rang out again. It was loud and resonated down the hall from all angles. She waited, refused to move. Then the figure knocked, paused again, and called out. "Mrs. Schofield? It's an urgent matter about your husband."

She stood there like a statue and waited for him to leave. The police in Indiana must have asked the local PD to send someone out to collect Schofield's wife. But they wouldn't be able to come into the house, even if they suspected that someone was inside. They would need a warrant for that. In one way, this new development hindered Maggie and in another it was a help. It would make leaving the house a challenge, but she figured that she could still sneak out through the back and make her way to her car through the neighbor's backyard. But this also meant that she had someone out front watching her back. If the Prophet or Schofield's family showed up, the officer would intervene.

After the cop had gone, Maggie walked back down the hall. At the end, she found a set of carpeted stairs just off the kitchen that led down into the home's basement.

99

THE HEADQUARTERS OF Schofield Security Associates looked to Marcus more like a hospital than an office building. It had that same large and ambitious glass feel that most new hospital boards seemed to prefer. A shopping plaza surrounded the building and made the police's job of containment more difficult. They had erected barricades and had uniformed officers holding back the onlookers, but a news crew was already on the scene and a crowd had formed. Local black and white squad cars mixed in with bronze and dark brown cruisers from the Lake County Sheriff's Department had the building surrounded, and Marcus noticed a large white truck and trailer marked with red and blue stripes and blue letters reading *Mobile Command Center—Indiana District One.* It was quite a set-up. He knew the command center was evidence of the estimated seventy-five billion dollars a year spent by federal and state governments for homeland security in response to the September 11th attacks of 2001.

They parked across the street in front of an IHOP, showed their IDs at the barricade, and walked to the command center. Marcus noticed a man that seemed to be in charge standing in front of another large truck labeled *Lake County Sheriff Tactical Unit.* The man wore a black BDU and a bulletproof vest with SHERIFF printed across the front in white block letters. He had a black mustache, thick eyebrows, and a boxer's nose with a wide and crooked bridge that looked as if it had been broken and not allowed to heal properly.

Flashing his ID, Marcus said, "It was my office that called

you in to apprehend this guy, but judging by the circus here, I'm guessing that it didn't go down as planned."

The cop's eyes narrowed, and his boxer's nose flared and looked even more crooked.

Andrew immediately stepped in, trying to defuse the situation. "My partner didn't mean to imply that your men are somehow responsible for the current situation. He was just commenting on the crowd. We have no intentions of trying to assume command here or question your decisions. We'd just like to know what's happening and what you're planning."

The man didn't seem convinced but said, "Your suspect has barricaded himself in one of the interior offices and has a hostage. He says that if we try to come in, then he'll kill her. He's refusing to speak with anyone other than an FBI hostage negotiator."

Marcus ran a hand through his hair and shook his head. "Make no mistake. This guy is a killer, and there's nothing more dangerous than a cornered predator."

The cop's mouth scrunched up, and his eyes narrowed again. "Well aware. We know what we're doing."

"What's your plan?"

"Right now, we're containing the scene and waiting for the negotiator. But I've already requested that the Jackson's Grove PD send some units to the suspect's house to see if we can get his wife and kids out here to try and talk him down. Other than that, we're drawing up contingency plans in case negotiations fail and we're forced to breach."

"What about the rest of the building's employees?"

"He pulled the fire alarm to get everyone out."

"Are we sure he's armed? Did anyone see him?"

"No, he barricaded the door and forced his hostage to call 911 and give his instructions. If you don't mind, I need to get on the phone and find out the status of our negotiator. I'll keep you in the loop."

Andrew said, "We appreciate it."

But Marcus just walked away. This could take hours, and they still didn't know the location of the abducted women or the Prophet. For all they knew, Conlan could have them and be making preparations to burn them alive at that very moment.

Flipping up his collar against the cold, he found an out-of-the-way spot at the inner edge of the barricades and stared up at the gray rounded end of the office building. He stamped his feet in an attempt to stay warm. It was an old beat cop's trick, but he had never been convinced that it actually worked.

To Andrew, he said, "Do you think he actually believes that he's the Antichrist like Crowley told Ackerman?"

"Don't know, but obviously Conlan believes it."

"How could anyone believe that they could start the apocalypse by killing a bunch of women?" Marcus's words came out in puffs of steam in the cold air.

"That's kind of a silly question."

"What do you mean?"

"You believe in God. Right, Marcus?"

"Of course, but the God I know would never want something like this."

"That's not what I meant. I'm saying that you have faith that there is a God even though you can't prove it."

Marcus thought of a quote from Paul the Apostle. "The substance of things hoped for, the evidence of things not seen."

"Right. You believe because you feel it in your heart. But imagine if you actually had faith in the fact that by killing a handful of people you would be saving the souls of everyone else in the world. Not saying that it's right or that I believe a word of it, but faith is a powerful thing. And misguided faith is an extremely *dangerous* thing. Just look at all the terrorist attacks and suicide bombings around the world."

Marcus said nothing. He just stood there and thought of all the people using God or religion or ideology as a crutch to prop themselves up and achieve their own selfish goals or desires. He had always thought of God as the source of all love in the world. If it involved hatred, then it wasn't of God. But unlike so many others who sowed the seeds of hate in God's name, he supposed that at least Conlan had never claimed to be doing God's work. The Prophet's master was the author of hatred.

His thoughts turned to Schofield. There was something about this whole situation that bothered him, but he couldn't quite nail down what it was. If he was being honest with himself, he couldn't concentrate on much else beyond the pounding in his skull.

"Do we have any Tylenol in the—"

A familiar voice interrupted him from behind. "Marcus, fancy meeting you here."

He turned to find the Director of the Shepherd Organization walking toward them through the crowd. Their boss wore a gray wool overcoat buttoned to the top and black leather gloves. A gray newsboy cap sat atop his head.

"What are you doing here?"

"Same as you boys, I suspect. Stan told me that you had the Anarchist cornered. I was in town visiting Allen."

"How is he?"

"Stable. What's the situation here?"

"He's in there with a hostage and only wants to speak with a negotiator from the FBI."

"We could set you up as the negotiator."

Andrew laughed. "I don't think that's a good idea, boss."

Marcus gave Andrew a dirty look but said, "Hate to admit it, but he's right. I'm not exactly the voice of calm and reason."

"That may be, but you're definitely a good investigator. You've done good work on this case."

Marcus just nodded. He had never been good at giving or accepting praise. But there was something that he needed to do that he *was* good at. He needed to get to the bottom of a mystery. "Andrew, could you see if we have any painkillers in the Yukon? I need to speak with the Director about a private matter."

Andrew mumbled something under his breath as he walked off. Marcus thought that he caught the words *damn* and *errand boy.* Once Andrew was gone, Marcus said, "Why was Francis Ackerman chosen for my recruitment?"

The Director hesitated. Not for long, but long enough to betray a lie. "We've been over that. He was just convenient. The timing worked out."

"So there's no connection between the two of us?"

"What did he tell you?"

"That you're a liar."

"And you believe him rather than me?"

"I'm going to say it one more time. Is there a connection between me and Francis Ackerman?"

"I think we should discuss it once this situation with the Anarchist is—"

"We'll discuss it *now.*"

"Fine. I'm not sure what he told you, but the truth is that Ackerman and his father murdered your parents."

Marcus suddenly felt dizzy.

"They played a game with them and would've killed you too if you hadn't heard the screams and hid. That's the reason why I chose him specifically to be part of your recruitment. If things hadn't gone wrong back then, you would have learned all this and been able to confront your parents' killer. That had been my plan, anyway."

Marcus steadied himself against a nearby police cruiser but couldn't shake the sensation of falling.

"It doesn't change anything. You'll catch him, and justice will be served. I would've told you, but I didn't want it to cloud your judgment."

Marcus closed his eyes and fought back tears. He should've been prepared for this. He had expected as much. But somehow it still felt strange and surreal. For most of his life he had wondered about that night. Tried to remember. Dreamed of finding the people responsible. Dreamed of making them pay. And now he finally had someone that he could line up in his sights.

His fists clenched and unclenched. He cracked his neck to the side, getting into fight mode. Without opening his eyes, he said, "Please leave. If I open my eyes and see you standing there, I'm afraid that I may do something that we'll both regret."

100

VASQUES HAD TAKEN Marcus's advice and called in the cavalry, but she hadn't wanted to involve the Bureau. Luckily, her partner, Troy LaPaglia, had friends in the Cook County Sheriff's office and was able to get their tactical unit out to help make the arrests. For obvious reasons, she hadn't wanted to involve the local police department.

Now she sat inside the same surveillance van that she had four days earlier when she had busted the human-trafficking ring in Elk Grove Village. The block vinyl letters reading MASCONI PLUMBING AND HEATING still clung to its exterior. It was still cramped and uncomfortable, and it still smelled of stale coffee and greasy takeout food. She was certain that Belacourt hadn't seen it; even if he had, the detective didn't have Marcus's memory.

Troy had set up a small electric heater that hummed on the desk beside him near the surveillance monitors. For some reason, he was always cold. Vasques was sweating and ready to throw the little heater out the window.

The parking lot of the Jackson's Grove mall was packed. Christmas was only a few days away and everyone was scrambling to cross the final names from their lists. The sight of all the cars and people heading toward the mall to purchase gifts for loved ones evoked both sadness and anger in Vasques. She would not be giving any gifts or receiving any that Christmas. Her brother's gift had been the little dog, and she hadn't bought him anything. Childhood memories of Christmas morning with her father only fueled her anger at Belacourt.

   She reached up inside her Level III-A body armor and
scratched at her chest. It would stop a .44 magnum round
traveling at fourteen hundred feet per second, but it was also
bulky and added to her discomfort in the stuffy interior of
the van. She popped in a third piece of Juicy Fruit gum. At
her side, Troy said, "I just bought a new pack of Marlboros
if you want one."

   "Thanks, Satan, but I'm fine."

   "You don't look fine. You look like one of those junkies
on that TV show where the person's family confronts them
about their addiction."

   Vasques shook her head, but she did it with a smile. "Shut
up and watch the monitors."

   They had a spotter posted on each of the entrances to the
mall and five officers waiting in unmarked SUVs ready to
converge on Belacourt and Jansen once they both arrived.
Belacourt had probably chosen the mall as a meeting place
because he wanted to blend in with the crowds, but it also
made it easier for their team to intermingle. She had called
Stan, and he would notify them as soon as Belacourt's signal approached the shopping center. Belacourt had told Jansen on the phone that he'd be driving a green Honda Civic
and would park along the back edge of the parking lot's far
corner.

   In her mind, Vasques ran through everything one more
time. The team would converge with overwhelming force,
blitzkrieg-style. With luck, that would ensure that they'd
meet no resistance. The very back corner of the lot had only
a sporadic dotting of cars, so they should be a safe distance
from any civilians. And she had parked the van close enough
to where she could rush up to Belacourt's car with the tactical team and be the one to make the arrest.

   They were ready. Now all they had to do was wait.

101

WHEN ANDREW RETURNED, he dropped two white extra-strength Tylenol tablets into Marcus's outstretched palm and said, "Where's the Director?"

"I don't care," Marcus said as he looked down at the tablets in his palm. "You only brought me two pills."

"They're extra-strength. You're not supposed to take more than two at a time."

"You're not supposed to shoot people or drive over the speed limit, either. But that's never stopped me."

"How many do you usually take?"

"I don't know. Four or five."

"That'll destroy your liver."

He popped the pills into his mouth and swallowed them dry. "If I live that long, I'll consider myself lucky. You think they have a coffee pot in that big command center?"

"Don't get any ideas. If you want coffee, you can get it your damn self."

Marcus chuckled. "You're getting cranky. Is it that time of the month already?"

"Hilarious. If you had coffee right now, I'd dump it all over you."

"Might feel pretty good in this weather."

Andrew's gaze traveled over the onlookers and police, and he said, "Does anything about this whole situation bother you?"

"Something doesn't fit. That's for sure."

"The Anarchist is so meticulous and likes to assess every situation and be prepared. So why wouldn't he be prepared for this? He had to have a plan in case the cops ever caught up with him."

Looking back up at the building, Marcus wondered what he would do if he were in a similar situation. He considered the facts, analyzed what he knew. The secretary had called in with instructions. They were barricaded in an interior office. Schofield had pulled the fire alarm. People were everywhere. They were right next to a strip mall, and it was the holiday shopping season. The police didn't know for sure if Schofield was even armed. They hadn't seen him. No one had seen him. No one had even talked to him.

Marcus's eyes went wide. He looked at Andrew and could tell from the look on his partner's face that he had followed the same line of thinking. "We need to go."

Andrew said, "Schofield's not in there." It wasn't a question, but a statement of fact.

"This is all just a distraction to cover his escape."

"He couldn't have taken his car. He must have walked out the back or through the underground garage and just blended with the crowd. But where would he go now?"

Marcus's head felt like a volcano about ready to erupt. He raised his hands and pressed hard against both sides of his skull. "I have no idea."

102

ERIK JANSEN HAD hated being a Marine. He didn't mind the actual training, but he had hated just about everything else. He hated the culture. Six-second showers for seventy-five recruits that had been sweating and crawling through salt marshes all day produced some odors that he could still feel clinging to the inside of his nostrils. He had once been punished for being late because he was only fifteen minutes early. The drill instructors treated him like a slave and nitpicked every move that he made. They yelled at him for asking too many questions. They yelled at him for not taking the initiative if he didn't ask questions and awaited instructions. He hadn't seen the point in any of it. He had been glad when they kicked him to the curb for knocking out the teeth of one of the drill instructors.

But he had acquired some valuable skills during his brief time in the Marine Corps. He had already been a good fighter, but they had honed his abilities. They had taught him about weapons. They had taught him how to kill, up close and from a distance.

He thought back on those lessons as he sat four hundred yards away from the back corner of the Jackson's Grove Mall. A wide swath of undeveloped land bordered the mall's lot and beyond that was a road lined on one side by small suburban homes and apartments. He had parked his maroon Dodge Caravan along that road in front of a little yellow ranch-style prefab. The minivan didn't seem out of place in any environment and had plenty of interior room. That was exactly why he had chosen it.

Inside the back of the van, he laid out his Remington 700 M24 sniper rifle between the second row of bucket seats. A Leupold Mk 4 LR/T M3 10×40mm scope sat atop the weapon. The rifle was loaded with M118LR 7.62 175-grain ammunition and had an effective range of about eight hundred and seventy-five yards. He would only have to shoot half that distance today.

He had it all planned out.

When Belacourt pulled up to the back of the mall, Jansen would slide open the side door of the van, sight in on the coward, and unleash a round traveling at 2,580 feet per second. The front glass of the car shouldn't be an issue, although he would have preferred to have another shooter there to pop the glass before he delivered the kill shot. But either way, he'd fire a second round to make sure that Belacourt was dead.

Then he'd turn the gun on anyone else nearby and kill a few more of the slaves, just for good measure.

103

AFTER STAGING HIS distraction, Schofield had slipped into a set of blue and white coveralls worn by SSA mechanics and system-installation technicians, placed a long blond wig over his hair, and covered the wig with a blue SSA baseball cap. It was the same outfit that he had stolen from the company to use when he'd installed his cameras. He kept it behind a ceiling tile in the men's second-floor bathroom just in case he was ever confronted at work and needed to make a hasty escape. He liked to plan ahead.

As he exited with the other technicians, he was afraid that someone would notice him. Mortimer, the garage manager, had glanced in his direction once as they hurried up the ramp as a group, and Schofield's hand had slipped around his pistol. But no one paid him any attention in the confusion of the fire evacuation.

After that, he had walked down the road a few blocks to the office of a local cab company. He paid a driver to take him just across the Illinois-Indiana border to the Lansing Municipal Airport. Several years earlier, he had paid $850 cash to a private seller for a beat-up 1988 Volkswagen Jetta GLI with 105,000 miles on its odometer. Then he had parked it in a long-term lot at the airport, ten minutes from his office. He had changed lots every month and practiced his escape route many times, hoping that he would never have to use it.

But he had been forced to do so, and now he sat behind the wheel of the Jetta, heading home. He knew that it was a risk to return to his house, and he didn't need to retrieve anything from the property. He had everything that he needed in the trunk of the Jetta, and his family had already gone. But he had unfinished business to take care of, and he finally had the strength to do something that he should have done a long time ago.

The police would be watching the house, but he hoped that it would only be one or two officers. That was manageable. Anything more, and he would keep driving.

He took Route 30 back to Jackson's Grove and then made two circles of his block without actually turning down the street in order to check for surveillance and police. He noticed two cars that he didn't recognize. One was a Kia Rio and unlikely to be used as an unmarked police vehicle. But the other was a black and white Jackson's Grove squad car sitting across the street from his house. It looked like there was only one officer inside. That would be protocol, since most small police precincts didn't have the manpower to have two officers per patrol car. Schofield guessed that they weren't actually looking for him, but just trying to locate his family.

Parking one street over, he cut through the backyards of two of his neighbors and came up beside a big house that looked a lot like his own only with cream-colored brick and no landscaping. The cop sat at the curb about fifty feet away. He could see the back of the officer's head. It looked like he was typing on the computer mounted over the center console of the cruiser, probably filling out one of the many reports that dominated police work.

He was a sitting duck.

Schofield considered his next moves carefully, choreographed them in his mind. He would approach from well beyond the field of view for the side mirrors. He would raise his P22 Walther silenced pistol at the last possible moment, keeping it behind his back until then. The glass could be a problem. A .22LR wasn't a powerful round and could be easily deflected. The officer would be wearing a bulletproof vest. It needed to be a head shot and even a slight obstruction could cause his first shot to miss. He could try to break the glass with the butt of the pistol, but what if it didn't shatter completely? Ultimately, he decided that it would be best to unload the entire clip at the man, just to be sure.

Taking a deep breath, he stepped away from the house and followed his plan to the letter. When he was within a foot of the window, he raised the gun and fired ten rounds into the vehicle. He couldn't risk the officer surviving even long enough to key the mic of his radio.

The cop didn't stand a chance. The rounds struck him in the head, and he simply shook from the impacts and fell forward.

But he bounced off his computer, and his left shoulder landed squarely on the cruiser's horn. The vehicle blared out an obnoxious and ear-piercing squeal.

Schofield swore and rushed forward to push the dead man away from the steering wheel, but the damage was done. Breathing hard, Schofield looked all around for any sign that a neighbor had heard the noise, but he saw no one, no movement in any windows.

He shoved the dead man over onto his side to make him less visible and then set off to take care of his unfinished business. This cop wasn't the last person that he planned to kill that day.

But unlike the officer, his next victim wouldn't die quickly and quietly. He would be burned alive. He would suffer terribly before death took him.

Schofield had come to realize that his son's experiments on the animal he had found in the shoebox and the dark drawings he had stumbled upon in the drawer weren't actually because Benjamin had no soul. The boy was being influenced by an outside source, and Schofield knew exactly who that was. And now the old man next door would learn that he should never have interfered with Schofield's family.

104

TWO THINGS HAPPENED within a moment of each other that added to Maggie's unease. The first was a text message from Marcus that read *Schofield is in the wind, watch your back.* The second was a car horn sounding out on the street. The prolonged nature of the noise seemed strange. If it had been someone pulling out of a driveway and nearly backing into another car or something similar, the horn's blare should have been quick and angry. She hadn't heard screeching tires or a collision. Still, it wasn't strange enough to warrant investigation.

The basement was large and open, half finished, half given over to storage. Shelves containing plastic totes of all sizes labeled with masking tape and marker filled the storage space. There was also a gun safe in one corner, but she lacked the skills to open it. There was no sign of the kidnapped women.

Once upstairs, Maggie crept into the foyer to see if the cop was still outside. Looking through the shades, she saw his car but not him. Maybe he was walking the perimeter. In which case, she was stuck inside the house. She couldn't let the cop see her leaving the house, federal agent or not.

She moved to the back of the house and peered out a window, but there was no sign of the officer in the backyard or near the garage. Then she moved into the kitchen and looked out through a window to the north side of the house. Her eyes scanned the neighbors' homes, since the officer might have decided to start asking questions.

And then she saw him. Walking into the neighbor's house

was a man wearing navy-blue and white coveralls. Stan had sent them all an image of Harrison Schofield that he had retrieved from the company's website, and although the guy in the coveralls was only visible in profile, she could have sworn that it was the same man. But why would Schofield return here? And why would the cop not have stopped him?

Unless the officer was already dead.

Maggie took her Glock 19 from the holster at her hip and ran toward the back door.

105

A TEXT MESSAGE from Stan appeared on Vasques's phone saying that Belacourt was approaching. A moment later, the spotter from the Cook County Sheriff's tactical team called out over the radio that the target was incoming. This was it. A part of her hoped that Belacourt would resist and choose suicide by cop, but she dismissed the thought. She wanted him to stand trial as an accessory to her father's murder and probably for the murders of his own wife and daughter. She wanted him to answer for what he had done. And she wanted to look in his eyes as they took him away in chains.

She watched the surveillance monitor showing the feed from a small articulating camera mounted atop the van. It showed Belacourt's stolen Honda Civic pulling through the mall lot and into a parking space near the mall's back corner. Vasques keyed her radio and said, "Hold positions. Wait for the second target to arrive."

Her phone vibrated again, displaying a message from Marcus. It read *Schofield is in the wind— We NEED Belacourt and Jansen.*

Working on it, she typed back. Then she popped in another piece of Juicy Fruit gum, checked her watch, and wondered how long they should wait before taking Belacourt if Jansen didn't show.

Troy said, "Hey, I was thinking that after this is all over maybe I could take you out to dinner."

She raised her eyebrows, and he added, "Not like a date, you know, just to celebrate."

But there was something in his eyes that she had never

noticed before. They had been partners for a long time. And she had never really thought about it, but he was probably her best friend. Still, something in Troy's demeanor and body language suggested that he hoped for more. The FBI had not rules against relationships between partners or even between supervisors and subordinates. She knew several agents who had met and married other agents or FBI support personnel.

Still, a relationship would change everything between them. How could they be partners and lovers at the same time? Vasques hated to think about spoiling what they already had.

But she was also damn tired of being so cautious in her personal life and being alone. So she smiled and said, "That would be great."

"Good, then it's a date. Well, not a date, but a…scheduled dinner…between co-workers."

She patted Troy on the shoulder and chuckled. "I know what you mean. Just shut up and watch the—"

The sound of a high-powered rifle shot split the air, the concussive boom and crack echoing through the interior of the van. She watched the monitor in horror as the front windshield of Belacourt's Honda exploded.

"No!" Vasques screamed. Then she threw open the back doors of the van and ran toward Belacourt. Maybe he was still alive? Maybe she could help him?

Her feet pounded through the brown slurry covering the asphalt of the parking lot. She heard Troy's voice at her back, but it sounded far away. He was yelling for her to get down, but she *needed* to reach Belacourt. He was their only lead on the location of the missing women.

She scanned the area for the shooter as she ran and pulled her gun.

Belacourt's car was only a few yards away.

She could see him. His head was slumped over to the side. He wasn't moving.

Across a large open piece of land was a residential area;

there was a minivan on the road opposite them. Was that the shooter?

Then she was falling. Something had struck her and stolen her feet out from beneath her. Her head cracked against the asphalt, and she felt very cold.

Confusion overwhelmed her. What had just happened?

Her mind replayed the events as she tried to make sense of it.

She had been running, and then something had hit her. A loud sound had followed.

Vasques touched her stomach. It felt warm and sticky. She couldn't breathe, and her whole body had started to go numb.

The air was cold and fresh against her skin and in her mouth as she gasped for air. Her sense of it seemed heightened. She felt as though she was suspended above the ground, not lying on it.

The sound of screaming reached her ears, and she couldn't tell if it was coming from her own mouth or from someone else.

She looked up at the sky. The different shades of gray and blue and white.

The numbness had crept over her whole body. Now she felt strangely calm as if she was floating on a tranquil sea, a million miles from anywhere, with an endless sky stretching out overhead.

And then she closed her eyes.

106

MAGGIE APPROACHED THE house at an angle, so as not to be visible from the front or the windows. The neighbor's home wasn't nearly as extravagant as the Schofield residence, but it was still a lovely and expensive-looking house, just on a smaller scale. It was a single-story ranch-style place covered with beige brick and surrounded by red rock landscaping. A white Ford Taurus sat in the driveway. The car was free of snow, as if it had arrived only a few minutes earlier.

There was little to block the wind in the space between the houses. It bit at her skin and pulled at her hair. The snow was deep, and it crept over the tops of her black ankle-high boots and soaked the cuffs of her jeans. Stomping up into the rocky flower bed, she rounded the corner of the neighbor's house.

A small porch ran along its front. With her Glock at the ready, Maggie stepped up onto the porch and peered through the front window. Her view of the room was partially obstructed by a thin white curtain, but the venetian blinds were open. There was an L-shaped brown and white sectional sofa facing a flat-screen TV mounted on the far wall. A big blue fleece blanket was draped over one arm of the couch.

In the center of the room, an old man was gagged and had been duct-taped to a kitchen chair. He had thick white hair that was soaked and clinging to his face. His clothes looked wet as well, and his eyes were wide with fear and confusion. She could hear Schofield but couldn't see him. He was yelling at the old man.

"You should have stayed away from my family!"

She inched farther around the edge of the window, and there he was. He paced back and forth in front of the bound man. A silenced pistol dangled from his right hand, and he held a bottle of Kingsford lighter fluid in the other.

Realizing why the man looked wet and what was about to happen, she rushed to the front door but found it locked.

Focusing on the area just below the knob, Maggie took a deep breath and prepared to strike. She stood sideways a few feet back with her leading foot facing forward. Then she executed a swift side kick, planting her heel into the space below the knob. She carried her momentum all the way through the kick, falling into her target and throwing all her weight behind the blow.

The door flew inward on its hinges and slammed into the drywall. Pieces of the ruined frame shot into the living room. Dust from the drywall and splintered wood filled the room as she raced in.

The air was thick with the smell of smoke and lighter fluid and burning meat. Maggie caught sight of someone moving, running from the room, but she had more pressing concerns.

In the center of the room, the old man was engulfed in flames. He was writhing in agony and screaming beneath his gag. He rocked violently and knocked the chair over onto its side.

Maggie didn't hesitate.

Dropping her gun, she jumped over the burning man and ripped the big blue blanket off of the couch. Then she flung it out over him and dropped her weight on him to smother the flames.

After several moments of frantic patting and rubbing, the fire was extinguished. He was alive, and he had only been on fire for a few seconds. She doubted that he had a hair left on his head or torso, but his injuries weren't life-threatening.

Once the fire was out, she didn't bother to undo the old

man's restraints. Her Glock had fallen near the ruined front door. She scooped it up and ran after Schofield.

She hurried toward a door at the side of the house and burst into the yard. The woods would provide the closest cover and a good escape route, and so her gaze moved in that direction first. But there was no sign of him.

Then she looked down at the snow. Long clumsy footprints showed a path from the side of the old man's house to the curb. Her gaze followed the tracks up and across the street, and she saw him.

Schofield was already nearly onto the next road over, charging through the snow in between his neighbors' homes in an awkward loping gait.

Maggie took off after him at a full sprint. The snow was thick and hindered her movements, but she was in good shape and light on her feet. She reached the street and crossed into the neighboring yard. She closed the distance between the houses and the next street quickly.

But she was too late.

She reached the street just in time to see an old Volkswagen spinning its tires in the slush covering the road as it sped away. She took aim with the Glock, but the car was already out of range.

Schofield was gone.

MARCUS PULLED THE Yukon up near the barricade blocking the road down from Schofield's big brick home. The street and the two houses were a swarm of activity—photographers, CSI techs, police, medical personnel, firemen. The Jackson's Grove police department had probably called in for help from Cook County, the surrounding precincts, and maybe even the State Police. They had at least three different scenes here containing potential evidence and needed all the manpower they could get. But of all the people on the scene, Marcus cared about only one of them.

As they walked up, he said to Andrew, "Give me a few minutes alone with her."

"Okay, I'll see what I can dig up about Mr. O'Malley. See if he and Schofield were enemies."

Maggie sat on the curb across the road from the house of the old man whom Schofield had tried to burn alive. Her hands rested atop her knees, and her eyes were glassy and unmoving. Marcus wanted to rush up and embrace her, but when she saw him, she made no effort to stand. So he just dropped down onto the curb next to her and said nothing.

They sat there for a long few moments as if they were two kids playing the quiet game and the first one to speak would be the loser. Finally, Maggie said, "I let him get away."

"So what?"

"So maybe you were right. Maybe I'm not cut out to be a field agent. I can help in other ways. After what happened today and in Harrisburg—"

"Maggie, please shut up. You did good today. I've come

to realize that our job isn't to catch killers. It's to protect innocent people. And that's what you did. You saved a man's life."

She met his gaze. Her cheeks were flushed, but he couldn't tell if it was from embarrassment or the cold. "Thank you."

"Don't thank me. You're a good agent, and if I were any kind of a team leader, you would already know that." Marcus blew out a long breath. "And if I were any kind of a man, you would also know how much I love you. But we—"

Her hands shot out and grabbed him by the sides of his head. Just as quickly, she pulled him in close and kissed him. It was a long and hungry kiss.

His arms folded around her. He could feel her heart pounding, and she was breathing hard. When she pulled away, she said, "Don't say anything else. You'll just ruin it."

108

Marcus found Stupak standing next to the Jackson's Grove cruiser containing the dead officer. The dead man looked young, probably only a few years out of the academy with a wife and kids waiting for him at home. When Marcus was a boy, not long before his parents died, his father had been hit with a baseball bat by two kids robbing a small electronics store. His mother had received the late-night call that the wife of every police officer dreads. When his father had worked nights, she liked Marcus to sleep in the bed with her, and so he was there when she received the call. Although his father walked away with only a slight concussion and a few stitches, Marcus would never forget the look on her face, and he wondered if there was another child out there at that moment seeing the same look of fear and heartbreak in their mother's eyes.

Stupak's overly expensive suit and overcoat looked rumpled. Both were unbuttoned. His tie was undone, and his shirt untucked. For the first time since Marcus had seen the detective in the Jackson's Grove briefing room, the man looked flustered.

"I'm sorry about your man," Marcus said.

Stupak nodded, but his stare didn't leave the technicians retrieving evidence from the cruiser. "He was a good cop. Young, but he took the job seriously. It was more than a paycheck." Stupak ran a hand over his perfectly shaved head. "This kind of thing doesn't happen here. Two of our own dead within a few hours."

"Two? You had another officer killed today?"

Stupak gave him a look of contempt as though he seemed to be trying to determine if Marcus was serious. "Belacourt. I don't care what anyone says that he did. He was a good detective…and my friend."

"Belacourt's dead?"

"You haven't heard?"

"No, I've been trying to call Vasques, but I haven't been able to reach her."

Stupak groaned and rubbed the back of his neck. "I'm sorry. You won't be able to reach her anytime soon. She had set up an operation to lure in a man named Erik Jansen by using Belacourt. Apparently it backfired. We think it was Jansen that shot Belacourt with a high-powered rifle. He died on scene. Vasques caught a round in the stomach. Her vest wasn't enough to stop that kind of round, but I'm sure it slowed it down. She's in surgery now. That's all I know."

Marcus felt like all the air had suddenly been sucked from the world. He couldn't breathe. Cold chills lanced down through the core of his body. But, within only a few seconds, the feeling of cold was replaced with fire. "I'm going to find these guys, Stupak. And I'm going to kill them. Conlan, Schofield, Jansen. All of them. You don't have to help me, but don't get in my way."

Stupak just looked at him for a long, hard moment. Then he said, "What do you need from me?"

"Have your guys been through the house?"

"Yeah, we found a gun safe in the basement loaded with some illegal weapons. A couple of automatics and a grenade."

"Grenade? Where the hell did he get that?"

"Not as difficult as you might think. Especially with him working in the security field. I'm sure their company employs a lot of ex-military. You can also buy disarmed grenades at just about any military surplus store. Then it's just a matter of having the know-how to put the guts back in."

"What about the family? Any word on them?" Marcus said.

"We contacted the cell company to track their phones. Led right back here. They left them behind. Then we spoke to Schofield's mother-in-law, and she said that her daughter called her late last night and said that an emergency had come up and they would be gone for a while. She tried but didn't get any details beyond that."

Marcus looked around at the expensive neighborhood and Schofield's house, which was the star of the block. It was the kind of house that raised everyone else's already bloated property values. The guy had a wife, three kids, and the biggest house on the block. But he still couldn't run from his past. The hunger that Schofield felt couldn't be filled with all the possessions and money in the world.

Marcus wondered why Schofield's family had run away. Had they finally learned his secret and fled in fear?

He retrieved a business card from the inner pocket of his leather jacket and handed it to Stupak. "I'm going to check out the house myself. If you find anything, call me."

Stupak took the card and replied, "Same goes for you."

Marcus moved up the stamped concrete walkway to Schofield's front door. One of the techs didn't want to let him in, and it took a showing of his credentials and some harsh words to gain access. Once inside, he did a quick walk-through of the first floor. There was a long hallway in the center of the house that was packed with family photos. Vacations, graduations, school events, candid shots, professional portraits. All variations were represented. It felt like a museum display, missing only the little info cards explaining what was depicted in each scene. It was a chronicle of the Schofield family and their lives together. They looked genuinely happy.

He thought of Vasques and wondered if she would get the chance to have a family like this. Husband. Children. A hall of fame commemorating each happy moment. Those bastards might have stolen that from her, and they needed to pay for it.

His phone rang, but he didn't recognize the number.

His teeth ground against each other, but he accepted the call and immediately said, "I have nothing to say to you."

"What did he tell you?"

"The truth."

Ackerman laughed. "I very much doubt that."

"He told me that you and your father killed my parents."

"Did he? Interesting. I guess that is partially accurate, but definitely not the whole truth. I was just a boy myself and had nothing to do with their deaths. I did, however, have something to do with how you lived past that night. Do you honestly not remember anything about what really happened?"

Marcus said nothing, but he knew exactly what Ackerman was referring to. He remembered the voice in the darkness that had helped him hide as his parents screamed on the floor below. He remembered someone holding his hand. He remembered the fear, the sadness, the emotions of that night. But he had been young, and it was all blurry and incoherent images that had either been blocked out or mostly forgotten. It had always bothered him how some memories from that time—trips to the Bronx Zoo and Coney Island or meals shared at Mazzola's bakery or Nino's pizzeria— could be so vivid and complete, but that night eluded him.

Ackerman continued. "I only learned the truth recently myself. I remembered that night, but I hadn't made the connection to you. I just remembered a scared little boy in cowboy pajamas. I was told to bring you down. But I remember there being something in your eyes that compelled me to keep you away from him. I hid you on the porch roof outside your bedroom window. Then I made the bed and told my father that you weren't there. He stormed up the stairs and checked for himself, but he couldn't find you. You're only alive today because of me. Because I saved you."

Marcus didn't know what to say. What the killer had told him coincided with his own scattered memories, and the new information didn't even necessarily mean that the Director had lied to him. His superior might never have known the whole story. Plus, the story rang true on another level that he couldn't quite identify.

"How did you figure out that was how we're connected?"

"Marcus, come on now. You can't expect me to give up all my secrets. Besides, we have more pressing concerns at the moment. How goes the hunt for our friend the Anarchist?"

"Goodbye, Ackerman."

"Wait, I can help you. I know how you can find him."

Marcus knew that he should have hung up right then. He knew better than to give in to the madman's fantasies or encourage him in any way. But curiosity, coupled with his desire to protect innocent life and avenge its taking, was too strong. He didn't say anything, but he didn't hang up either.

The killer accepted the silent acknowledgment and said, "If you want to beat someone or control them, you have to learn their weaknesses. Who or what does this person love? What do they want? What do they need? What is the most important thing in the world to them? If you can answer those questions about the Anarchist, then you can exploit his weaknesses and make him dance to your tune. And I think you already know what you need to do. You just need to have the necessary intestinal fortitude to step up and walk that path. This is what you are. Good hunting."

The line went dead, and Marcus closed his eyes. Ackerman was right. Marcus knew what Schofield loved, but he hated himself for being the kind of man who would use it against the killer.

He looked around at the pictures of smiling faces and happy memories one last time, and then he dialed Stan's number.

"Stan's Crematorium. You kill 'em, we grill 'em"

"Not in the mood, Stan. I need you to track down Schofield's family. They're running, but they don't know the game. I'm betting they've screwed up and left a trail some-where along the way."

"Okay, I'm on it. What are you going to do when we find them?"

"I'm going to kidnap them and hold them for ransom."

ELEANOR ADARE SCHOFIELD stared out the window of the Belmont Motel and thought about the perfect life that she had left behind. The motel was small with an orange and white faux-brick exterior. The big white and blue neon sign out front advertised telephones, air conditioning, and TV as though they were luxury items, but she supposed that just by looking at the place one would wonder about such things. The interior walls were bright yellow. The bedspread had a quilted white and yellow sunflower print that looked like something her grandmother had had on her bed when Eleanor was a child. The room had a faint musty smell like someone's basement that had been sprayed with disinfectant, but at least it was relatively clean.

The thought made her sick. Had she fallen so far that providing a place for her children to sleep that wasn't infested with cockroaches seemed like a victory?

Harrison had told her to go to the Belmont as if he had planned for it, as if he had considered such a thing before. He had told her to pay in cash, but she had been shocked to learn that a room in a dump like this was sixty dollars a night. She never kept much cash on hand—they always used their credit cards and paid them off at the end of the month— and so she had been forced to go across the street and withdraw the money from an ATM.

Eleanor had told the kids that they were going away on a surprise vacation. The younger two had accepted this with few questions, but she knew that Alison suspected something. She probably thought they were getting a divorce, and maybe they were. Alison had her earbuds in now. Benjamin played his little game system while Melanie watched *Dora the Explorer* on a small tube television with a washed-out picture. The little Pomeranian dog that Harrison had brought home rested on Melanie's lap.

When the phone on the nightstand rang, Eleanor jumped away from the window and cried out so loud in surprise that Alison pulled out her earbuds and looked at her mother with wide, startled eyes. Eleanor fumbled with the receiver and said, "Hello?"

"It's me. Are you okay? Have you had any problems?"

At first she felt relieved to hear Harrison's voice, but once the initial spark of warmth and safety faded, she wasn't sure what to feel. She fought back tears. While she'd been in the motel office paying for the room, she had seen the news about a hostage situation at SSA. She had heard the horrible things that her husband was accused of, and she knew that it was all true. A part of her had always known, and she blamed herself for not doing something about it sooner. But another part of her refused to believe that their entire life together had been a lie.

"Eleanor, are you there?"

She started to speak but her throat felt dry and she had no idea where to begin. She pulled the phone from the nightstand, moved into the bathroom, and closed the door behind her. The room was mint green and smelled like bleach.

The other end of the line was silent for a moment, but then he said, "You saw the news, didn't you?"

"Yes—they say that you're the Anarchist. That you're wanted in connection with over ten murders."

"I'm sorry, Eleanor. I wish you hadn't seen that."

"That way you could lie to me some more?"

"No, so you could hear it from me. So you could understand."

"There's nothing to understand, Harrison. You're a murderer. How could you?"

When he spoke, she could hear the pain in his voice. "Because I was born without a soul."

The statement shocked her. He had told her of the abuse he had endured as a child, but she never thought that he actually believed the things he had been told by his mother and the other members of that cult. Maybe she should have known? A sense of her own failure as a wife gnawed at her.

"That's ridiculous. Your mother and those people were insane. You know that."

"I don't know what to believe. All I wanted was to be whole for you. To be the husband and father that you and the children deserved. I'm so sorry that I've failed you." His voice cracked, and she could hear his tears.

She wanted to hate him, but yet a part of her pitied him. She had always known that his perception of the world had been scarred as a result of his childhood, but she had never realized how deep those wounds went.

"Harrison, we love you. We always have, and we always will. But you need to turn yourself in. We'll get through this together."

"I can't."

"Yes, you can. You need help. We can't get through this alone."

"You don't understand. The reason that I told you to run wasn't for my own good. It was because you're in danger."

"Danger from who?"

"The Prophet."

"The leader of that cult? I thought you said he was dead."

"No, he never let me go. He's always been there. He's been the devil on my shoulder since the day I was born. And now he wants you. He wants to sacrifice you and the kids."

She stifled a sharp cry, and her knees felt weak. "Damn you, Harrison. How could you put our children in danger?"

"I never meant for any of this to happen. You have to believe me."

"That's all the more reason for you to turn yourself in.

The police can help us. Maybe they'll give you some kind of a deal if you testify against him."

"The most I could hope for would be a mental institution instead of a prison. I won't subject you and the kids to that kind of humiliation. I know what that feels like, and I would never do that to you. I have money. We can leave this all—"

Eleanor jumped and dropped the phone as the sound of someone banging on the door echoed off the mint-green tile of the bathroom. She immediately opened the door, expecting to see one of the kids, but instead she found a strange man standing on the other side.

SITTING IN HIS own seedy motel room, Harrison Schofield gripped the receiver of the old rotary phone sitting on the nightstand and screamed his wife's name. He heard a banging noise followed by a clattering as though she had dropped the phone and then a stifled scream.

As he yelled for her, he felt his whole world fall down around him. He knew that the Prophet had found them. A vision of his children burning alive flooded his mind as he sank to his knees.

But then a man's voice came over from the other end of the line. The voice was deep and full of menace, and Schofield didn't recognize it.

The words were simple and straight to the point. "I have your family, and I'm going to kill them unless you do exactly as you're told."

THE BLIZZARD HAD come in the night. It swept over Chicagoland like a tsunami, and the flakes seemed to be flying in every direction. As Marcus walked up to the rented house, the snow stung his cheeks and eyes and made it so that he could barely see his surroundings. They had found a place on Artesian Avenue in Brighton Park ten minutes from downtown Chicago. The house was technically for sale, but some cold hard cash for a week's rental of an empty house was an easy choice for the owner. The man had described the place as a bungalow, but to Marcus it looked more like a small barn with bluish shingle siding and a bright red porch. It didn't surprise him that the house had been sitting empty for so long.

He knocked, and Andrew opened the door. Once inside, Marcus stamped his feet on the welcome mat to clear the snow and shook the cold from his shoulders. The interior wasn't much better. There was no carpet, just pale yellow linoleum and rust-colored wallpaper. Several of the interior doors had been inexplicably torn from their casings, and the whole house reeked of urine. He guessed that was the reason there were no carpets. Maybe some lady with a thousand cats had lived here before and just let her darlings defecate where they wished.

The look on Andrew's face illustrated his feelings about the place. "It's only temporary," Marcus said.

"It had better be."

"How's the family holding up?"

"About as you'd expect," Andrew said. "But I don't get

it. Why didn't we just let Schofield come to his family and grab him then? Why the ruse of a kidnapping?"

"Because if Conlan has those women, they'll be dead by tonight. We don't have time for an interrogation. Conlan is extremely unstable and delusional. There's no way to predict what he'll do. We need Schofield to believe that his family's lives are on the line. If we threaten to take away what he loves, he'll give us Conlan."

"I hope you're right, but I still don't like it. Maggie or I should be going with you."

"We don't have enough manpower. I'll have Stupak with me, and we'll need his help once we have a location on the women. Besides, I can handle Schofield."

Andrew's phone dinged, and he glanced at the screen and shook his head.

"What was that?" Marcus said.

Andrew laughed. "Nothing. I'm just playing Scrabble online with Allen. He's getting stir crazy in that bed. He's not used to lying around."

"How's the game going?"

"Allen's killing me. The Professor has a pretty impressive vocabulary. Maggie's on her way to visit him now, and she wanted to stop in and check on that old man who she saved. You should go see Allen, too. You've got some time before the meeting with Schofield. The hospital is on the way."

"I don't know. We'll see."

"What happened to him wasn't your fault. You know that, right? Nobody blames you. Least of all Allen."

Marcus said nothing. He just nodded and headed for the only closed door in the house. He knocked, and a voice on the other side told him to come in. When he opened the door, a little orange dog yapped at him. Eleanor Schofield sat on the yellow linoleum floor, playing Candyland with her son and youngest daughter. She was trying to smile and put on a good face for the kids, but he could see the sadness and pain behind her eyes.

"Can I have a word?" Marcus said.

She nodded and followed him into the living room where Andrew sat on the couch fiddling with his phone.

He closed the door behind her and said, "I just wanted to thank you for your cooperation on this."

"I'm doing it for those missing women, not for you." She gestured toward a lock that Andrew had installed on the outside of the door and said, "Are we prisoners here? You stuck us in a room with a lock and no windows."

"It's for your own protection. Hopefully, this will all be over very soon."

"My husband's not a monster."

"I never said that he was."

Marcus could see her eyes taking on a watery sheen. Her voice was hoarse and trembling. "I just can't accept that it was all a lie. He's a good man. I know he is. He's sick, and he needs help."

"I don't think your husband is a monster or evil. I used to think of men like him in those terms because it was easier to wrap my mind around. It's difficult to accept that we all have darkness in our hearts. We're all sinners and saints. Just to varying degrees. We're all capable of inflicting pain and hatred on this world, and we're all capable of showing compassion and love. I believe in evil, but I don't think that it lives in your husband. He is sick, but I also can't let him go on hurting people because of it."

Eleanor looked away and whispered, "I know."

"There's something else that you should keep in mind. I believe that this plan is going to work only because of how strongly your husband loves you and your children. And no matter what happens, you should hang on to that."

VASQUES LOOKED PALE. All manner of tubes and bandages coiled around her sleeping form, and her eyes fluttered behind closed lids. Marcus had grown accustomed to her sweet floral scent, but rubbing alcohol and cleaning fluids had bleached that away. Its absence made her seem like less of the person he had known, as though a part of her had already died.

A blond-haired man with pasty white features sat next to her bed, his hand folded around hers. The man wore a white button-down shirt. It was untucked and a black tie hung loosely around his neck. His eyes were bloodshot.

The blond man glanced in Marcus's direction but didn't say a word. Still, Marcus noticed his breathing change as if he were angry at being disturbed. "Are you Vasques's brother?" Marcus said.

"No, I'm her partner. Special Agent LaPaglia."

"It's good to meet you. I'm Special Agent Marcus Williams from the DOJ. Vasques and I were working this case together." He stuck out his hand, but LaPaglia didn't return the gesture. After a moment, Marcus's hand fell back to his side. He asked, "How's she doing?"

"She's stable. They think she's out of the woods." LaPaglia shook his head. "It's your fault that this happened."

"How do you figure?"

"It was your idea to use Belacourt to draw the others in. You should have taken him into custody like any other suspect and interrogated him. It's your little game that caused this."

"Vasques isn't the kind of woman that needs to be told

what to do. It was her call on how to handle Belacourt. But if I'd have been there at the scene, maybe this wouldn't have happened."

LaPaglia sprang from the hospital chair and shoved his hands against Marcus's chest, pushing him back. "You saying that I didn't have her back? Get out! You're not welcome here."

Marcus raised his hands in surrender and backed toward the door. He knew better than to argue with someone whose vision had been clouded by grief and doubt and a lack of sleep. He turned to leave but then stopped himself. "LaPaglia, someone recently gave me some good advice that I'll pass on to you. When she wakes up, tell her how you really feel."

ALLEN'S HOSPITAL ROOM was the same as Marcus remembered. The same antiseptic smell filled the air. Same shades of blue, same furniture, same machines beeping and whirring. But the mood was different. When he had been here before, there'd been a somber aura smothering everything and that had colored his memories of the place. But now Allen was sitting up and laughing along with his wife and Maggie. He still had the tubes connected to his arms and running into his nose and the doctors still weren't sure if he would walk again, but at least he was smiling and the color had returned to his cheeks.

Allen leaned over a rolling tray full of food that he was shoveling into his mouth as though he hadn't eaten in a week. "This food tastes like you cooked it, Loren," Allen said to his wife. "The meat has the tenderness of shoe leather, and I think someone spat in my mashed potatoes."

"If you know what's good for you, old man, you'll shut your mouth," Loren replied. "I have power of attorney. I can tell the docs to turn these machines off and let you wither."

"Teach not thy lip such scorn, for it was made for kissing, lady, not for such contempt," Allen said, quoting Shakespeare.

Marcus stepped into the room and joined the conversation. "In general, those who have nothing to say contrive to spend the longest time in doing it."

Loren laughed and gave Marcus a big hug. "Sounds like that guy knew you, Allen."

Allen gave a dirty look to both of them. "That was James Russell Lowell, an American poet. And I believe he died in the 1890s, so I never had the pleasure. You've been saving that one up for just such a moment. Haven't you, kid?"

"I have no idea what you're talking about," Marcus replied with a grin. "Where are the kids?"

"Down in the cafeteria. And if you wouldn't mind, ladies, I have something that I need to discuss with Marcus in private."

Maggie stood up from a recliner beside Allen's bed, and Loren grabbed her purse. On the way out, Loren patted Marcus on the shoulder and said, "Just smile and nod. That's what I do." Then she stuck her tongue out at Allen. Marcus could see the older man suppressing a grin.

Once they were gone, Marcus said, "So what's up?"

"I need to talk to you about Ackerman for a moment."

"We'll get him, Allen. He's getting bolder. He'll make a mistake, and I'll be there when he does."

"That's not what I meant. I just wanted to..." Allen sighed. "There's something that I should have told you a long time ago. And I'm sorry."

Marcus squeezed his hand. "Thank you, but it's okay. I know the connection between the two of us."

"You do?"

"Yeah, Ackerman hinted at it, and I confronted the Director. He told me that Ackerman's father killed my parents."

Allen closed his eyes and shook his head. "Oh, my boy, I'm afraid that's only scratching the surface."

MR. O'MALLEY'S ROOM matched Allen's, except that O'Malley's had two beds instead of one. The door was open and Maggie could see O'Malley carefully gathering his things. Bandages covered his face and hands. She could see the red, irritated skin around his eyes and mouth. His lips were cracked and bloody. But, all things considered, he was lucky to be alive.

She knocked on the door, and he turned toward her. His eyes were angry at first, and she couldn't fault him for the emotion. But the anger quickly drained away, and he forced a smile onto his cracked lips. When he spoke, his thick Irish brogue came out in a hoarse crackling like the crunching of dried leaves. "Miss Maggie, I hoped that I would get a chance to thank you properly for saving my life. When you checked on me in the ambulance, I was a bit out of sorts."

She smiled. "I would expect that you were, but there's no reason to thank me."

"Oh, now, don't give me a line about *just my job* or *all in a day's work*. I'd be dead now if it weren't for you. And not only that, but your quick reaction allowed me to escape with only second-degree burns.

A miracle, in my opinion. Saving a man's life is not a small thing where I come from. It's a debt that can never be repaid."

"I just wish that I would have caught the man that did this to you."

"Aye, I still don't understand why he attacked me like that. I had always sensed a bit of tension because I was so close to his kids. Maybe a little jealousy at our relationship, but nothing that would warrant something like this."

"Is there anything that *does* warrant setting another man on fire?"

"I suppose not. Speaking of Schofield's family, has there been any word from them? While I've been lying here that's been my biggest concern."

Maggie knew that Marcus wouldn't like her giving away any information about the family, but she truly felt for O'Malley. He was just a warm-hearted neighbor whose kindness had earned him a body covered in burns and a near-death experience. He deserved to know. But still, she hesitated. "I'm sorry. I haven't heard anything."

His face fell. Up to that point, he had seemed downright jovial for a man in his position, but now he seemed on the verge of tears. His voice cracked a bit as he said, "If you hear anything, please let me know. I don't think that I'll be able to sleep a wink until those kids are home safe. I had a daughter at one time, but she died before I could be blessed with grandchildren. But I think of Alison, Melanie, and Benjamin like they were my own kin, and I've been worried sick about them."

Her heart went out to him. He had been through enough, and he should be able to rest and recuperate in peace. "Mr. O'Malley, what I'm about to tell you is just between us. For their own safety, you can't tell anyone about this."

His eyes lit up, and he took a hurried step forward. "Do you know where they are?"

"Yes, we have them in a safe location."

"Oh, praise the Lord, you get to be my savior for the second time in as many days." His face took on a pensive look. "Do you think there's any chance that I could pay them a visit? I'm sure that poor Eleanor is feeling guilty about what her husband did to me. She may not seem so on the outside, but she's delicate. I want her to know that I hold no ill will. And at a time like this, those kids could really use some stability. Something to show them that their world hasn't been turned completely upside down."

"I don't think that would be possible."

"You've already done so much for me. I truly hate to ask for more, but I can guarantee you that it would be very much appreciated by us all. I know that I could help them to get through this terrible and dark time."

"I'm sorry. I can't—"

"Please, I'd be happy to wear a blindfold so that I won't know where you're keeping them. I'd do anything. Please, just a half an hour could make a world of difference."

Maggie crossed her arms and looked deep into the old man's eyes. The area of skin surrounding them was red and cracked, and she suspected that the bandages covered blisters and sores. O'Malley and the Schofield children had been through so much pain due to no fault of their own. And it couldn't really hurt for her to try and bring a little light into that world.

"Hold on a minute." She pulled out her phone and texted Marcus.

I told Mr. O'Malley that the Schofields are safe. He wants to see them.

She waited a few seconds, and then the reply came back. *What the hell were you thinking?*

She growled deep in her throat, and her fingers flew over the virtual keyboard.

Dammit, Marcus. He's been through a lot. They all have. I'm not asking. I'm telling.

She waited a long moment for his reply. *I don't like it, but you always do what you want anyway. Just make it quick.*

"Are you cleared to leave?" she said to O'Malley.

He grinned like a child at Christmas. "The doctor met with me a half-hour ago. I was waiting for an old friend to pick me up, but I'll just call on the way and let him know that I won't be needing a ride."

Realizing how much of a sucker she was, she said, "Okay, but you can't stay long."

ACKERMAN WATCHED AS Maggie exited the elevator and headed toward the Kia Rio parked nearby. She had a man with her who was all covered in bandages as though he was the Invisible Man. But it didn't really matter. Her guest was of little concern to him, whoever he was.

The killer's heart was racing now, and he felt almost giddy with excitement. They stood on a precipice at the edge of great revelation and enlightenment. Events that he had been planning for nearly a year were about to be set in motion, and Maggie was an integral part of that equation.

In his own way, he had warned Marcus that this would happen. He had said that in order to control another person, one needed to threaten or take away what they loved. And Maggie was one of the few things in the world that Marcus loved.

Which meant that Ackerman would have to take her away.

He smiled as her car pulled past him and down the ramp. Then he slipped his own vehicle into gear and slid into traffic behind her.

FOR THE MEETING, Marcus had wanted a location where Scho-field would be completely exposed and unable to escape. Somewhere public and accessible but still isolated. As he pulled down Columbus Drive and parked in view of Buck-ingham Fountain, he knew that he had made the right de-cision.

Nestled in the heart of Grant Park in downtown Chi-cago, Buckingham Fountain was one of the most famous landmarks in the city and the world's largest illuminated fountain. Normally, one and a half million gallons of water filled the wedding-cake-style fountain, but every year in mid-October it was shut down and the water replaced with festival lights. With the blizzard in full force, there were no tourists piling from double-decker buses or snapping pic-tures of the landmark. The fountain had been completely abandoned, giving Marcus an unobstructed view of the en-tire area. He could see only one man in the distance stand-ing at the rendezvous spot.

"Are you ready for this?" Marcus said to his passenger.

Stupak nodded, but the detective's stare didn't leave the man near the fountain. Marcus had instructed Stupak not to wear his suit, so the cop had come dressed in an elegant black button-down shirt tucked into designer khakis. Mar-cus wore a black zip-up hoodie and jeans and wondered if Stupak owned a simple sweatshirt.

"Stupak, you keep your mouth shut and follow my lead or you stay in the car. Do we understand each other?"

"Maybe we should have called in backup units to surround the area."

"We don't have time for that. This guy's smart and wealthy. We bring him in, he'll lawyer up instantly, and we'll get nothing out of him."

"What if he has friends up there waiting for us? It could be an ambush."

"He wouldn't risk his family. Besides, according to Schofield's wife, Conlan wanted to sacrifice them and so Schofield isn't drinking the Kool-Aid anymore. Who else could he get to back him up?"

"I just don't like it."

"We're trying to trick a multiple murderer into helping us save the lives of a couple women that are going to be sacrificed to the devil within a few hours if we don't find them. What's to like about it?"

As Marcus pulled open his door, the cold wind assaulted him. He pulled his hood up over his Yankees cap and looked toward the city, but all he could see in the distance were vague outlines of buildings whose details were obscured in a white mist. The snow was falling so fast and hard that it made the city look like it was shrouded by a blanket of fog. There was a steady stream of traffic flowing on Columbus, but he still felt strangely isolated. It was as if some supernatural force had shaken a snow globe and made the millions of other people in the city disappear.

Shaking off the feeling, he headed toward the fountain and passed a long line of large stone pots. He guessed they were normally filled with flowers, but now they were compacted with mounds of snow. White-capped mazes of shrubbery formed the outer perimeter of the path leading to the fountain. There were no other footprints in sight. No one else was crazy enough to venture out into the park in weather like this.

By the time they had trekked halfway there, Marcus's hands were freezing and his nose was running. The snow seemed to be pelting them from every angle. He kept his head low so the brim of his Yankees cap would take the brunt of the barrage.

Schofield stood beside the fountain, watching them approach. He wore a wool coat over a pair of blue and white coveralls and a baseball cap adorned with the SSA logo. His hands were in his pockets, and Marcus could see a bulge that could have been a weapon. When the distance between them had narrowed to about ten feet, Schofield said, "That's far enough. Where's my family?"

The other man's directness impressed Marcus, especially since he knew how Schofield felt about confrontation. "They're safe for now. You tell us the location of the Prophet and the missing women, and I'll make sure they stay that way."

Schofield eyed them through the snow. "I've seen you before. Both of you. I watched you at the crime scenes before you found my cameras. You're cops." The killer's gaze swept over the surrounding area. Perhaps he was expecting to see other officers converging on their position. "You won't hurt my family."

"I know that Conlan wanted to kill them. Why protect him?"

"We're done here."

Schofield started to back away from them, but Marcus pulled the Sig Sauer from his coat. "You're not going anywhere. Show me your hands."

"I'd be careful what you ask for," Schofield said. Then he slowly removed his hands from his pockets. There was a grenade in each fist, and the killer had already pulled the pins.

115

MAGGIE PULLED THE Kia up to the curb in front of the ugly blue house in Brighton Park. Marcus felt that he had gotten a great deal on the place, but in her opinion, the owner should have burned the little blue barn to the ground a long time ago. At least she didn't have to sleep there. It made her skin crawl just having to step inside, and she felt even more sorry for the Schofield family that they were stuck in such horrid accommodations.

She had considered blindfolding O'Malley as he had suggested but decided against it. The sidewalks and stairs would be slick, and the last thing she wanted was to cause the old Irishman to fall and have to take another trip to the hospital.

The snow beat down on her as she made her way up the bright red steps onto the safe house's porch. O'Malley's coat had a hood, but Maggie suspected that the little projectiles of snow would still slip underneath. The pinpricks of cold had to be torture against his inflamed skin. She slipped on the walkway a few times and nearly went down. But O'Malley was surprisingly sure-footed and had no such problems.

She knocked, and within a moment, Andrew appeared at the door. He gave her a strange look and said, "Who's your friend?" But the look in his eyes said something more like *Who's the mummy?*

"This is Mr. O'Malley. He's the neighbor that Harrison Schofield attacked. I stopped in to visit him at the hospital, and we felt that it would be good for the kids to see a familiar face." As she spoke the words, she realized that her choice of phrasing was odd since O'Malley's *familiar face* was actually disfigured and covered with bandages.

"Does Marcus know about this?"

"I let him know. Can we come in now? It's freezing out here."

"Sure. Sorry about that."

Andrew stepped back from the door, and Maggie followed him in. The smell assaulted her immediately, and she suppressed a shiver at the thought of the germs teeming over every surface. There was a kitchen table in the middle of the living room. It had been ripped from the 1970s with its light faux-wood top, along with four green chairs the color of pond scum. She stripped off her coat and reluctantly laid it over the back of one of the chairs.

"Are the Schofields here?" O'Malley said.

Andrew nodded. "They're in the back bedroom. I'll go get them."

But O'Malley just smiled and said, "Allow me."

Then, before Maggie even realized what was happening, O'Malley's arm shot out and grabbed her sidearm from its place on her hip. He moved with startling speed and precision. In one smooth motion, the gun was in his hand, and he was bringing it up and against the side of her skull. Hard.

She saw it happen, but her mind still couldn't comprehend the images passing in front of her eyes.

The pain lanced down the side of her face, and she stumbled back against the retro table.

When she looked back at her attacker, she saw Andrew reaching for his own gun. And then she saw Mr. O'Malley use her Glock to fire three 9mm bullets directly into Andrew's chest.

116

THE SIGHT OF the two grenades shouldn't have shocked Marcus as much as it did, and he cursed himself for it. He had known that the police had found M67 fragmentation grenades in the killer's basement, and he had even looked up their specifications. Schofield liked to plan ahead, but Marcus hadn't expected the killer to try anything with his family on the line. But then again, he hadn't considered the possibility of Schofield recognizing them as cops either. He considered that maybe his migraines and the lack of sleep were finally starting to take their toll on his thought processes and ability to reason.

Schofield said, "If you come any closer, I'll drop one of these at your feet and throw the other out into the traffic on Columbus."

Marcus slipped his gun back into its holster. "Let's not do anything crazy. You don't want to die here." He took a step forward.

"Don't move! I've considered all the variables! If there are other cops out there, I'll use these to kill myself. If I drop one grenade, you could kick it away or run before the timer runs out and it explodes. But you wouldn't be able to stop the one that's going out onto the street. Odds are good that it would go off right underneath one of those cars. And if that doesn't convince you to stay back, then I also have a backup plan."

Schofield pointed at one of the large green sea-horse statues sitting inside the fountain, and a loud boom echoed over the park. A bullet ricocheted off the sea horse, sending up a puff of snow.

Marcus jerked instinctively at the sound, and Stupak nearly hit the deck. Normally, a hundred tourists and park-goers would have been running and screaming at that moment. But in the midst of the blizzard, Grant Park was as desolate as the moon, and the only other people around were the ones driving past inside their cars on Columbus and Lake Shore Drives. Marcus recognized the sound of a 7.62 mm round, but most people would have dismissed it as a car backfiring.

"My grandfather Raymond. He's a good shot," Schofield said. "Maybe on the range, but lining up a person in your sights is a whole different ball game."

"That's true. He actually wanted me to turn myself in, but when I explained that the kids' lives were on the line, he agreed to do whatever it took. We're pretty much the only family he has left, and he'd do *anything* to protect us."

Marcus held up his ID, deciding to change tactics. "I'm not a cop. I'm from the Attorney General's office. I have the authority to make you a deal. You give us Conlan and the women, and you can avoid prosecution."

"Right, great idea. Then I'll just walk away now and have my lawyer contact your office to draw up the papers. Do you think I'm an idiot?"

"No, I think you're scared. I think you've been scared your whole life. Scared of the Prophet, of your mother, of other people in general. But, most of all, you're scared of yourself. You're scared of what you're capable of."

"You don't know me. We're done here. Don't try to follow me." Schofield took a step back, but Marcus matched the movement.

He said, "I know more about you than you know yourself. I know that you think that you were born without a soul. I know the things that they told you as a child. The things that the Prophet did to you. I know about your friends up at the compound. About you sitting in the circle and watching them burn."

Schofield moved back toward him and screamed, "You don't know anything!"

With micro-glances, Marcus scanned the area. The park was full of places where a shooter could set up, but there was one that stood out. Less than a hundred yards over Schofield's shoulder, there was a small green building topped by a metal roof with large awnings on all sides. A sign read Fountain Cafe. The place would have been shut down and empty during the winter, and it provided the perfect angle and a protected spot to shoot from.

"Really? I know who your father is. Do you?"

Schofield looked as if an angel had just descended from heaven and punched him in the gut. The look was equal parts awe and confusion. Schofield whispered, "You shut up."

Marcus took another step forward. "Come on, Harrison. You're a smart guy. You honestly didn't believe that you were the product of some immaculate conception, did you? That Lucifer really crawled up from the pit and knocked up your mom? Come on. You've always had your suspicions."

"You couldn't possibly know."

Marcus moved forward again. "I found your mother in the Will County Mental Health Center and paid her a visit. She broke down and told me the truth. Her dirty little secret."

"You're lying."

Schofield held the grenades out in front of him like a barrier. His arms trembled, but Marcus didn't think it was from the cold.

"You have a soul and a father just like everyone else, Schofield. And I think you know who it is. I think you've always known, but you've been too scared to admit it."

"The Prophet is not my father!"

Marcus edged closer to the killer. "Your mother told me everything. How Conlan would bring her into his private quarters for a special lesson. I'm sure she wasn't the only one. He was probably screwing every little girl in the compound. What was she, twelve? Thirteen? Did he take you in there for private lessons too?"

Schofield stepped forward and screamed, "Shut up!" And then Marcus made his move.

117

MAGGIE HAD HEARD cops who'd been involved in shoot-outs talk about time slowing down and extreme events unfolding around them in slow motion as rushes of adrenaline kicked in. But that wasn't the case for her. In fact, it was exactly the opposite. The events inside the small house in Brighton Park happened so fast that her mind struggled to keep up with them.

It was all just a flash of images and emotions. The gun in O'Malley's hand. Something striking her face. Stumbling backward against the table. O'Malley firing into Andrew's chest. Her ears ringing from the shots. The smell of burnt gunpowder in the air. Andrew falling back against a ratty old couch. The entire thing tipping over as gravity pulled him down to the pale yellow linoleum. He smashed into a small end table, causing an antique lamp with no shade to fall over on top of him.

Then O'Malley started to turn and bring the gun to bear on her. Her first instinct was to run, but she fought the impulse. Instead she grabbed hold of one of the green chairs around the table and swung it against O'Malley's back.

He cried out in pain but stayed on his feet.

Marcus had taught Maggie to use her environment as a weapon, always stressing that *anything* could be a weapon in the right hands. She followed that advice now as she grabbed the edge of the faux-wood table and flung it at O'Malley.

It struck him, and he stumbled backward. But he shocked her again by not going down. The man who only a few moments before had appeared frail and old in her eyes now seemed to have shed twenty years and was surprisingly strong and quick.

She went for the backup pistol concealed at her ankle, a .357 Glock 33 subcompact. But, as she pulled it free, O'Malley lunged forward and slammed her with an upper-cut from the butt of the gun in his right hand.

Maggie felt the flesh on her face tear open as she slammed back against the linoleum. The impact drove the air from her lungs. Her Glock 33 slipped from her grasp and skidded across the floor and out of reach.

Her mind registered vaguely that she had been played, but she didn't have time to consider the possibilities. O'Malley was raising the gun in her direction.

She rolled toward the back door as he opened fire. It was heavy and wooden, its paint white but flaking from age. The sensation of flying hot metal searing the air around her head and the noise of plaster exploding propelled her through the door. She staggered onto an old porch that had been closed in and converted to a laundry room. She fell to the floor and kicked the door shut behind her. Three more 9 mm bullets smashed through it, splintering the wood.

Scenarios flew through her mind. Should she run out the back door and go for help? But she couldn't just abandon the Schofield family in the house. It was her job to protect them, not just save her own skin.

Marcus's words returned to her again. *Anything can be a weapon.*

Maggie glanced quickly around the small porch. There was an old yellow dryer and a mismatched white washer. The room smelled of water damage. A shelf hung above the washer and dryer. It contained a dusty bottle of fabric softener and a big jug labeled Clorox with white letters over the shape of a red and blue diamond.

Anything can be a weapon.

Maggie grabbed the bottle and spun the cap. Then she squatted low and waited, another trick she had learned from

Marcus. People expected others to be at chest and head level with them, which was where humans' gazes naturally traveled first. Getting low and catching the old man unaware could save her a split second, and a split second was often all that was needed to turn the tide in a battle.

The respite lasted only a few breaths. It ended when O'Malley kicked open the door and aimed the Glock inside. She didn't hesitate. She tossed the contents of the jug up at the man's face.

He saw her at the last second and jerked back, which probably saved his eyes. But the bleach still landed on his face and arms. In his condition, with already damaged and exposed skin, the bleach must have felt like acid in an open wound. It soaked his clothes and bandages.

O'Malley wailed in agony. It was a high and penetrating sound. But the trauma didn't slow up the old man's attack. Instead, it whipped him into a frenzy. His eyes were wild and insane as he rushed toward Maggie, and his mouth was wide open and screaming a banshee's wail.

She stumbled back from her crouch, and he tackled her to the ground. His bandaged hands found her neck, and he squeezed while simultaneously lifting her from the ground and pounding the back of her skull against the linoleum.

There was no defense against such fury and violence. She kicked and clawed and gouged at his burnt flesh. But his rage eclipsed his pain, and the more she fought, the tighter he squeezed.

After a moment, Maggie could feel consciousness slipping away as her lungs cried out for air. She fought and tried to suck in a breath through her nose but was only rewarded with the pungent smell of bleach.

The darkness closed in, and she felt numb all over.

But then the back door of the small room burst open, and snow and light flooded into the room. The cold breeze felt good on her skin. She saw an indistinct figure in the doorway.

Maybe a neighbor who had heard the shots? Or a cop who was in the area?

The newcomer kicked O'Malley away from her.

Then the man stepped into the room and closed the door behind him, shutting out the cold and snow. A massive stainless-steel revolver was pointed directly at O'Malley. Maggie recognized it as a Taurus Judge, a pistol that could be loaded with five shotgun shells.

She gulped in a mouthful of air and looked up at her savior. The breath caught in her already irritated throat. She coughed and gasped at the sight of him.

The man smiled down at her with a charming grin on his handsome face, a face that she had hoped never to see again.

118

MARCUS HAD HOPED to distract Schofield with talk of his childhood and the terrible events that had taken place at the Wisconsin compound. And it had worked. But before he could make his move, two things had to happen. First, he needed to slowly close the distance between them, and second, he needed Schofield's body lined up between him and the Fountain Cafe, effectively blocking the view of the shooter inside.

At the mention of the abuse the killer had suffered at the hands of the Prophet, Schofield stepped forward and thus met both of Marcus's requirements.

Marcus had learned a long time ago not to hesitate when your enemy gave you an opening. So when Schofield moved into position, Marcus quickly latched on to Schofield's fists, clamping his hands over the killer's like two vise grips.

Then he squeezed.

It took only around twelve pounds of pressure to break a bone in the hand of an adult man, but he wasn't worried about breaking Schofield's hands. He was more concerned with the two grenades held in the killer's fists.

With both his hands occupied, Marcus tilted his head downward slightly, clenched his teeth, and stiffened the muscles in his neck. A headbutt sounded like a pretty straightforward maneuver, but in reality it could easily cause more damage to the person attempting it than the one receiving it. In principle, the concept was simple. The forehead is a large hard bone, but the face and nose are soft, fragile areas. A hard forehead crushing into a man's nose could be a formidable blow if executed correctly.

And, unluckily for Schofield, Marcus had always been good at hurting people.

He thrust his head forward, bending his back and throwing all his weight into the attack. His forehead collided with the bridge of Schofield's nose, and the killer's head snapped back from the force of the blow.

Schofield's grip on the grenades slackened, but Marcus kept hold of them as the killer let go and stumbled backward. Blood poured down Schofield's face from his shattered nose. His eyes were dazed and glassy, and he nearly toppled over as he staggered away from the fountain in an unsteady run.

But Schofield wasn't the only problem.

Marcus could feel the cross-hairs of a 7.62 mm rifle lining up on him and Stupak at that very second, so he drew back his right arm and threw a grenade toward the sniper's location. His main concern was to distract the man, not blow him up. And unless Schofield's grandfather was some kind of hard-core Spec Ops rifleman, he'd be hitting the deck the second he saw an explosive flying through the air in his direction.

"Get to the fountain," Marcus yelled to Stupak as he jumped over a waist-high black wire fence and headed for the lip of the landmark.

He pictured the grenade lofting toward the small building, striking the snow-packed ground, and rolling up to the cafe's outer wall like the world's deadliest snowball.

Stupak was on his heels as they slipped over the edge and landed on their hands and knees in two feet of snow that had accumulated in the bottom of Buckingham Fountain's outer ring. The fountain was only four feet deep, but it was more than enough to provide them with cover.

The sound of the explosion thumped against his ears as the grenade filled the air with snow and concrete dust and fragmentation projectiles. Marcus felt the wave of pressure in his bones.

His left fist still held a live M67 fragmentation grenade, but he pulled his Sig Sauer with his right hand and scanned the cafe and park for signs of movement. He didn't see Schofield. The Anarchist must have made it to cover. But he did see a flash of something in the window of the cafe and dropped back below the fountain's concrete lip. He was thoroughly outgunned at this distance, pitting his .45 ACP pistol against a 7.62 mm rifle. If they were going to stand any chance, he needed to get closer.

He scanned the interior of the fountain. Normally, water would have been above their heads, but during the winter the fountain was just an empty shell with its pipes, jets, catwalks, lights, and supports all exposed. Snow covered the decorative statues and obscured their details. Marcus couldn't see anything that could help them, only the ornamentation and framework. No manhole covers indicating drains or tunnels that could lead them to safety.

Staying low below the fountain's lip, Marcus moved toward the other end of the bowl. Then he chanced a quick look over the edge. There was a line of benches backed by shrubbery and small trees maybe a hundred feet away. Beyond that was a walkway bordered by a section of the park filled with several large trees. The wooded section butted right up against the back of the Fountain Cafe. If he could reach the benches and then the trees, he could flank the shooter.

But in order to do so, he would have to cross over a hundred feet of snow-covered open ground, and he would be completely vulnerable and exposed.

He poked his head up over the edge again and caught sight of Schofield limping from a line of trees toward the cafe. The killer's impaired movement suggested that he might have taken some shrapnel from the fragmentation grenade.

Then a bullet ricocheted off the lip of the fountain just to the right of Marcus's head, driving him back down.

"Dammit," he said.

"This isn't working out very well," Stupak commented at his side. "You think?"

Marcus searched for a solution and found one gripped firmly in his left fist. The first grenade had bought them enough time to reach cover, and he assumed that the second would do the same. But if Raymond Schofield was smart enough to realize that Marcus's throw from even closer had fallen well short of the building, the older man might not take cover as he had the first time. He might take aim and squeeze the trigger instead. But it was a risk they'd have to take.

"Okay," Marcus said. "Get ready to lay down some covering fire on that building. I'm going to toss this last grenade and then make a break for the trees. You keep them pinned inside, and I'll work my way around to their backs."

Stupak nodded, a .40 caliber Glock 22 held ready in his right hand. Marcus took a deep breath and prepared to throw the grenade.

119

WHILE SITTING OUTSIDE and contemplating how best to secure his target, Francis Ackerman Jr. had heard the familiar sound of gunshots coming from inside the blue house. He had quickly made his way through the yard and peered in through one of the windows in time to see Maggie rushing toward the back door with the bandaged man in pursuit. He wasn't sure who this fellow thought he was, but nobody messed with Ackerman's friends.

"I would suggest that neither of you move," he said, staring down the sights of his Taurus Judge. "It's good to see you again, Maggie, but I don't believe that I've had the pleasure of making the acquaintance of your friend."

She stared up at him with fire in her eyes and said nothing. "What's your name?" he said to the bandaged man. "Your real name."

The man got to his feet. His eyes were intense and bright behind the bandages. Ackerman recognized the look. It was one of utter insanity. The bandaged man's cracked and burned lips curled up in a snarl of contempt.

"Listen, friend," Ackerman said. "I don't really care who you are. To me, you're just another cockroach."

"You shut your damn mouth. You have no idea the power that I hold." The man's voice was harsh and strained but hypnotic and soothing nonetheless. It was a deep Southern baritone that rolled from his mouth like honey.

Ackerman noticed Maggie's head whip round toward the bandaged man in shock. "You're not Irish," she said absently, almost to herself. "Oh my God, you're the Prophet.

You were faking. That's why Schofield was trying to kill you. He was just protecting his family."

"Schofield has lost his way. But that's none of your concern, slave. You'll burn tonight with all the rest in *The Great Fire.*"

Ackerman said, "Excuse me. This is all very fascinating. But I'm still here, and I still don't care who you are or what you want." Ackerman tossed a syringe of clear liquid in the bandaged man's direction. It rolled to a stop near his feet on the yellow linoleum. "You have a choice. You can either inject that into Maggie, or I can shoot you and do it myself. Though I would prefer that you do it. She'd fight me and cost me extra time."

"Who are you?" the bandaged man said.

"Does it matter? I'm not sure how it works around here, but normally when someone fires a gun in a populated area, the neighbors call the police. I'm sure they're on the way as we speak. So although I would genuinely like to hear about this *Great Fire* that you referred to, I simply don't have the time. So inject that into Maggie, and we'll be on our merry way."

"What about me?"

"If you inject her with that, then I'm perfectly happy to let you go about your business."

The bandaged man picked up the syringe and gave Ackerman a cracked and bloody smile.

120

THE DISTANCE BETWEEN the fountain and the line of benches was the longest hundred feet of Marcus's life. After throwing the grenade, he took off in a sprint toward cover. But with every shot that Stupak fired, Marcus wondered whether the next one would come from the sniper and would tear through his body and shred his internal organs.

Four seconds passed, and the grenade exploded just after Marcus reached the benches and shrubbery. He didn't look, but he felt the jolting wave of pressure shoot through his body. His ears rang from the gunfire as the wind and snow pelted his face.

He wasted no time in heading across the walkway to the relative protection of the trees. Then he weaved in and out among the bare elms until he reached the back of the Fountain Cafe. He hugged the wall of the green and gold structure and edged around to the other side. Stupak was still laying down covering fire at the cafe's south end and, with any luck, the sniper might not even have seen Marcus's dash from the fountain.

The north side of the cafe, where Marcus now stood, had one window near the building's front edge. He peered inside. There was a deli counter and chairs, but there was also a man directly opposite him at another window.

Schofield was nowhere in sight, and that worried him. Last he had seen, the killer had been limping off in this direction. Schofield could have been inside the building, guarding the entrance. Or he could have kept on going right past the cafe while Marcus was sprinting to the trees. There was no way to know for sure. But, in either case, he didn't have time to stand around.

The sniper's back was to him as the older man leaned over the cafe's sink with the rifle at his shoulder. Marcus took aim and opened fire through the glass.

Several .45 caliber bullets tore into Raymond's legs, and the man dropped to the ground, screaming in pain. His rifle clattered to the floor, and he made no attempt to reach for it.

Marcus wasted no time. He raced inside the building and secured the older man. "Don't move," he said. Raymond didn't seem to hear him. The floor was slick with blood, and Marcus could see that his shots had struck Raymond's femurs. He would pose little threat. Still, Marcus pulled out a pair of plastic cuffs, secured the older man's hands, emptied the rifle, and tossed it into the corner.

Then he yelled out the open window. "Stupak! You're clear. Get up here."

He watched Stupak climb over the fountain's lip and move toward the cafe. Schofield's grandfather rolled around on the tile floor and banged his head against the ground from the pain. The bullet impacts had probably broken both his legs and the projectiles' collision with the bones would have fragmented the rounds, causing more tissue damage. They needed to get him to a hospital, or he could easily die from blood loss.

"Where's your grandson?" Marcus said.

"Go to hell," Raymond said in a harsh whisper.

Marcus clenched his jaw and swore. He hadn't gone through all this just to let the Anarchist escape. Maybe Andrew had been right? Maybe they should have taken Schofield at the hotel?

Then Marcus thought of the way Schofield had been limping, and he bolted toward the door. Stupak was just approaching as Marcus burst outside and started to scan the ground. He could hear police sirens growing closer. The noise echoed through the park in a Doppler effect and made it impossible to determine from which direction the cops were approaching or how far away they were. The grenade blasts must have finally drawn some attention.

"What's going on?" Stupak said.

"The grandfather's in there. He's down. He needs an ambulance."

"What about Schofield?"

"He couldn't have gone far."

"He got away?"

"Just cover the grandfather and get him some help. I'll find Schofield."

And then Marcus found what he was searching for. The ground was a bright white, and the trail of crimson showed up like a neon sign. He followed the small drops of blood down a set of steps to a path that cut through the park. It led off to the east, toward Lake Michigan.

Marcus stared ahead as he ran down the path, trying to see through the snow flurries. Bare elms and cast-iron lampposts bordered the walkway. The sirens were growing closer.

He heard a frenzy of angry honking coming from the road ahead—and then he saw him. Schofield was two hundred feet ahead, hobbling through nine lanes of traffic on Lake Shore Drive. Cars were skidding to halts and sounding their horns.

Marcus weaved his way across the busy road, trying to avoid getting run down. A white Chevy S10 screeched to a stop just a few feet from him, and the wind from a passing semi took his breath away. But then he was across and scanning for his prey.

Schofield was only thirty feet away now, hobbling toward the waters of Lake Michigan. Marcus wondered where the man thought he was going. Did the killer still have another trick up his sleeve?

Pounding through the snow with his Sig Sauer aimed at the killer's back, Marcus closed the distance between them and said, "That's far enough!"

Schofield stopped, and his shoulders took on a defeated hunch. But he didn't turn around. Marcus could see his body shaking as his lungs dragged in short ragged breaths.

"It's over, Schofield. Put your hands up and turn around, slowly." Schofield complied, and when he turned, Marcus could see a large gash in his right thigh and holes in his coat where small pieces of shrapnel or chunks of concrete had struck him. All in all, it didn't look like anything life-threatening.

"I won't let you take me alive," Schofield said. His voice was eerily calm, like a man who had accepted that he was about to die and the world couldn't touch him. "I know what it's like to have a parent locked away somewhere, and I won't put my family through that. Right now, the best way I can protect them is by dying."

"Where are the missing women?"

"I don't know."

"Tell me!"

"I don't know."

"Where's the Prophet?"

"I don't know."

"Does he have the women?"

"Yes. He has a small antiques shop on the north side of town, but I doubt that he's there. You need to understand. I'm not his partner or his accomplice. I'm his pet. He expects me to do as I'm told. He doesn't share his plans with me. I wish I'd had the courage to kill him a long time ago."

"It's not too late. Help me find him, and I'll make sure that he never harms another soul."

Schofield laughed, but there was no humor in it, just regret. "I tried to kill him once already, but that woman stopped me. Hell, they would have killed him back at the compound when I was a child. The others were turning on him, but he was too smart for them. You have no idea what he's capable of. He—"

"What woman are you talking about? The one who stopped you."

"Yesterday I tried to burn him alive, just like he ordered me to do to all those women. Just like he did to my friends when I was a boy. But this blonde stopped me."

The gun trembled in Marcus's hands. He hadn't understood why Schofield had attacked the old man, but now it all made sense. And Maggie's kindness and sympathy for someone she had thought to be a victim had placed them all in danger. She had delivered the Prophet to his next sacrifices. A vision of Maggie burning alive filled his mind and made him feel suddenly nauseous.

Schofield must have sensed his unease. "What's wrong?"

"Conlan is your neighbor?"

"Yes, he's always stayed close to me. Like my own personal devil watching me from the shadows."

Marcus kept his gun trained on Schofield but managed to pull out his cell phone. "I think Conlan might have your family."

Schofield took a step forward. "What are you talking about?"

Marcus's heart thundered with every ring of Maggie's phone. She didn't answer. It went straight to her voice mail, and he hung up after leaving a clipped message.

To Schofield, he said, "Your family is in terrible danger, and if you really love them, you're going to help me put that bastard in the ground. Now, what was your escape plan?"

MARCUS NEEDED TO avoid the police. He had just been engaged in a shoot-out at one of Chicago's most famous landmarks. His credentials would clear him, but they'd want to file reports and take statements, and he didn't have time for that. He considered explaining the situation to the officer in charge, but there were no guarantees there. If he got a good cop who grasped the severity of the situation, they might let him continue with his pursuit of the Prophet. But if he got a bureaucrat or a Boy Scout, they'd insist on following protocol to the letter. Plus, he needed Schofield, and the Chicago PD would never let him waltz off with one of the worst murderers in Chicagoland history.

So he had found himself moving along the banks of Lake Michigan in the middle of a blizzard. Schofield had parked his car in a secluded lot beneath Route 41. That was where he had been headed when Marcus had caught up to him, and for the first time, Marcus was glad that Schofield liked to plan ahead.

The wind off the water was even colder and harsher than what he had experienced in the park, and it drove the snow into Marcus's face and blew hard into his ears, making them ache. His clothes and shoes were soaked, and his feet were numb and stinging with tiny needles of pain. The exhaust fumes from the cars on Lake Shore Drive mixed with the clean scent of cold air carried on the wind and formed a clashing natural and industrial combination of odors.

Even though Marcus wasn't sure if he'd be able to hear over the wind, he tried to call Andrew but received no response.

After several minutes of slogging through the snow, they finally reached the parking lot beneath Route 41. It was a dark and menacing place that Marcus thought would be somewhere more suitable for a shanty town of cardboard boxes populated by homeless men and women. But instead, someone had decided to fill the space with parking spots for workers in the nearby skyscrapers. He didn't see any security and imagined that it would be fertile ground for the area's muggers.

He still didn't trust Schofield, even though the lives of the man's family were on the line, and so he had kept the killer in front of him and one hand on the gun in his jacket pocket. Schofield led the way to a beat-up older-model Volkswagen Jetta.

"You're driving. I'll ride in back," Marcus said.

They climbed inside and Schofield said, "I'm not going any farther until you tell me what the hell is going on. Where is my family?"

"I don't know. But let's get something straight right now. You don't have the right to ask questions or make demands. If you don't do exactly as I say, I'll snap your neck and leave your corpse out in the snow." Schofield's eyes shot to the rearview mirror. Marcus placed the freezing cold barrel of his Sig Sauer against the back of the killer's neck and continued, "Make no mistake, you're only alive right now because I've allowed it. Because I need your help to find the Prophet and those missing women. That doesn't make us partners, friends, or accomplices. You lost your basic rights as a human being the second you chose to take the lives of innocent people. I know that you've been through hell and that not all of this is your fault. I don't hate you for what you've done, but I am going to make sure that you pay for it. If you help me, you may get a chance to save your family and kill the Prophet. Cross me, and I won't hesitate. Are we clear?" Schofield said nothing.

In a swift and violent movement, Marcus slammed the

butt of his pistol into the side of Schofield's head. The killer's left temple smacked against the driver-side window, and he gasped in pain.

"Are we clear?"

"Crystal."

"Good. Now exit the lot and take 55 south."

Schofield pulled the Jetta out from beneath the overpass and headed toward the exit to I-55. They would be passing right past Buckingham Fountain, but Marcus didn't expect them to have set up any kind of roadblocks, at least not yet.

As they passed the fountain, Marcus looked out his window and saw that it was buzzing with activity. The Chicago PD cruisers and an ambulance were parked along the opposite side of the park, coming from the city. As if on cue, his phone rang. It was Stupak, but he didn't accept the call. He wasn't in the mood for explanations.

They pulled onto the interstate, and Marcus tried Maggie again. There was still no answer, so he dialed Andrew. This time, he received a response. "Hello?" The voice on the other end sounded as though it was straining for air, like someone suffering from emphysema.

"Andrew?"

"Yeah, I'm here."

"What happened to you? Is Maggie with you?"

"I took three in the vest. Came away with two broken ribs and some nasty bruises. It also knocked me back, and I hit my head. When I woke up, the cops were here, but everyone else was gone. It was Schofield's neighbor, the Irish guy. He must have taken them. I don't know what happened. I feel like I've been hit by a truck."

"The neighbor is really Anthony Conlan. The accent and innocent-bystander routine was all for show. That's why Schofield tried to take him out."

"And we led him right to the family. I'm sorry."

"It wasn't your fault. I should have figured it out. Where are you now?"

"They took me to the hospital."

"Okay, just stay there. I'm going to try and figure out where they're headed. I'll call you when I know more."

Marcus clicked off and said to Schofield, "Take me to Conlan's antiques shop."

122

ARAMARK WAS A leader in professional services, including facilities management, food services, and uniform and career apparel. It was also the company where Erik Jansen was employed as a driver under a false identity. His job was to deliver uniforms to health-care institutions. But the large white truck used for those deliveries also provided the perfect means of transportation for five bound and gagged women.

The Prophet sat in the back with the boy, Benjamin, while Eleanor Schofield and her two daughters, along with the other two slaves, had been tied and thrown in a heap on the floor of the truck's storage compartment. The Prophet's plan was to stay mobile until the hour of the final ritual. It was only a matter of time until the police or the feds searched his antiques shop and home, but he reckoned that if they remained on the road they should have no problems.

Benjamin's stare was locked on his mother and sisters. His eyes were filling with tears. The Prophet reached out and gently turned the boy's head away from the sacrifices. "They're not your family, Benjamin. You'll be united with your true father tonight when the ritual is complete. These are merely the slaves that have cared for you until the time of your ascension. This is what we've been preparing for."

"I know...but I don't want to hurt them."

"Their pain will only last for a moment, and it's completely necessary. Once the ritual is complete, you will be king of this world and usher in a new golden era for mankind. You will wipe the tears from every eye. You will be our glorious savior, and then no one will ever need to suffer as the slave of a false god. These people have been put on this Earth to test you. To try and stop you from ascending to your rightful place. Don't be fooled by their hollow words and counterfeit sentiments of love. They don't love you, Benjamin. They know that you are *The Chosen*. They're jealous of you. They hate you."

Benjamin's gaze fell to the floor of the delivery van. The Prophet placed a hand on the boy's knee and gave a tender squeeze of affirmation. "Don't worry, Benjamin. I believe in you. I know how strong you are. I know that you are *The Chosen*, and tonight you will be my king. Do you believe it?"

"I guess."

"Don't guess. Mean it, boy. The other kids at school tease you, don't they?"

"Sometimes."

"That's because they sense how special you are. Look what they've done to me, Benjamin. They tried to kill me. These slaves will do the same to you, if you give them the chance. But I know that you won't let that happen. You're my strong king. After tonight, you will be loved by all. You will never have to be afraid or sad or feel left out or different again. We'll set everything up. All you have to do to take your rightful place at the throne is to make a simple choice. Do you believe it?"

Benjamin raised his eyes to meet the man's gaze. "Yes, Prophet."

123

CONLAN'S ANTIQUES SHOP was a surprisingly elegant gallery located in Chicago's River North area. The place was closed down, but Schofield had a key and knew the alarm code. The interior reminded Marcus of some centuries-old shop transplanted from the south of France. It was filled with beautiful antique glassware, furniture, sculptures, and pottery. The floors were made from a very light and worn hard wood like that of an old barn. Cream-colored brick lined the walls. The ceilings were all exposed beams, but with sophisticated chandeliers hanging every few feet. It all combined to create an atmosphere of old-world elegance. Marcus at least had to give it to Conlan: he had taste.

Marcus started with Conlan's office. He rifled through filing cabinets and stacks of papers scattered on the killer's old mahogany rolltop desk. There were a myriad of small drawers and shelves in the antique. But it was all business-related, nothing to indicate what Conlan was planning.

Then Schofield led him to the back of the shop where a large rug of intricately woven red fibers concealed a trapdoor. It was padlocked, but Marcus was able to break the lock free using a tire iron retrieved from the trunk of Schofield's Jetta.

As soon as the door came open, the smell bombarded them. Marcus could tell by the scent of excrement and body odor that this was where the women had been held. Descending the concrete stairs, he saw the large blocks of sound-proof foam covering the walls. It was similar to the material that Marcus and his colleagues used in their shooting range back in DC.

No one would have been able to hear the women's screams.

He pictured Conlan entertaining upper-class clients just above the spot where he was holding a group of women that he planned to sacrifice to the devil later. By all accounts, Conlan could be charming and charismatic. No one would have suspected his true nature. Marcus wondered how someone that could appear so normal to the outside world could actually be so utterly insane.

There was a large homemade cage in one corner, but it contained nothing more than a bucket filled with foul-smelling liquids. Bare bulbs lit the space and illuminated a massive black pentagram drawn onto the floor and surrounded by body-length mirrors. There was also an old wooden table covered with a few scattered pieces of aluminum foil, a cardboard box, some plastic baggies, and a spool of thin wire.

Marcus picked up the box and examined it. It was labeled *AlphaFire 1Q—Wireless Radio Firing System—For Fireworks Pyrotechnical Display*. But the box was empty. Then he picked up the spool of wire. The words *Resistance heating wire, Nichrome, 32 awg, 50ft* were typed in a plain font onto a white address label attached to the spool.

"Where is he going, Schofield?"

"I told you. I don't know."

Marcus swore and ran a hand through his hair. This was a dead end, and he had no idea where to go from here. Everything was crashing down. Vasques, Andrew, and Allen were all in the hospital, and Maggie was MIA. He had failed them all. But there had to be something he was missing, some clue or avenue of investigation that was still open.

Schofield said, "Did you really talk to my mother?"

"No. I just knew about her from your file. I made the rest up."

"So Conlan's not really my father?"

"I can't tell you for sure, but I'd be willing to bet that he is. It fits. You have to have wondered the same thing."

"I've tried to get her to tell me for as long as she's been in the home, but she still says that I'm the child of the devil. And that I have no soul. That I'm an abomination. I've tried to be something more, but I've failed."

Schofield's gaze was fixed on the floor, and his eyes glistened in the light from the bare bulbs burning overhead. He looked like a broken man, and Marcus couldn't help but feel sorry for him. "Your family loves you, Schofield. Your wife, your kids. You've done right by them—in that part of your life, anyway. Despite all that you've done, they still love you. And that counts for something."

"All I wanted was to be a whole person for them."

"We're all the sum of our collected experiences. And your experiences have been about as bad as they can get. You're sick, broken. But that doesn't make you a monster or an abomination. They love you for the man that you are, not the one that you wish you were. Besides, we're all broken in one way or another."

"Then how do we get fixed?"

"We don't. Not on our own, anyway."

Schofield was quiet for a moment. "Do you think that God can forgive me for the people that I've killed?"

Marcus thought of all the lives that he had taken. His hands were just as bloody as Schofield's, and he had often asked himself the same question. In a whisper, he replied, "I hope so."

Schofield closed his eyes and leaned against the old wooden table. Marcus continued to examine the basement. There had to be something more that he was missing. He looked around at the pentagram and the mirrors and thought of the compound in Wisconsin where Conlan had performed the first ritual.

"Schofield, the last ritual that Conlan performed, is this where it took place?"

"No, but I know now that he never intended for that to be the final ritual. He was just trying to prepare me. He wanted me to choose to sacrifice my own family willingly."

"But where did it take place?"

"There was an old church in the west suburbs that was closed for renovations. He wanted it to be on holy ground."

"So he'd want this ritual to be on holy ground as well?"

"I suppose," Schofield said, "but do you have any idea how many churches there are in the Chicago area?"

"Two thousand, nine hundred and eighty-two churches and places of worship in Chicago. But there has to be a way to narrow it down. He wouldn't want to be disturbed, and so it would have to be somewhere isolated. Has he said anything else about the ritual?"

"Just something about the abomination standing in the holy place." Marcus thought of a verse from the Book of Matthew.

When ye therefore shall see the abomination of desolation, spoken of by Daniel the prophet, stand in the holy place, (whoso readeth, let him understand): Then let them which be in Judaea flee into the mountains.

"Did he say anything else?"

"He did mention something about the ritual being on the darkest, longest night in the highest place. But I don't know if that means anything."

Marcus thought about that for a moment and then pulled out his phone and dialed Stan.

On the third ring, Stan answered and said, "Thank you for calling Procrastinators Anonymous. Leave a message, and we'll call back...eventually."

"Cut the crap, Stan."

"Gee, somebody's in a mood."

"I need you to find out if there are any churches in the Chicago area currently undergoing renovations. Or a church that's currently closed down for any reason."

"Okay, give me a few minutes."

Marcus hung up, and then he said to Schofield, "How much time do we have?"

"He'll start the ritual at three in the morning."

"You know that for sure?"

"It's the devil's hour—according to him, anyway. He says that's the time when the barriers between hell and Earth are at their weakest. Something to do with three in the afternoon being the time when Jesus was crucified, so the inversion of that is the devil's time."

Marcus nodded, but he found it strange that someone would attach supernatural significance to a specific hour like that. After all, Jesus would have been crucified in an entirely different time zone. It was always three a.m. somewhere. But he didn't have to buy into the Prophet's beliefs or even understand them in order to use them against the killer.

Giving up on finding anything in Conlan's shop, they went back to the car and waited for Stan's call. Time seemed to be ticking away, the clock working against them. Marcus was both keyed-up and dead tired at the same time. He wished that he could close his eyes and sleep for a few moments while they were waiting, but there was no way he was going to take his eyes off Schofield.

His phone rang, and Stan's number appeared on the screen. "What did you find?"

"I've got a ton of churches that have gone defunct and been converted into condominiums and houses."

"No, nothing like that. Somewhere isolated."

"Okay, there's one small church on the north side of town that just had a fire destroy part of the roof. It's closed for renovations, and they've moved their worship services to another location."

"That could be it. Send me the address," Marcus said. "Maybe we'll get lucky and finally be one step ahead this time."

But in the back of his mind, he sensed that they were still missing something.

124

As the Prophet stared up at the night sky, he saw that the eclipse had already begun. The surface of the moon was seventy-five percent dark. Normally, when a lunar eclipse reached its apex the moon wouldn't disappear from the sky. Instead, it would turn blood red as sunlight refracted through the Earth's atmosphere. The blood moon on a winter solstice would still mean that this would be the longest, darkest night in five hundred years. But, because of volcanic eruptions in Iceland and Indonesia during the past year, there were two clouds of ash and dust floating high up in the atmosphere. As a result, the eclipse would be even darker and might cause the moon to disappear completely.

Everything was falling into alignment, a perfect storm of celestial forces coming together to make this an unparalleled moment to finally break down the walls of this reality and forge a new one. And soon he would stand in the highest place of worship in all the land and complete *The Work*.

The Prophet fitted an Osprey sound suppressor to his FNP .45 Tactical handgun and loaded the clip with subsonic ammunition. He wanted to ensure that their entry went undetected so that they wouldn't be disturbed during the ritual. Jansen parked the delivery truck down the street a short distance from their destination, and the Prophet stepped out.

"Wait here for me. I'll call when I'm ready to bring in the sacrifices."

Jansen nodded reverently. "Yes, Prophet." The younger man's eyes were blazing with excitement. Tonight would be one of great joy and triumph. The excitement even allowed the Prophet to momentarily forget the pain and stinging from his burns.

He followed the sidewalk to the front of the skyscraper and entered through a set of large glass and bronze doors. Inside was a long corridor with white block walls and ornate archways. It was dimly lit and had white and bronze accents over a dark marble floor. The sparse illumination reflecting off the bronze gave it a glowing, candlelit feel. A security guard sat behind a small desk in an alcove along the right side of the corridor and a bank of elevators was on the left.

The security guard was a small Asian man with red-dyed hair that hung down over one side of his face. He wore a blue blazer jacket with a small bronze name tag that said his name was Ronald. As the Prophet approached, Ronald gave him a big smile, but then his eyes went wide for a second. He was probably surprised by all the bandages. He said, "May I help you?"

The Prophet returned the smile until he was close, then he pulled the silenced FNP from his pocket. He fired twice into Ronald's forehead before the man could speak. The shots were muffled but were still loud enough to draw attention as they echoed down the corridor. For a moment the Prophet watched for anyone coming to investigate—even though he didn't expect anyone else to be around at this hour—and then moved behind the small desk and retrieved Ronald's keys. He had done extensive research on the location for the ritual and knew that he would need a special key to insert into the elevator in order to gain access to the appropriate floor.

Once he had the key in his hand, he called Jansen. "Bring the sacrifices and the boy. We're ready to begin."

125

THE NORTHWEST CHURCH of Christ sat within the Mayfair neighborhood on Chicago's north side. It was a mid-sized white and tan brick building. Scaffolding had been affixed to the building's periphery, alongside stacks of shingles, but the repairs would have to wait for warmer weather. A red sign out front had the name of the church listed in English, Spanish, and Korean.

Something about the church didn't seem right to Marcus. He was sure that it was a fine place to be a member or in which to worship, but it was nothing extravagant. It wasn't unique or special in any way. It didn't stand out, and he couldn't work out why the Prophet would choose it for his magnum opus, despite the fact that its renovations meant it was closed at present. He couldn't shake the feeling that they were in the wrong place.

During the hours of waiting, Andrew had checked himself out of the hospital and picked up Marcus and Schofield in the Yukon. The three of them sat together and kept watch on the church. Marcus sat in the back. Andrew was behind the wheel. And Schofield sat in the passenger seat with his hands secured uncomfortably by a pair of plastic cuffs fastened to the handle next to the window, a handgrip which was used to let passengers pull themselves up into the high vehicle. The cuffs were yellow one-time-use models made from a polycarbonate resin. They employed a roller-lock retention system similar to that of zip ties and could only be removed by cutting them off.

"We're in the wrong place," Marcus said.

The other two men didn't respond, but he knew that they were both thinking the same thing. And they all had something to lose. Schofield needed to save his family. Andrew wanted to save his friend. And Marcus wanted to find out what had happened to the woman he loved. He couldn't stop his imagination from conjuring images of Maggie burning alive.

The lives of many people were on the line, and Marcus and the others had no idea if they were even in the right location. He checked his watch. Less than an hour until the ritual, but there was still no sign of Jansen or Conlan.

He closed his eyes and considered what he knew about the ritual.

Conlan would want it to be performed somewhere isolated that could at least give him some assurance that they wouldn't be disturbed. Somewhere on holy ground. But somewhere special. Everything that the killer had planned for was an extreme. The darkest, longest night. Schofield making the ultimate sacrifice. Committing the ultimate blasphemy against God by defiling a church sanctuary.

The Prophet would want the location of the ritual to be extreme as well.

There was something just on the edge of Marcus's consciousness, something he had read or seen. But it was like a shadow in his peripheral vision that disappeared whenever he tried to catch sight of its source.

What was he missing?

Schofield's words in the Prophet's basement floated to the surface of his mind. *The abomination standing in the holy place... The darkest, longest night in the highest place...*

The Highest Place...

When Schofield had spoken the words, Marcus had just assumed that the Prophet was using *highest* as a term of spiritual significance, like a holy altar or a church of historical importance. But what if he actually meant the *highest* church?

And that was when he knew where they needed to go.

The skyscraper Chicago Temple Building was the tallest church building in the world, and at its top, four hundred feet above ground level, sat the Sky Chapel—the highest place of worship on Earth.

126

THE SKY CHAPEL wasn't a large sanctuary. It was quite the opposite. The intimate yet beautiful place of worship seated only thirty people and was used for prayer and reflection, weddings, and special services. Situated at the base of the steeple, it was octagonal in shape and was surrounded by sixteen stained-glass windows depicting various scenes from the Bible and the history of the Church. In the center of the ceiling, there was a large blue illuminated recess surrounded by golds and reds and Christian symbology. Backlit glass depicting rays of sunlight stretched out to each of the recess's four quadrants, symbolizing the power of God reaching out to all four corners of the world.

The Prophet had been here many times and knew that it was the perfect setting for the final ritual, the holy place where the abomination of desolation would soon stand.

He and Jansen had rearranged the chapel's small benches for their own purposes. The seats normally sat facing an altar adorned with an ornate and intricate wooden carving of Jesus staring out over the city of Chicago and weeping because the people did not know what brought peace. But now they had positioned the benches to sit at the five corners of a crude pentagram spray-painted in black on the center of the chapel's floor. Each of the five sacrifices remained gagged and had been secured to the benches using specially constructed harnesses similar to straitjackets. The women's faces were streaked with tears, and they moaned and sobbed behind their gags. A bench for the boy also sat in the center of the pentagram. A large black cloth covered the middle bench.

The Prophet stroked Benjamin's dark hair and, in his honeyed Southern tone, said, "Are you ready, my child?"

"Yes, Prophet."

"Then lie down."

Benjamin lay back on the bench, and Jansen secured the restraint straps around the child's body. The Prophet said, "Benjamin, you will be the spark that ignites *The Great Fire*. Like the legendary phoenix, you will rise from the ashes of this world and start a new one, a better one. It will be a glorious new beginning. Here, on the darkest, longest night in the highest place, you will become a god. Do you choose to accept your place as *The Chosen*?"

"Yes, Prophet."

The Prophet squeezed the boy's shoulder. "I'm so proud of you." Then he and Jansen finished dumping the five gallons of lighter fluid over the sacrifices and the chapel.

All that was left was to wait for the proper hour and watch the world burn.

127

THE CHICAGO TEMPLE was a five-hundred-and-sixty-eight-foot-tall skyscraper church located in the heart of downtown Chicago. The structure looked to Marcus like a strange amalgam of an office building topped by a Gothic cathedral. It contained the First United Methodist Church of Chicago as well as several floors of rented office space.

As they pulled up to the building, Marcus glanced across the street at the distinctive red and brown facade of the Richard J. Daley Center which housed more than a hundred and twenty court and hearing rooms as well as the Cook County Law Library. Daley Plaza sat between Daley Center and the Chicago Temple and was currently home to the city's official Christmas tree, a seventy-foot fir covered with red and green lights.

Marcus pulled open his door and was nearly overwhelmed by the snow and wind. Sitting in the warmth of the Yukon, he had actually forgotten how cold it was outside.

As Marcus began to slide out of the big SUV, Schofield said, "Wait. You said that I could help." He tugged at his restraints and shook the seat.

"I said that you could help save your family, and, hopefully, you've done that. Consider yourself lucky."

Marcus slammed the vehicle's door, and he and Andrew pushed through the snow to the bronze entryway of the Chicago Temple. Once inside, they shook off the cold and examined the area. Andrew was the first to find blood behind the security desk. "We're in the right place," Andrew said. "Where to from here?"

Pointing skyward, Marcus replied, "All the way up."

He pressed the elevator button, the shining bronze doors parted, and they stepped inside. The highest number on the control panel was for the twenty-second floor, but when Andrew pushed it, nothing happened. The button didn't light up.

Marcus swore and tapped a keyhole beside the button. "You must need a key to access it."

"What do we do now?" Andrew reached up to the ceiling and tried to find some kind of hatch.

"It won't open," Marcus said. "It'll be locked from the other side. But have you ever heard of elevator surfing?"

"No. It sounds like an Olympic sport for stockbrokers."

"Here's what we'll do. We'll take the elevator up to the twenty-first floor, and I'll get off there. You take the car back down to the twentieth floor and push the emergency-stop button to hold it in place. I'll wedge open the doors and step out on top of the elevator car."

"Then I take off the emergency stop and push the elevator up to the twenty-first floor?"

"Actually, I'll control it by using the maintenance panel on the roof of the car."

Andrew gave him a curious look and said, "It sounds like you've done this before."

"I grew up in a city with a lot of skyscrapers and plenty of time on my hands."

Marcus pressed the button for the twenty-first floor, and the elevator started to rise. The lights above the door cycled their way to twenty-one, and the door dinged and slid open. With a nod, he stepped out and watched the doors close.

He waited a few seconds and then flipped out his knife. With the blade wedged between the two bronze panels of the elevator, he applied leverage until a crack appeared. Then he slipped his fingers into the crack and pulled the doors open the rest of the way.

A faint buzzing sound filled the inside of the shaft, and it smelled of hydraulic fluids, grease, and rust. He flipped

on a work light located on the right-hand side of the car.
The walls were worn concrete. The shaft contained several
tracks for additional elevators, separated by only a few metal
beams running the length of the shaft at ten-foot intervals.

A metal railing had been placed around the top of the elevator car but it was only about three feet tall and provided
little obstruction to prevent anyone from falling down the
shaft. The roof was made of flat gray metal and featured a
few blue conduits, the tarnished blue sheath containing the
hydraulic ram, and a yellow control panel the size of a shoebox. A red light glowed on top of the box.

Marcus stepped onto the top of the car and bent down to
the control panel. He twisted a toggle and pulled out a red
button to put the car into inspection mode. This transferred
control of the car's movement away from the inside panel to
the switches on top of the car. Then he flipped the control
switch up and rode the elevator to the doors leading onto
the twenty-second floor.

The inner side of the doors had a lever near the top that
the car would trip to slide open the panels when it reached
the proper floor. He placed his palm against the bottom of
the lever and pushed it up. The doors parted slightly.

As he had done previously from the other side, Marcus
slid his fingers into the crack and started to pull the panels open.

But unlike before, this time he was immediately greeted
by a silenced black pistol pointing at his face.

128

MARCUS JERKED BACK quickly from the opening as the heat of a subsonic round passed close to his face. His hand shot into the gap and closed around the suppressor attached to the gun's barrel. He yanked hard, throwing his whole body weight into pulling the gun away.

A large object slammed into the outside of the elevator doors as he jerked the weapon. There was a muffled cry of pain, and then the gun came free. Marcus's momentum and the force he had put into the movement nearly caused him to topple head first down the elevator shaft.

He dropped the gun and steadied himself against the low railing. The sound of the gun clanging off the concrete walls of the shaft echoed up to him, producing a feeling of vertigo.

Turning back to the doors, he found a hulking man shoving the panels the rest of the way open. Erik Jansen's eyes were ablaze with fury, and the big man screamed as he shot forward onto the top of the car. He was charging, and Marcus knew that he couldn't withstand a frontal attack by the larger man. Jansen had to be at least six foot five inches tall, probably weighed two hundred and seventy-five pounds, and had fists the size of cement blocks.

Marcus dropped as low as he could and placed his back against the low railing to keep from being knocked from the car. He tried to use Jansen's momentum against him to send the big man careening over the edge. But Jansen quickly recognized the danger.

He kept low as well and threw his momentum into pounding both his fists down onto Marcus's back.

With his weight already shifted forward to accept a head-on charge, the blow knocked Marcus flat against the roof of the car. Jansen wasted no time in grabbing him from the floor and slamming him face-first into the concrete side wall near the elevator doors.

Marcus felt pain surge down the side of his face as his flesh grated against the wall. But Jansen was far from done with his assault. He continued by pounding his meaty fists into Marcus's kidneys and back.

The pain was immense, and it shot down through Marcus's legs. Then Jansen grabbed a handful of Marcus's leather jacket and, lifting him from the floor, threw him into the open elevator shaft.

129

Marcus felt weightless for a second, as though gravity had suddenly lost its hold. Then the pull kicked back in and dragged him downward into the shaft. The darkness of twenty-two stories and several hundred feet of empty air clawed at him, but his instinct for survival was quicker than any rational and calculated action could be.

His hands found the steel hoist cable in the adjacent shaft, but his weight continued to pull him down. The friction between his palms and the cable burned like fire as the metal dug into his skin. He screamed in pain, the sound echoing through the depths of the concrete pit. But, after dropping a few feet, he was able to halt his fall.

He looked back up at Jansen. The big man stood grinning on top of the elevator car. A meaty fist wagged an invitation. The gesture's meaning was clear. *Come get some more.*

Gladly, Marcus thought.

He considered reaching for the .45 pistol resting inside his jacket. But the thought of dangling over the precipice, holding on with one injured hand, thwarted that idea.

Fist over fist, Marcus pulled himself back up to eye level with Jansen. Then he swung his legs and used the momentum to kick at his opponent. Jansen jerked back enough for Marcus's feet to clear the railing and reach the top of the car.

Jansen lunged forward again, but this time, Marcus was ready for him. He dodged to the side, and in a blur of motion, he slammed his elbow into Jansen's temple. He followed the blow with four strong punches to the other man's acne-scarred cheeks.

Blood poured from Jansen's jaw and stained the top of the elevator. But the giant turned swiftly and grabbed Marcus in a vicious bear hug. The massive muscular arms wrapped around his torso and started to crush him. It felt like a large truck had just backed over his chest. He gasped for air, but none could be squeezed into his compacted lungs.

His heart pounded, and he could feel the blood flow throbbing through his skull.

His fists hammered, driven by panic, against Jansen's back and head. His legs kicked out ineffectually against the man's shins. He could see Jansen grimacing in pain, but there was no sign of him letting go. Marcus's attacks were accomplishing nothing except expending his own limited supply of oxygen.

He could feel his rib cage compressing, cracking, separating.

The words he often preached to Maggie came back to him. *Anything can be used as a weapon.* And not just any object in your surroundings, but also any part of your body.

Marcus couldn't gain the necessary leverage to deal a brutal enough blow to get Jansen's grip to relent. At least, not with his arms or legs. But anything could be used as a weapon.

He had learned long ago that human beings have short jaws with thick masseter muscles and blunt, chisel-shaped incisors. With that knowledge in mind, Marcus sank his teeth deep into Jansen's cheek and bit down with all the force the human jaw could attain.

Jansen screamed, and the pressure lifted from Marcus's chest. He came away with a chunk of flesh in his mouth, but he quickly spat out the foul metallic, salty taste as he gasped for air.

With both hands clamped over the side of his face, Jansen stumbled to the back of the elevator car's roof.

Marcus didn't hesitate.

His hand flew inside his jacket and came back out holding the Sig Sauer pistol. He fired a shot into each of Jansen's kneecaps, dropping the big man to the metal ceiling of the elevator car. The blasts echoed like thunder down the shaft and made Marcus's ears ring as the smell of burnt gunpowder filled the air.

Jansen rolled around in agony, and Marcus wiped the blood from his mouth onto his black shirt.

"That was for me," he said. "And this is for Vasques."

Marcus fired one more shot into Jansen's skull and then kicked the body over the edge of the elevator car. He watched as it twisted into the darkness of the shaft. A wet thump came a few seconds later.

Marcus bent down, took the elevator out of inspection mode, and stepped through the doors onto the twenty-second floor. He pressed the elevator call button and waited as the car came up. The doors dinged open.

Andrew looked him up and down, taking in Marcus's injuries and the blood staining the area around his mouth. Then Andrew said, "What took you so long?"

130

THERE WAS A large glass entryway on the twenty-second floor that had already been unlocked. It led up a set of stairs to a tiny white elevator. With their weapons at the ready, Marcus and Andrew climbed inside and rode it all the way to the top. They exited into a darkened foyer that had four tall windows behind a set of monstrous wooden beams in the shape of an X.

Another set of stairs with dark gray carpeting and red and gold walls ascended to the Chapel in the Sky. The stairs curved up to a landing, and Marcus walked up quietly backward, so he could watch the railing above them. He clung to the outside wall with Andrew following close behind.

They scanned what they could of the chapel from their vantage point and then moved up one final set of stairs into the sanctuary. The room's natural, soothing tones—pinks, golds, blues, creams—radiated an aura of elegance and serenity. The women bound and crying at the points of a crude pentagram quickly shattered that illusion.

Marcus scanned the entire room, staring down the sights of the Sig Sauer, but there was no sign of the Prophet. Maybe he had slipped past them somehow? Or maybe Conlan had convinced others to do his dirty work as he had in the past?

Either way, Marcus didn't like it. Why would Jansen have been guarding the elevator if he'd been supposed to start the fires?

Marcus moved cautiously through the sanctuary. In the center of the pentagram, he saw the boy bound by the feet and arms with leather restraints and lying flat on a bench.

A black cloth covered the bench and hung all the way to the floor, making it look like some dark sacrificial altar. Benjamin's gaze was distant and was fixed on the recessed ceiling.

The smell of lighter fluid was strong in the air, and there was more than had been found at the other scenes. The room was soaked in it, and the quantity of accelerant had turned the entire chapel into a tinderbox. When the fire was set, it would burn anyone inside to ash.

It didn't make sense. Conlan would kill the boy as well. But then again, none of what Conlan did was supposed to make sense to a normal, sane person. Such was the nature of insanity.

Marcus thought of Conlan's elegant antiques shop with the torture chamber in the basement. It was just like the man himself: charismatic and charming on the outside with a darkness at the core.

Then he suddenly realized the significance of the items he had found in the basement of Conlan's shop. He pictured the cardboard box and the spool of wire.

The box had read *AlphaFire 1Q—Wireless Radio Firing System—For Fireworks Pyrotechnical Display*. It was a remote igniter triggered by a hand-held radio-control unit designed for use in commercial fireworks displays.

The spool of wire had been labeled as *Resistance heating wire, Nichrome, 32 awg, 50ft*. Nichrome was the material that lit up inside a toaster. When electric current passed through it, the wire would glow and burn extremely hot.

Hot enough to ignite the lighter fluid.

Which meant that by linking the igniter and the wire, the Prophet could start the fire from anywhere that was in range at any moment.

131

SCHOFIELD HAD TUGGED at his restraints until his wrists were chafed and bleeding. But he hadn't made any headway with brute force and had ultimately given up. He would have to trust Marcus to save his family. The man definitely seemed capable.

And a part of Schofield was glad. He wanted to be the hero for his family, to stand up against the Prophet and save them. But he also feared that confrontation. He felt powerless and hollow. His head fell against the window, and he wept against the glass, the cold surface at least making him feel something other than pain and regret.

Opening his eyes, he wiped the tears on the sleeve of his blue coveralls and then looked across the road at Daley Plaza. He had always found the design of the red and brown building strange because its support pylons were on its exterior.

As he examined the building's facade, he squinted through the snow into a protected recess in front of the center's lobby. There was someone standing there. He looked closer, and he felt his stomach climb into his throat.

The man was looking up expectantly at the Chicago Temple Building. Schofield could just barely see the bandages covering the man's face. It could only have been one person. The Prophet.

The man who had destroyed his life—the man who might have been his real father—was just across the courtyard. And Schofield knew what he had to do. Maybe he'd get to be the hero after all.

But he was still restrained and powerless.

Schofield tried to calculate the variables. If he couldn't break free by force, maybe he could by other means. Examining the yellow plastic cuffs, he noted their similarity to zip ties. They operated using the same roller-locking mechanism. He had once seen his wife unlock a zip tie using a straight pin. He examined the retention block of the cuffs. It looked like there would be just enough room to fit something small between the roller lock and the straps. That would block the roller lock from contacting the teeth on the straps and allow him to pull slack into the restraints and slide his hands free.

But he would need something small to slide between the straps and the lock.

He checked the time on the Yukon's dashboard. Less than three minutes until three a.m.—the devil's hour.

132

WITH HIS TUNGSTEN-coated knife in the closed position, Marcus tossed it to Andrew and said, "Cut the women free, and get them out of here. I'll find the igniter."

He checked his watch. If Schofield was right about the timing, Conlan would be sparking the fire in less than two minutes. His gaze traveled over their surroundings. If he could find the device, it would be easy to disarm. After all, it was just a cheap remote fire-starter designed for firework displays. It didn't have fail-safes or sophisticated circuitry like a bomb. But it would also be fairly small, and there were a lot of places to hide such a device.

Marcus's heart was pounding, and his stomach was churning in knots. He needed to find the detonator, but something else was bothering him and clouding his thoughts. Maggie wasn't there in the sanctuary. The two abducted women, Schofield's wife, and his two daughters were all bound in place around the pentagram, but Maggie wasn't among them.

Did the Prophet kill her? Is she a hostage?

But he couldn't afford to worry about that. He needed to concentrate on the task at hand and attack the problem logically and methodically.

First, he scanned the areas he could see. Nothing.

Then he ran around to every recess, nook, and cranny. He checked behind the X-shaped support pillars that surrounded the chapel. He checked behind and around the altar and behind a small electronic piano shoved against one wall.

But there was nothing there.

His breathing was quick and ragged. The adrenaline pumped through his system at high speed and made his muscles shake. He resisted the urge to check his watch. The Prophet could be igniting the fire at any second.

Andrew had freed the first two girls, but he couldn't just undo the harnesses that held them in place. And so he had been forced to saw through them with the knife. It wouldn't be fast enough to get them all out.

Marcus knew it was up to him. He had to find the igniter before time ran out. But there was nowhere else that it could be hidden.

He scanned the room again. Then a third time. Still nothing. No obvious hiding spots. But it had to be there. He just wasn't seeing it.

Willing himself to stay calm and logical, he asked himself where he would have hidden it. He forced himself to think like Conlan. He thought of the words in Conlan's writings that he had found in the Wisconsin compound. Words like *The Chosen* and *The Great Fire*.

The boy was the center. The key. The spark.

Conlan would want the fire to originate from Benjamin.

Marcus rushed forward to the center of the pentagram and slid to the ground beside the boy. Benjamin's eyes now looked frightened and confused. Marcus couldn't imagine what the boy had been through. Benjamin would need extensive counseling, but first he would have to survive beyond this night.

The lighter fluid saturating the floor soaked up into Marcus's jeans. It felt slick and oily and cold.

He pulled up the black cloth that had been draped over the bench beneath the boy's bound form. And there, beneath the shroud, he saw it. The igniter was a simple black box with a silver antenna and a few buttons and switches on its face. A small LED light was shining bright green. Below that Marcus found a switch with three positions marked *Test, Off, Fire*. It was in the *Fire* position.

Marcus switched the unit to *Off*. And, just to be sure, he pulled out the length of nichrome wire from the device's black and red electrical ports and snapped off the receiver's antenna.

Then, for the first time in several hours, he allowed himself a deep sigh of relief.

But the sensation was short-lived as his worry for Maggie crept back over him. Where was she? And where was the Prophet?

133

PROTECTED FROM THE elements inside a recess in front of Daley Center, the Prophet watched the highest place, awaiting the proper moment. The anticipation had caused his heart to race and sweat to form on his body despite the cold. *The Work* would finally be completed tonight, and in the new world that rose up from the ashes of the old, he would be a god.

He checked his watch. The hour of reckoning had come, and it was time to spark *The Great Fire*. From his jacket pocket, he removed the remote for the igniter system. It was a simple device made from hard black plastic with a silver extendable antenna and a sliding plate that covered the ignition button.

The Prophet used his thumb to guide the protective cover gently back, revealing a bright red button. He stepped into the falling snow and stretched his arms out reverently at his sides. He dropped to his knees on the cold ground and raised his gaze to the highest place. Then he pushed the button.

But nothing happened.

He hadn't expected an explosion, but he had imagined that he would see the fire burst to life within the chapel's windows. But there was nothing there. No fire. No sign of anything out of the ordinary.

He heard the sound of approaching police sirens and knew that he had failed. Somehow the slaves had discovered the site of the ritual and had ruined everything.

A wave of sadness so abysmal that it made him consider taking his own life on that very spot swept over him.

The Colt Anaconda .44 Magnum pistol resting in his jacket pocket felt heavy against his side. He imagined putting the cold barrel of the gun against his temple and squeezing the trigger.

But he couldn't do that. This was just another test. He had come so far, but he had failed again. It wasn't the first time, and it wouldn't be the last. He would do *The Work* until the last breath of life was torn from him by the slaves and their false deity.

The Prophet would never give up. He would find a new *Chosen* and start again.

134

RAGE DRIVING HIM, Harrison Schofield searched for a way to free himself from the restraints. He needed a small piece of metal like a pin, but with his hands bound above the dashboard, he couldn't even search for one.

He checked the clock. It was time.

He looked across the courtyard at his father. The Prophet was on his knees, his head hanging low. Something must have gone wrong. Marcus must have succeeded.

Schofield wished that he could feel joy, because in that moment he knew that it would have been a marvelous explosion of relief and happiness. But those emotions couldn't penetrate his damaged heart and tainted soul. He felt a sense of relief but no joy, just the same hollowness. He realized now who was responsible for placing that sickness inside him, and it was his job to ensure that the man atoned for his many sins.

Schofield raised his right foot to the dashboard and pulled off his shoe and sock. Then he used his toe to pull back the release on the glove box directly in front of him. The compartment fell open, and he scanned inside for anything that he could use. It contained only a few papers and vehicle manuals. But there was one stack of registration documents bound together by a small silver paperclip.

Contorting his body to its limits, he slid his foot inside the dashboard and pushed the stack of papers out onto the floor mat. Then his feet fumbled over the papers until he reached the stack containing the paperclip. It took a few seconds of his toes groping blindly over the papers until they could find a hold. But he was able to maintain a tenuous grasp on them and slowly bring the stack up to the dashboard, where he could reach it with his hands.

He quickly removed the paperclip and straightened it. With some effort, the small piece of metal slipped between the roller lock and the straps, and when he tugged the straps against the grain, he found that the locking teeth had lost their grip. He pulled his right hand free and didn't bother with the left. Time was running out. The Prophet would soon realize that the ritual had failed and would slip into the night to destroy the lives of some other family.

He couldn't allow that to happen.

Earlier in the evening, he had seen Marcus retrieve ammunition from a set of hard plastic boxes in the back of the Yukon. Schofield's hope was that there would be weapons within the boxes as well.

With the plastic cuffs still dangling from his left hand, he threw open the passenger door and ran to the back of the black SUV. Inside the rear compartment, he found the containers and searched inside them.

Schofield was shocked at what he found. It was a veritable smorgasbord of weaponry and ammunition. There were thousands of rounds and several handguns, but the weapon that caught his eye was a compact and futuristic-looking automatic rifle.

Quickly loading a long magazine with thirty rounds of .45 ACP ammunition, he slammed it into the weapon and took off after the Prophet.

He could see Conlan moving away from Daley Center, heading north on Dearborn Street. Schofield could guess where the man was headed. One block north and one block east and the Prophet could slip into the Red Line subway station on State Street.

The air was cold and felt heavy in his lungs as he ran down Dearborn. The snow stung his cheeks. The Prophet was walking slowly and calmly, trying not to arouse suspicion. Schofield could hear the sirens coming. Police would be swarming over the Temple Building and Daley Center in just a few seconds.

Willing his legs to pump harder and faster, he fought to close the gap between himself and the Prophet. The older man was only a hundred feet away.

Then Conlan glanced over his shoulder and saw Schofield. Their eyes locked.

But Schofield didn't slow down. He pressed forward even faster, closing the distance to seventy-five feet.

Conlan pulled a massive pistol from his coat. Its long stainless-steel barrel shimmered under the street lamps.

Fifty feet.

Conlan raised the pistol and fired. The powerful handgun roared and bucked and shot flame from its tip. Due to the late hour and the blizzard, the Chicago streets were as quiet as Schofield had ever heard them. The crack of the gun filled the silence and echoed off the glass of the neighboring buildings.

The first bullet sailed wide, just over Schofield's shoulder. He heard it strike a car that he had just passed. He didn't allow himself to stop or even hesitate.

Thirty feet.

He watched as Conlan aimed the .44 magnum.

Schofield aimed too and squeezed back on the trigger of the rifle. He saw Conlan's gun buck in his bandaged hand. Schofield's weapon thundered to life. It was in fully automatic mode, and within just two seconds, the entire magazine of .45 ACP rounds had been exhausted.

Not all the rounds struck their mark, but enough of them did. Conlan's body shook from the trauma, and he wailed in pain as the bullets pierced his flesh.

Schofield watched events unfold, even as he fell to the ground himself. He felt warm and confused and nauseous. It took a few seconds for the pain to register in his abdomen. But, for some reason, he couldn't feel the snow stinging his

cheeks anymore. He felt light-headed, and a numb floating feeling spread through his legs and penetrated his core.

He knew what was happening. Death had its cold fingers around him, probing his body, searching for a soul to
carry away. And it was for the best. The circle was complete. He had ensured that the Prophet would never harm
another person. It was as happy an ending as he could have
ever hoped for.

A part of him wished that he could have seen his family one last time. Telling them that he loved them. Holding
them close. Saying he was sorry.

But another part of him knew that they were better off
without him. Their lives would continue. Eleanor would re-
marry. The kids would grow up. They would be happy. He
wouldn't be there to see it, but in that moment, he knew that
it would come to pass.

As Schofield thought of those happy memories yet to be
created, he felt strangely at peace.

He looked up into the night sky. The snow falling through
the darkness seemed to glow in the light of the street lamps
and looked like a million shooting stars.

He wondered if God was looking down at him. He asked
for forgiveness and was reminded of a story from the Bible.
He had never read the book himself, but he was familiar
with the story of the thief on the cross. As Jesus was being
crucified, a thief sharing the same fate asked the Lord to
remember him. Jesus told the man that he would be with
him in paradise.

Schofield wondered if God could also forgive him or if
he would be cast down with the devil.

With that question still hanging anxiously in his mind,
the numb feeling overtook him, and he slipped away.

THE DISORIENTATION SWIRLING in Maggie's mind from the drugs that Ackerman had administered made her surroundings seem vague and blurry. She floated in and out of consciousness, but images penetrated the haze in small flashes. She saw the inside of a car, felt the bumps of a road, heard the tires sloshing through the snow and the engine humming.

Then it seemed as if she blinked and was somewhere else, on a sidewalk. But she wasn't walking. She was moving forward, but not by her own volition. She looked down and saw a red and orange afghan blanket covering her body and wheels moving across the sidewalk. A wheelchair?

The world seemed dark and brown, and she realized absently that she must be wearing sunglasses. There was a heavy weight on her lap beneath the blanket. It felt cold and metallic. She tried to move her arms but found them paralyzed and held in place, either by the drugs or some kind of restraints.

A nauseous fluttering burned in her guts, and she opened her mouth to speak but no words came out. There were several people passing by on the sidewalk and cars were zooming down the street, but no one paid her any attention.

Maggie blinked again, and more time slipped away. Now she was in a building, riding on an elevator and then moving through some kind of atrium. People packed the space. There were hundreds of them, all moving quickly and holding shopping bags. She tried to call out to them, but no sound could penetrate the fog enveloping her mind. The atrium was tall and open and surrounded with glass and storefronts. A shopping center? A mall?

The wheelchair came to rest in front of a silver and glass barrier in the center of the open space, and she felt herself spin in a circle until her back was placed against the railing.

She recoiled in fear from the face that greeted her. Ackerman wore a dark gray wool overcoat atop a black button-down shirt. He was handsome and blended in perfectly with the other patrons.

"Hello, Maggie," Ackerman said. "It's been wonderful getting to spend more time with you. But I'm afraid that we've come to the end of our journey. The drugs I've given you will begin to wear off soon, but I would suggest that you stay quiet and don't move. Nod your head if you can understand what I'm saying."

With some effort, she bobbed her head up and down.

"Very good. I've attached a specially designed bomb to your body. Only Marcus will possess the knowledge to disarm it. Once I leave you, I'll call him and tell him where you are. There's a cell phone beneath the blanket. My number is already programmed into it, so when he arrives, just tell him to hit send. Please nod again if you're following me so far."

Her jaw trembled and her pulse raced, but she nodded her head in acceptance.

"That's good, Maggie. You're doing so well. But please don't try to get cute and attempt to save yourself. Don't call out. Don't try to bring in the police or the bomb squad or try to warn anyone. If you do, innocent people will be needlessly harmed. I'm going to give Marcus an opportunity to save you. Let him take it. And remember, I'll be watching. So you just sit tight and wait for Prince Charming to arrive."

AFTER PARTING COMPANY with Maggie, Ackerman took the escalator down to Michigan Avenue, removed a fresh disposable cell phone from his pocket, and made two phone calls. The first was to Marcus. Ackerman gave him the details of where to find Maggie and told him that he would be in contact with further instructions.

Ackerman ended that call and placed the second. This one went to the Director of the Shepherd Organization. The message was simple. The Director should tell Marcus the truth or both his golden boy and Maggie would soon be dead.

THE CHICAGO WATER Tower rested between the skyscrapers along Michigan Avenue like an old-world castle. It was constructed from white limestone blocks and dotted with neo-Gothic spires. Just north of the landmark sat Water Tower Place, an eight-story shopping mall occupying seven hundred and fifty-eight thousand square feet.

Andrew dropped Marcus off in front of the mall. There were glass entry doors between two massive swirling-gray marble pillars. Once inside, Marcus immediately bounded up an escalator that ascended toward the main area of the mall. Between each set of escalators and stairs, there was a multi-tiered black granite fountain that trickled water toward the street in a steady stream. At the top of the escalators, a replica of the Water Tower made entirely from Lego blocks marked the actual start of the shopping plaza. The aromas of the mall were all around him—perfumes, coffee shops, greasy fast food, cinnamon rolls.

His pace slowed, and his gaze darted around the large space. Ackerman could have been hiding anywhere, watching. It was only days before Christmas, and the mall was a mass of humanity. They shuffled and scuttled, their arms loaded with bags and boxes, across a tile floor that had been colored to resemble hardwood. But Marcus could see Maggie through the gaps in the stream of shoppers. She sat in the center of an atrium that rose the entire eight stories of the mall across from a giant bank of glass elevators.

Marcus's phone rang, and he fumbled it from the pocket of his jeans. It was the Director. "Hello."

any

"

peri

H

reach

bled

she s

"D

"H

should

Ma

beneat

was ab

display

a blue a

gie's le

man an

you, there was some familiarity that I couldn't
tify. Now I know what it was. You look like
Same eyes, same smile, same facial str
"The first time I saw you, I was af
"That's rare for me. They say that
with my brain that makes it so
in the way that normal peop
made me afraid. Later, I
resemblance to our fa

The words we
heart. Ackerma
but Marcus
around h

It's

"Hello, Marcus. I'm sure Maggie has told you the dire nature of your situation. We'll wait for the Director to arrive. He'll have the code to disarm the device. Just tell him that you need to type the name of your real father onto the keyboard. He'll have the answer for you."

"I know that there's really no bomb."

The other end of the line went silent for a few seconds, but then Ackerman said, "Of course there is. You should know better than to question my resolve. I'm a monster. I'd kill every person in that mall without blinking an eye."

"You'd even kill your own brother?" Ackerman didn't speak.

"You didn't have to do any of this. I know you wanted to trick the Director into telling me the truth, but I already know."

"How?"

"Allen told me at the hospital. He told me everything. But I guess I've always had my suspicions. When I first saw

t quite iden-
her, our mother.
cture."

aid," Ackerman said.
there's something wrong
can't feel fear. At least, not
e do. But something about you
ealized that it was because of your
her. It's in your eyes."

e like a dagger plunged into Marcus's
continued on about destiny and connection,
wasn't listening. The world had melted away
m. He braced himself against a nearby railing.

in your eyes.

He had always known that he was different. He had always felt a certain anger and hunger, but he had fought to
keep it buried. Still, Ackerman had seen it raging just below
the surface, the monster clawing its way to freedom.

The world spun. Tears fell. A tidal wave of fear and anger
and doubt slammed against the foundations of his soul.

Francis Ackerman Sr., his real father, was a madman
who'd tortured his own son and killed many others. And now
Marcus knew *that* was his true legacy. He wasn't a third-
generation cop. He was a second-generation serial killer.

MAGGIE USED ANDREW'S key to enter the hotel room he'd shared with Marcus back in Jackson's Grove. The first room of the suite was empty except for the rearranged furniture, their touchscreen display board, and various cups and food containers. It smelled of old grease and cold coffee. The door to the bedroom was closed. She pushed it open and found Marcus sitting on the bed in the dark, staring absently at the wall. His bag was packed and resting on the bedspread behind him.

After Marcus's phone call with Ackerman, he had barely said a word to any of them. It was as if he were engulfed in some kind of fugue state. Maggie had never seen him like that. He just walked out onto Michigan Avenue and flagged down a taxi. It took a phone call to the cab company to track him down, but not until after the Director had explained the situation to her and Andrew. When Marcus's mother was pregnant with him, she had run away from her abusive and disturbed husband, Francis Ackerman Sr. The pain of her loss had been the stressor that initiated a chain of events ultimately leading to countless deaths and immeasurable suffering.

Marcus didn't seem to register her arrival. His stare didn't leave the wall. His eyes were bloodshot. She could tell that he had been crying.

She said, "It doesn't change anything. You're still the same man you've always been."

His eyes didn't move. "You're right. I've always been a man of violence, a killer. Now I just know why."

"That's not true. You've helped a lot of people. You're a hero. It doesn't matter who your father was. What matters is—"

He held up an outstretched palm to stop her and then said, "Did you know?"

"What? Of course not."

"How am I supposed to believe that?"

"Because it's the truth. You know how secretive the Director is. He never tells us what's really going on."

"And you don't see a problem with that?"

Maggie said, "Of course I do, but what I am supposed to do about it."

"I don't know. I don't know what to think anymore, but I can't keep going like this. I'm done." Marcus stood, looked into her eyes, and said, "I love you, Maggie. I always have. I'm just not very good at showing it."

His hand found her cheek, and she pressed her face into his palm as her own tears fell.

Marcus continued, "Come with me. We can start a new life, a normal life. I can't promise you that it'll be perfect, but I'll do my best." She swallowed hard and thought of her younger brother and the man who had stolen him away. Her mouth was dry, and her voice trembled. "I don't want a normal life. We help people. Think of all the people that would have died this week if you hadn't have been there to save them. I can't leave that behind, and you've said it yourself: you can't run from what you are."

He leaned in and kissed her long and hard. Then he whispered, "I can try."

MARCUS FELT LIKE he was wandering through a nightmare somewhere between awake and asleep. He had felt depression before. He had felt sadness before. But nothing as deep and destructive as this. It felt as though a black hole had opened up inside of him and sucked out all his desire to go on living.

As he stepped into the hallway and left Maggie behind, he found Andrew leaning against the wall.

"Where do you think you're going?" Andrew said. "Anywhere but here."

"I hear Vasques is awake and doing well."

"That's good."

"You going to pay her a visit?"

"No," Marcus said, thinking of his recent run-in with her partner.

Andrew clasped his shoulder. "We need you. You realize that, right? You're the best investigator that I've ever worked with. You just need some time to clear your head, let all this process."

Marcus forced a smile. "You've been a good friend. I'll get in touch once I'm settled somewhere. Take care of Maggie for me."

Andrew nodded, and Marcus stepped past him and headed for the elevator.

"Marcus, wait. If you're leaving anyway, then there's one more thing that you should know."

THE SNOWSTORM HAD broken in the early-morning hours, and the day had actually shaped up to be rather pleasant. The Director stood beneath the car port of Marcus's hotel, enjoying the climate shift. He puffed on a Marlboro. It had been nearly fifteen years since he had given up smoking, but that morning he had caved in and purchased a pack of his old brand.

After checking the time on his cell phone, he wondered how Maggie was handling the situation with Marcus. This was exactly the reason why he had concealed the truth in the first place. Marcus simply couldn't handle the knowledge of his true lineage. It was human nature to hold certain truths beyond reproach, and when those truths were questioned or outright shattered, it was naturally a jarring and life-changing experience. Some could recover from such things, while others could not.

The Director leaned on the hood of his rental car, a silver Buick LaCrosse, and took another drag off his cigarette. But, as the warm smoke flowed into his lungs, something struck him from behind and slammed him against the car.

His attacker spun him around and pressed the barrel of a large black handgun against his neck.

The Director tried to remain calm, but there was murder in Marcus's eyes.

"You could have gotten us all killed a hundred times over!" Marcus's body shook with rage, and his jaw was clenched tight.

"Let's just settle down now," the Director said. "I have no idea what you're talking about."

He tried to ease himself away, but Marcus slammed him back against the car.

"Andrew told me everything. Stan discovered that Ackerman had hacked our system months ago, but you told him to let it happen.

You've been feeding Ackerman information through a back door. Why in the hell would you do that?"

The Director exhaled harshly and considered his next words with care. "Listen, Marcus. There are simply some things that you can't understand unless you can see the big picture. You just don't—"

Marcus slammed an elbow into the Director's jaw. His teeth slammed together, and he could taste blood in his mouth. Then Marcus dug the barrel of the gun even harder against his neck. "I should blow your head off. The world would be a better place."

"Dammit, boy. What do you want me to say? I used you as bait. Ackerman had gone underground. Our best chance of catching that madman was to use his obsession with you against him. So yes, I allowed him to access our systems. It was the right move."

Marcus shook his head. "You reckless son of a bitch. You're out of your mind. You could have gotten us all killed. Allen may never walk again because of you! But sure, it was the right move."

"You would have done the same thing. And I had every confidence in the abilities of your team to bring Ackerman to justice."

Marcus shoved him back again and stepped away. "We're not just pawns on your chessboard to be moved around and sacrificed when it serves your needs."

"You're right. I should have told you. I've made mistakes, just like everyone else. But I didn't want to risk tipping off Ackerman."

With a shake of his head, Marcus jammed his Sig Sauer back into his coat and raised his hands. "I'm done."

"What are you talking about? This isn't just something that you do. It's who you are. You've tried to run from that before, but it hasn't gotten you very far."

"I can be better than this. Better than you. I quit. Is that clear enough?"

Marcus headed toward the street, and the Director knew that he had a very difficult choice to make and not much time to decide. He swore under his breath and called after Marcus. "If you leave now, you'll never learn the final piece of the puzzle. Something that even Ackerman doesn't know. He's alive, Marcus."

Marcus continued to walk away, but gradually he began to slow down like a freight train that had thrown on its brakes but took time to halt its forward progress. He turned back and said, "Who are you talking about?"

"The man who tortured your brother and murdered your mother and stepfather. Francis Ackerman Sr. The man who brought you into this world. He's still alive."

* * * * *

About the Author

WHEN A FIREMAN or a policeman would visit his school, most of his classmates' heads would swim with aspirations of growing up and catching bad guys or saving someone from a blazing inferno. When these moments came for Ethan Cross, however, his dreams weren't to someday be a cop or put out fires; he just wanted to write about it. His dream of telling stories on a grand scale came to fruition with the release of his first novel, *The Shepherd*.

Ethan Cross is the pen name of a thriller author living and writing in Illinois with his wife, two daughters, and two Shih Tzus. In addition to *The Shepherd* and *The Prophet*, he has published two novellas—*The Cage* and *Callsign: Knight* (with Jeremy Robinson)

REQUEST YOUR FREE BOOKS!
2 FREE NOVELS PLUS 2 FREE GIFTS!

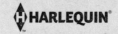

ROMANTIC suspense

Sparked by danger, fueled by passion

YES! Please send me 2 FREE Harlequin® Romantic Suspense novels and my 2 FREE gifts (gifts are worth about $10). After receiving them, if I don't wish to receive any more books, I can return the shipping statement marked "cancel." If I don't cancel, I will receive 4 brand-new novels every month and be billed just $4.74 per book in the U.S. or $5.24 per book in Canada. That's a savings of at least 14% off the cover price! It's quite a bargain! Shipping and handling is just 50¢ per book in the U.S. and 75¢ per book in Canada.* I understand that accepting the 2 free books and gifts places me under no obligation to buy anything. I can always return a shipment and cancel at any time. Even if I never buy another book, the two free books and gifts are mine to keep forever.

240/340 HDN F45N

Name _____ (PLEASE PRINT) _____

Address _____ Apt. # _____

City _____ State/Prov. _____ Zip/Postal Code _____

Signature (if under 18, a parent or guardian must sign)

Mail to the **Harlequin® Reader Service:**

IN U.S.A.: P.O. Box 1867, Buffalo, NY 14240-1867
IN CANADA: P.O. Box 609, Fort Erie, Ontario L2A 5X3

Want to try two free books from another line?
Call 1-800-873-8635 or visit www.ReaderService.com.

* Terms and prices subject to change without notice. Prices do not include applicable taxes. Sales tax applicable in N.Y. Canadian residents will be charged applicable taxes. Offer not valid in Quebec. This offer is limited to one order per household. Not valid for current subscribers to Harlequin Romantic Suspense books. All orders subject to credit approval. Credit or debit balances in a customer's account(s) may be offset by any other outstanding balance owed by or to the customer. Please allow 4 to 6 weeks for delivery. Offer available while quantities last.

Your Privacy—The Harlequin® Reader Service is committed to protecting your privacy. Our Privacy Policy is available online at www.ReaderService.com or upon request from the Harlequin Reader Service.

We make a portion of our mailing list available to reputable third parties that offer products we believe may interest you. If you prefer that we not exchange your name with third parties, or if you wish to clarify or modify your communication preferences, please visit us at www.ReaderService.com/consumerschoice or write to us at Harlequin Reader Service Preference Service, P.O. Box 9062, Buffalo, NY 14269. Include your complete name and address.

HRS13R

REQUEST YOUR FREE BOOKS!
2 FREE NOVELS PLUS 2 FREE GIFTS!

◆ HARLEQUIN®

INTRIGUE®

BREATHTAKING ROMANTIC SUSPENSE

YES! Please send me 2 FREE Harlequin Intrigue® novels and my 2 FREE gifts (gifts are worth about $10). After receiving them, if I don't wish to receive any more books, I can return the shipping statement marked "cancel." If I don't cancel, I will receive 6 brand-new novels every month and be billed just $4.74 per book in the U.S. or $5.24 per book in Canada. That's a savings of at least 14% off the cover price! It's quite a bargain! Shipping and handling is just 50¢ per book in the U.S. and 75¢ per book in Canada.* I understand that accepting the 2 free books and gifts places me under no obligation to buy anything. I can always return a shipment and cancel at any time. Even if I never buy another book, the two free books and gifts are mine to keep forever.

182/382 HDN F43C

Name	(PLEASE PRINT)
Address	Apt. #
City	State/Prov.	Zip/Postal Code

Signature (if under 18, a parent or guardian must sign)

Mail to the **Harlequin® Reader Service:**
IN U.S.A.: P.O. Box 1867, Buffalo, NY 14240-1867
IN CANADA: P.O. Box 609, Fort Erie, Ontario L2A 5X3

**Are you a subscriber to Harlequin Intrigue books
and want to receive the larger-print edition?
Call 1-800-873-8635 or visit www.ReaderService.com.**

* Terms and prices subject to change without notice. Prices do not include applicable taxes. Sales tax applicable in N.Y. Canadian residents will be charged applicable taxes. Offer not valid in Quebec. This offer is limited to one order per household. Not valid for current subscribers to Harlequin Intrigue books. All orders subject to credit approval. Credit or debit balances in a customer's account(s) may be offset by any other outstanding balance owed by or to the customer. Please allow 4 to 6 weeks for delivery. Offer available while quantities last.

Your Privacy—The Harlequin® Reader Service is committed to protecting your privacy. Our Privacy Policy is available online at www.ReaderService.com or upon request from the Harlequin Reader Service.

We make a portion of our mailing list available to reputable third parties that offer products we believe may interest you. If you prefer that we not exchange your name with third parties, or if you wish to clarify or modify your communication preferences, please visit us at www.ReaderService.com/consumerschoice or write to us at Harlequin Reader Service Preference Service, P.O. Box 9062, Buffalo, NY 14269. Include your complete name and address.

HIDIR13R